D0405707

Marcia

Come Back
TO ME

Come Back TO ME

Josie Litton

Bantam 🐓 *Books*

New York Toronto London Sydney Auckland

COME BACK TO ME

A Bantam Book

ISBN 0-7394-2173-5

Published simultaneously in the United States and Canada

Bantam Books are published by Bantam Books, a division of Random House, Inc. Its trademark, consisting of the words "Bantam Books" and the portrayal of a rooster, is Registered in U.S. Patent and Trademark Office and in other countries. Marca Registrada. Bantam Books, 1540 Broadway, New York, New York 10036.

PRINTED IN THE UNITED STATES OF AMERICA

FOR

H

FOR LONG WALKS AND

HAPPY TALKS

Come Back
TO ME

Chapter

ONE

A RIM OF FIRE RISES AT THE EDGE OF THE
world, searing away gentle night, setting the sky
aflame. The Dragon watches it come, welcomes
it. He moves silently over the soft earth. A stag
flees before him, crashing through the brush, ignored.

The fierce Viking warrior Dragon Hakonson has not
come to the forests of Essex to hunt today. Today, he seeks
the quiet of the pines at the edge of the sea for a different
purpose. On the verge of taking a step he can no longer
avoid, he has sent his attendants on ahead and given himself
this small chance for reflection.

But his solitude is about to be interrupted. Golden eyes
watch him from the protection of the trees. A slim, lithe body
holds very still, hardly breathing. Slowly, oh, so slowly, the
intruder tries to creep away. A twig snaps. His senses honed
by a lifetime of struggle and danger, Dragon reacts at once.
Swifter than the saying of it, he pounces, dragging the
struggling, squawking creature out to study at his leisure.

So quickly! The speed with which the stranger moved
stunned Rycca. One moment she was kneeling in the cool

moss where she had slept a few fitful hours, watching with wary care the man who had appeared without warning, and the next was only a blur. She was clasped so tightly she could scarcely breathe. Pain radiated up her arms and along her ribs. A little more pressure, only a little, and they would snap as readily as the treacherous twig.

She had no idea who the man was, nor did she care. Nothing mattered save wresting free of him. Growing up a victim of her brothers' casual cruelties, she had honed her skills. She grabbed hold of the powerful arm within easiest reach and bit down hard. In her experience, the surprise of such a counterattack caused the miscreant to loosen his grip quickly.

Yet now a different surprise awaited her, darkly circled with shock. The man did not so much as grunt. He merely tightened his hold on her enough to prevent her from breathing altogether.

She held on as long as she could, until colored lights whirled before her eyes and unconsciousness was scant moments away. Only then, fearing what total incapacity would mean, did she let go. For an instant he did not, and she felt herself plummeting into nothingness. Absurdly, she clung to the same arm as though it might anchor her in the world. Even as her lungs screamed for air, it was granted. She inhaled long and deeply, gasping.

"Fool," the man said. His voice was a deep rumble out of his chest, felt against her back, oddly pleasant for the circumstances. He shifted his hold to her shoulders and turned her to face him. "What were you thinking, boy? All I want is a look at you. A man likes to know who's lurking behind his back."

Rycca stared up through the thick fringe of her lashes, up . . . and up yet more. Her legs refused to stay straight, thus she was not at her full height, but all the same he was very tall. She had known that even as he crouched beside the river, yet the full realization of his

size almost made her stop breathing again. His shoulders
and chest were massive, shaped of solid mucle and bone
clearly visible beneath the sleeveless leather tunic he
wore. His face was square, blunt-featured, lit by eyes that
looked like shards of half-buried gold. Dark brows arched
above them, the same hue as the golden brown hair pulled
back at his nape. His skin was burnished by the wind and
sun. Gold of hair, eye, and skin, he was easily the most
handsome man she had ever seen. Indeed, he might have
been a pagan idol cast in the fiery furnace of a master
smith but for the purely human touches that clung to him.
He had gone long enough without shaving to have the beginnings of a beard. He smelled of woodsmoke, sea air,
and pine, a not unpleasant combination. Human, all
right, all too human, too real, and much too close.

He thought her a boy, thank heaven. In her frantic
haste to escape, she had seized clothes Thurlow left behind when he departed for Normandy. They were too
small for the twin who had grown inches beyond her in recent years, but they fit Rycca with room to spare. Her
form was well concealed, as was her hair, tucked out of
sight beneath a felt cap. She had even smeared dirt on her
face in an effort to conceal the softness of her skin. Still,
she was not so foolish as to trust her disguise overmuch. It
would not hold up to more than the merest scrutiny.

The boy's silence and seeming docility surprised
Dragon. At his age—he judged the lad to be about thir-
teen—he'd been a hell hound spitting fire and willing to
take on all comers even if it meant being pounded into the
ground. It was part of growing up in a wild and violent
world. Where then had the boy acquired wisdom enough
not to offer further challenge? The little cuss could bite,
that was certain, but now he seemed too stunned to do
anything but stare.

"I ask again," Dragon said in Saxon, presuming that
was what the lad would understand. Norse was the

Dragon's native tongue, and with that he was understood by Danes and Swedes as well. On his travels he had picked up other ways of speech so that he could converse with Franks, Germans, and even Moors. Languages came to him easily, perhaps because he loved the music of words.

"Why did you lurk in the underbrush and spy on me?" He looked more closely at the lad, observing the good quality of his garb made of finely spun wool and sewn too big for him, but that was not surprising. Children's garments were usually made with growing room. This was no peasant boy but a young lordling likely to be in fosterage at a local manor. Why then was he here in the forest without companions and on foot?

Essex was at peace on this sunny spring morning, a happy circumstance still fresh enough not to be taken for granted. Such tranquility had been wrested from decades of war by the wisdom of the great King Alfred and the iron will of the noble Lord Hawk of Essex. That same Hawk was brother to the Lady Cymbra, who was wife to Dragon's own brother, the Norse Wolf. The ties of family were further strengthened by genuine friendship, a fact of which Dragon had to remind himself every time he dwelled on the reason for his presence in Essex. For all its blessing, peace could not be counted on and even a young boy had to explain himself.

"Why are you here?" Dragon demanded, and because the lad had been tardy in answering, he gave him a good shake.

Rycca's teeth rattled. Inwardly, she cursed the poor judgment that had put her at such risk. If only she had remained still, not tried to escape, she might have gone unnoticed. Too late for such thoughts and too late for much of anything save a last, desperate effort to break free. There was something to be said for having two brutal louts for older brothers and another, her beloved twin, who had taught her to defend herself.

"Don't hesitate," Thurlow had advised when he ignored her scarlet face and remorselessly continued his instruction in the finer points of self-defense. "Give no warning and act quickly. Then, for God's sake, run like the wind. The pain, though intense, does not last forever."

She had never made use of his teaching, for Thurlow had promptly informed the elder siblings who were the bane of both their existences that she was armed with knowledge they wished no woman to have. He had endured the beating they administered in retaliation, merely the latest of uncounted punishments, and laid plans for escaping to a better life.

"I will send for you when I am established in Normandy," he had promised Rycca. "We have kin on our mother's side there and I hear opportunity abounds. It will not be long."

Not long yet too long, as the floodtide of events overtook Rycca far sooner than either of them could have expected and threatened to sweep away all hope. Terror filled her. She would never get away. She would be trapped within the fate her family intended for her. Anything was better than that, absolutely anything.

She still had not answered; her captor was scowling. He looked unaccustomed to defiance. Mayhap this would be a salutary lesson for him.

She took a breath, closed her eyes, and rammed her knee up between his legs with all the considerable force she could muster.

The stranger stiffened. She looked up to confront him as he stared at her in blank shock. He did not, as Thurlow had assured he would, howl in agony. But he did groan very deeply even as his hands fell from her. His legs gave way and he went down slowly onto his knees, reminding her of a mighty oak felled by an ax.

She was free yet she hesitated, battling the sudden, overwhelming need to help him. Truly, she would never live to see Normandy if she entertained such mad notions. The impulse passed, survival ruled. Like the wind, Thurlow had said, and like the wind she ran. Her legs were slim but well muscled. She had the grace of a seasoned colt and used it to leap over every obstacle. Her breath was strong and steady. Having faced fear and escaped danger, she felt charged with confidence. After a while, convinced the stranger could not possibly catch her, she ran for the sheer pleasure of it. Ran and ran through shadowed glens and across sun-drenched fields, through copses of pine and oak and along shell-strewn shores. Rycca ran until finally, more at peace than she had been in longer than she could recall, she slowed and stopped.

She was at the edge of a wood hard by the glittering sea. Wind rippled over the blue-gray water turned silver beneath the sunlight. Gulls circled overhead, their wings scarcely moving. Rycca shaded her eyes, staring out to the distant horizon where sea and sky merged. Until coming to Essex scant days ago, she had never before seen more water than could be contained in a river or lake. The sea enthralled her. She was at once afraid of it, for she could not swim, and enchanted by the prospect of escape it offered. Somewhere beyond that distant horizon was Normandy and the chance for a new life. All she had to do was reach it.

All she had to do was unfold her wings like the gulls above and soar into the sky. Such was scarcely less mighty a task than that she had set herself. Yet it made no matter, for the alternative was unthinkable.

Rycca shook the thought away and gave herself up to the enjoyment of sun and sea. She had slept little and her stomach was empty; she was alone and without help in a land where she could expect nothing save to be hunted down and brutally punished. Yet for all that, she was swept by a shining sense of well-being as bright as the sunlight shimmering on water. She was *free*.

When in her life had she ever been free or even dared to think that such a blessed state might someday be hers? When had she ever hoped to do other than hide her true self behind a mask of endurance? Only with Thurlow had she ever lowered her guard and even with him she had pretended her misery was less than it truly was, as she suspected he had done for her.

Free. She flung her arms wide and laughed suddenly. To be still was beyond her, she had to move, turning around and around, laughing into the sky. Gloriously, stunningly *free*. However difficult the future might prove, anything was worth this single, exhilarating moment. Absolutely anything.

A BSOLUTELY NOTHING WOULD STOP HIM FROM wreaking vengeance on the menace who had brought him to his knees. Grimly, Dragon set his mind apart from the waves of pain still resonating within him and turned to the far more pleasant contemplation of the punishment he would inflict. No one, not even a green boy, could be pardoned for such an assault. He would have to pay and pay dearly. The only question was how.

First he had to be caught, but that was no matter. Had the imp of hell deliberately set out to mark his trail, he could not have left it clearer. Granted, Dragon was a hunter of rare skill, but it required no special talent to see where the boy had gone. His way was littered with broken branches, trampled grass, even bits of wool caught on prickler bushes. By the length of his stride, he had run as fast as a bat out of hell, which suggested he at least had a brain, much good that it would do him.

Dragon did not run for he had no need. His legs were longer than the boy's and he did not tire. Long after the shortened stride showed that the lad was flagging, Dragon continued easily. He stopped only once to drink from the clear-running brook where, he saw, the boy had rested. Then he went on as the trail veered east toward the sea and he came at last within sight of the shore.

Having lived almost all his life by the sea and spent a fair measure of those years actually on it, Dragon did not pause in admiration. He continued walking, noting where the water-slick stones were turned and the wild roses disturbed. He even happened upon a stretch of sand dotted with slender footprints. Near there the beach narrowed as cliffs began to rise above it. He found the bushes the boy had seized hold of to pull himself up, saw where he had almost lost his grip and tumbled down, and after a moment's hesitation he followed that path. The sun was almost at its zenith when Dragon hoisted himself onto the top of the cliff and, with his back to the sea, looked around. From the corner of his eye he caught a glimpse of movement near the edge of the forest. Cautiously, staying out of sight behind trees and rocks, he took the trail into the woods.

The boy was tiring more quickly now, he could see that by the closeness of his footprints and the increasing frequency with which he stumbled. But the lad seemed disinclined to stop. Perhaps he was making for somewhere in particular. Where?

Dragon considered how far he himself had traveled since morning, did a quick calculation, and decided he was within reach of Hawkforte, the stronghold of his host, the Hawk of Essex. Built to withstand the ravages of the Danes, who of late had not been so intemperate as to challenge its master, Hawkforte protected a prosperous town and port. Although there were other settlements in the area, none rivaled it in size. In all likelihood, the boy was headed there. Conveniently, it was also Dragon's destination, although he was in no hurry to attain it. Once he did, his freedom would be gone and his head well and truly in the noose.

Dour thoughts for another time. He wondered again in passing why the lad was traveling alone. Not that it mattered. Soon enough, he would be made to explain himself. Dragon quickened his pace through the woods and began closing on his quarry.

R YCCA SLUMPED DOWN ON A MOSS-DRAPED ROCK and drew a pained breath. She was footsore and weary yet determined to press on. Springs there were aplenty but she was famished and had found only a few handfuls of berries. The small sack of food she had carried with her lay where she had abandoned it when she fled from the golden giant. What a foolish way to think of him! Clearly, fatigue had disordered her thoughts. He was merely a man and a damned inconvenient one at that. Besides, she had no reason to think of him at all. Even if he had wanted to follow her, she had fled too quickly and too long. He was far behind, somewhere in the woods, perhaps still cursing her but not destined to cross her path ever again.

More's the pity.

She raised a slanted brow and scowled. What imp of mischief put such wayward notions into her poor head? True, she was dog tired, but that was no excuse for such foolishness. She had important matters to consider, her whole life for one and how she was to manage it. There was neither time nor energy to be mooning over a man.

The most handsome man she had ever seen.

"Stop!" She was startled to realize she had spoken out loud and clamped her lips together sternly. Enough and enough again! Her unruly self needs must be silenced while she got on with matters of true import.

Coward.

She was not! No woman who would refuse the fate her family intended for her and strike off on her own, determined to reach a far shore about which she knew almost nothing could possibly be termed a coward.

Fool, then.

Damn, damn, and damn again! The cursed habit had followed her all her life since tenderest childhood. How she loathed being different, how she despised always *knowing*. Lie to her and she would be happy, trick her into believing what was not and she would be delighted, prevaricate, falsify, fib, and palter, nothing would thrill her more. To be in blissful ignorance, never to know or at least not to know beyond the ordinary ken whether someone spoke the truth or lied, that was her great dream as much as freedom itself, for it was a kind of freedom all its own. Let her be done with truth!

He was a man, nothing more. A stranger and a threat. She was glad to be done with him.

Lies.

Her mouth set thinly, she came away from the moss-draped rock and launched herself back upon the course of least resistance through the wood. She would reach Hawkforte before dark. She would wrangle her way onto a merchant ship bound for Normandy. She would find Thurlow there and together they would make a new life far from the loathsome threat that hung over her were she foolish enough to remain in England.

And that, for anyone who cared, was *truth*.

There was silence in her mind and in the wood, as though nature itself stilled before her blind determiantion. She drank it in, nodded once, and hurried on. It did not occur to her to glance back or even train her hearing in that direction. Not that it mattered. Had she done so, she would have perceived nothing. The Dragon moved over the land like smoke, fathomless and irresistible.

He caught up with the lad scarcely an hour after the first sign of movement. It would have been quicker but he'd hung back awhile, making sure he hadn't been spotted and waiting for the right moment to take him by surprise. He intended to make this quick and get it done with before the boy could hurt himself struggling. After that there would be time for the customary courtesies.

And so it would have been but for one of those vagaries of nature that can never be anticipated. A family of grouse was at home in the underbrush. Dragon's sudden passing roused the parents to protective fury. The male flew from the nest batting his wings and squawking furiously. The female arched her neck, stretched out her wings protectively, and hurled her own dire threats.

The clamor was answered by a slew of other birds who lifted into the air, cackling, cawing, hooting, shrieking, and scolding until the hitherto tranquil wood fairly rang with their outrage. The noise penetrated even the fog of Rycca's fatigue and made her look around in surprise.

Surprise that turned swiftly to shock.

The handsomest man she had ever seen.

A shiver of disbelief rippled through Rycca. She did not linger to contemplate the stranger's sudden reappearance or her own absurd thoughts. Instead, she turned and ran with all the desperate speed her weary body could muster.

Dragon followed swiftly. He saw no reason to let the boy exhaust himself any further. Best he face what he rightly had coming and be done with it. Then they would settle the matter of why he was alone and where he was heading. Dragon would see him safely there whether his destination be Hawkforte or not, and whether the lad wanted the company or not. Not mere protectiveness alone dictated that he do so. There was also the matter of

curiosity. He sensed a story behind the lad's solitary journey, and if there was one thing Dragon loved, it was a
good story. Indeed, people claimed he had a collection of
them to rival that of any skald or bard. There were even
some who said Dragon should have been one of that
happy fraternity, traveling from manor to manor pro-
claiming the great tales of the age. Fate had called him to a
different life, that of warrior and leader. So be it. He still
enjoyed those evenings spent around the fire when the ale
flowed freely and he held an audience spellbound in the
magic of his words.

The lad truly was desperate, Dragon realized suddenly, for he was moving far more quickly than he should
have been after the miles he had already covered. With a
shake of his head, Dragon closed the distance between
them. The boy had strength and stamina, there was no
doubt of that, but Dragon was a man full grown, trained
to hardship and war, at the peak of his power. His legs
were steel, rippling with muscle, devouring ground. He
ran without effort, moving easily over every obstacle, remorseless and inescapable.

The boy seemed to realize that suddenly as he darted
a glance over his shoulder. Dragon was so near that he
could see shock in the eyes so wide and thick-fringed they
must surely provoke teasing. A sudden, dark thought
flashed through his mind. Perhaps the boy had a particular reason for taking such desperate measures to escape.
A memory rose sharply despite its being long years old.
Little more than a child, torn from his home by the
ravages of war, Dragon had set sail upon the world's seas
in the company of his older brother. In the hold of a ship,
at night, a man . . . Even now, Dragon grimaced in disgust. He had fought and fiercely so, but alone he would
not have escaped. It was Wolf, already big for his age and
with the skill that would make him one of the most

renowned warriors of their day, who had saved him. Striking with savage intent, he gutted the attacker, leaving him to writhe in his death throes as he hugged Dragon fiercely and swore they would survive against all enemies and all dangers.

So they had done, rising to vast wealth and power, but not climbing quite so far that Dragon had forgotten how it felt to be young, helpless, and very afraid.

Mildly chagrined by his own kinder self, he nonetheless called out to the boy, "There's no need for this. I'm not going to hurt you. Just stop and we'll talk."

The look this earned suggested that Dragon must have suffered a recent head injury in addition to that done his nether parts. With a last backward glance, the boy redoubled his efforts to get away.

Dragon sighed. He took half a dozen more strides and flowed smoothly into the air, bringing his quarry down in a single motion. Even then, he rolled as they hit the ground, taking the impact himself and sparing the boy all but a simple jarring. He might have done better to knock the wind out of him for the brat struggled furiously, kicking out in every direction and doing his damnedest to get his teeth into any portion of Dragon that presented itself.

"Oh no you don't!" Dragon exclaimed. "I've had enough from you." He bounded to his feet, hauling the boy up with him, and gave him a good shake. "Calm down! All I want to do is talk."

That accomplished precisely nothing. Flush-faced, wide-eyed, the lad continued to struggle with all his might. Prudently, Dragon held him off at arm's length and even so kept a careful watch on his flailing limbs as they slowly but inexorably wound down. He waited until the miscreant had scarcely enough strength left to twitch before he tried again.

Pleasantly, he asked, "Are you ready to talk now?"

The boy was panting so hard he probably wasn't capable of speech but he did manage a glare of pure venom.

"No? I can wait." He continued to hold the boy a few inches above the ground, dangling at the end of a very long, very strong arm. At the same time, he repeated quietly, "I am not going to hurt you."

When the boy looked at him in utter disbelief, Dragon added, "Oh, I considered it rightly enough. You deserve a thrashing for what you did. But I'm willing to allow that you may have thought you were acting in self-defense, even as I myself was when I seized you. Any man has a right to protect himself." Deliberately, he awarded the stripling a title he would not merit for many years yet. On closer appraisal, the lad might be even younger than Dragon had thought. Cheeks that had been red with exertion were paling rapidly, revealing damask smooth skin without the slightest trace of even an infant beard. The boy's features were delicately drawn, a straight and slender nose sitting above a full mouth and gently rounded chin. But it was those eyes, those huge, slightly uptilted eyes the precise shade of clover honey, that sent a prickle of apprehension down Dragon's back. A sudden, hideous suspicion stirred in him.

Without warning, his free hand darted out and snatched the cap that swaddled the imp's head.

"*Noooo!*" Slender fingers flew to stop him, too late. Masses of silken hair glinting with the sheen of copper tumbled free. Dragon stared in disbelief. A girl. He had been brought to his knees by a *girl*. The realization stunned him if only because in all his experience with women—his very long, very considerable experience—nothing remotely similar had ever happened. In all modesty, no female had ever looked upon him with other than warm encouragement and affection. That may have been because of his appearance although he'd never thought anything of how he looked one way or another. And perhaps his wealth and position had impressed some. But he suspected it had much more to do with the simple fact that he adored women. Utterly, completely, unreservedly *adored* them. Women were the greatest of the gods' considerable accomplishments, the best gift, the most marvelous delight that could be bestowed upon the earth and upon man, including his own lucky self. Women were soft and strong, they smelled good and had beguiling smiles, they gave life and made it count for something. In bed, out of bed, he delighted in them. Old, young, in between, he found their presence a constant source of comfort and enjoyment. That one of these marvelous creatures might actually seek to do him harm left him stunned.

Not that he could blame her. She must have been absolutely terrified, and while he was thinking about it, what in hell's name was she doing traveling alone? No wonder she was gotten up as a boy, but that was scant protection. If he'd had more than a few seconds to look at her earlier he would have realized at once what he had finally discovered. *A girl.*

"It's all right, sweetling," Dragon said gently. He set her down with the utmost care, watchful lest in her exhausted state she topple over. "There's nothing for you to be afraid of. No one's going to hurt you. I'll see you safely to wherever you're going and—"

She turned and, fleet as a young doe, ran. He stared after her in amazement. Where had she possibly found the strength to try to escape yet again? It was truly amazing and just one more testament to the extraordinary mystery of women. Not that he could let her go, of course. She might get lost, or have trouble finding food, or be cold once night came, or run into some man with altogether the wrong sort of attitude toward women. Dragon couldn't allow any of that to happen. Nor could he allow her to harm herself by dashing through the woods probably paying no attention at all to her surroundings.

Frowning with concern, he hurried after her.

Rycca's breath came in labored gasps. Her legs were lead; the effort of running was agony. Only the desperate courage deep within her kept her from slumping to the ground in defeat. Of all the cruel tricks for fate to play upon her. She had escaped the brutality of her family and their nightmare plans for her future only to find herself in the hands of the most terrifyingly powerful warrior she had ever seen in her life.

And the handsomest man.

If she had possessed even a whisper of breath to spare, she would have laughed in sheer disbelief at herself. Even now, fleeing for her life, she could harbor such a thought. She must be possessed of some inner demon.

Only truth.

Truth be damned! And with it all the rest that life had inflicted upon her. She would not fall to the warrior or to her own weakness. She would run until her heart burst if she had to but she would never, *ever* give up. Surrender was for the craven and meek. She was neither. Heedless of the tears of exhaustion and fear that streamed down her cheeks, Rycca ran on. She did not see the ground change around her, did not notice the trees thinning away, paid no heed to the sea shining below the cliff that suddenly loomed before her. Nor did she hear Dragon's frantic shout. Drained of strength, bereft of hope, driven only by despair, she tumbled straight over the cliff face. A strangled scream broke from her. Grasping at bushes, she tried to halt her headlong plunge. The effort failed, and with a last sob of terror she glimpsed the white-foamed breakers rushing up toward her.

Dragon saw the girl disappear over the cliff and fought the wave of sickness that clawed at him. He could scarcely believe what his stubborn pursuit had wrought but there was no denying the brutal result. The girl was gone, might even at that moment be dead or dying, and it was his fault. With a horrified groan, he flung himself over the cliff, scarcely controlling his fall as he slipped and slid until leaping the last dozen feet to the beach.

The sight that greeted him made bile rise in his throat. She lay crumpled at the edge of the water against the boulder that had finally stopped her. Tendrils of copper hair drifted on the incoming tide. Another few minutes, and the water would be deep enough to drown her. As it was, her slender form was unmoving. A thin trickle of blood oozed from a wound on her forehead, flowing away into the sea.

Scarcely breathing, Dragon lifted the girl and carried her a safe distance up the sand. He laid her down carefully, then hesitated, momentarily uncertain of what to do. The man who had seen more injuries on the battlefield than he could count, and who had prevented his own death a year before by swiftly dealing with a wound that would have killed him, found himself at an utter loss. She looked so fragile lying there, all the strength and courage suddenly gone from her. Swallowing thickly, he opened the small pack hanging from his belt, drawing from it the supplies that good sense and his sister-in-law, herself a renowned healer, assured he always carry with him. The soft, clean cloth he pressed against the wound on the girl's forehead slowed the bleeding. He left the makeshift bandage in place and quickly checked her limbs, relieved to find none of them broken. In the process, he could not help but discover that the loose boy's clothing concealed a body of strong, flowing curves. Firmly putting that discovery from his mind as best he could, he carefully slid his hands beneath the tunic and, ignoring the odd trembling that inexplicably struck him, confirmed that her ribs were also intact.

With a deep breath, the first in several moments, he drew back and regarded her cautiously. Her only injury seemed to be the blow to her head. She might recover from that completely . . . or she might never wake and simply slip away into eternal sleep. He had seen both happen with men similarly struck down. Only time would tell.

Fortunately for Dragon's peace of mind, before he could do much more than begin to consider how he might get her to a place of greater comfort and safety, the girl moaned softly. Thinking perhaps he had imagined the sound, indeed had merely willed it into being, he leaned closer and closer still until the soft exhalation of her breath brushed his bearded cheek. His gaze focused on her intently, he watched as her eyes slowly fluttered open.

Chapter

TWO

HER HEAD HURT. RYCCA WINCED BUT HER instinct was to move, to get up, to get away even if she couldn't quite remember what she was fleeing from. She tried to rise only to be pressed gently back onto the sand.

"Easy, sweetling. You had a bad fall. There are no bones broken but you need to take it slowly."

The voice was a deep rumble, soothing, seductive, and . . . all too familiar. *Him.* He had done this to her, chased her down, driven her right off the edge of the cliff. He'd damn near killed her and now he thought her helpless, prey no doubt to whatever it was he had in mind.

He had a nasty surprise awaiting him.

But not, unfortunately, until her head stopped spinning. With a frustrated moan, Rycca subsided. Dragon took the sound to mean she was suffering and bent over her in concern.

"Does something hurt besides your head? I checked and you seem to be all right but I could be wrong."

He had checked. What did that mean? She stared directly into his eyes, which looked like ancient gold suddenly revealed to sunlight. Worse, his voice rippled through her, setting off odd little shivers at the same time as it made her feel strangely content.

His hand touched her brow very lightly. She scarcely noticed, so absorbed was she in his look of tender concern. Not that she was fooled by that for a moment. She knew warriors, had lived among them all her life. They were rough, crude men who took what they wanted with no thought but the satisfaction of their own urges. To have fallen from the heady heights of freedom into the very hands of such a man was worse even than falling from the cliff. That, at least, she had survived.

Long experience had taught her the terrible folly of ever showing fear or doubt. Accordingly, she met the warrior's gaze squarely, ignored the strange fluttering of her heart, and snarled, "Get away from me."

Dragon sighed. He didn't blame her in the least for being angry with him; she had every right to feel that way. What he regretted was his inability to do as she wanted. "I'm sorry," he said sincerely, "but I cannot. You've been hurt and you need help."

Truth.

No, it couldn't be. Men didn't apologize, at least not to women. Nor did they extend themselves to help someone unless they expected something in return. The candor and compassion she felt in him had to be false. And that prompted a sudden thought: The tumble down the cliff might have done something to her strange, unwanted gift. Perhaps she no longer had any greater ability to tell truth from lie than did any other person. For that, she would fall down a dozen cliffs.

Yet there was still the tantalizing possibility that the warrior meant exactly what he had said. She eyed him cautiously. "I need no help. Let me up and I will be on my way."

Patiently, he shook his head. "It is not safe for a woman to be traveling on her own."

"I was perfectly safe until you crossed my path."

"Well may you see it that way, but if I hadn't come along, someone else would have and you could be in great difficulty right now."

If she hadn't known it would hurt, she might have laughed. As it was, she had to content herself with a grimace. "Oh, you mean I could have been chased over a cliff?"

The warrior reddened, not with anger, which she would have understood in response to her derision, but with what looked very much like regret.

"I thought you were a boy in need of better manners. Had I realized you were a girl . . ." He paused and shrugged. "I would still have come after you because you really should not be without escort. But I would have tried to take you by surprise so you would not run off and get hurt."

Truth.

"Yes, well, that's fine, but there is no need for you to be concerned. I am meeting my . . . my brother just a short distance from here."

Strictly speaking, Normandy was a far journey. But there were much greater distances to go, all the way to fabled Byzantium or even to the lands farther to the east and south. If that weren't enough, there were tales of a land to the west where mountains ran with molten fury and vast vents of steam rose from the sundered earth. Some of those who claimed to have seen such a place told stranger stories yet of a land yet farther to the west, endowed with rugged coastlines and endless forests. Besides all that, Normandy might as well be the neighboring village. So she wasn't really lying . . . not entirely.

"Fine," the warrior said. "I will take you to him."

Rycca closed her eyes in frustration. She opened them again to find him about to lift her into his too-strong arms. "There is no need! I can walk perfectly well. Besides . . ." She looked around quickly even though it hurt to move her head. "You have no horse."

He smiled and when he did . . . oh, sweet heaven, this was so unfair. He was by far the most compelling man she had ever seen, that was truth she could no longer deny. But when he smiled he undid her completely. She had to battle the sudden, mad urge to give him anything and everything he might desire. There was only scant comfort in the knowledge that her head injury might excuse her not being in her right mind.

He stood up, dusting sand off his steely thighs bare beneath his short tunic, and said, "Where does your brother await you?"

"My who?" Her mouth was very dry. That too was because of the fall and had nothing whatsoever to do with his nearness. Her heart was beating too fast probably for the same reason. A fall could do a lot of damage. Stranger yet was the sensation that she still had not touched ground and, indeed, might never do so.

"The brother you are going to meet?" He bent down again and looked at her closely. "Are you having trouble with your memory?"

"No! I'm perfectly fine." Except that she couldn't tell him where her brother was or he might decide to take her all the way to Normandy. She absolutely would not yield to the temptation that presented.

For that matter, she could not tell him *anything*. If he discovered who she was and why she was alone, he might take her straight to the very fate she was trying so desperately to elude. A warrior such as he had to be in service to some great lord. Her stomach roiled at the thought. He could be bound by oaths of loyalty that would make him act unquestioningly, no matter how hard she tried to convince him otherwise.

Slowly, ignoring the pounding in her head, she forced herself to sit up too swiftly for him to stop her. Staring into the most perfectly formed male features she had ever seen, she asked the question that was suddenly uppermost in her mind. "Who are you?"

Such a simple question and one he would normally have answered without thought. Yet Dragon was silent. The girl was hiding something, of that he was certain. But what? She had told him nothing about herself save for the mention of a brother he doubted existed. Who then might she be?

She was young; no longer misled by her boy's garb, he judged her to be perhaps seventeen or eighteen. She could be wed and fleeing a husband she thought unkind. Or she might have absconded from a convent, having decided the cloister was not to her liking. If he was going to look at the situation honestly, he had to consider also that she might be escaping prosecution for some crime.

The thing to do was to take her to Hawkforte with him and let Hawk sort it out. Yet he was oddly reluctant to do so. Partly that was because of her beauty, which, the longer he looked at her, became ever more evident. But he knew himself too well to believe he could be swayed by beauty alone. It was her spirit that drew him as well, her courageous if foolhardy daring and her refusal to fawn upon him as women had always done.

The plain fact was that she puzzled him. Almost as much as he loved women and stories, Dragon loved puzzles. That was likely not coincidence. He had thought to steal a few days to hunt and generally distract himself from the fate looming over his head. But now he considered an even more pleasing prospect. He could do right by the girl and divert himself at the same time. Once she understood she had nothing to fear from him, she would confess her secret, whatever it was, and he would see her to safety as recompense for having so endangered her.

That was only fair, but what he would not do was let the darling creature have her way in all matters. He needed no further evidence beyond the fact that she was traveling alone to conclude that her judgment was not the best. He would protect her even from herself.

Having settled the matter in his mind, Dragon acted promptly. "I will tell you who I am when you have told me who you are."

She scowled at him. "It's just a simple question. Why can't you answer it?"

"Why can't you?"

At a loss for a moment, Rycca recovered quickly. "I asked you first."

Dragon grinned. He was enjoying this. Better yet, he saw his challenge had distracted her from the pain in her head, which he guessed was considerable. She was still very pale and dark shadows were creeping beneath her eyes. The sooner she accepted that he was going to take care of her, the better.

"I don't think you remember who you are."

"I do so!"

"Then tell me."

Rycca started to reply, caught herself, and pressed her lips together in frustration. He had her neatly trapped. The longer she refused to divulge her identity, the more chance he might conclude the worst about her and take her to the authorities. Yet if she let him believe she was impaired from the fall, he would likely be even more determined not to leave her. She couldn't win in either case. Best then to seem to go along with him and wait for a chance to get away.

"My head hurts," she said. Again not a lie, for her skull pounded savagely. Yet she knew full well he would take it as an admission that her mind was not working properly.

His arms were around her before she could draw breath. He lifted her very gently and with no apparent effort. She was not a small woman but he made her feel absurdly like thistledown. Mayhap there really was something wrong with her mind.

"Where are you taking me?" He could tell her at least that much.

Dragon was already walking, feeling much happier now that he had her where she belonged. He stepped carefully to avoid jostling her. She was trying to keep her head up but that didn't last long. Soon enough she was leaning against his shoulder. "To a lodge no great distance away."

"Yours?"

"It belongs to a friend but I have the use of it. You can recover there."

"Then you are from here."

He looked down at her with a smile. "Did I say that?"

She winced, not up to more banter and feeling very weak. He saw it and was instantly repentant. "Enough chatter. You need to rest."

She subsided, but before long another question occurred to her. He had said the lodge was no great distance away, yet he had already carried her perhaps half a mile, as far as she could guess. That he did so with no sign of the slightest strain was not something she cared to dwell upon. Instead, she turned her thoughts in another direction.

"Why don't you have a horse?"

He looked at her chidingly but answered anyway. "I do have a horse."

"Where is it?"

"At the lodge. Enough now, be quiet and rest."

She obeyed but only because she had no choice. The shock of what had happened to her was finally setting in and she felt unutterably weary. Deciding she would close her eyes for just a few moments, Rycca slept.

H ER FEATURES BECAME SMOOTH AGAIN AS THE awareness of pain slipped away. That was good. If only she would stay asleep until they reached the lodge, she might awaken feeling much improved. The lodge was about another hour's walk at the pace the Dragon was keeping. No great distance by his standards. Truth be told, he could have gone on carrying her much longer. There was undeniable pleasure in holding her, despite the circumstances. Of course, he would much rather have had her in his arms awake and amorous, but he wasn't going to think about that.

Instead, he mulled over the mystery she presented. Obviously she'd been headed for somewhere, and Hawk-forte still seemed the likeliest place. What could a lone girl, probably of good family, hope to accomplish there? Was she, perhaps, intending to petition Hawk for redress of some injury? Possibly, but then why hadn't she just said so? Had she really lost her memory? Probably not, for there was too much awareness in those honey-hued eyes. But he was willing to allow that the brother might be real. Perhaps she meant to meet up with him in Hawkforte, but again, why not just say that? Could she have some reason for concealing her brother's identity, more even than her own?

In his most recent letter, Hawk had written of putting down an attempted rebellion by a Mercian lord. Mercia was allied to Wessex, ruled by the great Alfred, who had extended his dominion in other directions including Essex, where men of good sense, Hawk chief among them, were glad to acknowledge him as king. Mercia had done the same but not, apparently, without discord. Could the girl's family have been involved in that?

Dragon frowned, thinking on. Since his brother Wolf's marriage to the Hawk's sister, Dragon had visited Essex several times. He knew it fairly well now but the rest of England was a little hazy in his mind. If he remembered correctly, Mercia was landlocked. Anyone seeking to flee from there would have to go south into Wessex or southeast to Essex. Any other way out would mean going through territory still held by the Danes.

He glanced down at the girl. Sooner or later, he would find out how much trouble she was in. He would not let her go until he did.

The realization that somewhere in the course of the last hour he had come to that decision didn't surprise him. His mind often worked beneath the layers of his awareness. Nor did he much care that acquiring the company of a beautiful Saxon girl would raise eyebrows, at the very least. He was prepared to do his duty. If that didn't satisfy everyone, too bad.

Having decided on a course of action, Dragon continued on in better humor. It did not escape his notice that for a man who had been kicked in the balls only a few hours before, he was in a remarkably good mood. Indeed, he felt far more cheerful than he had in months, ever since realizing he could not dodge what fate had in store for him. Nothing had really changed yet somehow he felt more the master of his destiny. After all the lovely, accommodating women he had known in his life, why being assaulted and snarled at by a copper-haired spitfire should improve his outlook bewildered him. But he did like a challenge and she was that.

However, she was also injured, and honor demanded he put aside all other consideration until she was healed. That being the case, he was relieved to see the roof of the lodge come into view beyond a copse of pines.

It was a small building of rough-hewn planks roofed in thatch. Another, smaller structure was nearby, meant to house the horses that, as he had expected, had already arrived. His attendants had left them as arranged before continuing on their own way to Hawkforte. They would also have fed and watered the beasts since Dragon had no fondness for doing either.

He pushed open the door with his shoulder and stepped inside. There was only one room but it was spacious and comfortably appointed. A large iron brazier sat in the center of the floor below the smoke hole in the roof. A fire had already been laid and awaited only the addition of the glowing embers left in the metal box beside the hearth. Near the fire, set along one wall, was a sleep bench covered with a down-filled mattress, coverlets of finely woven wool, and a lush fur throw. If that was not sufficient indication that the lodge was the property of a wealthy lord, the choice selection of shields and banners hanging from the walls would have informed the least tutored eye.

A finely carved table with chairs and several chests completed the furnishings. From previous visits, Dragon knew there was a shed at the back for food storage and a sauna dug into the nearby hillside. Hawk had built the lodge as a gift for his beloved wife, the Lady Krysta. The pair of them with their baby son used it when they felt the need to escape from their duties and enjoy a few days together. They were also generous about lending it to friends, including Dragon.

He crossed the room and laid the girl carefully on the sleep bench. She scarcely stirred. After a moment's hesitation, Dragon removed her sandals but left the rest of her garb undisturbed. She was skittish enough as it was. Covering her, he went out to check on the horses.

As he expected, his attendants had seen to the animals. There was nothing left for him to do save to look at them warily. There were two, both chestnuts with coats so glossy they held a silver sheen. They were brothers born a year apart to the same mare. Oversized brutes, they could gallop tirelessly all day and charge straight into battle with rambunctious glee. They could also cavort as though they were still colts. When Dragon was fool enough to come near them with apples, they would give him no rest until he fed them, rubbed their velvety noses, and told them how wonderful they were.

He despised them. No, that wasn't fair. He despised the need to have anything to do with them. The animals themselves weren't to blame for that. It wasn't their fault he hated to ride and would never feel at home on the back of a horse no matter how much time he grimly and stubbornly spent there. Not that anyone knew his secret. He rode with the same power and grace he brought to everything but he took no credit for it. The gods had seen fit to endow him with unusual size and strength; he thanked them for it and went about his business. Every chance he got, he planted his feet firmly on the ground and counted on them to get him wherever he was going. They had never failed him, nor did he have to find fodder for them.

The horses, dumb animals that they were, had no hint of his true feelings. They thought he liked them, which probably explained why they were always glad to see him. Even now, they were butting against him, vying for his attention, and making slobbering fools of themselves. He bore it as long as he could, checked again to make sure they had everything they needed, and retreated to the lodge.

The girl was still asleep. She looked to remain that way for quite some time. Dragon plucked a bow and a sheaf of arrows off a peg on the wall and headed out the door.

RYCCA WOKE AS THE SUN WAS DRIFTING LOWER in the sky. She sighed luxuriously and turned over onto her side. What luxury to be in a comfortable bed. Truly, she could not remember the last time she had felt so utterly relaxed. Not at home certainly because she had fled from there and . . .

Her eyes shot open. She sat up abruptly and looked around. There was no sign of *him*, for which she was much relieved, and she did not at all feel a small pang of alarm. Absolutely not. Her head still hurt but not as much as it had. Yet did she feel bruised all over, as though the full effects of tumbling down the cliffside were only now making themselves felt.

This must be the lodge he had mentioned. Her brows drew together. The appointments were far more luxurious than she had expected. The bed she was lying in was bigger, softer, and the covers . . . She plucked the blanket, noting that it was of finely spun wool skillfully woven. There was a large table near the fire. Its sturdy legs were carved in a spiral design and the whole was well polished. Two high-backed chairs startled her for she had never seen but two others like them in her life, her father's chair and the one he kept for honored guests. Yet not even he could boast the beautifully made pillows embroidered with bright flowers that graced each chair and assured the posterior of anyone seated in it would be well content.

Pillows? Slowly, Rycca rose from the bed. The lodge boasted several windows equipped with ox-hide coverings that were rolled up to admit light and air. Beneath them were intricately carved chests. She walked over to one, tentatively lifted the lid, and was surprised when it opened. Instantly, the scent of honeysuckle and lilac rose to greet her. Eyes widening, she bent closer. Directly below the lid of the chest was a wooden tray and in that tray was . . .

Soap? Perfectly formed circles of soap scented with honeysuckle and lilac replacing the usual smell of rendered animal fat and lye. Astounded, she lifted one and sniffed deeply. Instantly, she felt transported to a summer meadow. As though burned, she dropped the soap and slammed the chest shut. But that could not stop her from scanning the lodge anew, seeing now all the myriad little touches that signified a woman's presence. There were dried flowers hanging from the rafters. The sleep bench was draped with lushly embroidered curtains drawn back by tasseled ties. The iron brackets set in the walls were designed not for torches that would smoke but for precious candles.

No mere woman then but a lady. She must be somewhere nearby, for the chest had been left unlocked. Suddenly acutely conscious of her dirty face, rough clothing, and bruised forehead, Rycca hesitated. Realizing there was nothing to be done about any of that, she steeled herself and eased open the door.

A freshening breeze riffled the tops of the trees. She stepped out and glanced to either side. No hint of movement, no sound of footfall to suggest where the lady might be. But she did hear a low nickering coming from the building she assumed was the stable.

Slowly, she went in that direction. She had almost reached it when a gleaming chestnut head popped out the window. Rycca found herself being gazed upon by the most appealing pair of brown eyes she had ever seen. A rapturous sigh escaped her, escalating to a blatant groan of delight when a second head appeared. There were two of them! A matched pair of magnificent chestnuts, as she discovered when she hurried into the stable. The horses nickered a welcome from their adjacent stalls.

"Oh, look at you!" Rycca crooned in sheer delight at the lithe, powerful animals. She adored horses, had ever since as a tiny child she had clambered aboard her first mount when no one was watching. That it was a warhorse only the strongest men could manage meant nothing to her at all. On the back of a horse, she felt safe and secure, protected from the violence of the world around her and at one with the swift galloping wind. Heaven could not offer anything better.

What a strange day this was turning out to be. Awakening to the sight of the most compelling man she had ever seen, fleeing from him, running right off the edge of a cliff, and now encountering these glorious horses.

Her aches and pains forgotten, Rycca smiled. "Aren't you just wonderful! Aren't you the most beautiful horses ever?"

They agreed with her heartily, tossing their proud heads and nuzzling her until she burst out laughing. "You're such sweethearts! Who owns you? Who deserves a pair like you?"

He had said his horse awaited him at the lodge but the stable contained only these two. Either his mount wasn't here after all or . . .

Her smile faded. Only a warrior of lordly rank could possess such horses. Likely, they would be the gift of a great noble in thanks for services rendered. There was only one such thane in this part of England, the man called Hawk. A shiver ran through Rycca. She had heard her father and brothers speak of him with fear and envy. Such was his power that people from all walks of life flocked to his side. His stronghold of Hawkforte had become a thriving port and market town as the wiliest merchants prospered under his protection. Rycca herself was making for it because it offered the best possible chance of getting a ship to Normandy. Yet did Hawkforte also pose the greatest possible danger to her should her identity be discovered.

The warriors of the Hawk were said to be the most fearsome in the land. *He* would certainly fit that description, which made it likely he was a sworn man of the Hawk himself. Praise be to heaven that she had told him nothing!

The realization of how close she really had come to disaster banished the daze of uncertainty that had clung to her since awakening in the unknown bed. She had to get away and quickly before he returned. The horses posed an undeniable temptation. On the back of one of them, she could cover miles in scarcely any time. But so, too, would she be the focus of all eyes. A lone boy riding a horse known to belong to a sworn man of the Hawk could expect to be stopped and challenged.

But she would have no better chance on foot. Belatedly, she realized what should have been starkly evident to her when he appeared hours after she thought she was safely away from him. He had tracked her easily and he would do so again unless she could find some way to conceal all trace of herself.

The problem made her head hurt even more. She left the horses reluctantly and continued to explore around the lodge. There was still no sign of a lady, which, now that Rycca thought about it, was probably fortunate. *He* had said the lodge belonged to a friend. Likely it belonged to the Hawk himself and unlikely that his lady would be anywhere about without his own presence. Rycca shuddered. She had seen the Lord Hawk once; more to the point, he had seen her. That she might encounter him again chilled her to the bone.

Her head was throbbing by the time she spotted a glint of water just visible through the trees. A narrow trail led down to what proved to be a river. Hope flared within her. If the water was not too deep or fast running, she might be able to escape undetected after all.

Might, if she wasn't half blinded by the sunlight and weak as a day-old kitten. She took a deep breath, trying to find within herself the strength to step into the river, make her way over slippery rocks and fallen branches, and trudge mile after mile for however long it took to reach Hawkforte, presuming the river went that far.

Sooner begun, sooner ended. She had never been one to put things off. Barely had she learned of her family's plans for her than she had laid her own plans for escape. There was no sense waiting around for things to get worse. Yet try though she did, she could not take that first necessary step into the water. She could stare at it, all right, and think about how important it was for her to get away. But there she still was on the riverbank, leaning against a tree and blinking dazedly in the overbright light.

Her whole body hurt. She felt as though she had . . . fallen off a cliff. The realization made her laugh weakly. How else could she possibly feel? Not that it mattered. She still had to do what she had to do.

Just that first step . . .

She managed to push herself away from the tree that had been holding her up but the moment she did so, she swayed alarmingly. Reaching out to the sturdy trunk, she steadied herself and took several deep breaths. That seemed to help. Mayhap if she went very quickly, the shock of the water would revive her enough so that she would be able to keep going.

Mayhap she would fall flat on her face and drown. She had escaped death once that day by a hair's breadth. Did she truly want to tempt fate again?

Yet what other choice was there? Stay where she was and wait to recover her strength? In company with a sworn man of the Lord Hawk. Oh, yes, that was a splendid idea. Why not simply tell him everything right now and go like a lamb to the slaughter?

Damn herself for being so weak! If she had a man's strength, she could push on, but no, she was trapped in a woman's body and prey to all the vulnerabilities that brought. Even now, her eyes burned with tears of sheer weakness. Furiously, she scrubbed a hand across her face. At the very least, she could spare herself the ignominy of crying.

No, it seemed she couldn't, because the tears continued to trickle down her cheeks. Worse yet, her legs were giving way. Even as she grabbed hold of the tree and tried to stay upright, her knees seemed to dissolve right out from under her. She slid down onto the mossy ground and stayed there, too weary to move.

Thus did Dragon find her a short time later when he returned from the hunt. At first glance inside the lodge, he was alarmed to find the bed empty. But it was easy enough to see where she had gone. Shaking his head at such folly, he went after her.

She was sitting beside the river, her legs drawn up and her chin resting on her knees. He had a moment to enjoy the pure line of her profile and the tumble of coppery hair down her back before she sensed his presence. She turned her head very slightly, looked at him, then looked back at the river.

Dragon sighed. He sat down beside her. Silence drew out between them until he said, "Do you like rabbits?"

"Hopping around or on a stick?"

"I was thinking more of rabbit stew."

Her stomach growled.

He grinned, stood up, and offered her a hand. She stared at it for a moment before her shoulders slumped. With obvious reluctance, she allowed him to help her up.

"Are you strong enough to walk?" he asked.

"Of course I am." She took a step and sat right back down on the ground.

Dragon cursed under his breath. He scooped her up, ignoring her protests, and started back to the lodge. She frowned the whole way, including when he set her on the bed.

Gently, he said, "You'll feel better after you've eaten."

She looked up at him and he saw for the first time that she had been crying. His heart turned over. She might not have much sense but she had courage aplenty and he admired that. "Look," he said, going down on his haunches and taking her hands in his, "you've been through a bad time and I suspect I don't know the half of it. But things will get better now. You just have to trust me."

Truth.

He actually meant it. This fierce warrior intended to help her. She studied him with the same intensity as she would have given to a marvel of nature never before encountered. Her twin, Thurlow, had a kind heart, but that made him unique among all the men she had ever known. Never before had she met a man who had the power to compel others to his will yet acted with compassion.

For a moment, the temptation to unburden herself to him was almost overwhelming. She was stopped only by the knowledge that if she told him who she was, he would be caught between duty to his lord and desire to help her. That was no way to repay kindness.

She stared down at the powerful hands holding hers and felt an odd tightening in her throat. Such strength and yet such gentleness . . . Locked in the tumult of her emotions, she did not notice the single silver tear that fell like a sparkling star against his wind-roughened skin.

THREE

THE TEAR SEEMED TO SCALD HIM. DRAGON gazed at it for a long moment before he released her hands and rose. A little gruffly, he said, "Lie down and rest now. I'll wake you when supper is ready."

She nodded, too drained to do anything else. He drew the cover up over her and waited as her breath became slow and deep. Only when he was certain she was asleep did he go back outside to see to the stew. Swiftly, he built a small fire and set over it an iron tripod from which he hung a pot filled with water drawn from the nearby well. As the water warmed, he added the meat, as well as wild carrots, turnips, cabbage, and a handful of herbs and spices. Leaving the whole to simmer gently, he went around the back to the larder, finding there the skins of wine, loaves of fresh-baked bread, golden rounds of cheese, and baskets of summer fruits left by the servants of his thoughtful host.

Let it never be said that Hawk did anything halfway. But then besides being a good friend, he had every reason to want Dragon in a reasonably decent mood. If it took a few days at the hunting lodge, holding the world at bay, so be it.

A few days in the company of a beguiling Saxon girl. Oh, yes, that was a good idea. There was a real risk he would end up even less reconciled to his fate than he was already. Yet it was a risk he would take willingly, determined as he was to make amends for running her off the side of a cliff.

A proper meal would be a good start. By the time the stew was ready, the girl was stirring again. Carrying the pot into the lodge, he watched with amusement as first her nose twitched, then her eyes opened. She sat up and looked at him curiously.

"What is that?"

He hoisted the pot a little before setting it on the table. "Come and eat."

She came but cautiously, not taking her eyes from him until finally she bent over the pot, took a long sniff, and blinked dazedly. "You can cook."

He shrugged modestly. "The credit is not mine. A friend showed me how to make this."

She was back to looking at him. "You seem to have a lot of friends."

Dragon grinned and held out one of the chairs for her. "It's true, I'm fortunate in that regard. Likely it comes from being a friendly sort of person."

"A friendly warrior. Do you hug your enemies on the battlefield? Crushing the life from them in an excess of amicability?"

Ladling stew, he paused before answering. He had heard the thread of bitterness beneath her words. Not surprising in a land where one even as young as she might well have known war. But not of late. "Haven't you heard? We are at peace."

"Ah, yes, the peace of blessed Alfred. Do you know

some say he will be made a saint? Of course, he will have to die first."

He concealed his surprise but with difficulty. She spoke so easily of the king, almost familiarly. Were all English like that? Or did it reflect her upbringing in a noble house? A house perhaps not loyal to Alfred?

Dragon set her bowl before her along with a spoon carved from oak. He served himself before replying. "It is not wise to speak of the death of kings."

She looked surprised by the reprimand, mild though it was. "I wish the man no harm—to the contrary. I am merely . . . skeptical."

He picked up the bread, tore off a hunk, and handed it to her. "Of Alfred or of peace?"

She did not answer directly and he had the sense she thought she had already said too much. The stew provided a ready distraction. She took a spoonful, then another, and sighed deeply. "Your friend is a genius."

Dragon laughed. He thought of one-eyed Olaf, the old Viking who had joined up with Dragon and his brother while they roamed the world and stayed with them through the long climb to power. The recipe was his and he was rightly proud of it.

"I will tell him you said so. Try the wine." He filled a goblet before she could object. She took a sip cautiously. It was very good wine, brought all the way from the land of the Franks, but Dragon did not expect her to be surprised by it. He had already concluded that she was the daughter of a noble house, therefore likely well accustomed to such luxuries. Yet, contrary to his expectation, she looked first startled, then amazed.

"Surely, you have tasted such before?"

She spared him a quick glance before returning her attention to the food. "It is good enough."

They ate in silence, both hungry and doing justice to

the meal but aware of all that lay unspoken between them. While yet she refused to tell him who she was, he would reveal nothing of himself. Never before had Dragon realized how very little that left to talk about. Several times he thought to speak but did not. She was still very tired, the bruise on her forehead a constant reminder of what she had suffered. He could not bring himself to press her.

When they had finished, he rose from the table and gathered up the dishes. The sun had almost vanished beyond the western hills. Soon it would be dark. "I think you will find a night robe in the chest, if you look."

Her head lifted at that and she scrutinized him. "Do you think the lady who obviously comes to this place would approve of my using her things even if she is so foolish as to leave them here and unlocked?"

"She is generous, not foolish, and she would not mind."

"Who is she?"

The question came so suddenly that he was on the verge of answering it when he caught himself. "Who are you?"

She scowled and looked away. He sighed, loudly and exaggeratedly, and continued clearing the table. "When you are better rested, I'll expect you to help with the chores."

Her head whipped around so quickly that hair like copper silk lashed his arm. "What makes you think I will be here long enough for that?"

"I am paying you the compliment of assuming you are intelligent." Before she could conceal her wary surprise, he added, "Or if not, that you have at least enough common sense to realize that you would not get very far." Ominously, he added, "If I have to go after you again, I will put aside any concern I have about why you are concealing your identity and take you straight to the authorities. Is that clear?"

She paled slightly, making him twinge with guilt, but he ignored that. The threat was as much for her own good as for his peace of mind. When she murmured under her breath, he bent closer. "What was that?"

Their eyes were level. Hers blazed. "I said," she repeated, enunciating very clearly, "you'll have to catch me first."

Dragon recognized desperation when he heard it. "It wouldn't be much of a contest right now," he said gently. "Perhaps when you're recovered."

He was being kind to her again, not throwing her defiance back in her face as she had half expected, not even getting angry at it. Truly, this wasn't fair. He looked like a god of ancient yore, was remarkably good-humored and genuinely kind, and, miracle of miracles, he cooked. Men like that did not exist in Rycca's world, at least not as far as she had ever seen.

Perhaps in going off that cliff, she had leaped into a new land with as yet unsuspected marvels. Wasn't that a thought?

But not for her aching head. The wine had not been a good idea. She was duzzled enough as it was. Duzzled wasn't a word, was it? Ought to be, though, for it perfectly described what she felt—dazed and dulled.

A god of ancient yore. Really not fair at all.

"Let me help you," he said and eased her gently from the chair. A few steps and she was back to the bed—the so big, so comfortable bed so obviously built for two. Never, ever had she thought of sharing a bed with a man and she wasn't thinking of it now. Absolutely not. He was very close, holding her elbow lightly. His touch seared her. She was fevered and chilled all at the same time. She was coming down with the ague, she decided, and who could blame her after the day she'd had? But she was as hearty as the horses she loved and likely to throw off any ailment swiftly.

"I will sleep outside," he said, "but if you need anything, call and I will hear you."

That was a twinge of relief she felt, not disappointment. Her nature was not so bold, at least not in such
matters. It was merely the duzzling that had made her
mistake one emotion for the other.

After he had left, closing the door quietly behind him,
she sat for a while on the edge of the bed. The food had
given her a little strength and she had already slept far
more than was usual, so she was content for a time to
merely take in her surroundings. The lodge fascinated her.
Never before had she seen such evidence of a woman's influence. Or for that matter any influence at all. Her father's
holding was starkly shorn of feminine touches. If any had
ever existed, they had died with Rycca's mother. That
pale, silent woman had perished in childbed when Rycca
was eight, her death the result of the last in a long series of
miscarriages. No trace of her remained but for the grave
visited only by Rycca and her twin. Certainly there was no
sign that she had put her mark upon her husband's holding, nor had any other woman done so. There, all that was
feminine was decried as weak and contemptible. But not
here, in this place where the womanly seemed not merely
allowed but celebrated.

Mulling that over, Rycca stood and made her way to
the carved chests beneath the windows. Slowly, she bent
and opened the one in which she had discovered the marvelous soaps. The man had said something about a night
robe—

She had never slept but nude or in a rough shift. Certainly she had never seen anything like the confection of
finely woven linen and lace she drew from the chest. On
impulse, she raised it to her face and inhaled deeply. The
garment smelled of sunshine and roses. The yearning
to wear something so extraordinarily feminine just once
overwhelmed her. She was about to remove her tunic

when a knock at the door stopped her. Quickly, she stuffed the night robe back into the chest.

"What is it?"

Dragon cracked the door open. He was carrying a bucket of toughened hide filled with water. "I thought you might want this." He stepped inside and set the bucket on the table. "But be careful, it's hot. Let it cool a little."

She nodded, trying to absorb the fact that he had brought her water to wash. A warrior drawing water, heating it, and not even for his own use. Truly, this had to be a different world.

"Thank you," she murmured but he was already gone, closing the door behind him.

A short while later, scrubbed from head to toe and clad in the night robe, Rycca slipped back into bed. She had cleaned up carefully after herself though it took what little strength she had left. The lodge looked just as it should, which was to say perfect. She lay on the softest mattress she had ever known, beneath cloud-light covers, and watched the long summer twilight fade to gentle dark. Her last thought before drifting off was that she was already dreaming.

Dragon required longer to get to sleep. He lay on a bed of pine needles, his arms folded behind his head, and looked at the stars. From long habit, he picked out the shapes men saw in them, recalling the stories associated with each. But his mind kept drifting far closer to home.

He'd been right to think her a puzzle. She wore the garb of a highborn youth and had the manner to go with it, defiant and confident. But she had never tasted good wine before and the smallest courtesy seemed to take her by surprise. Was this merely typical of the English or were her circumstances unusual? That he had no way of knowing did not stop him from wondering. But the day had been long and eventually he, too, drifted off.

Only to wake abruptly in the thick of night, shocked upright by a scream that interrupted the drone of summer insects and sent a prowling fox scurrying for its den. Dragon was on his feet, reaching for the sword that lay beside him, when he realized the scream came from inside the lodge. In a single motion, he tore the blade from its sheath and hurled himself straight through the door. Any intruder would have been hacked down in a breath but there was no one to be seen save Rycca. She was sitting up in the bed, gasping for breath, her eyes wide but sightless. A long shudder ran through her as she tried to fight free of sleep that had become the gateway to terror.

Dragon was at her side in a heartbeat. He set the sword down on the floor and gathered her into his arms. Perched on the edge of the bed, holding her, he rocked her back and forth, crooning to her softly. "It's all right, nothing's going to hurt you. There's nothing to be afraid of, you're safe."

She shuddered again but clung to him, her head burrowed against his chest as though she was trying to shut out all the world. Sobs racked her. Bewildered and deeply concerned, Dragon tightened his hold. Perhaps she had dreamed of falling off the cliff. That possibility stabbed through him and he resolved to do anything necessary to calm her. Truly, he could not bear to see a woman in distress. Carefully, he eased her back down on the bed, fitting himself in beside her, protecting her within the curve of his body as he sought to soothe her.

Rycca did not hear his murmured words but she felt his hand lightly stroking her hair. It penetrated the fog of her terror, reaching not the woman he held but the little girl locked inside her memories.

Such terrifying memories . . . smoke rising from burning huts . . . bodies sprawled everywhere . . . people running in every direction, screaming, falling . . . and Aelflynne . . . dear, sweet Aelflynne, only Rycca's age, also without a mother, the best friend ever for creeping into hay racks to play with precious poppets and exchange secrets. Aelflynne . . .

"Nooooo!"

She struck out desperately, hammering against Dragon's chest, tears streaming down her pale cheeks.

The breath caught in her throat as it had that terrible night. She was choking, unable to breathe, fighting her way through smoke to reach her friend's side, slipping on dark blood oozing away into the greedy ground. And Aelflynne so still . . . eyes wide and staring at the uncaring sky.

She wanted to die, as she had yearned to then, to escape a world that held within it such horror. Yet caught within memory's grip, she was also aware of something else holding her . . . someone . . . speaking to her softly and urgently, surrounding her with gentle strength, drawing her back from the precipice of despair.

Someone . . . him . . . the hero of the strange new world in which she had found herself. Beneath his hands, in his arms, she felt terror flow away. She opened her eyes once, saw his gazing at her, and slipped into blessed dreamlessness.

Dragon exhaled slowly. The girl was a limp weight against him but he scarcely noticed. He was glad that whatever nightmare had troubled her was gone. Yet could he not think to leave her lest it return. A deep sigh escaped him. With the girl nestled against him, he found it impossible to return to sleep. His response to her was predictable enough, for clad only in the thin night robe, no illusion of the boy remained. Yet for once he did not wish to be blessed with quite so ardent a nature. Still he was as he was and he could be grateful she was unaware rather than afraid or shocked. What he would do in such eventuality he really didn't know for he had no experience with women who were other than . . . friendly. This one was

not. Indeed, she put him in mind of a prickly little creature, all sharp points sprouting in every direction.

She stirred against him just then and he was reminded that, prickly or not, she was also very soft and
smooth, gently curved and lithe in his arms. He smoth-
ered another sigh that was really more of a groan and
schooled himself to fortitude. It was going to be a long
night.

R YCCA WOKE GREATLY REFRESHED. HER HEAD
hurt scarcely at all compared to the pounding of the
previous day. Her limbs bore the faint echo of an ache but
a little luxurious stretching eased that away. She left the
bed, carefully removed the night robe, and was washing
with water from the bucket on the table when she remembered the dream. A shudder ran down her back but she
wasn't really cold. The day was already balmy, and besides, the water she was using was warm.

Which it could not have been if it was the water left
over from the night before, which meant someone—*he*—
had brought her fresh water not long ago while yet she
slept as she had all night in that bed, which, now that she
noticed, bore in its soft mattress the mark of two bodies—
not one—resting side by side.

Water she forgot to wipe away trickled down her face
as memories of the night overtook her. That the dream
had come did not surprise her for it always did when she
was especially tired, in pain, or frightened. Yet surely it
was a trick of memory to think *he* had also come, holding
her gently, murmuring reassurances so that the haunting
terror faded far more swiftly than it ever had before. Had
he truly done all that and remained with her throughout
the night, chastely and protectively, holding her fear
at bay?

Good food and hot water were unusual enough; such comfort as she imagined he had given her was surely impossible. Yet there was the depression in the bed to say otherwise. On impulse, she bent down beside the bed, put her head to the smooth linen, and inhaled. Sun . . . wind . . . sea . . . whispers of wildness and power that were purely male. Her own spirit—proud, strong, female—rose in instinctive response. She swallowed hard and spun away from the bed. Quickly she dressed, retreating into her boy's garb.

When she was finished, pride made it impossible to remain inside. Yanking open the door, she stepped into dappled sunlight.

D RAGON CROUCHED ON THE GROUND, STIR-ring the fire. He looked up as she emerged and slowly stood. She looked well, he thought, better than might be expected after a haunted night. But she would not meet his eyes and her self-consciousness was palpable.

None of the women of his vast acquaintance would have felt the least self-conscious for having merely spent the night in bed with him. At least not unless chastity embarrassed them. Yet there she was, her cheeks aflame, and her gaze skittering off to anywhere other than where he stood.

He hid a smile and returned his attention to the fire. "There's porridge if you're hungry."

She shrugged but came nearer. Taking that as encouragement, he ladled porridge into a wooden bowl, added a drizzle of honey, and topped it off with a scattering of wild strawberries picked that morning. When he handed it to her along with a spoon, she blinked in surprise.

"Another of your friend's recipes?"

"No one needs a recipe for porridge."

Her swift glance suggested otherwise but quickly she turned her attention to eating. After a tentative first taste, the rest of the porridge disappeared with speed he could not help find flattering.

"There's more," he offered, but she shook her head, self-consciousness returning.

"About last night—" she said.

Hurrying to put her at ease, he said, "You had a bad dream. I held you and you quieted, that's all."

"It was very kind of you." She looked at him once, quickly, and looked away again. "Thank you."

"You seem little accustomed to kindness."

She took the bowl to a pail of water near the fire, rinsed it out, and returned it to him. Perhaps she had taken to heart what he'd said about helping with the chores. Or maybe she was buying time to reply to a question that, answered carelessly, might reveal something of her identity.

"I am as I am." Unconsciously, she echoed his thoughts of the night before. The similarity startled him. Were they alike then in some way? He would not have thought so but beneath the obvious differences of man and woman, he sensed her pride and strength, her courage and fortitude, all virtues he liked to think he possessed.

A sudden smile lit his sculpted features. She stared, caught herself, and frowned. "What is it?"

"I was just thinking you are like a warrior, a woman warrior. There are legends of such beings, you know."

"Boudicae was no legend. She was real."

Boudicae. She was . . . ? Wait, he remembered. An ancient Briton queen who had stood against the Romans of legend, people Dragon had thought mythical until he went to Byzantium and discovered otherwise. Were he Saxon, he would know of her as the girl did.

"Well, yes, of course, there's Boudicae. But what about the Amazons?"

"The who?"

"Amazons. Mayhap I will tell you of them. What do you wish to do today?"

Caught unawares, she said what first came to her mind. "Leave."

His smile turned swiftly to a grimace. "You are honest, at least."

Of course she was honest, she who dealt with truth as others dealt with breath. She had no choice in the matter. But that he perceived such in her, saw the intrinsic honesty, surprised her. Suddenly he was closer even than he had been in the bed, touching the very essence of her.

Bluntly, she said, "You could have lain with me last night. We both know I could not have stopped you. You did not; therefore I ask you, why do you keep me here?"

"I owe you a debt for injuring you. I will see you to safety if you but allow it."

"I release you from your debt. Let me go."

There was the crux of it. She released him, he could simply walk away or let her do the same. Yet could he not. His concern for her safety was genuine. An unprotected woman, especially one who looked as she did, faced obvious risk. But something else was at work besides concern for her, something about her that drew him despite the reckless complication she presented in his life just then.

As a reasonable man, he could not be swayed by the undeniable attraction he felt for her. How fortunate then that there was also the matter of her safety. He seized hard hold of it and refused to let go.

"Go where?" he challenged. "To your brother, wherever he may be? How do you propose to get there safely? For that matter, how do you even plan to feed yourself?

You have no means of hunting food, and if you have coin to pay for it or anything else, you have it well concealed."

When she did not respond but only looked at him, he pressed harder. "You almost died yesterday. Are you so anxious to depart this life that you would go on alone, taking such risk when there is no need?"

"There is need. I cannot stay here."

"Tell me who you are and I will see you forthwith to safety."

She worried the grass with her toes but faced him squarely. "It must be obvious to you that if I could do that, I would have done it yesterday."

Dragon nodded. He understood full well that she could not trust him. He was a stranger and a warrior, but that was not the sole cause of her distrust. She also harbored a secret that he suspected would drive her to conceal her identity from anyone.

"All right then," he said. "I offer a bargain. Stay here a few days. I promise no harm will come to you, and if at that time you still will not tell me who you are, I will take you wherever you wish and ask no further questions."

Truth.

The tight coil of tension present within her since she had first awakened began to ease a little. He meant what he said. For whatever reason, he truly did want to help her. Heaven knew, she needed help aplenty. Her situation was terrifying, her prospects grim. Without help, she might never reach the coast, much less take ship for Normandy.

Yet she hesitated for right alongside the recognition of her need was need of another sort. She who had never taken any notice of men except to avoid them could scarcely take her eyes from him. She who had thought the strongest emotion she was capable of feeling was fear had just begun to discover the power of desire.

He tempted her, this man of gentleness and truth,

tempted her as she had never before been tempted in her life. Indeed, it was a new world of temptation he presented such as she had not known could exist. If he had been merely handsome, even devastatingly so as he was, she might have managed better. It was the combination of his sheer physical beauty and the beauty of his nature that undid her.

Or threatened to, at least. She tried to imagine herself undone but, lacking any such experience, failed. She would be all right then . . . most likely . . . and besides, what choice did she really have? A few days in his company, protected and cared for, her secret still locked safe within her, and then his help to accomplish what she would be hard-pressed to do alone. What else could she possibly say but . . .

"A bargain then." She held out her hand, slim, summer tanned, her palms callused. He gave his own, swallowing hers with gentle care. Touching, they stood and stared at each some little time before remembering themselves. Their hands parted, they each took a cautious step back. Dragon cleared his throat.

"I ask again, what would you like to do today?"

Something well and thoroughly distracting so that she did not have to drag her gaze from him continually. A sudden, happy thought occurred to her. "There are two wonderful horses here."

"You are not well enough to ride." He spoke so quickly and looked so wary that Rycca could not help but wonder why.

"Are they your horses?" she asked.

Reluctantly, he nodded. "They are."

"I have never seen more magnificent steeds. You must be very proud of them."

"They are well enough, I suppose. You will do better with a gentle walk."

"I will not! I am fully recovered. If you are concerned

I might damage them in some way, I will assure you that I ride well. Please do not think me immodest for saying so, but I love horses and they seem to know that."

He continued to look at her skeptically. "You get along with them?"

"Oh, yes! Truly, if you will only trust me, I promise I will do no harm."

Dark brows rose above topaz eyes. "Trust? I thought that singularly lacking between us."

He had her there, Rycca thought glumly. Now he would throw her lack of trust in him back in her face and that would be that. No chance to ride like the wind on a creature almost as beautiful and compelling as its master.

"All right."

What was that he'd said? "All right?"

Dragon nodded. He did not look happy about the prospect but seemed resigned to it. "Trust has to start somewhere. I will trust you with my horses. *One* of them, at any rate, for be assured I will be on the other and right beside you. Do not even consider going off on your own—"

"I would never!" Actually, she had, but rejected any such notion as foolhardy. He didn't have to know that.

He had agreed. He was actually going to let her ride one of those glorious, thrilling steeds. For just a moment, giddy excitement threatened to overwhelm her. She came *that* close to flinging herself at him in burbling thanks. Praise be to heaven, she caught herself in time, but the nearness of her escape made her heart hammer. Not his nearness, that had nothing to do with it at all.

Quickly, before he could change his mind, Rycca turned toward the stable. Over her shoulder, she called, "I'll saddle yours, too. You don't have to do a thing."

Joy. The most fascinating woman he could remember meeting had kicked him in the balls, refused to tell him even her name, and loved those slobbering, four-footed dolts forever poking about for apples and wanting their manes combed. What were the gods about? Was this all some plot by Loki to resign him to his fate, mayhap even make him grateful for it? The god of mischief was capable of doing that and worse. Mayhap he would be well advised to find himself a plump goat and sacrifice it to the prank-prone deity. At the very least, it couldn't hurt.

Resigned, he trudged after the girl, arriving in time to help her hoist the heavy saddles into place. She gave him a smile of such sheer delight as to rock him back on his heels. Barely had he recovered from that than she was leading the horses out.

"What are their names?" she called.

Dragon thought fast. Both horses had Norse names but he was disinclined to tell her that. She believed him to be Saxon, as why should she not since he spoke Saxon as well as she did. Let her go on believing that there was at least that much bond between them.

"Their names are . . . Romulus and Remus."

"Strange names. How came you to think of them?"

"Those two were brothers and supposedly the founders of Rome."

Listening, she handed one set of reins to Dragon and, before he could so much as blink, lightly sprang onto the back of the other horse. The horse was taller than the girl herself. For her to mount him without assistance suggested both strength and skill. From her perch, she grinned at his bemusement and asked, "Which one is this?"

"Romulus . . . that's who he is." Determined not to be outdone, and by a girl no less, Dragon mounted quickly. The newly dubbed Remus shied a little, cursed beast that he was, but he settled down quickly enough.

"I have heard of Rome," she said, "but know little of it. Do you know more?"

"Somewhat. What would you like to know?"

"Anything . . . everything. Whatever you would tell."

Skald-souled as he was, Dragon could not resist. Would that all audiences were so uncritical and so eager.

Chapter

FOUR

L ONG YEARS AGO," DRAGON BEGAN, "MORE
years than men know, two infant brothers were
abandoned near where a great river runs. They
were left to die there by the jealousy of their
great-uncle who had usurped their grandfather's throne.
Fortunately, they were found by a she-wolf and a wood-
pecker, who suckled and fed them until a herdsman discovered the boys and took them into his own home to be
reared. When they came to manhood, they banded together with other youths, overthrew their treacherous
great-uncle, and restored their grandfather to his throne.
However, their adventures had only begun. In time . . ."

So they went, riding through the summer forest beside the silver river while Dragon spun images of fierce
struggle, betrayal, death, and glory. Rycca forgot her wish
to gallop like the wind. Never had she heard such a tale so
vividly told. His voice flowed over her like silken rain, beguiling, entrancing, making her forget all else.

"And so," Dragon concluded at length, "having
killed his own brother and conquered the Sabine people,
Romulus ruled for a time as king of Rome. But one day a

mysterious storm descended upon the land. It came not as storms do, with at least some warning, but suddenly and it turned day into night. Wild lightning rent the sky, and the seven hills of the city shuddered from the force of the thunder. A strange, whirling vortex of wind danced upon the ground, right up the steps of the palace and into the building itself. There it seized up Romulus and carried him away. He was never seen again."

Rycca sighed with pleasure. The spell of the story still clung to her. "Mayhap the wind was his brother's spirit come for revenge."

"Mayhap," Dragon agreed, "but the Romans of old thought it was the gods who came for Romulus, to make him one of them."

They had come along the trail to a pleasant glen. Dragon drew rein, glad of the excuse to dismount. "We should water the horses."

Rycca nodded and slipped from the saddle. She rubbed her horse's nose affectionately, cooing over him. "You're such a good boy, aren't you? You have such a splendid gait, so smooth and steady. I'll bet you could run all day and never tire."

"Romulus"—the four-footed one—was taking all this in with the delight he would give a big juicy apple. He butted his head against the girl, which only prompted her to laugh and stroke him all the more. "Remus" could not stand missing out. He shouldered up against his brother, trying to push him out of the way. That several thousand pounds of horseflesh were shoving and jostling right in front of her did not seem to trouble the girl at all. It bothered Dragon mightily. He had seen men crushed beneath such animals in battle.

"All right," he said, stepping between her and the unruly pair. "Let's get them watered."

Rycca looked at him curiously but complied. As the horses drank, then grazed, Dragon made himself comfortable against a moss-draped rock. He was thinking that he should have brought a fishing line when the girl asked, "Who were the Amazons?"

"Don't tell me you want another story already?" Dragon teased.

She shrugged. "Do you have another?"

"I suspect I have hundreds, maybe more. It seems all my life I have been collecting or creating them."

"Perhaps you should have been a bard."

"I have thought of that but . . ." He paused. "I have been called to a different path." Patting the ground beside him, he said, "The Amazons . . . what a tale is that."

She sat, he spun.

"The Amazons were a race of women warriors, very fierce in battle, it was said. They lived without men for the most part, associating with them only to get children. The females they kept, the males they sent back to their fathers. Many great stories are told of them. For instance, they warred with a mighty hero called Heracles, who was set tasks by the gods, including to steal the girdle of the Amazon's queen."

"Some hero," Rycca scoffed, "stealing a woman's girdle."

"Better than her head, wouldn't you say?"

"I suppose."

Dragon continued. "At another time, a great war was being fought at a place called Troy. The Amazons were allied with the people of that city. They battled with another hero, called Achilles. He slew their queen in battle only to realize after he had done so that he loved her."

"He should have thought of that first, wouldn't you say?"

"He should have indeed. Another Amazon queen, I think it was the same one who had her girdle stolen, ended up marrying yet another hero after he defeated her in battle."

Rycca rolled her eyes. She plucked a piece of sweet grass and chewed it thoughtfully. "For women who wanted to live apart from men, it seems they had to spend a lot of their time fighting them."

Dragon shrugged. "It's just a tale. Obviously, they never existed."

She looked up quickly, caught the laughter glinting in his eyes, and smiled. "Must I mention Boudicae again? She led her men—and women—into battle on her war chariot and fought right alongside them. Nor was she alone. Many women on this isle have taken up arms."

"But an entire race of women choosing to live without men? That's unbelievable."

He hadn't brought a fishing line but he had brought bait and he was enjoying dangling it. She started to speak, caught his teasing smile, and laughed. "I suppose we might want to keep one or two of you around. Only the good ones, of course."

Rycca watched the play of light over his face and body. He was stretched out on the grass, looking completely relaxed, but she was vividly aware of the power coiled within him. Aware, too, of how very odd he made her feel, safe and excited all at once. No doubt if women were to decide to go off on their own, they would likely insist on bringing him along.

He reached out suddenly and brushed a stray wisp of hair back from her forehead. His touch lingered, lightly caressing. "That's a bad bruise."

"I scarcely feel it." Indeed, she probably could have been smacked over the head with a log just then and would scarcely have noticed.

"Even so, you should not overdo."

"Does that mean a gallop is out of the question?"

Dragon moved a little closer to her, the more easily to look at her hair. He felt entranced by the sparkle of sun-

light in the fiery depths. Absently lifting silken strands
and letting them trail through his fingers, he said, "We are
in a forest, there is nowhere to gallop."

Her voice wavered slightly. "The land is open near
the cliffs. How far are we from there?"

He gave her hair a little tug and let it go. "I can't believe you would want to go back there."

Bereft of his touch and astonished to feel that way,
Rycca answered tartly, "Think you I will fall off again?"

"Anything is possible on one of those monsters." He
gestured toward the horses, who were lunging at each
other, supposedly playfully, in between snatching up
great chunks of grass.

She looked at him in amazement. "You can't mean
that. They're darlings."

"They're horses. I see no reason to get foolish about
them."

A long moment of silence followed, ending finally
when Rycca said, "You don't like horses." She spoke with
utter astonishment, as though she had just stumbled upon
the strangest, most outlandish discovery possible. "You
own the two most wonderful horses I have ever seen and
you *don't like them?*"

"Why must I like them? Is it not enough that I care
for them well?"

That he did so she could hardly deny, yet she was still
amazed. "How can you possibly not like horses? You ride
well enough." At the prompting of a raised eyebrow, she
amended that. "You ride very well. How can you do that if
you don't like horses?"

"I suppose the same way I can hack men to bits on a
battlefield when I don't really like doing that either."

"No," Rycca said quietly, "I suppose you don't." She
had never thought of that before, never imagined there
were warriors who disliked war. Her own family seemed

to relish it for surely they sought every opportunity for conflict, at least those they thought they could win. Of late, the pickings had been slim.

"But why horses?" she asked. "Did you have a bad experience with one?"

"Yes," Dragon admitted. He was distracted, watching the graceful movement of her body as she settled more comfortably on the grass. The oversized boy's clothes concealed much but not the lithe slimness of her legs. She had really wonderful legs. Too easily, he imagined himself lying between them.

"What happened?"

"When?"

"When you had a bad experience involving a horse," she explained patiently.

"Oh, that. I got on one."

"And then . . . ?"

"Then it did what they do . . . walked, ran, the usual things."

"Did you stay on the horse?"

"Of course I did. I wasn't foolish enough to jump off while it was moving."

She was looking at him oddly. "You weren't thrown?"

He shook his head. "I've never been thrown. It's easy enough to avoid."

"Really? How?"

"You just have to hold on with your legs and stay properly balanced." His tone said she must surely know that.

"If you've never been thrown by a horse, why don't you like them?"

"If I tell you, will you be satisfied and stop pestering me about this?"

"Likely, but it will have to be a really good explanation. I simply cannot believe that someone who rides as well as you do doesn't like horses."

"It isn't really the horses, it's . . . being on them."

She peered at him through the thick fringe of her lashes. Tiny wrinkles appeared between her brows. "I really am trying to understand."

"Up on them."

"Up?"

Dragon nodded glumly. He could not believe what he was telling her, that which he had never confessed to a living soul, not even his brother. But if it helped her to trust him, it would be worthwhile, or so he hoped.

"Up," she repeated, and suddenly understanding dawned. "You don't like heights."

"Hate them."

"And horses are high up, at least horses big enough to carry you are, so therefore you . . ."

"Don't like horses."

She nodded slowly. "I can see how that would be a problem, but why don't you like heights?"

"I thought you were going to stop pestering me."

She shrugged unapologetically. He sighed. There was no getting around it.

"When I was very young, my brother and I left home. On board ship, I took it into my head to climb the mast. For some unknowable reason, I thought when I got to the top I would be able to touch the stars. I found out otherwise and I wanted to get down, but it was dark and the weather had turned suddenly. Wind was howling and the ship pitched violently. It was all I could do to hold tight to the mast and wait for dawn when my brother found me."

A child seeking to touch the stars. Rycca's throat tightened. "Where were your parents?"

"Dead in a raid, the usual kind of thing. Or at least it used to be usual. Thankfully, that's changed."

Without thought, she reached out and touched his hand. He saw the sheen of tears in her eyes and knew she was remembering again. Cursing himself for taking her back into that memory, Dragon sprang to his feet, drawing her with him. "The beasts will get rambunctious if we leave them alone much longer."

They were standing very close together. He could smell the perfume of her skin, fresh grass mingling with hints of honeysuckle. His gaze drifted to the fullness of her mouth. White teeth worried her lower lip. He raised a finger, touching lightly. "Don't."

He felt her sigh, saw her uncertainty, knew what he was about to do was wrong. Worse yet, mad. Yet nothing could have stopped him save the girl herself. He bent his head, dark against the brightness of hers, and lightly, tentatively touched his mouth to hers.

Rycca stood utterly still, too stunned by sensation for so paltry a thing as breathing. *Pleasure* jellied her joints. Her reason, poor thing that it was, whirled away forgotten and she became again the woman who had knelt beside the bed that morning, breathing in the scent of him. She swayed closer . . . seeking. . . . His lips were smooth, warm, hard . . . careful. She had seen men kiss women with the same finesse they brought to gorging themselves on a haunch of venison, greedy mouths slobbering and devouring. It so repulsed her that she had thought herself cold. Fool's fool! She was on fire, trembling with the dual shocks of discovery and need. . . . God's blood, such need! How was it possible to yearn so suddenly and so much?

She had to touch him, press her palms against the solid wall of his chest, had to taste him with a little flick of her tongue and oh, the delight when she felt the shudder that ran through him. His hands were big and hard on her back, drawing her closer. He deepened the kiss, parting her lips, his tongue penetrating swift and sure. Had she breath, she would have cried out in sheer, exultant delight. That the world held such marvels and she all unknowing all these years!

She raised her arms, sliding her palms up his chest to stroke the breadth of his shoulders before twining around his neck. His hair was pulled back at the nape; it brushed over her fingers like thick silk. Beneath the boy's tunic, her nipples ached. Helpless, she yielded to the need to move her hips against his.

He held a column of fire in his arms, Dragon thought dazedly. Pure, incandescent flame leaping from her body to his. He was an ardent man well schooled in the amorous arts but never had he felt such raw hunger as overtook him now. His warrior woman, for so he had come to think of her, had a sensual nature to match his own.

Yet was she an innocent, of that he was certain in the way of a man who knows women. It was the realization of that piercing the haze of desire that finally made him draw back. Even so, he could bring himself only to break off the kiss, not to let her go. He pressed her head to his chest, stroking her hair gently, as he struggled to control the near-overwhelming urge to lay her down on the soft grass and give them both what they so obviously wished.

He had compelled her to come with him. He wanted her to trust him. Two stone-hard truths that stood as sentinels to buttress his wavering conscience. No matter that they were both willing participants, honor demanded he do that which was right.

"I should not have done this," he said softly.

She looked up at him in bewilderment until the meaning of his words sank in. Instantly, she stiffened and pushed against his chest. He had to force himself to release her. Even so, he reached out a hand as she moved quickly away. She eluded him, cheeks flaming, but she could not elude his words.

"Listen to me," he said urgently. "You are a girl, young and untried. I am a man. I have pledged to keep you safe. Therefore, I should not have done this, but in truth you tempt me as I have never—" He caught himself. Best not to frighten her too much. "You tempt me deeply. Yet do I pledge you have nothing to fear from me. I swear this to you."

Truth.

Rycca stopped, turned, looked at him. She saw a man indeed, one of breathtaking beauty and virility who had held her gently through the night to keep her terror at bay, put aside his own feelings to take her riding, set them aside yet again to keep her safe even from her own turbulent desires. The hero of this strange world. Truly, there was no better way to think of him.

Softly, she said, "You went over the cliff."

Indeed, he did feel as though he had fallen a great distance, but somehow he didn't think that was what she meant. She saw the question in his eyes and smiled a little. "You hate heights, yet you followed me right to the edge of the cliff and over it. You climbed all the way down to get me."

His mouth quirked. The weight was coming off his chest. She was not angry. "I climbed up it, too, to get you."

Her smile broadened. "A determined man."

"Yes," he said, and went for the horses.

T HEY RETURNED TO THE LODGE AT MIDDAY. Rycca claimed to feel fine yet offered no protest when Dragon insisted that she lie down and rest for a while. Intending to do no more than close her eyes, she slept until close on to evening.

She woke to find no sign of him. Romulus and Remus were in their stalls, happy as ever to see her. If he had left, it was not on horseback, but then he preferred his own two feet. Not that she truly believed he had left, she was merely being foolish. Yet was her foolishness relieved when she saw the fish left gutted and scaled, ready to be put on green branches over the fire. Where was he then? The river? She was turning in that direction when she noticed smoke rising from the side of a small hill not far from the lodge.

She had heard of saunas but they belonged to the Danes, therefore were not a thing honest Englishmen indulged in. Why was there one here? She was just starting toward the sauna when the low door in the side of the hill opened and a man stepped outside. A naked man.

Oh . . .

Oh, my . . .

Heaven . . .

Rycca's cheeks flamed. They felt hot enough to light tinder but she scarcely noticed. Without allowing herself to think, she slipped behind a tree and stared. Although, to be honest, "stared" really didn't get close to it. She gaped . . . she gawked . . . she practically ogled. She was enthralled, fascinated, deeply impressed, and positively tingling.

He was glorious. Far and away, the most beautiful thing she had ever seen in her life. Her palms itched. She wanted to run them over every inch of his magnificent body, over broad shoulders that rounded into chest and arms taut with muscle, over thighs and calves that looked corded with steel, and back up again to . . .

She'd forgotten to breathe. Inhaling painfully, she watched him turn toward the river. Even his back was beautiful, and his buttocks . . .

When had the day turned so horribly hot? Indeed, it was a marvel the grass wasn't igniting before her eyes. Perhaps the sun had suddenly moved closer. Yes, that must be it.

No, it wasn't, it was she, feeling as hot for a man as any of the wanton women of whom she had heard drunken tales when eavesdropping on her father and his louts. Women she had always assumed did not exist, for surely no woman could desire a man like that. But yes, she could. And did. Moreover, he was a man who had no reason to suspect he was being looked upon in such an untoward fashion. If their positions were reversed, and she found him invading her privacy like that, she would be furious. Also excited. Oh, no, that wasn't true. Well, yes, it was, but she absolutely wasn't going to think about it.

She ought to be ashamed of herself. And as soon as she was breathing regularly again, she probably would be.

He was going to the river, to swim no doubt after the heat of the sauna. That was how it worked, wasn't it? First stifling heat, then a dip in water, the colder the better. Crystal droplets of water running over that big, hard body, trailing where she wished her fingers to trail . . .

She could have used a good, cold dunking right about then but she wasn't going anywhere near that river. That much sense she still had. Or had again now that he was safely out of sight. Ah, but the memory lingered, turning over in her mind in lovely, exquisite detail.

Breathe . . . in . . . out . . .

He was just a man just a man just a man. If she could only remember that, she would be all right.

Except he wasn't and, try though she did to convince herself otherwise, she was too intrinsically honest to manage it.

Which left her with a problem. He was going to come back; she was going to have to face him. She would die first, absolutely curl up into a little ball of embarrassment and go *poof* away. No, she would not. She had far too much pride for any such thing. She would . . . manage . . . somehow.

Dragon returned from the river a short time later. He wore a fresh tunic of finely spun brown wool that left his arms comfortably bare and came a little more than halfway down his thighs. It was his customary garb in warm weather. Around his waist was a thick leather belt from which dangled a sword and scabbard. The path to the river was strewn with soft pine needles, thus he had not bothered with sandals. His hair was still wet and tied back at his nape. He had shaved earlier and felt much refreshed for being clean. Hawk could be a treacherous, manipulative bastard, but he was enlightened enough to have a decent sauna. He was also, Dragon reminded himself, a good friend who was going to have a damn difficult time understanding how Dragon had gotten himself sidetracked in thé direction of a fiery-haired enchantress he had no business looking at twice.

Much less kissing.

One kiss. One small, ought-to-be inconsequential kiss.

He had wallowed in sensual delights with some of the most accomplished courtesans of the day, such being one of the great pleasures and benefits of travel. He had also enjoyed the shared joys of bed and body with women who made up in ardor what they lacked in art. He had long since passed the stage when a single kiss meant much of anything.

Hadn't he?

It did not matter overmuch now, when he had more immediate concerns, including how to manage what was suddenly a precariously unmanageable desire for her.

He had to persuade her to tell him who she was. Once he knew that, he could weigh the danger she was in and arrange for her safety. Even if her family was involved in the recent attempted rebellion against King Alfred, her future need not be bleak. Hawk could give her his protection and present her case to the king. Alfred was not a vindictive man when it came to women and children. Dragon knew she would be fine if only she would trust him with the truth.

It was getting her to that point that was the problem.

He was still mulling that over when he reached the lodge. The girl was nowhere in sight. He supposed she was still asleep. But the fish could not wait much longer and besides, she must be hungry. He was about to wake her when Rycca came around the corner near the stable. She held her head high and smiled at him matter-of-factly. Her cheeks looked flushed—by sleep, he assumed—but otherwise she seemed fine.

"You're back," she said.

"I went for a swim. By the way, there's a sauna here in case you'd like to use it."

That seemed to discomfit her, perhaps because it was foreign. "I'd prefer the river," she said. "It must be warm enough."

"It's perfect, very refreshing." In another moment, they would be talking about the weather. She had not been so uneasy with him after that kiss as she seemed to be now. Indeed, she had appeared somewhat preoccupied but nothing more. Now she was oddly self-conscious, obviously having to make a real effort to look directly at him. With time to consider what had happened between them, no doubt had come regrets.

He was sorry about that, for it made gaining her trust even more difficult, but the kiss itself he could not wish away. The memory was too sweet.

"I'll see to the fish," he said.

She gathered wild greens and berries while he prepared the rest of supper. They ate largely in silence except for her praise of the fish and a brief discussion about how to catch the best trout. She favored nets, he preferred lines. It was all very polite.

Night was falling by the time they finished eating, still did they sip the crisp Rhenish wine Dragon had also found in the larder. Even for an openhanded lord, Hawk was being uncommonly generous, well that he might.

Mars had risen, glowing red, and near it was the bright star Spica. There would be no moon that night and the sky was clear. A good time to study the heavens.

"Do your stories include any about the stars?" Rycca asked hesitantly. She saw where his attention had turned and felt the answering stir of curiosity she had experienced so often when contemplating the pinpoints of light that hovered above the world. Sometimes they really did seem close enough to touch, as he had yearned to as a child.

"A few," he said and smiled. Let him lull her with tales as a mother soothed her child. Let him spin marvels of legend, fable, and mayhap even truth until she forgot all else. He reached over and refilled both their cups again.

"See there? Those two bright stars there, one almost on top of the other, and the other stars trailing away to their left? That is Cassiopeia. She was queen in Ethiopia, an ancient land far to the south. A boastful woman, she is chained to her throne for annoying the gods. Sometimes she hangs upside down."

"That's awful."

He shrugged. "I suppose, but the Arabs say she's really just a kneeling camel, so who knows? See there to the right of her? That's her daughter, Andromeda. When Cassiopeia was trying to avoid her own fate, she thought to sacrifice Andromeda to appease the gods. She chained her to a rock by the sea where she would be devoured by a monster. Fortunately, the hero Perseus swooped down out of the sky on a great winged horse and saved her just in time."

"Lucky Andromeda," Rycca murmured.

Dragon saw his chance and took it. Quietly, he said, "Sometimes people need help. Sometimes they need to trust somebody to get them out of a difficult spot."

"I am not chained to a rock."

She was quick; he gave her that. "You might as well be, trying to manage on your own as you were."

"What happened to Andromeda after Perseus rescued her?"

Dragon shifted slightly. "What matters that?"

"It's part of the story, isn't it?"

"I suppose."

"Then finish it, please."

She said *please*. That undid him. He hated to deny women. "They fell deeply in love and married. Andromeda bore Perseus six sons and a daughter but their life was not untroubled. Perseus unwittingly fulfilled the prophecy made at his birth that he would slay his grandfather. He had to flee from his homeland but he ended by founding a great new kingdom from which many heroes sprang. Thus ends the tale."

What little was left of the long twilight was almost gone. He saw her face in shadows and streaks of flame. "A happy myth," she said, "nothing more."

"It could have happened."

She said nothing. He knew she disagreed.

And so to bed, Rycca within the lodge and Dragon without. Night deepened. Deer rose from the mossy clefts of banks where they drowsed away the day. Foxes crept from their dens. An owl glided overhead, her wings scarcely moving on whispers of air. A few small bats fluttered among the trees. In the stable, Romulus and Remus dreamed of endless meadows.

Dragon watched the heavens turn. He saw his namesake, Draco, the Dragon, arc across the sky. There were men who said the brightest star in Draco had once been the constant star by which men measured the way north. It was no longer, but the heavens changed in their own slow time, far beyond the brief ages of man, so perhaps it once had been so.

He drank more wine. A star streaked across the sky,

burning brightly in its swift flight. Then it was gone, extinguished as though it had never been.

Life was too damn short.

R YCCA PUNCHED THE PILLOW YET AGAIN. WHAT had previously been so comfortable now felt lumpy. The so-soft covers irritated her skin. She was too hot with them, too cool without. The bed was too wide, the air too still, the night too long.

Andromeda, indeed. And he an unlikely Perseus, not about to get up on any winged horse. Seven children . . . a lost kingdom and a new land. What a tale.

She hurt inside, a dull ache of emptiness. Why was life so hard? She and her twin had made common cause and tried to help each other as much as possible, but apart from that all she remembered was callousness, strife, and outright cruelty. Was that to be the sum total of her days? Even if she made it to Normandy, what life awaited her? Thurlow had his own way to make; she could not count on him for everything. Odds were she would have only two choices—the convent or marriage, both prisons of a sort.

She *knew* more was possible, sensed it with every fiber of her being, had even felt it within her grasp when she whirled, turning and turning, on the beach, savoring her freedom. But what good was freedom if it meant being alone? What good was companionship if it meant captivity?

Damned pillow.

She got up, walked to the windows, walked back again, ran her fingers over the long edge of the table, remembered the kiss.

The ache inside got worse.

Likely, she would be caught. For days she had refused to admit that, but the cold truth of it stuck in her mind, remorseless. Reaching Hawkforte was difficult enough. Doing it when word of her escape might already be about and people looking for her could be well nigh impossible. Even with his help, her chances of reaching safety were very small. And if she did not . . . She shuddered at the thought of the fate that awaited her.

She guessed she would be locked away, perhaps left to die. Her family could do that; it would not trouble them. Death then might be her only freedom.

Her throat tightened. She yearned to hold fast to life, to savor every moment and claim the joy she sensed it could offer if only . . .

If only what?

Fly, her mind whispered, and her heart answered, soaring.

FIVE

I T WAS COOLER OUTSIDE THAN IT HAD BEEN all day but not unpleasantly so. The air caressed Rycca's skin through the thin night robe. It seemed very daring to be outside so scantily clad, for though the gown came to her ankles, it was sheer enough for starlight to pass through. She thought for a moment of the woman for whom it had been made and felt a sudden kinship with that unknown lady. Barefoot, her hair tumbling around her shoulders for she had not troubled to braid it, she approached the fire beside which Dragon lay.

He was asleep, she saw that in an instant, lying on his back with an arm thrown out toward the . . . hmmm, empty . . . jug of wine. His head was turned toward her, his chiseled lips slightly parted. A low, soft rumbling came and went in rhythm with the deep rise and fall of his chest. Her eyes widened and she smiled. That he snored ever so slightly was a human touch she welcomed. It made him seem just a little more approachable. Approach she did, slowly, content for some little time to look upon him.

She was surprised that she had no doubts. She would have expected some had she ever anticipated such a moment. Yet there was only certainty in her. The future looked too bleak. If she could have nothing else, she would have this night.

And this man.

He stirred slightly, drawing her eyes down his length. She breathed in the sweet night air and felt the fierce need building within her. Oh, yes, she would have him. Honor, duty, and the rest be damned. Her life would be her own, if only for this tiny space of time.

But how to begin? She had never touched a man save for the occasional affectionate cuffing in Thurlow's direction. And for that kiss. That shocking, scintillating, oh so inspiring kiss that with the gentleness of him had led her to this moment.

Another kiss, then. She went down on her knees next to him. A lock of hair had fallen across his brow. She reached out very lightly and brushed it aside. When he did not react she was emboldened. Moving just a little closer, she lowered her head.

Even in sleep, his mouth felt firm. She touched her lips to his carefully, little more than the brush of a butterfly's wing. This close, the heat radiating from him warmed her all the way through. Or maybe the heat was within herself and he merely the spark.

As the sun sparked the heavens, she thought, and deepened the kiss. Only a little, still so cautious, yet this time he moved. The hand tossed out rose, hovered, fell back. She smiled against his lips. Lowering herself beside him, she stroked his bare arm. Beneath her touch, his muscles rippled reflexively.

Her fascination expanded. Never had she imagined the freedom to touch a man. Women were handled and mishandled, taken without thought. It was assumed that a woman's body was not her own. But a man's . . . that was different. Even the poorest peasant thought himself king of his own hovel. Woe betide anyone who said otherwise.

But now the initiative was hers, never mind that she had only the vaguest notion what to do with it. He was dressed, more's the shame, in the tunic he had donned after bathing. But the night was pleasant enough—or he hardy enough—that he hadn't bothered with a cover. Her fingers drifted over his broad shoulders, down along the contours of his chest. He felt like sun-warmed rock. There was no give in the man at all.

Heart thumping at her daring, she slipped her hands down his thighs, her palms tickled by the light furring of hair along his legs. At the bottom of his tunic, she hesitated. It would be oh, so easy for her to ease up the garment and . . . Her cheeks flamed. That would be shockingly bold.

A wry shake of her head sent a spill of copper silk over his chest. Truth had hold of her, as always, and would not let go. She had passed over the borders of proper behavior the moment she decided not to accept the fate her family decreed. Now she was beyond bold, shocking or otherwise, in a realm where desperation and desire could hardly be told apart.

Such a beautiful man. Such a beautiful memory to warm her in the dark, cold time she was sure was coming.

Shocking then, so be it. She rose on her knees and quickly, before she could reconsider, lifted the night robe over her head. Cool air touched her skin but she did not feel it. The heat within was too strong. Taking hold of his outflung hand, she drew it to her breast.

He was dreaming, of course. A particularly erotic dream inspired by an excess of wine. Erotic . . . yet different somehow. He had a store of sensual memories upon which to draw but did not seem to be doing so. He should have been reclining on a silken couch enjoying the sublime skills of a beautiful houri as he had in Byzantium. The Circassian, perhaps, the one with the flame-red hair, or the Nubian who had trained as a gymnast and could . . .

Yet he seemed instead to be lying upon hard ground, and the houri, if such she was, wore the scent of honeysuckle that reminded him of . . .

Dragon's eyes flew open. He stared at his hand curved over the alabaster mound of a perfectly formed breast, at the delectable rose-hued nipple peeking through his fingers, up past the firm set of a certain chin and straight into honey-hued eyes that somehow failed to appear the least abashed.

"Uh . . ." he said, which he rather thought was as articulate as any man could be expected to be under the circumstances, skald-souled or not.

"Don't think," she said, rather unnecessarily since he could only vaguely recall what thinking was and not at all why he should want to do it.

Her shining head bent, he felt the brush of her lips, tentative, seeking. Her small, smooth tongue tasted his.

He was rock hard, close to bursting. She was in his arms and he was drawing her beneath him when some faint whisp of reason reared against the pounding hunger of his fierce need.

"Can't . . ." he muttered, the best he could muster for an eloquent argument as to why their present behavior was ill-advised.

She ignored the protest and concentrated on the man. Her hands, strong after all the years of holding reins, tugged at the bottom of his tunic. He tugged back in the opposite direction, caught himself doing it, and groaned. Of all the ludicrous situations to be caught in, as though they had reversed roles and he the modest maiden.

Just then it dawned on him that she really was naked, he hadn't imagined it—or if he had, he was also imagining the delight of silken skin pressed all along his length. A deep groan broke from him as his big hands stroked down the arch of her spine to the firm roundness of her bottom. She made a soft whimpering sound and moved against him.

He couldn't . . . absolutely, positively couldn't. Not after his vow that she had nothing to fear from him, that he would keep her safe, that she could trust him. Blessed Frigg, queen of the gods, help him now!

But the goddess seemed disinclined to intervene. He was on his own, just him, his conscience, and the girl herself, who appeared to have taken leave of her senses.

"Have to stop," he gasped, exhausting what little breath he had. His chest felt gripped in a vise, his heart pounded wildly, and as for his cock, that merry fellow was bent on having his own way at all costs.

"No," the girl said very clearly, and "no" again on a whisper, sweetly pleading. It was the second *no* that reached Dragon through the red mist of the struggle he was waging within himself. He looked again into those glorious eyes and saw no fear, not a shred of it in his warrior woman. Yet did some demon drive her.

"Why?" he murmured, cupping the back of her head, stroking her hair gently. The last of the wine-fog was fast fading, leaving him all too alert and aware.

Her mouth moved against his. "A memory." With artless innocence, she reached beneath his tunic and cupped him. A soft gasp of surprise broke from her. He groaned, caught her hand within his, but did not deny her touch. They both wanted this far too fiercely.

A memory. That he understood. There had been times when he had yearned to lock forever in his mind the turning of every star, the exact delicacy of tendrils of cloud across the moon, the scent of the wind, the flutter of a bird's wing, every tiny, exquisite detail of the world. But those times had always been on the eve of battle or during a sudden lull when he thought his time amid such beauty might be counted in hours if not minutes.

Where did she see her own end? That she saw it he did not doubt. She had weighed the danger that faced her and his own offer of help, and chose to seize life while yet

she could. It said little for her confidence in him but much
for her courage. All the same, he couldn't let her do
this. . . . Could he?

In his experience, nothing brought men and women
so close together as did bed sport. If he could bring her to
pleasure, give her the memory she sought, yet still protect
her from harm, would she not then be drawn to trust him
as she surely must were she to have any chance of survival?

If . . .

At the very thought, his merry fellow reared in
protest. The girl gasped again but did not draw away.
Dragon inhaled deeply, summoning control from the
deepest reaches of his being. In the perfumed chambers of
Byzantium, he had studied arts unknown to the ordinary
run of men. His diligence then had seemed to have no
greater purpose than dalliance; now he thought otherwise.

He could do this . . . he really could. A memory she
wanted, a memory she would have.

R YCCA ARCHED HER BACK HELPLESSLY, HER HEAD
pressed into the firm ground. Sweat dewed her skin,
her breathing came raggedly. Cresting waves of pleasure
gave her no respite. Scarcely did she begin to descend than
his questing mouth and too-skilled hands drove her upward again. Her nipples were painfully hard, her thighs
quaking from the force sweeping through her. She stared
down the length of her body to the dark head resting between her legs and gasped anew as remorseless pleasure
seized her yet again.

*Never, ever had she imagined . . . never could she
have . . .*

In the rough disregard of her father's keep, she had
seen men take hold of women, grab at their breasts, some-

times even put their mouth to them likes babes suckling. Rycca usually absented herself right about then but once she had lingered on the curve of the stairs, peering down into the hall. She had seen a man pull a woman's skirts up to bare her flanks, push her on top of a table, free his member, and plunge directly into her. A few thrusts, some grunts, and he was done, not unlike horses mating but without the power and beauty.

She had thought it was like that for all.

Fool! Oh, sweet heaven, silly fool!

Her fingers dug into his immense shoulders. She cried out hoarsely as the world exploded yet again.

Dragon raised his head, gazed up her exquisite body glowing pale in starlight, and observed her with satisfaction. Not the satisfaction he burned for but the only kind he would allow himself. She was a virgin, he had confirmed that by the simple expediency of slipping a careful finger into her. Her passage was so hot and wet as almost to end all hope of his control right then and there, but the unmistakable barrier of her innocence had strengthened his resolve just when he needed it most.

She was exquisitely responsive. Every inch of her came alive beneath his touch. Her breasts were not large but perfectly shaped to fit his hands, the nipples swelling yet further beneath his caress. Her waist was small, exaggerating the graceful sweep of her hips. The taut skin of her belly was acutely sensitive, as was the velvet smoothness of her inner thighs. At their apex, she was like a lovely pink shell opening to him, moist with the sea.

He tasted her with light, flicking touches and deeply, driven to know her in this way and rewarded with her swift waves of passion. That first kiss they shared had not misled; she was fire in his arms, holding back nothing, taken again and again by pleasure's relentless fury.

But not taken by him. Somehow, though it killed him,

he would get through this. His body screamed for relief but he ignored it, all his attention focused on his enthralling warrior woman.

Rycca gazed into his features cast in sharp relief by the glow of the fire's embers and knew a moment's helpless fury. He was doing this deliberately, denying her what she most wanted even as he gave her what she had never imagined could exist. The revelation of ecstasy was yet one more discovery in this strange land but it was not enough. She wanted . . . *Sweet heaven, yet again* . . .

She was panting, scarcely able to bear anything more, yet she knew full well it was the man she wanted, not simply the shattering release he gave her.

With strength she would not have thought still to possess, she twisted suddenly beneath him, gripped his shoulders again, and pressed him down onto the ground.

"Enough, lord," she whispered against his burning skin as her lips skimmed down his chest to the dark whorls of hair circling his navel and beyond. "Enough and enough again. You cheat us both."

"No!" he said and made to stop her but she was swifter just then. His love play had taught her well but her instincts might have been guide enough. He gasped and fell back at the first stroke of her tongue, shivering like a man struck down by fever. Good, she thought, he felt the same, then thought nothing at all as she yielded to the most primal need to savor him.

Somewhere far in the back of Dragon's fire-drenched brain the realization occurred to him that he *really* could die from this. Then the roar of his blood drowned out all else and he became for some lost time only pure sensation.

When next he was aware of anything, the girl was straddling him. She tossed her hair back, away from the twin moons of her breasts. The sight of her would have stolen his breath had he any left. Frowning slightly, with determined concentration, she lowered herself toward him.

Suddenly realizing her intent, Dragon tried to stop her but the effort proved stunningly feeble. She merely seized his hands, laid them upon her breasts, and brought the tip of him within her tight, wet heat.

He knew he had to halt this, absolutely knew it, and could do nothing. His passion had become paralyzing, save for his merry fellow in which all strength and will were focused.

Dragon stared, helplessly fascinated, as she lowered herself onto him. Her concentration was intense. Small white teeth dug into her lower lip as she frowned. She hesitated, adjusting herself, struggling to accommodate him. He thought certainly she would stop when she came to the moment of it but he should have known better. His warrior woman did not so much as pause but took the pain and him together.

Dragon cried out; she threw her head back and made a keening sound that struck him to the bone. His big hands clasped her hips. Vainly did he try to hold her still but her inner muscles proved no match for him. She clasped him firmly, stroking rhythmically, and the world dissolved. His orgasm came on him in a fierce rush, the essence of his life pouring into her. He fell back against the ground, gasping, and fell further still into sweet oblivion.

R YCCA STIRRED SOME TIME LATER. HER BACK was chilled. She lifted her head slowly and realized she had collapsed on top of the man. His chest was her hard pillow. She hurt inside but it was a strange, exultant pain that seemed to have far more to do with the excesses of pleasure than the gifting of her virginity.

Gifting . . . given . . . gone. Truly, she was a fool, for only now did she realize what she might well have thought of sooner but had not—her value had just become as

nonexistent as her maidenhead. She was—glory of glo-
ries—a fallen woman. And as such, she just might be dis-
owned by the enraged family no longer able to barter her
for kingly favor. She would no longer exist to them and
she might—just might—be able simply to disappear. It
was a slim hope but more than she had felt earlier in the
night and it spurred her to action.

She had involved the man far too much already, taking advantage of his willingness to help her. However
high he stood with his lord, and she did not doubt it was
high indeed, he might be blamed if his part in what had
happened between them became known. Honor demanded that she put him at no greater risk. Yet it was still
a struggle to force herself from him. Slowly, reluctantly,
she drew away from him and rose to her feet. With a last,
lingering glance, Rycca squared her shoulders and hurried into the lodge.

Moments later, dressed once again in her boy's garb,
she slipped out into the darkness. She did not allow herself to look back at him for she knew that to do so would
be to shatter her brittle resolve.

D RAGON WOKE TO THE SQUABBLING OF SQUIR-
rels. Wincing in the bright sun, he threw a hand
over his eyes. He was halfway to his feet when memory
flooded back. Thought, motion, purpose, everything
stopped as he stood riveted, stunned by recollection. The
girl . . .

He shook his head, struggling to clear it. Surely he
must have imagined her coming to him, incandescent
with passion, exquisitely responsive, defeating his noblest
intent. A dream, no more— No dream, for just then,
glancing down at himself, he saw the evidence of her vanished virginity. A low, virulent curse broke from him.

His life had just become vastly more complicated. So be it. She was Saxon and of a noble house. That would have to suffice. Hawk, Alfred, even brother Wolf would simply have to accept it.

A faint smile eased the grim set of his features. All in all, this might work out for the best. The more he thought of it, the more it seemed so. Had there been any wine left in the jug, he would have poured a libation in Frigg's honor, for he suspected the goddess had played her part.

That would have to wait, for first he had to find the girl. Let the minx try to withhold her identity from him now. He grinned, thinking he would inform her that she could tell him or wait and tell the priest, it mattered not. He could just imagine her reaction to that.

But imagine was all he could do, for not quite half an hour later he accepted that she was not in the lodge or the immediate area. Romulus and Remus were in their stalls, happy to see him as always. He paused just long enough to give them fresh water and grain before continuing his search.

She was not in the sauna or at the riverbank though he could track her as far as the water's edge. There her trail vanished.

Dragon stood for a little time, staring down at the slowly moving water, before he turned abruptly and rammed his fist into the nearest tree trunk. The pain of the blow would have felled a lesser man. He did not even notice it. Damn her! Twice and thrice damn her! She had lain with him, gifted him with her virginity, given him every reason to believe she was, at the very least, in lust with him, only to vanish into thin air without so much as a fare-thee-well.

He had been duped by a scheming, treacherous, cold-hearted maiden who had played him well and truly for a fool. And he'd thought getting kicked in the balls was bad.

This was vastly worse, a wound to the heart he could not admit even to himself. Only anger was allowed and he gave full vent to it.

She would pay and pay dearly for breaking her promises to him, both explicitly to remain the few days for which he had bargained and implicitly in the gifting of her body. He would find her, wring the truth of her identity from her, and then decide how the most exquisitely sensual woman he had ever met would pay for her transgressions against him.

Scant moments later, Dragon was ready. He rode Grani, who had been called Romulus but was really named for the mount of the god Sigurd, and was followed by Sleipnir, formerly Remus, named for the mighty Odin's own horse. Never mind his dislike of horses, they offered the swiftest way to track her.

One more quick sweep of the ground in all directions confirmed what he already knew. She had learned from the experience of two days before. There was not a trace of her beyond the few footprints at the water's edge. She had entered the river. He could not do the same without risking the horses in the uncertain footing of the stream bed. He would have to follow as closely alongside as possible, knowing there would be times when the path veered inland through the forest. Yet was there also advantage, for there were only two directions in which she could have gone—upstream or down.

Upstream meant north, against the current and into the hinterland from which she had fled. Downstream was Hawkforte, its port and the chance, however remote, of escape.

Grim-faced, the Dragon turned south.

RYCCA STUMBLED, STRIKING HER KNEES YET AGAIN on the treacherous rocks. She bit back a curse, hauled herself upright, spat out a mouthful of water, and went on, just as she had every other time she had slipped and fallen in the hateful, damnable, seemingly endless river. She was soaking wet, half blinded by the hair trailing in her eyes, and hurting in every inch of her body that wasn't outright numb. She was also chilled to the bone, for despite seeming to have swallowed enough water to turn the river into a dry bed, she was still submerged to her waist.

The temptation to just crawl up onto the bank and lie there in a huddled mass of misery was almost overwhelming, but some part of her, as she observed with a certain dazed detachment, was too pigheaded to give up. No, she would plod on likely to the ends of the earth, slipping and sliding, gasping and groaning, until either the river won or she did. Had she been inclined to wager, she would have bet on the river.

A soundless laugh broke from her, mute because she had scarcely any breath left. To think she had been afraid of drowning. With hindsight, that might have been merciful if only for being swift, unlike the seemingly endless torment into which she had plunged. She could not even say her heart ached unless emptiness could be said to resonate with pain as a cavern does when sound pours into its void.

Never to see him again, not even to know his name, how was that to be borne? Yet what else could she have done? He was already at too great a risk merely for being with her and vastly more so now that they had lain together. What poor thanks it was for his care of her to place him in such danger. Yet she had done so selfishly, without thought to his welfare, merely to seize a memory.

She tasted salt on her lips and knew it did not come from the river. Enough then, what was done was done. Whatever anguish filled her, whatever longings dogged her every breath, she was still driven to live. Step after painful step, grasping on to branches and rocks yet falling many more times, Rycca made her way downstream. Not until she judged that she had covered several miles did she drag herself from the river. Lying panting with exhaustion on the bank, she tried to think. Surely by now she had gone far enough to elude pursuit? Even so masterly a tracker could not follow where there was no trace at all. Could he?

Best not to think of that, for truly she could not endure the river any longer. Sitting up, Rycca glanced around, trying to gain some sense of where she was. All around was forest, revealing nothing. With a sigh, she rose to her feet and began wringing water out of her tunic and hair. When she was no longer quite so wet, she girded what strength she had left and plodded on.

An hour or so later, when the sun had dried her almost entirely, she came to a bend in the river where the bank simply disappeared. Nothing was left save a sharp incline along which she could not crawl, much less walk. Carefully marking the position of the sun to guide her, Rycca struck inland.

The forest was dense and the going hard but at length she emerged onto what appeared to be a well-traveled road. That was both good and bad. She could make much faster progress but the chances of being caught were vastly greater. Listening constantly for the sound of anyone approaching, she hurried along as quickly as she could.

She managed several more miles, her pace slowing as weariness crept over her. Despite her best resolve, she was sinking into a daze of mingled fatigue and sorrow. Through it, the sound of approaching horsemen did not reach her until long and precious moments after it should have. Even so, once she recognized her peril, Rycca responded swiftly. She had almost reached the safe obscurity of the trees when the lead rider spotted her and called out.

"Halt! You there, boy! Halt!"

Not for an instant did Rycca consider obeying. One swift glance at the banners carried by the outriders told her that she was in far more danger than she had been when she fled from the unknown man. She darted into the forest and ran, zigzagging among the trees, praying to find a route a horse could not follow. But her efforts were in vain. She felt the ground tremble beneath pounding hooves just as she was snatched up. The horse turned, she was scratched and snapped at by swiftly passing bushes, and in scarcely a heartbeat she was dropped, firmly and unceremoniously, back on the road.

"Boy—" The voice was harsh and haughty. It reverberated through Rycca, casting up in its wake fragments of haunting memories. Swept with cold, struggling to show no fear, she got to her feet slowly. Slower still, she raised her head and faced her fate.

The man before her, mounted on a proud war horse, had known forty and more years, most violent, even more dissipated. He was balding, with tufts of gray-streaked hair clustered in an unruly fringe around his ears. He had a big head but it went with the rest of him. His skin was weathered and creased, his jowls drooping. What had been muscle had long ago turned to fat, yet he was still formidable if only for a will that did not hesitate to kill or otherwise dispose of anyone who challenged, annoyed, or merely inconvenienced him. Of late, with the peace of blessed Alfred, he had enjoyed little chance to vent his spleen. Hence was he unusually ruddy and narrow-eyed as he looked at what he thought, at first glance, to be a lone boy.

Alas, that mistake did not last long. He knew her too well.

The eyes, set deep beneath layers of folded skin, widened with effort. The small mouth twisted.

"Rycca." He said her name with a mixture of loathing and satisfaction that sent a shudder down her spine.

"What?" A younger version of himself appeared at his side, cruelly yanking at his horse's reins. "*Rycca?*"

"Look for yourself." The older man waved a hand contemptuously in her direction. "I knew we'd find her." He rested his hands on the pommel of his saddle and nodded, well pleased with the turn of events. "You stupid bitch. Did you really think you could get away? Gad yourself up as your weakling brother and hie for Hawkforte? What were you thinking, to take ship for Normandy?" He laughed, a deep and rasping sound. After a moment the younger man joined in, grinning broadly as he surveyed her.

"By God, you were right. She and Thurlow are in this together. First he takes off and then she disappears. They plotted this as one to humiliate and harm you."

"No!" Despite her fear, which was sensibly real, Rycca could not let such libel pass. "Thurlow had nothing to do with this. I acted alone."

At once, the younger man reached out to strike her. She sidestepped him quickly and his blow fell on empty air, which only infuriated him more. He began to dismount, obviously intent on chastising her.

There was nowhere left to run, nowhere to turn, and no strength left. For an instant she remembered how it felt to be held and cherished, protected and pleasured. Her eyes welled with tears even as she fought to restrain them. Yet did her heart, which had so lately seemed to be absent, suddenly fill with yearning so great that she was unable to contain it. It built and built, filling her entirely and finally soaring beyond her in a simple, terrible, and utterly silent cry for the hero of the strange land in which she had too briefly dwelled.

"Bitch," Ogden said, echoing their father, and

smashed his hand across her face. Burning pain tore through her. She stumbled and fell onto the hard earth.

Above her, the Lord of Wolscroft reached out to the true son he had managed to get off his craven wife, one of two good ones to be fair and thankfully nothing like the twin whelps she bore him last, before dying in childbirth. From one hand to the other passed a black, coiled whip.

"Make it quick," he said. "We cannot linger here." As an afterthought, he added, "Do not kill her. She may still have some use."

Sprung into the air, the whip cracked. Rycca lay unmoving, curled in as tight a ball as she could manage. She did not have to see Ogden's face to know how much he was enjoying this. Worse yet, she did not need to see her father's cold anticipation of her suffering. She knew both all too well. Desperately, she sought the only escape still left to her. Down and down into her mind she went, as she had from tenderest childhood when cruelty and callousness became overwhelming, down and down away from the world into a place so much gentler, so much better, and so very still that she scarcely had to breathe.

A place that had never before had more than the most indistinct shape yet now, suddenly, had clear form. The lodge, the perfumed bed, the soft murmuring of the nearby river, the smell of woodsmoke, and above all, warming her with his smile and his arms, the man.

She was almost there, almost curled tight within herself, when a sudden sound ripped through the fabric of her mind and hurled her back into harsh reality.

"Hold."

Dragon drew rein before the party stopped on the road. Even as disbelief roared through him, he looked from the girl lying facedown in the dirt to the man poised above her with a whip and farther to the older man who was clearly in command. A man of some substance that one, judging by his garb and by the men-at-arms who attended him. They were all looking at Dragon with some surprise and, not unexpectedly, concern. But not too much of the latter for he was, after all, only one lone man.

So did the older one obviously think, for he gestured contemptuously to several of his men, sending them in Dragon's direction. They came with clumsy speed, yanking their swords from their scabbards. Watching them, Dragon sighed. He released Sleipnir, who trailed behind him, and the well-trained horse immediately moved off to the side. Beneath Dragon, Grani tensed in happy anticipation. The attackers were almost upon him when Dragon reached behind without undue haste and drew the blade sheathed across his back. At the same instant, he dug his heels into the stallion.

The first man to reach Dragon fell before he could do more than swing his sword a few inches. He landed hard on the ground and groaned, clasping the wound to his shoulder, which, though not fatal, would most likely end his career as a man-at-arms. The second followed an instant later. The third lasted just a little longer, enough to actually engage so that steel rang against steel for a scant moment before that man, too, tumbled. All three lay cursing and moaning, yet alive for so it had pleased the stranger to leave them. True, compassion played some role in his thinking, yet he was also disinclined to allow such carrion the passage to Valhalla that death in battle would grant them.

Wolf, brother to the Dragon, was said to be the greatest warrior ever to come out of the northlands since the ancient gods themselves strode forth, but Wolf himself said that he had only trained the greatest and his name was Dragon. That sunlit spring day in the peace of blessed Alfred, no man on the Hawkforte road would have disagreed.

Certainly Ogden did not, for he tumbled backward as

Dragon approached, kneeing Grani forward slowly as his ruddied blade flashed in the sun. Tripping over the whip, landing hard on his ass, Ogden held out his hands in panicked surrender.

"No, don't! Just a misunderstanding . . ."

"To send armed men against an unknown stranger who has done you no harm?" Dragon looked from the craven lordling lying in the dirt to the older man who watched from his mount, his formerly florid complexion now paled with shock and there, in his eyes, the light of swift calculation as he reassessed the situation. Brutal to be sure but not stupid.

"Yes, I would call that a misunderstanding," Dragon said. "And this, too . . ." He pointed the tip of his sword at the girl, who rose from the ground, threw the hair from her eyes, and looked at him in stunned amazement as though the sun and moon together had just appeared before her.

That was rather gratifying but he wouldn't let it appease his anger quite yet.

Ignoring the lordling, Dragon gave his full attention to the older man. "What do you here?"

"A sad but necessary task, the chastisement of an errant daughter, for daughter she is despite her boy's garb, should that have fooled you. Therefore, this is no concern of yours. Go on your way."

Daughter. Dragon stiffened but as quickly concealed his reaction. That put rather a different twist on the matter and required some delicate handling. Keeping his expression blank, he said, "I would know to whom I speak."

The older man frowned but he could hardly refuse, faced with a warrior who had single-handedly disabled three of his men and made his own son whine in the dirt. Ogden would pay for that, to be sure, yet he truly could not be faulted overmuch for he had always been raised to do whatever was needful to survive, even crawl to an over-wheening king who imagined himself a peacemaker.

A cold smile preceded his response, as though he anticipated the warrior's reaction when he realized whom he had challenged. "I am Rudyard, Lord of Wolscroft in Mercia. Does that satisfy you, whoever you may be? You handle a sword well enough but I have not seen you in the levies of the king nor those of the Lord of Essex. Mayhap you seek to make some reputation for yourself by standing against your betters."

The warning implicit there, even the threat, should have brought any man up short. Yet Dragon scarcely heard it. He stared at the Mercian in darkly forming shock before swiftly turning his gaze upon the girl.

"Wolscroft . . . ?"

Frowning, Rudyard nodded. "Now sheathe your sword and stand aside. We will be on our way."

Dragon made not the slightest move to comply but he did return his attention to the older man. "Then your daughter would be . . . ?"

Rudyard frowned as well he might for surely this up-start stranger had no business asking anything at all about his daughter. Yet, if it would compel him to move on, he would have his answer. "The Lady Rycca of Wolscroft and you would be well advised to take your eyes from her. She is betrothed to a Norse lord who comes soon to claim her."

Slowly, Dragon sheathed his sword. Slowly, he dismounted from Grani. Never taking his eyes from her, he walked toward Rycca. Ogden had stumbled to his feet and foolishly thought to interpose himself. A single cuff from Dragon's mighty fist returned him to the ground.

Rycca did not move. A horrible thought, so dread as to be almost beyond grasping, began to form within her. The hero of her strange land had recognized her family's name. That she saw clearly even as she struggled desperately to see nothing beyond. But the veil of her ignorance would not remain. Before the fire deep within topaz eyes, it shredded and dissolved away.

"You are Saxon . . ." she said desperately. "You must be. You speak Saxon as well as I do and—"

"I speak many languages. They come to me easily."

"You were without attendants!"

Yet gifted with use of a lodge that must belong to the Lord of Essex himself, provided with every luxury and comfort, and possessed of the two most magnificent horses Rycca had ever seen. *Sweet Mary and all the saints, why hadn't she realized?* Who else would dare to go alone about the countryside, certain of his own overwhelming skill as a warrior as she had just seen but certain also that no man would dare raise a hand to him without answering to the Hawk and even the king himself? Yet how then could he have been so kind to her, so patient and caring? That fit with nothing she knew buried deep within in her darkly haunted dreams.

"So did I choose to be. I wished for a few days to myself." His mouth twisted. "To contemplate the future. Yet contemplation seems not to have been enough for you. You preferred action."

Cold dread filled her yet still it warred with disbelief. Exactly whose arms had she lain in, whose body had gifted hers with nearly unbearable pleasure, whose tender strength had led her to spin dreams of gossamer that now threatened to choke her?

"You cannot be . . ." she moaned, staring into hard-set features and eyes that swept her with cold derision.

"What is this?" Rudyard demanded. "You two have met? By God, identify yourself or all your skill will not save you from the wrath of the most feared Viking to come out of the northlands in a generation or more, a man savage as a devil, drenched in blood, a man who—"

"Has a name," Dragon interrupted. He whistled for

Grani, sprang up onto his back, and from that height spared a moment's stern scrutiny for Rycca, who was still staring at him ashen-faced.

Fighting the insane temptation to comfort her, he regarded her loathesome father. Though quiet, his voice filled the shadowed road where all men had suddenly fallen silent.

He spoke simply, without boastfulness and his words rang all the harder for their simplicity. "I am Dragon Hakonson, Lord of Landsende, and I have indeed come to claim my bride."

Scarcely had he uttered those words than Rycca began to laugh, at first softly, then helplessly. She doubled over, holding her waist, as the sheer, horrifying absurdity of it all overwhelmed her. She had risked her life to flee from the very man to whom she had given herself and who stood now before her, outraged because she had betrayed him with . . . himself.

What could possibly be funnier except perhaps life itself?

Rudyard cursed virulently and from the saddle made to strike her. So he would have had Dragon not blocked his way. "No," he said in a tone that brooked no argument.

The Lord of Wolscroft looked disposed to argue but even he saw how foolish that would be. Dragon was not a man to be challenged, and in any case, a father's rights must give way before the authority of a husband.

"A thousand pardons, Lord Hakonson," Rudyard said. Swiftly, he assumed the demeanor he used with Alfred, humble and sincere. "My daughter has betrayed us both. Were it left to me, she would be shut away forever. As it is—" Raw hatred and grim pleasure mingled in the look he shot her.

"As it is, obviously no man of your high standing can be expected to take her to wife when there is no knowing where she has been or, more to the point, who she has been with. If you encountered her, so may others have done the same. Should you be willing to even consider going forward with this marriage, she will be examined. I pledge to you that if she is no longer virgin, she will die."

A father's hideous promise hung on the air, drifting like rank fog over the silent road. Dragon glanced at Rycca; their eyes met. Unspoken between them was the understanding that he had been handed the weapon to free himself from a marriage he had not wanted and a bride he could not trust. Examined, proved unchaste, no one would believe her if she claimed the very man she had lain with was the man she was supposed to marry. All he had to do was keep silent and she would die.

Dragon did not hesitate, nor did he draw out the moment. Merely, he spoke with implacable will. "No one touches her. Our marriage is the pledge of peace between our peoples. It goes forward regardless of her feelings." Quietly, he added, "Or mine."

Before anyone could reply, Dragon leaned over, hooked a steely arm around Rycca's waist, and deposited her on the saddle in front of him. His face grim, he whistled to Sleipnir, set his heels to Grani, and set off at a gallop for Hawkforte.

Chapter

SIX

K RYSTA WAS IN THE WALLED GARDEN NEXT
to the great hall when she heard the shouts.
She broke off planting a row of dill, grabbed
up Falcon, who promptly chortled at the prospect of amusement, and hurried inside. Servants were
swarming about, having been distracted from their work,
which was odd in so well tended a manor as Hawkforte.
She stopped a serving maid and asked her what was happening.

"Someone's come, my lady. I don't know who but
seems unusual, don't you think?"

Unusual indeed, for Hawkforte was a busy port and
seat of one of the most powerful lords in England, second
only to the king himself, some said. All sorts of people
came and went on the average day, royal heralds, clergy,
traders from as far away as Byzantium. The population
took pride in being accustomed to them.

What then could stir them so?

Holding her baby son more closely, she passed
through the hall and out into the bright day, quickly spy-
ing a man-at-arms. "Has anyone sent to his lordship?"

Hawk was on the training field, yet further honing the army that helped keep Alfred on the throne and the peace he had brought in place. Only the previous year, that same army had hunted down the traitor Lord Udell of Mercia, who had thought to unseat the king. Hawk himself had killed the miscreant, not in the least because he had dared to make off with Krysta. Never mind that they hadn't been married at the time, though she, unknowing, carried their child. Everything had worked out splendidly, for which not a day passed without her giving thanks.

The soldier nodded quickly, a hardened man well bloodied in battle who was nonetheless disconcerted to be addressed by the wife of the Hawk. Flushing slightly, he said, "Yes, my lady, that's been done."

Satisfied that all was in hand, Krysta spied her old nurse Raven fluttering nearby. "Here," she called, "take Falcon for me while I see who's come."

The thin, black-garbed woman obliged, cradling the babe gently and bestowing upon him a warm smile. "And how's the little chick this morning? I swear he's grown another inch or two in the night."

The baby burbled and waved his arms, and Krysta grinned. Her son was the picture of health and already hinting that he would attain his father's size. His tawny hair was nearer the shade of Hawk's, slightly darker than Krysta's, but of late his eyes had turned from the blue of birth to the forest green of his mother's. None of this surprised Krysta, for she carried within her the memory of the strange vision that had come to her months before her child's birth when her own life and his were in terrible danger. Then had the image of a young man she knew to be her son appeared before her, offering vital comfort and strength. She shivered at the thought of how very close they had come to dying at the hands of a madwoman, but the fear that could still spark within her faded quickly, as it was likely to do these days. She lived surrounded by the

love of her husband, the esteem of his people, who were
now also hers, and the joy of motherhood. Nothing dark
could truly touch her.

Yet still she felt a flicker of apprehension as, crossing
the field before the hall, she saw the rider who had just entered through the well-guarded gates. Dragon Hakonson
was well known to her. He had visited Hawkforte on
several occasions and was always warmly welcomed.
Hawk's sister, the Lady Cymbra, was married to Dragon's
brother, the Wolf. Thus were they all united by ties of
family as well as friendship.

It was not Dragon who sparked Krysta's instant concern but rather the girl he held on the saddle in front of
him. That she was a girl was clear only from the copper-
hued hair that tumbled over her shoulders. She was clad
in boy's garb but that was only a passing oddity. Of far
more importance was her obviously bruised and bedrag-
gled state.

"What happened?" Krysta asked as she hurried forward. The closer she got to the girl, the more her concern
grew. There was a bruise across her brow and another,
uglier one on her left cheek. Her clothes were filthy, looking as though she had rolled in the dirt, as well as torn and
tattered. Scratches could be seen on her arms, hands, and
legs. She was very pale and looked beyond exhaustion.

Dragon handed the girl down to a man-at-arms, dismounted, and immediately reclaimed her. He nodded
cordially to Krysta but did not smile, unusual for him,
and there was a grim light in his eyes she had never seen
before.

"Is Hawk here?"

"On the training field. He's been sent for. Come,
bring her inside."

When she thought it necessary, Krysta could be every
inch the lady of the manor. Whoever the girl was, she
needed care immediately. Dragon would not be foolish

enough as to think otherwise but Krysta wasn't about to give him the opportunity to do so in his present odd mood.

He followed, however reluctantly. Krysta went directly to the guest quarters on the second floor. On the way, she gave orders to several servants to bring hot water, her medicine kit, bandages, and the like. Pushing open the heavy wooden door, she gestured Dragon inside. Only belatedly did she realize that she had come to the quarters meant for him, perhaps not appropriate for a young woman who was presumably—hopefully?—a stranger to him. But Dragon quickly erased any such thought.

He set the girl down on the bed, stepped back, and said, "This is the Lady Rycca of Wolscroft." Nothing in his tone or manner suggested he was the least pleased about that.

The girl herself said nothing at all, yet her averted gaze held such a wealth of misery that Krysta could not help but be moved. There was a mystery here to be sure, for Dragon Hakonson was not a man to spark misery in a female, but explanations would have to wait. It was of far more immediate importance to see to the young woman's injuries.

Servants began bustling into the room. Dragon took the opportunity to nod curtly and remove himself.

He got as far as the great hall before walking straight into Hawk. The two men were of similar size, both tall, powerfully built warriors at the peak of their powers. An unfortunate caught between them would have been crushed. They clasped hands.

"Dragon! We didn't expect you for several days yet. Tire of hunting so soon?" Hawk grinned as he spoke, his manner more relaxed and at ease since his marriage. Yet there was still a hint of caution in his eyes for already he had received reports of the girl who arrived with his Viking friend—his soon-to-be-married friend.

"I never got to hunt unless you count a few rabbits.

Look, something's happened and I'd just as soon you hear it from me as from anyone else."

"Like that, is it? Would this be the sort of tale that goes down better with a horn of ale?"

"More like a vat," Dragon said grimly and followed his host to the large oak table at the far end of the hall. A servant appeared, as they always seemed to do since the Lady Krysta had taken over management of the household from her crazed sister-in-law. In scarcely as much time as it took to give the order, they were seated with the ale before them, as well as a platter of fresh-baked breads, cold meats, and cheeses, for Krysta believed drink should not be taken without food. His task completed, the servant withdrew discreetly, leaving them alone.

"Well now, what's the problem?" Hawk asked after a long swallow to banish the dust of the training field.

Dragon hesitated but, to his credit, not for long. "I brought a girl with me. Krysta is seeing to her now. She's Lady Rycca of Wolscroft."

Hawk's brows rose slightly. "Your betrothed."

"My *errant* betrothed. I met her a few days ago, apparently after she donned boy's garb and fled from her home rather than come here and be married to me."

Hawk cleared his throat, decided this was a good time for more ale, and emptied the horn. He finished up with a deep breath before attempting a response. "I see . . . Well, I don't actually. She was dressed as a boy, you met several days ago, but you didn't bring her here until now?"

"I didn't know who she was. She wouldn't tell me her name so I—" His mouth thinned sardonically. "I decided not to tell her mine. Clever, don't you think?"

"Why do I have the distinct impression it was anything but?"

"*Not* knowing who I was—" Dragon broke off. His

gaze sought a distant corner of the hall. Quietly, he said, "Not knowing who I was, she lay with me."

Hawk whistled softly yet he was not particularly surprised. "Look . . . Dragon . . . you've always had great success with the ladies without even trying, isn't that so? A young girl, confused in her thinking, was bound to be seduced by you. Now granted, she shouldn't have been, but even so, you shouldn't have either—"

"It wasn't like that. I didn't seduce her." A flush darkened his cheeks. "The truth is she seduced me."

"She did?" Hawk couldn't hide his shock or the cause behind it. "But when I went to Wolscroft and saw her, I assumed she was . . . innocent."

"She was." Having said that, Dragon finished off his ale, accepted another round, and generally made it clear he had nothing further to say on that particular aspect of the subject.

After a moment or two, Hawk asked, "She was running away?"

"That's right. She'd left Wolscroft garbed as a boy and was making her way alone, I suspect to Hawksforte. I can only think that she meant to take ship for somewhere."

"Alone?" Hawk shook his head in amazement. "She took a hell of a risk."

"I thought her courageous but I was wrong. She is afraid, I suppose because I am unknown to her and she thinks all Vikings are alike. Even so, fear must be overcome especially when it threatens the peace between our peoples." Dragon said all this sadly for it was hard for him. Giving up the vision of his warrior woman was proving surpassingly difficult.

"She thought only of herself," he concluded regretfully.

Hawk did not pretend to misunderstand, nor did he

try to minimize the problem. The long struggle of recent decades had a single purpose, a better future for those to come. But to reach it, all of them from the king on down had to do what was needed for the greater good regardless of personal wishes, needs, yearnings, and even fears. Hawk himself had married against what he thought were his better instincts, only to find himself stunningly happy. Such were the strange twists of fate sometimes.

"I thought she would suit you," Hawk said slowly. "She is very beautiful, and beyond that, the ordinary folk of Wolscroft speak well of her."

A sudden memory flashed through Dragon's mind and he grimaced. "You were always fond of getting people to talk to you."

Both men were silent, remembering when Hawk had gone to the lair of the Wolf at Sciringesheal in Vestfold, there to learn if his sister taken in battle was captive slave or willing wife. To that end he had sent his men among the common folk of the town, from whom came a litany of tales that led Hawk to a stunningly wrong conclusion.

"It seems I may not be good enough at listening," he said regretfully.

"Don't blame yourself. At least you tried. I appreciate that."

Hawk was silent for a long moment. He leaned back in his chair and contemplated the horn of ale in his hand but did not drink from it again. Finally, he said, "You know, you don't have to marry her."

Dragon jerked his head as though he had been struck. "What?"

"Just what I said. Wolf, myself, and now you, we've all seen marriage as a means to further the alliance between Norse and Saxon. But Wolf and I have also found great personal happiness. I'd hate to think you couldn't do the same."

"Didn't you believe love as rare as hen's teeth? How now do you imagine it can come to me?"

Hawk shrugged. "When I saw Wolf and Cymbra together, and realized how much they loved each other, I thought it was just a fluke, something unique to them. I was glad for my sister, of course, but I never imagined the same could happen to me. At least, not until I met Krysta."

"I thought she bewildered and enraged you at first," Dragon said with a faint smile. He had visited Hawkforte during that time and well remembered the tension between the pair now so blissfully content.

"Well, yes, that's true but I got over it. At any rate, I meant what I said. You do not have to marry Lady Rycca of Wolscroft. When she ran off as she did, she violated the betrothal contract. No man will gainsay you should you choose to put her aside."

"After lying with her?"

"That was her choice . . . and her mistake. Another bride can be found. Mayhap not quite as comely, but more settled and predictable."

"A meek little woman to rub my feet?"

"What?"

Dragon smiled wanly. "That's what I used to tell Wolf I wanted in a wife. He warned me I'd be dead of boredom before the wedding flowers wilted."

Hawk tried, he truly did, but he could not suppress a grin. Yet he grew serious a moment later. "I have learned for myself what a marriage founded in love can mean. I would be less than a friend if I encouraged you to wed where there is only mistrust and acrimony."

"Even so," Dragon said slowly, "I pledged to make this marriage. Now it is a matter of honor."

"Honor is a cold bedfellow."

Dragon was on the verge of remarking that Rycca was anything but cold when he caught himself. He did not want to think of what had passed between them at the lodge, for it was still far too painful. His sense of having been abandoned by her hurt him as he would not have believed possible. So did the realization that she had rejected him before they'd even met. Rather than dwell on either, he concentrated on more recent events.

"Besides, what would happen to her if I wed elsewhere? I met her despicable father. He was just about to have her whipped."

"The marriage stands," he said, and drank his ale to the dregs.

H ERE," KRYSTA SAID GENTLY, "DRINK THIS." She held the cup of herbal tea to Rycca's lips and waited for her to swallow. The girl complied but slowly, as though she drifted some great distance from herself. Clearly she was dazed, possibly from exhaustion or from the blow to her head. She seemed also to be in shock.

"Lady Rycca," Krysta said gently, "whatever has happened, you are safe now. You will have every care and comfort." She lifted the hair falling across the girl's brow and frowned at the bruise there. "How did this happen?"

Rycca looked at her with wide, vacant eyes. Once again, Krysta had the impression that she was very far away. Several moments passed before the words seemed to penetrate what could only be described as her absence.

"I fell," she replied, so softly that even close as she was, Krysta had to lean closer to hear her.

"You fell? Where?"

"Off a cliff."

She had heard her correctly, Krysta was quite sure of that. Concealing her own shock, for she had no wish to alarm the girl, she asked, "How did that come to be?"

Rycca looked at the cup. Krysta took that as encouragement and immediately held it for her again. "This is a

good restorative made from willow bark, parsley, and a
few other things. The recipe is from my sister-in-law, the
Lady Cymbra. No doubt you have heard of her. She is a
renowned healer."

Having drunk a little more, Rycca nodded. She had
heard of Lady Cymbra. Who had not? Even her father
spoke of that lady with grudging care, perhaps because
she was both wife and sister to two of the most feared warriors ever known. She was also said to be the most beautiful woman in all of Christendom. As though that were not
enough, there were rumors about her, strange rumblings
that she had some unusual gift that enabled her to heal almost any illness or injury.

Rycca knew about strange rumors. Until she had
learned to conceal it, her unerring ability to sift truth from
falsehood had set her apart from others at Wolscroft and
led to rumblings from her father that she was bewitched.
Once or twice, when he was even more deeply in his cups
than usual, he had looked slant-eyed at her and muttered
that she might need burning. So had such paternal regard
led her to become expert at concealing herself, but there
was a price to be paid for that. Someday, she feared, she
would withdraw so far from the world as not to be able to
return. Even now she had to struggle for awareness of the
room, the woman, and all else that was real and tangible.

"Yes," she said, finally managing to speak above a
weak whisper, "I have heard of her and also of you, Lady
Krysta."

That seemed to fluster the beautiful, golden-haired
woman. She blushed a little and laughed a shade ner-
vously. Even as she did so, a raven landed on the windowsill and peered in. "Good heavens, I can only imagine
what tales have filled your ears."

That the Hawk was besotted with her, that she was
lovely as the moon, even that she sailed with skill to out-
strip a man's. How could any of that discomfort the lady?

Of course, there had been something about her having odd servants, but Rycca hadn't paid attention to that. Nor had she listened much when her father ranted on and on about Lord Udell, a fellow Mercian, who had boasted he would unseat the king only to take as hostage the last woman on earth he ever should have gone near, be tricked by her in some strange encounter people swore involved a troll, and finally fall before the vengeful sword of the enraged Hawk. If nothing else, the lady seemed to have an adventurous life.

"Nothing to your disrepute," Rycca said. Yet the lady was one of that hated and feared race that haunted Rycca's nightmares. Never had she imagined she could be at ease with a Viking, but then neither had she ever imagined that she would willingly lie with one, however unknowingly.

Weariness threatened to overcome her but the tea was reviving. She took another sip.

"About your fall off a cliff," Krysta said, quashing any hope Rycca had that she had forgotten her question. "How terrible that must have been. Were you coming here to Hawkforte when it happened?"

Rycca nodded slowly. Even had she had the strength to try, she saw no point in concealing anything. Lord Dragon would surely make known to all and sundry what had happened. Not for a moment did she believe that his pledge to her father that the marriage would stand could be taken seriously, although it had, strangely enough, held the ring of truth. She must have been mistaken about that. He could not possibly want her for his wife now, after all that had happened. She presumed he had merely brought her to Hawkforte to be punished, yet the gentle care she was receiving seemed at odds with that. Likely it would stop soon enough. There would be a knock at the door or someone would simply barge in, perhaps even the Hawk himself. She shivered at that thought and at the revulsion the Lady Krysta would no doubt feel when she realized to whom she had ministered.

"The night robe is yours," she said suddenly, her weary mind careening from one thought to the next. "I must ask your pardon for I borrowed it. That was wrong, I know, but I had never seen anything so lovely."

Krysta shook her head in bewilderment. "That matters not. When did you fall from the cliff?"

"A few days ago." A soft sob broke from her but she managed to swallow enough of it that it sounded only like a gulp. "A lifetime ago."

Now Krysta truly was worried. She knew what head injuries could do. Lady Rycca was behaving most peculiarly. Not for a moment did Krysta think Dragon might be responsible for the girl's condition. He was kindness itself to women. But something terrible had happened and she meant to get to the bottom of it.

"Have you been dizzy since that fall? Have you fainted? Do you find yourself being forgetful?"

Rycca laughed painfully. "Yes to all, so dizzy as to be out of my senses, fainting away from the world, forgetful of everything good sense and reason should have told me. But no, not as you mean. I suffered little ill effect, amazingly enough."

This left Krysta less than reassured. Very lightly, she touched the side of Rycca's face. That bruise looked fresher, yet she was not sure. "Did this happen at the same time?"

"No, today. My brother struck me."

Krysta grimaced. She had never heard anything good about Wolscroft or his elder sons. "I am sorry, but it will heal. Now you need a warm bath and a proper meal—that with a night's rest and I believe you will be much improved come morning."

"Where is your husband?"

"With Dragon, I suppose. Why do you ask?"

"Then he will be here soon. He will not be pleased that you are caring for me."

"Of course he will be. Why do you think otherwise?"

Rycca took a breath, sought courage, realized she had none, and did without. "I ran away because I did not want to marry the Lord Dragon. Yet fate caused our paths to cross. He pursued me, I fled, and in the doing I fell down the side of a cliff. He took me to your lodge and there we stayed together several days." She sighed deeply, closed her eyes for a moment, and opened them again to find Krysta regarding her gently. It was the kindness she saw in the forest-green eyes that enabled her to continue, that and the desperate wish that someone might somehow understand what she had done and why. "I did not know who he was, nor did he know me, but I . . . I wanted a memory, something bright and good to hold on to no matter what happened. It was my fault what passed between us yet I cannot even now regret it."

To Rycca's surprise, the Lady Krysta did not look shocked or dismayed. Instead, she merely nodded and even smiled, as though considering her own memories. "Ah, yes, the wish to seize something perfect in this imperfect world even when it must be done against all reason and good sense."

Struggling to cope with so unexpected a reaction, Rycca was startled by the sudden knock at the door. At once, she stiffened. Now she would be dragged away, denounced, made to pay for what she had done. . . .

But at the lady's summons, the door opened to admit a stream of servants carrying buckets of water, garments, food, and drink. Within minutes they had filled the bath and departed.

"We will sort all this out later," Krysta said. "For now, you will feel a great deal better when you are clean."

Dazed and bemused, Rycca found herself led to the

tub. The torn and stained boy's garments, smelling less than pleasant thanks to their time in the river, were removed and she was helped into silken water scented with . . . what was that? Roses. The water was scented with roses. Never in her life had she known such unbridled and utterly feminine luxury.

"Heaven," she murmured.

"It is, isn't it?" Krysta agreed. She looked at the boy's clothes and tossed them into a corner. "Let me help you with your hair."

Careful of her bruised face, Krysta gently washed and rinsed the coppery tresses while Rycca simply sat still in the tub and tried to absorb what was happening to her. The Lady of Hawkforte seemed in no way dismayed by what she had told her. Ragamuffins fleeing state marriages might turn up on her doorstep every day for all the concern she showed. That could not possibly be right.

The water was cooling when Krysta helped Rycca from the tub, wrapped a length of sheeting around her, and sat her down next to the table. With care, she brushed out her hair and dried it. When that was done, Krysta held up a night robe.

"Put this on and you'll be done."

Rycca complied, too weary and bewildered to do anything else. In the huge bed, warmly covered and propped up by down-filled pillows, she watched as Krysta's servants arrived to tidy up. This they did with admirable speed, not one of them even so much as glancing at her. When they had gone, Krysta brought a tray of food and drink to the bed.

"You really must eat something," she said. "The soup is very good. It's another of Lady Cymbra's recipes. She very kindly sent me a veritable book of them, for, truth be told, I have no particular talent with such things."

Obediently, Rycca accepted a spoonful of the soup only to discover that it was as good as Krysta said and that she was truly hungry. She cupped the bowl in her hands and ate as rapidly as decorum allowed. When she was finished, she lay back against the pillows. Outside, the twilight was fading. Krysta rose, struck flint to tinder, and lit the twin iron braziers that stood on either side of the bed. "You should go to sleep soon," she said quietly.

"You have been very kind. I don't know how to thank you." Tears like a rain of sorrow glistened within her eyes but did not fall. That much control she still had left.

Krysta shrugged. "People were kind to me when I was in need. Someday you will do the same for another person. That will be thanks enough."

She turned to go, but Rycca reached out and clasped her hand. "Please, stay a moment."

"Yes, of course." Krysta sat down on the side of the bed. She presumed the young woman was simply afraid to be left alone after everything she had been through, but in this Rycca surprised her. Her thoughts were not of solitude but of marriage.

"You married for the alliance?"

Krysta smiled. "I came here to Hawkforte because of that, but the truth is, I married for love."

Rycca's eyes widened. "How could that have happened? No one weds for love."

"It's rare, to be sure, but it happened nonetheless. How is a rather long story and I don't think you're up to it right now. Is it love you seek or do you have some other reason for not wanting to marry?"

"I don't believe in love," Rycca said flatly. "Or I didn't. If you say it exists, I will believe you. I just think it must be extremely uncommon. As for the alliance, you are Norse and I do not wish to offend you."

"But you don't believe Vikings mean to make peace?" Krysta spoke without acrimony. She was well aware of this view of her countrymen. While she knew it to be unfair generally, she understood that those who had been the

target of Viking raids for generations found it hard to believe that the wild men of the north were willing to give up
their warring ways.

"Vikings have ever gone adventuring," she said gently.
"It is in our spirit, but besides that, we've really had no
choice. The northlands are beautiful but can support only
a small number of people. If a farm is divided among too
many sons, soon it will support no one at all. Thus do many
of us become traders and venture to the farthest reaches of
the world."

"The Vikings who came to England did not do so to
trade," Rycca said.

"That is true and terrible things have happened because of that. Moderation is needed. Therefore did the
Lord Wolf propose this alliance. He believes that friendship between Norse and Saxon will encourage all concerned to turn their hands to more peaceful pursuits."

Her deep green eyes scanned Rycca's face for a moment. She smiled sadly. "You do not believe me or at least
you do not believe it will work. Life offers no guarantees,
but surely peace is worth the effort?"

*Burning huts ... smoke rising into air filled with
screams ... terror so great she could scarcely breathe. Aelflynne
racing toward her, clutching the doll she loved so well ... a
shadow over her ... the sudden cry and her arms outstretched
toward Rycca hiding in the stable, their gazes locking for a
fateful moment until a knife flashed, blood oozed into the
ground, a small body went limp, and Aelflynne's eyes dimmed
forever.*

"Peace," Rycca said emphatically, "comes only with
power. When we are strong enough to crush our enemies,
they will be our friends, not before."

Krysta did not mince words. "That is a terrible view
of life."

"Nothing I have witnessed contradicts it."

Nothing save the kindness of a man who had no idea

who she was yet pledged to protect her while asking nothing for himself.

A fluke, nothing more.

Not true.

"Stop," Rycca murmured.

"I'm sorry, I've kept you talking too long."

"No, not you, that isn't what I meant. . . . It is I who must apologize. You've been very good to me and I've repaid you with rudeness."

Krysta smoothed the covers. "I take no offense. You are very tired." Softly, as though to her own child, she said, "Sleep now, Lady Rycca of Wolscroft. Tomorrow is a brighter day."

Y ET MUCH LATER, AS KRYSTA LAY IN BED BESIDE her husband, drowsily content in the aftermath of their lovemaking, she wondered if her hopeful promise could possibly be fulfilled. Stirring in Hawk's arms, she sat up and gazed at him. His eyes were closed, his rugged features relaxed, he looked like a man with nothing more on his mind than a decent rest.

She poked him lightly with her elbow. "You aren't asleep, are you?"

Without opening his eyes, Hawk sighed. "Why is it women always want to talk?"

She poked him harder. "Women?"

He opened one eye, cautiously. "Did I say that? I mean woman, of course, just one very singular, very adorable, occasionally maddening woman."

"Is Dragon very upset?"

"Men don't get upset. We get angry, enraged, irritated, bewildered, amused, and, very rarely, flummoxed, but never upset."

"Which is he?"

Hawk hesitated. He stopped pretending to sleep and

gathered his wife closer. When her head was back down on his chest where it rightly belonged, he said, "I think he's hurt."

"I was afraid of that. She's very beautiful."

"It's not the beauty, or not mostly. He thought she was brave and other things as well, I suspect. Now he sees himself saddled with a wife too selfish to care about peace."

"She does care, she just doesn't think the alliance will work."

"What will then, more war?" Hawk spoke with the disdain of a man who has left too much of his youth on battlefields.

"This isn't a good beginning for them," Krysta said with a sigh.

Hawk nodded. "But a beginning it must be all the same."

Just then, Falcon made a little snurfling sound in the cradle close by their bed. Both parents stiffened, wondering if rest would prove elusive that night. But a moment later he settled back down, and shortly thereafter so did they.

But not quite completely. In the haven of her husband's arms, Krysta murmured softly, "A wounded dragon."

Hawk was almost asleep. "Seems to be."

Dangerous, her mind whispered, but she was no longer awake to hear. In any case, it was not her concern.

The same could not be said for the Lady Rycca, who lay in the sumptuous bed in the immense guest room, counting the long hours of night and wondering what day would bring. Krysta's promise was kind, as was the woman herself, but not for a moment did Rycca think anything good lay ahead of her.

Chapter

SEVEN

YET WITH MORNING CAME MORE OF THE cosseting of the night before. Rycca woke from belated sleep to a daze of sunshine, fair breezes, bustling servants, and a determinedly smiling Krysta. The day looked scrubbed clean and so did Rycca feel by the time she emerged from her second bath, donned the shift Krysta held out for her, and sat herself at the table by the windows. From there she could see beyond the roofs of the many dependencies and the high stone walls against which they clustered, all the way down to the town itself with its busy port. Only Winchester, seat of the king, was larger, and she had seen that but once.

Hawkforte compelled even her gray and disordered thoughts. Shops lined the streets, often of two stories to provide living room above and with large gardens in the back. Here and there a goat nibbled grass or a pig lolled in cool mud. A sudden flash of white drew her notice to a small herd of sheep being led through the streets to market.

Half-a-dozen ships rocked gently beside the town

quays. Gazing at them, Rycca wondered which one might have carried her to Normandy had fate so willed. Perhaps none, for her scheme was fraught with danger from the beginning, yet her mind still lingered a little while longer, reluctant to give up forever the hope of freedom so fleetingly found.

Krysta drew her back into the moment, but gently as though she sensed the regrets that had left shadows beneath Rycca's eyes.

"Your father arrived this morning," the Lady of Hawkforte said quietly. The firm set of her usually soft and generous mouth made clear what she thought of that. "He met with my lord. I know not what was said, though Wolscroft seemed much calmer when he emerged."

"Calmer?" Rycca's slanted brows rose. She looked away from the tray of food set in front of her for in truth she could not imagine eating anything. This latest news only increased the weight of anxiety that hung upon her. Events were spiraling beyond any hope of her influencing much less controlling them. She felt trapped within a cage with the walls growing ever tighter. "I do not believe I have ever heard that word used to describe my father."

"Ah, well, Hawk can have a remarkably soothing effect on people when he wants to." Krysta's smile suggested *soothing* perhaps did not best describe what had gone on.

"Even so . . ."

"Your dowry has been deposited with our priest, Father Desmond. He has agreed to marry you and Lord Dragon this afternoon."

What little color had been in Rycca's face vanished. She darted a quick look at Krysta and saw true sympathy in her eyes but determination as well. Sitting down beside her, Krysta took chilled hands in her much warmer ones and said earnestly, "I wish these were happy tidings for you but I know they are not. Yet do I beseech you, accept what must be."

"Why must it?" Rycca asked faintly. "I would have thought the Lord Dragon had reconsidered by now and decided the marriage not to his liking."

"He has done nothing of the sort, nor will he."

"Yet he did not want this marriage to begin with, he was merely resigned to it. And now he must have the worst possible opinion of me. . . ." Her voice trailed off. She could scarcely bear what the man in whose arms she had lain and who had gifted her with such joy must think of her now. Bad enough that she had fled from a marriage meant to make peace, how much worse that she had given the virginity that rightly belonged to her husband to a man she believed to be a stranger. He must think her a coward, selfish, uncaring, and a wanton without a scrap of morals.

What a marvelous beginning to a marriage. She pressed her lips together tightly lest the groundswell of distress growing within her become known to all the world.

Krysta stood up. She gestured to the servants who hovered a discreet distance away, waiting to dress the bride. Not unkindly, for she was never that, but with simple directness, she said, "As to that, Dragon will not refuse but you still can. If you stand before Father Desmond this afternoon and refuse his blessing, there will be nothing anyone can do, not Dragon, Hawk, your father, or even the king himself. The Church is quite clear about that—no marriage without consent." She looked at Rycca frankly. "Of course, you must realize what will happen if you do that."

"I will remain under the authority of my father."

"Precisely, and he will punish you as he sees fit. The law gives him that right."

To Krysta's surprise, Rycca smiled faintly. "There is irony to this. My father would be pleased to have the marriage stopped."

"Because of the dowry?"

"No, not that. I think in an odd sort of way he takes pride in showing his wealth. But his hatred of Vikings knows no limits. So too does he despise Alfred for seeking terms with the Danes and for making this alliance with the Norse. Yet he would still punish me, mayhap even to death."

Krysta was silent for a moment. Quietly, she asked, "Do you know, was Wolscroft in alliance with Lord Udell?"

"The traitor? Your husband killed him, did he not?"

Krysta nodded. Her face grew somber as she remembered the events of the year before. How very close they had all come to tragedy. "There was not a breath of suspicion about Wolscroft, yet if he hates Alfred . . ."

"He thought Udell was a strutting fool, always bragging about what he could do. But the truth is Udell had the will to act, however misguidedly, while my father does not. He may rant and rave, yet survival matters most to him."

Krysta looked relieved. "No doubt that is why he was *soothed* by Hawk."

A tiny laugh escaped Rycca. The sound startled her. She looked from Krysta to the hovering servants and felt inevitability wash over her.

THE GOWN WAS BEYOND BEAUTIFUL. THE FABric seemed crafted of moss-draped glens, shards of sunlight dappling through trees, and, here and there, embroidered into the sleeves and hem, shy wood violets and twining vines. Never had Rycca seen anything like it.

"I cannot," was her first reaction.

Krysta dismissed that. "Of course you can. It suits your coloring perfectly, indeed far better than it would have mine."

"It was made for you."

"Yes," Krysta acknowledged, "but not yet worn and now yours, my gift to you. Come, we must see if it needs any alteration, although I think perhaps it will not for we are of the same height and it may be . . ."

She dropped the gown over Rycca's head, helped her slip her arms into the sleeves, quickly laced up the back, then took a long look.

"Ah, yes, just as I thought. It is perfect." Behind her, the servants beamed their agreement. They stepped aside to reveal an object Rycca had never seen before. It was almost as tall as herself, half an arm's span wide, and glowing within it . . .

A soft gasp escaped her. She stepped closer, reaching out a hand and watching as the ethereal woman caught within the gleaming metal did the same.

"It's a mirror," Krysta said. "Brought all the way from Byzantium."

"Incredible," Rycca breathed. "I have never seen one that was bigger than a few inches—" She was caught by the image of her other self speaking just as she did. Yet that could not possibly be herself. *She* looked like something out of a dream, fire-lit hair framing a face of unnatural calm above a willowy body that the gown managed to both conceal and reveal. The mirror did much the same, displaying her appearance yet muting any imperfection. Rycca stepped a little closer, touching fingers lightly to her bruised cheek. It still hurt but not as much as the day before and she could see no trace of the injury. Even the bruise on her forehead was almost gone.

"You look lovely," Krysta said with a reassuring smile.

Rycca took scant comfort from that. Dragon might be moved by beauty under ordinary circumstances but she doubted he would be in her case. It was the nature of her character, not her face and form, that would concern him.

She took a deep breath and turned away from the mirror.

"Can you drink a little?" Krysta asked.

Rycca honestly tried, if only to please the woman who was being so kind to her, but a few mouthfuls of water were all that she could manage. For once, she was glad of the fast imposed before mass.

Too soon, Krysta was ushering her out of the room and down the stairs, where they were met by a wave of noise rising from the great hall. Rycca stopped, her hand pressed hard against the wall, and stared. So many people! Prosperous merchants and their wives mingled with stern men-at-arms and their own ladies. She caught a quick glimpse of her father and his retinue standing off to one side, scowling but impotent under the watchful eye of the Hawk's men. And there was the Hawk himself, towering over almost all the men in the room save for just one, who was beside him, the two deep in conversation.

Her throat so tight that she could scarcely breathe, Rycca stared at the man to whom she was shortly to be given. Aside from the rugged symmetry of his perfectly formed features, and the graceful power of his body, he looked very different from the man she had so briefly known. To begin with, he was far more richly dressed, garbed in a tunic of somber black that gleamed with threads of gold, gold visible again in the thick bands around his neck and in the torque that encircled his throat, symbol of his rank and power. Perhaps in deference to his host he wore only a short dagger at his waist but he looked nonetheless dangerous for that. His somber expression made it clear he did not come as a lighthearted bridegroom to his nuptials.

Nor did the men clustered near him appear any more pleased. Almost of a size with the Dragon, his Viking attendants were without exception fierce men, keen-eyed and vigilant. If they were uncomfortable in this crowd of

Saxons they did not show it, but neither did they appear inclined to relax their guard for even a moment.

No wonder her father and the others from Wolscroft were huddled off to the side. For just a moment, she entertained the mad wish that she might join them. Better she leap from the cliff again.

Just then, Dragon saw her. He stiffened slightly but otherwise gave no sign. He made no effort to greet her, nor did he so much as smile. Rycca had expected nothing else, yet her spirits dipped still further. Averting her gaze, she continued on to the bottom of the stairs, where she abruptly became aware that all conversation in the great hall had ceased.

Rycca's hands clenched at her sides. Her stomach roiled and she was deeply grateful for its emptiness. With an effort of will, she kept her head high and her back straight. The temptation to flee into the safety of her mind was almost irresistible but she knew she must not. She must walk through this crowd, to the side of her betrothed, as serene as though she strolled through a pleasant dream. For if she did not, truly she feared she would be ripped apart.

Their eyes were so avid. Men and women alike, they looked like hunters at the moment when the prey is brought to ground and there remains only the blooding. Not of her, though, not this time. Her virgin's blood was gone yet she was to be kept alive, to go through with this mockery of a marriage.

Behind her, Krysta murmured, "It's all right."

Rycca scarcely heard her but the cool clarity of truth sounded deep within her all the same. The Lady of Hawkforte did not merely hope, she believed. Had there been time, Rycca might have puzzled over that but there was none for just then the tall, fair-haired man with the piercing gray eyes stepped forward. He smiled at Krysta, a smile of such all-encompassing gentleness that Rycca was filled with sudden longing for what her better sense told her would never be hers. Then he turned his attention to the errant bride.

"Lady Rycca," he said, not unkindly but in a tone that brooked no resistance, "you are welcome at Hawkforte. Our priest, Father Desmond, is eager to meet you."

As he spoke, he gestured to a young man tonsured and garbed as a cleric. His youth surprised her. To be house priest to a lord so high as the Hawk of Essex at so young an age was unusual indeed. Perhaps the intelligence she saw gleaming in his dark eyes had something to do with his swift promotion.

The priest stepped forward and offered his hand. "If you would, my lady, I ask only a few minutes of your time."

He could have the entire rest of the day and into the next as far as Rycca was concerned. She nodded and went with him, glad to be away from the eyes of the crowd and determined not to think about the fact that Dragon had said nothing at all.

They went to a small, graceful chapel a little distance beyond the great hall. Here the light of day gave way to soft shadows chased by beeswax candles that were already lit. The scent of flowers hung heavily on the air. The center of the chapel was empty, for it was there that the congruents would stand. There was also a beautiful altar draped with an embroidered cloth and set with vessels of silver and gold.

"Decked already for your bridal," Father Desmond said with another smile. Two steps led to the altar. He sat on the upper one and gestured for her to join him. His informality surprised her even as she felt it slipping beneath the edges of her dread.

"You know why I wished to speak with you?"

She nodded, watching her clasped hands twist in her lap. "I must give consent."

"Exactly. Church teaching is quite clear about that."

"Yet I would hardly be the first bride to wed unwillingly."

The young priest stiffened. He looked at her with concern. "Are you unwilling?"

She shrugged. "It does not matter."

"Oh, but it does, on pain of your immortal soul, it most certainly does matter."

When she did not respond, he stood up and began to pace back and forth before her, using his hands for emphasis as he spoke. His fingers were long and slender. Two on the right hand were stained with ink. Knowing she must listen to him, wondering at her waywardness, Rycca found herself staring at those ink-stained fingers.

"You are a scribe?"

He paused suddenly, in the midst of saying something about the marriage at Cana. "I do still make books although my duties take me in other directions as well."

"You are young for such a post. May I ask how it came to be?"

Father Desmond colored slightly. "I was in the scriptorium at Winchester. His lordship engaged me to make a book for the Lady Krysta. When it was done, they were both pleased with the results. As it happened, they were also in need of a new house priest. The invitation was made to me to come here and I happily accepted."

"I was at Winchester once and saw the library there. It is magnificent."

"It is indeed and a great joy. But to return to the matter at hand, I assure you, your consent is essential. Do you mean to withhold it?"

"No," Rycca said and saw his instant relief. Man of God that he was, Father Desmond clearly did not relish the notion of angering both his patron, the Lord Hawk, and the fierce Lord Dragon. Yet Rycca had the impression he would risk exactly that if he believed she did not consent to the marriage.

"There seemed to be some . . . irregularity in your coming here," the priest said delicately. Thus did he characterize her arrival, bruised and battered, in the arms of her betrothed rather than under the decorous escort of her family.

"I had some trouble on the road. Lord Dragon was most helpful."

Father Desmond nodded, smiling. "Everyone speaks very well of the jarl. I believe he and Lord Hawk are fast friends."

"Friendship between Norse and Saxon seems much the fashion these days."

The priest looked at her quizzically. "Do you think so? I have little knowledge of fashion, despite being at court. There was never time to notice such things."

"I meant because of the alliance. Everyone seems to have an opinion about it."

"Oh, as to that, I cannot imagine anyone would object. Surely we all want peace."

Rycca's smile was a little wry. "You would be surprised, Father. There are actually some who prefer war. But beyond that, do you take it as given that this alliance is genuine, that the Norse really do mean for there to be peace between us?"

Father Desmond thought about that for a moment. Slowly, he nodded. "Yes, so far as it goes. The people of Vestfold, those we call Norse, want peace. Moreover, I think they want the land-hungry Danes to understand that should they cast covetous eyes toward Vestfold, they would be met with all-out resistance not only from the Norse themselves but right here, on the Danes' southern flank, from the Saxons. The Danes would quickly find themselves fighting a war on two sides, something I am quite certain they do not want."

"But what if the Danes and Norse decide instead to act together? After all, they have far more in common than do Norse and Saxon. They speak the same language, worship the same gods, follow the same customs. Surely they are more natural allies?"

"So it might seem," Father Desmond agreed, "yet they are also competitors for land, fishing ranges, trade routes, and the like. Besides, those differences that exist between Norse and Saxon are the reason for the marriages that secure the alliance, of which yours will be the third. The binding together of families offers assurance that the peace will be kept."

"I pray you are right," Rycca said softly.

Father Desmond held out his hand to her. She took it and together they knelt on the steps before the altar. He prayed quietly, his voice leading her into realms of calm she had not thought available to her. For a few moments, she felt at peace.

Then it was over and he led her back to the great hall and the feasting eyes.

D RAGON WATCHED HER COME AS HE HAD watched her from the moment she appeared on the stairs, a vision of feminine grace and beauty that sucked the breath right out of him, damn her. His desire for her was immediate and all but overwhelming. He cursed himself for it as he fought to project some semblance of calm. Incredibly for one so inured to battle, his chest hurt as though constricted by bands of steel. His palms felt very hot, even sweaty.

What had she told the priest?

Hawk had said their holy man could not perform the

wedding unless he was sure the bride was willing. Had there ever been one less so?

Her eyes were downcast, she would not meet his gaze no matter how fiercely he willed her to do so. But the priest was smiling. He nodded to Dragon even as he addressed Hawk.

"Ah, well, now that is taken care of. We will proceed as you wish, my lords."

"Immediately then," Hawk said. He did a decent enough job of hiding his relief but Dragon wasn't fooled. Until that moment, not even the Lord of Essex had been sure the marriage would take place.

Krysta appeared at Rycca's side. She spoke to her softly, distracting her as she guided her to a small room off the great hall. There the bride would wait while the guests, her scowling family, and one stern-faced groom assembled in the chapel.

Father Desmond led the way. Dragon followed even as it dawned on him that he was well and truly about to be wed. All through the sleepless night he had thought of it, pondering why he had refused to call off the marriage. She had betrayed him, with himself true enough but it was betrayal all the same, not merely with her body but with the far more important matter of her spirit.

He had thought her courageous and found her cowardly, he who knew the deeply engrained torment of fear but knew also the conquering of it. So, too, had he believed her honorable in her own fashion and discovered she cared for naught save her own well-being.

Why did it matter so much? Why didn't he simply laugh at the absurdity of it all? He had not wanted to marry to begin with and once reconciled to the need, he had allowed himself no expectations. Or so he had thought. Never had it occurred to him that he might not be able to trust his wife or at least respect her. Without so basic a foundation for their life together, he truly wondered how they would manage.

Yet there he was in the flower-scented chapel, giving the appearance of listening as Father Desmond instructed him in what was to happen.

"I will serve mass. I realize you are not Christian so perhaps I should explain . . ."

"I understand the mass. You commemorate the sacrifice of your savior."

"Essentially, yes. Before that occurs, I will ask you and the Lady Rycca to come forward and to tell me what you wish. Your part is to say that you wish the blessing of Cana upon your marriage. To all intents and purposes, the two of you have been wed since the marriage documents were signed, but the Church believes it is important to sanctify the union."

"Fine . . . What is that you said?"

The priest looked at him shrewdly. "I thought it was the same in the northlands. With or without the blessing of a holy man, a couple is legally wed when the appropriate documents have been signed. Is that not so?"

Dragon nodded curtly but his mind was turning over the notion. So he had lain with his *wife* before the lodge, in that star-lit night of passion beyond his imagining. He suspected the priest meant for him to be mollified by that but it made no difference. No matter that she had not known his name, rank, even his very right to her. She had *known* him in the ancient sense, known the man he was and how it was between them. And she had left him all the same.

He did not doubt for a moment that she would do the same again were she to be given the chance. He who had pleased uncounted women had not been able to please her enough to persuade her to stay. Or so it seemed.

"Let's get this over with," Dragon said and went to his nuptials with that black cloud hanging over him.

How strange that it should be so simple, Rycca

thought. For so transforming an act as marriage, it was accomplished very quickly. The priest said a few words, asked if they agreed to be "boon companions" and abide with one another, then made the sign of the cross above them. They were wed.

She turned, her hand gripped hard in Dragon's, and saw her father glaring at her. He looked smaller somehow, as did Ogden beside him, as though they had shrunk. That was impossible, of course. It was only the imaginings of her addled mind.

They were back out in the golden sunlight. Dragon had said nothing to her nor had he looked in her direction. But there was the warmth, nay even the heat of his skin against hers. Krysta came up, smiling, and said something to them both. She hugged Rycca, who could only stare back at her, not having heard a word. Lord Hawk took his wife's arm. He, too, spoke, and Dragon answered him but their voices were only a low rumble in the far distance of Rycca's mind.

With a start, she pulled herself back into the moment. Dragon was leading her to the great hall. Servants swarmed everywhere. Only now did she notice the wide tables that had been set up, draped in white linen and gleaming with precious plate. Hawk and Krysta took their places at the high table with Dragon and Rycca beside them and Father Desmond to her right so that she was between her new husband and the priest. Wolscroft was seated to Hawk's left, close enough to be kept under scrutiny. Ogden looked to be already drunk as he stumbled into the chair next to his father's.

Hawk offered a gracious toast, musicians began to play, and pages hurried about with platters of food as serving girls refilled the drinking horns. A moment's strained silence fell over the high table in sharp contrast to the joviality already evident throughout the hall. Krysta moved swiftly to remedy it. She turned to Dragon and asked a question about his voyage that he could hardly neglect to answer. An instant later, Father Desmond asked Rycca to tell him about the time she had visited Winchester. That left Hawk, who, after a flicker of irritation soothed by a dazzling smile from his wife, sighed deeply and inquired of Wolscroft if he was still fond of boar hunting.

So did the next few hours pass. Rycca ate almost nothing. Dragon spoke not a word to her, nor did he give the slightest hint that he was even aware of her presence. This despite the fact that, as custom dictated, they were sharing a plate. Once, when her hand accidentally brushed his, she felt him stiffen but he did not so much as glance at her.

She sat in misery, grateful for the company of Father Desmond, who proved as interesting as he was kind. He was a scholar, trained in the schools King Alfred was creating across the land, and he took a special delight in the study of nature. After a particularly long but thoroughly engaging discourse on the habits of the titmouse, he broke off suddenly and blushed. "I fear I rattle on far too much, Lady Rycca. You are most patient to listen to me."

"Not at all," she assured him quickly. "There has been little opportunity in my life to observe much of nature beyond the ordinary day-to-day activities common to any manor. But there have been stolen moments when I've watched a bird make her nest or seen a doe caring for her young. I treasure such times."

The priest nodded. "Such are precious to me as well. I am very fortunate in that the lord and lady encourage me still to draw the animals I observe. Lord Hawk has even commissioned another book and wishes to expand the scriptorium here."

Rycca was about to comment on this when a disturbance at the other end of the high table distracted her. Red-faced with drink, Ogden was trying to pull a serving girl into his lap. With one hand he gripped the girl around the waist while with the other he was pulling down her bodice. The girl looked terrified as she struggled to get away from him.

Instantly, Hawk and Dragon were on their feet. Hawk, being closer, got hold of him first but Dragon was not far behind. Hawk freed the girl by the simple expediency of removing Ogden's arm from her and twisting it sharply behind the man's back as he lifted him onto his feet. Wolscroft belatedly realized what was happening and started to rise, only to be pressed down into his chair by Dragon's heavy hand on his shoulder.

"What's this now?" Wolscroft demanded belligerently. "My lad's not doing any harm, just wants a bit of fun."

"Not here," Hawk said firmly. He gestured to two of his men-at-arms, who came forward immediately. "Lord Ogden is indisposed. See him to his quarters."

"What th'hell?" That was too much for Wolscroft, who struggled to rise, found he still could not, and turned on Dragon. "Get your hand off me, boy. You may think you call the tune now but I'm not about to be insulted by the likes of you."

Rycca gasped. She too had risen and was staring at the scene in horror. Ogden's being drunk and pawing at serving girls was nothing new, nor was her father's overbearing manner. Both men considered such behavior their right and would not take kindly to any suggestion otherwise. Neither would their attendants, ranked at tables nearby and watching what was happening with bleary-eyed interest. Several were already on their feet.

Dragon and Hawk exchanged a quick glance. Ogden was being removed, there was still a chance the matter could end peacefully. Dragon let go of Wolscroft and stepped back but he did not take his eyes from the older man, who was now rising from his chair. "I have no quarrel with you," Dragon said, "but your son is too deeply in his cups to sit at table with ladies. It is well he withdraw."

"Well?" Wolscroft repeated angrily. He swayed a little as he rose but regained his balance. He fumbled for the sword usually at his waist but it was missing, Hawk having insisted that all such be removed. There was only a small dagger on the table, the same one he had used for his meat. This Wolscroft seized and, before Rycca's horrified gaze, pointed it at Dragon.

"Only went along with this 'cause high-and-mighty Alfred said I had to an' then this one"—he waved the dagger toward Hawk—"this king's lackey tol' me there weren't no choice. But if I'd wanted a Viking son-in-law, I'd have given her to a Dane." He spared a sneering glance at Rycca. "The Danes are always sniffin' around, lookin' to keep Alfred lyin' awake at night. I could've had my pick."

"That would have been a very poor choice on your part," Hawk said quietly. He was moving to his right, slowly so as not to alert Wolscroft, but obviously determined to put himself between the armed man and Krysta, who was now closest to the Mercian. Dragon saw the same danger even as Rycca did, and with a mere flick of his eyes he signaled to his men to hold. They had been moving closer, ready to intervene at his signal, but now they froze in place. Hawk's retainers did the same, although they were positioned close behind the other Mercians, ready to take hold of them in an instant. The great hall fell silent, poised on the verge of a battle that might well prove one-sided but could be bloody all the same.

Sickness rose in her throat. She had ever been at odds with her family, save for her twin, and ever been horrified by them. But now she was well and thoroughly humiliated. Dragon was controlling himself admirably but he had the look of a man who has found something unpleasant on his boot. Ogden, slumped between the men-at-arms, was oblivious to the havoc he had sparked, but Wolscroft had his face set in bulldog belligerence. Little flecks of spittle shone at the corners of his mouth. Again he waved the dagger.

"Danes would be better 'an this," he said. "Led about like a damn eunuch. Alfred's after cuttin' the balls off all of us."

"Put the dagger down," Hawk said.

Wolscroft seemed not to hear him. He was too far gone in drink and his own resentments. "What's the point havin' a daughter if you can't marry her for profit?" He waved the blade at Dragon again. "He gets the dowry and I get . . . what? Norse scum for a son-in-law."

When still Dragon did not react, Wolscroft's sneer deepened. "I just called you scum, boy. Don't you think you ought to do somethin' about that?"

"Do what, old man?" Dragon asked quietly. "Fight you? At your daughter's wedding feast?" He shook his head in disgust. "Just put the dagger down and go to your bed. You're finished here."

"Finished?" Wolscroft sputtered in rage. "I'm not *finished*, boy! I say you're not man enough. Speakin' of eunuchs . . ."

"That's enough!" The sound of her own voice surprised Rycca but she was beyond fear, driven to desperation by the shame clawing at her. All day she had dwelt in misery, caught in the web of her own deficiencies, recalling over and over how poorly Dragon must think of her. This was the last straw. One way or another, the man who had made her life a hell of cruelty and fear was going to stop.

Wolscroft turned on her in surprise. The instant he did so, she struck out with her heavy drinking cup, smashing it against the protruding bone of his wrist. He squawked as his hand flew open. She caught the dagger by its hilt as it fell. Gripping it firmly, she pointed it at him even as she began to tremble, not with fear of him, for he suddenly did look like the old man Dragon had called him, but rather with fear of herself. What was she that she could behave like this? Certainly not the gentle, caring lady she was supposed to be.

"Go away," she said to her father and heard the thickness of tears in her voice.

Dragon was suddenly at her side. He took the dagger from her. She yielded it willingly, wishing never to see the repulsive thing again. There were other men beside Wolscroft, leading him away. He was still protesting but the fight had gone out of him. Maybe the consequences of creating such a scene in the home of the feared Hawk were finally dawning on him. Or perhaps being disarmed by his own daughter, she whom he had always treated with such contempt, deflated him more effectively than anything else might have done.

It made no difference to Rycca. Her shame was complete.

As was Dragon's bewilderment. He had just seen his cowardly, selfish, untrustworthy bride behave with rare courage and strength. She had disarmed an enraged warrior, her own father, and done it in the blink of an eye. Moreover, Dragon could not shake the unsettling impression that she had acted to protect him.

It made no sense. Who was this woman?

Besides, of course, his wife.

Chapter

EIGHT

D RAGON WOULD HAVE TIME TO PONDER
the matter, perhaps the rest of his life. But just
then he had the night to get through. His wedding night.

He glanced at Rycca. She looked pale, exhausted, and
deeply unhappy. A long sigh escaped him. How could he
possibly expect her to lie with him after everything she
had been through and given all that lay between them?
How could he not? Certainly everyone at Hawkforte
would expect it and take it very amiss if the marriage was
not properly consummated. To hell with them, he'd worry
about that later. Right now, all he wanted was to get
Rycca out of the room before her misery became any more
apparent.

From Hawk's arms, Krysta met his gaze. She understood at once. With a reassuring smile for her husband,
she left him and went to Rycca.

"Come, my dear," she said softly. "It is time for you
to retire."

Any doubt Dragon might have had about his noble
plan vanished when he saw the sudden look of dread on

his bride's face. So too did any doubt about the involvement of Loki, god of mischief. That capricious deity was
clearly up to his old tricks. How else to explain how a man
who adored women—and who was adored by them—
found himself with a bride who faced the marriage bed
with less enthusiasm than she would a viper-infested den?

And not because she feared lovemaking. He could
not even comfort himself with that excuse for he knew
damn well she most certainly did not. No, it was merely
her distaste for him now that she knew who he was that
explained her antipathy. Loki might be vastly amused;
Dragon was anything but. He watched his reluctant bride
leave with Krysta, promptly emptied his cup, and held it
out to be filled again.

Hawk laughed, partly with relief that Wolscroft and
his son were gone, the matter settled without bloodshed,
but also with the amusement that the happily wedded
man feels for the nervous bridegroom.

"You want to go easy with that," he offered. "Too
much wine and even the best of men—" He shrugged.

Dragon took another long swallow and wiped his
mouth with the back of his hand. "That's the least of my
problems." He slumped back down in his chair.

"My son," Father Desmond ventured, "if you are
troubled . . ."

"Prayers for a pagan, good priest?"

"Oh, I pray for everyone," the young man said cheerfully, "and everything, for that matter. The bird in her
nest, the child in his bed, God cherishes all."

"Your god should meet my god," Dragon muttered.
"At least the mischievous one."

The priest laughed. "They are but one and the same,
my lord, for there has ever been but one God. However, if
it is any consolation, what seems like divine mischief is always to a good purpose."

"Damned if it is."

"Oh, well, as to damnation, I hardly think that is an issue here. After all, you and the Lady Rycca are pledged to bring peace to both our peoples. The Lord has told us that peacemakers are blessed."

"And that the meek will inherit the Earth. I hardly see that happening."

Hawk took a seat next to Dragon and let his cup be refilled. It was looking to be a long night. "I did not know you were versed in such things."

Dragon shrugged. "Hard not to be. Wolf's had a house priest for years now and he's not even Christian. . . . Wolf, I mean, not the priest. Or at least he hasn't admitted to it but I think it's only a matter of time. Besides, that holy book of yours has good stories."

Hawk laughed. At Father Desmond's puzzled look, he said, "Be advised, priest, if you wish to convert this one, do it with stories. He cannot resist them."

The younger man nodded slowly. "I see . . . Well, then, what stories interest you the most, my lord? I've always liked the tale of Jonah, myself, but it isn't to everyone's taste. What about Samson, have you heard that one?"

Despite himself, Dragon was caught. He truly could not resist a good tale. "Who was Samson?"

Father Desmond told him. Dragon protested that Delilah wasn't really so bad, she was merely trying to help her own people, which led on to the story of Esther. Dragon had heard that one but not the one about Ruth, which he thought an excellent example of the courage and sacrifice of women. The three men, for inevitably Hawk became involved, argued about Salome, with Dragon insisting she couldn't have possibly been that bad, although not even he could find a good word to say about Jezebel.

At length, Father Desmond exchanged a look with

Hawk, cleared his throat, and said, "My son, your knowledge of Holy Writ is impressive, especially taking into account that you are pagan. And heaven knows, no one likes such discussions more than myself. However, I feel rather guilty having kept you here so long."

Only then did Dragon notice that the wedding guests had either departed or were asleep in their seats. Father Desmond did look as though he could carry on all night, but Hawk had the air of a man who wants to seek his bed or, more likely, his wife.

Pox on him, then. But no, such envy wasn't to be borne. Dragon was genuinely glad of his friend's happiness. He just wished that even a small measure of the same did not seem beyond his own reach.

With the eagerness of a man approaching a battle that is already lost, Dragon rose. He bade both men good night and mounted the steps to his quarters.

R YCCA LAY ON THE FAR SIDE OF THE BED WITH her back toward the door. She had finally settled on that position after tossing and turning for several hours. Several times she had gotten up and paced the floor only to be afraid he would come in suddenly and find her like that. Not for the world did she want him to know that she was discomfited.

Oh, lord, what a polite word! And so utterly wrong. She was terrified, excited, filled with dread and longing all mixed together, bewildered, apprehensive, and . . . married.

Married.

She didn't want to be married. She wanted to be back at the lodge, lying by the fire, with the freedom to explore his body and discover the possibilities within her own. To be happy for the first time in her life, making choices for

herself and determining her own future as much as anyone could.

Free.

Married.

Night and day, black and white, win and lose.

She had lost; she was quite certain of that. Lost the
freedom she had tasted so briefly and lost the chance to
make a marriage that might actually have brought a measure of happiness. Her stomach twisted as she contemplated the irony of her situation. Had she stayed at home,
played the obedient daughter, and acquiesced in her family's plans, she and Dragon might have discovered that
they could like each other.

Or might not, really who was to say? And what was
the point anyway? Done was done. Surely it was craven
and foolhardy to lie in a heap of misery with hot tears
trickling into the pillow. Immensely irritated with herself,
she sat up and rubbed her cheeks hard.

He wasn't coming, that was obvious by now. He was
drinking downstairs with Hawk and the others, or even
more likely amusing himself with some appreciative
wench. God, that hurt! For a moment she truly lost her
breath. Sucking in air, she struck the pillow hard, then
froze suddenly at the faint sound of a footfall outside in
the passage.

She'd imagined it. Or it was some servant.

Coming closer . . .

Slowing . . . hesitating . . .

The door opened.

Rycca flattened herself under the covers, closed her
eyes, and forced herself to breathe slowly and deeply. In
and out . . . in and out . . . fast asleep, dreaming pleasantly, not a care in the world . . .

He was very close to the bed and she could feel him
looking at her. "Just as well—"

Dragon's muttered words shot through her. Oh, it was, was it? Just as well she was asleep and he didn't have to deal with her.

He sounded weary. Not that she cared, not at all.

He went to the washbasin. She heard splashing, then the rustle of clothes. The covers on the other side of the bed were pulled back. Rycca stiffened as the mattress depressed. Hardly breathing, she waited. . . .

And waited. The bed was huge; several feet of open space lay between them. She could not even feel the warmth of his body. He shifted once, twice, and was still.

Really, the fuss people made over wedding nights. You'd think there was supposed to be something special about them.

At least she wasn't crying again. The distressing tendency she'd shown of late to do so filled her with self-loathing. No more of that. She wouldn't let him or anyone else see how hurt she was, much less the regrets and fears she felt. She would be the perfect picture of Saxon pride, hold her head high and take whatever came her way without flinching.

What she wasn't likely to do was sleep, yet exhaustion slowly crept over her. Weariness drove a wedge into the wheel of worry and stopped it. Lead weights tugged at her eyelids. Twice, she caught herself drifting off. The third time, she did not.

D RAGON WAS NOT SO FORTUNATE. HE LAY awake through the long night, listening to his wife's rhythmic breathing and cursing himself for thrice a fool. His faults were all too easily enumerated. First, he had agreed to marriage with an unknown woman. For the laudable goal of peace, to be sure, but he should have insisted on picking out his own bride. Then he had neglected to arrange to meet her before their wedding. In the privacy of his mind, he acknowledged that as a cowardly act born of his fear of disappointment. And then, worst of all, it had not occurred to him that the copper-haired beauty in flight across the English countryside could be fleeing from *him*. Scant comfort that he was hardly the first man done in by vanity; it hurt all the same.

But then what could he expect? Real life never worked out as it did in stories where everything was brought to a neat conclusion. Real life was messy, uncertain, and capricious. The gods always rolled dice with the fate of humans. Did the one God do the same? He'd been listening to Father Desmond too much. Still, the priest could be persuasive. Could there truly be a purpose to life, something beyond struggle and suffering?

What if God were a skald? What if the world and everything in it was but the tale of a divine storyteller?

His head hurt. Must be from the wine. But he hadn't drunk that much, really.

A story . . . the miserable bride, the disappointed groom, the pair of them locked in unhappy matrimony for the good of their peoples. It had possibilities. Not very cheerful ones but possibilities all the same.

Things would be better when he got her to Landsende. There, she would be in her own home and have charge over it. Women liked that, he thought. His confident understanding of the fair sex had taken a bit of a dent but all the same, she had to be happy just to be away from the loathsome Lord Wolscroft. In the meanwhile, she needed time to come to terms with the huge change in her life. Hell, so did he.

She wasn't the only one with feelings, after all. His had taken a hard hit too. But he was a man and supposed to conceal any such weakness. Conceal, as well, the fear that still ate at him. She had fled him twice would she do so again?

How not? He had no reason to think her reconciled to

their marriage, quite the contrary. Whatever else she was, she was clever and resourceful. He could not be absolutely certain she would not get away—again.

In the dark of night, haunted by such grim thoughts, Dragon found consolation. He had a fleet of ships at the ready. Before his unwilling Saxon bride could don boy's garb, run off a cliff, or plunge into a river, he would have her safely aboard and at sea. Damned if he wouldn't.

He felt better after that and even dozed a little but was up and dressed before dawn's gray fingers peeled night away.

S O SOON?" KRYSTA ASKED. SHE LOOKED FROM Dragon to Rycca, who sat silently at his side, and frowned. They were at breakfast in the great hall. Everyone else had finished and gone. Casting a quick glance at Hawk, who appeared unperturbed, she said, "I had thought you might linger here a little while longer."

"Ordinarily, I wouldn't hesitate," Dragon said smoothly. "But my people are anxious to meet the Lady Rycca, as are Wolf and Cymbra."

"Of course," Krysta said, "I should have thought of that. Even so, a day or two wouldn't really make a difference, would it?" She looked at the men hopefully. "And it would give Lady Rycca and myself a chance to do something about her wardrobe."

"Wardrobe?" Dragon asked.

"Wardrobe?" Hawk echoed.

"I don't have a wardrobe," Rycca said with honest bewilderment. These were practically the first words she had spoken since the meal began. Having eaten almost nothing in several days, she found herself famished. It seemed not all the dread in the world could occupy her stomach forever, although her appetite might have been helped along by the departure at first light of her father and the other Mercians. That Wolscroft did not think it necessary to bid his daughter farewell was no surprise. Indeed, being spared the sight of him was a rare blessing. All the same, the notion that she might possess such clothes as to constitute an actual *wardrobe* was so bizarre that it caught her in the midst of nibbling on a wedge of cheese.

"My point exactly," Krysta said. "You must have proper clothes." Observing the blank response this evoked in Rycca, who truly could not imagine such a thing, the Lady of Hawkforte turned her attention to Dragon.

"Surely you can see that? How can Rycca possibly be presented to your people if she isn't properly garbed?"

"Well . . . I never actually thought about—"

"Dragon, I'm surprised at you! You know women so well, how could you have overlooked something so vital?"

"I've been preoccupied?" he suggested wryly.

"You won't find a better selection of fabric than what is available right here. We have the loveliest linens and wools, rare fabrics brought from the fabled lands of the East, everything imaginable."

"Two days," Dragon said. He knew when he was beaten.

Two days. He could keep himself busy that long. Turning to Hawk, he said, "What about a turn on the training field?"

Their chairs scraped as they were pushed back.

Left alone, Rycca looked at the serenely beautiful lady beside her. "I must tell you," she said softly, "I have not the faintest idea what a wardrobe would involve."

"Oh, don't worry about that. I know exactly what you need. Besides," Krysta added shrewdly, "you want him to be proud of you, don't you?"

That struck home as nothing else could have done. While Rycca privately thought there was scant chance of

Dragon feeling pride in a wife who came from a contemptible family and had behaved with such dishonor as
to flee their marriage, she was desperate enough to seize
on any hope. Therefore, she set aside her concerns and put
herself in Krysta's hands.

Two days later, Rycca was debating the wisdom of
that. She was exhausted, her feet and legs ached from
standing so much, and the world seemed to have become a
blur of colors and textures each more exotic than the last.
Never had she seen such things. The most finely woven
linens and wools were only the beginning. There were
fabrics she had barely heard mentioned, much less ever
imagined actually holding in her hands.

"The silk is from Byzantium," Krysta said as she
eyed a length of shimmering blue embroidered with gold.
"At least it comes through there, but I believe it was
brought all the way from the fabled lands to the East."

Rycca shook her head in amazement. "It looks like
the sea rippling in wind under bright sunshine."

"It will look even better on you," Krysta said and
proceeded to direct the seamstresses as they draped the
fabric. There were a dozen such women in the room just
then but many more labored elsewhere, rushing to complete the extraordinary quantity of shifts, tunics, and
mantles Krysta believed were necessary. Late in the afternoon, when Rycca's worries about cost were mounting,
Krysta insisted she come down to the great hall to look at
something. Whatever it was remained unseen for just
then the men returned from hunting. Later, Rycca was to
doubt that their presence together in the great hall was a
coincidence, for by then she had realized that the lovely
and genuinely kind Lady Krysta was also very clever, but
at the moment she thought of nothing except Dragon's
sudden appearance.

She had scarcely seen him since the previous morning. He spent all his time on the training field, hunting or

sailing with Hawk, retiring very late, and once again staying to his side of the bed. She told herself she was relieved. Her mind rang with the lie.

But there he was, striding through the great hall, bringing with him the scents of wind and leather, sunshine and man. He looked in good spirits although she fancied she saw shadows beneath his eyes. What foolishness.

"My lord," Krysta called, and having his attention, she gave a little curtsy that made Dragon laugh and caused her own lord to raise his eyebrows.

"Be careful," Hawk advised. "She wants something."

Krysta swatted him lightly. "Stop that, this is important."

"A big something," Hawk amended and took another swat from his wife with a grin.

Rycca watched all this with amazement. Never had she seen such easy byplay between a man and woman, but that the man was easily the most feared warrior in all of England, known for the steeliness of his will and his prowess on the battlefield, left her stunned.

Yet there was Krysta going on blithely while Hawk looked at her with fond amusement. Such must be the power of love, Rycca thought, and felt stabbed through the heart.

"Your lady has proper respect for your purse, Lord Dragon," Krysta said. "She fears we are depleting it too much."

Dragon looked genuinely surprised. "I doubt that. How much are we talking about?" He addressed Rycca but Krysta hurried to answer.

"A dozen shifts, the same in tunics, several mantles, shoes, belts, gloves, veils, the usual."

"There is no time for more?"

"Alas, I fear not, my lord, unless you are willing to extend your stay."

Hawk laid a gentle hand on his wife's arm. "Krysta . . ."

"Oh, all right, I won't start that again. Then you do not think we have overdone, my lord?"

Dragon was looking at Rycca quizzically. "No, not at all. It seems adequate for the next few months."

Adequate. Garments of such quantity and luxury were merely *adequate*.

"I thought you would prefer to select the furs yourself," Krysta was saying.

"Of course," Dragon replied as though that was the most ordinary thing in the world.

Turning to Rycca, Krysta said, "You will be glad of those come winter. Cymbra tells me it is fierce cold in the northlands for much of the year. But she doesn't mind. The fires are always lit, there is great jollity, and Wolf gave her a wonderful sleigh that is pulled over the snow by reindeer trained by the Laps. Isn't that amazing?"

Rycca nodded mutely. Dragon was still looking at her and she found she could not meet his gaze. At length, he cleared his throat. "Well then, Hawk, what do you say to a sauna?"

Hawk said that sounded fine to him but the swift look he exchanged with his wife suggested both were more than a little concerned about the behavior of the newlyweds.

That concern was still in evidence the following day as they all gathered on the quay. Coming down from the stronghold, riding beside her husband, Rycca tried very hard not to stare at the ships awaiting them. There were three in all, long and sleek with center masts for the sails and row after row of benches for the oarsmen. Trading might have made the Lord Dragon rich but it was not in trading vessels that he himself ventured forth. The ships were drakars, dragon ships for the dragon lord, with curving double-ended hulls the sight of which struck terror into the most valiant heart.

Rycca took a deep, shuddering breath and struggled to calm herself but the vision was too real, the image too deeply rooted. Smoke and mist . . . the moon obscured . . . silence overall save for the soft rustlings of sleep until . . . the thud of a ship's hull striking shore . . . clatter of metal . . . feet pounding . . .

The church bell was ringing, ringing, ringing, not the slow and stately cadence of the call for prayers but frantically as it had when the mill caught fire and everyone streamed out into the night to fight the flames.

There were flames on this night, too. Flames and blood and screams . . . Aelflynne . . . shying from that anguished image, she encountered Wolscroft, younger to be sure but still the same, shouting orders, flailing with his sword, calling for his horse . . . the terrified face of the boy just before Wolscroft ran him through, silencing the tongue that might speak of how the lord fled when the Vikings came.

And later, in the dawn, crawling from the stable down to the river, hearing the men laughing as they finished their work, loading the last of the spoils and the slaves before the dragon prow vanished into the mists.

"Rycca?"

Her husband spoke to her, her *Viking* husband. From Sleipnir's back—she had learned the horses' true names from a groom—Dragon looked at her with concern. "You are ill?"

Hide quickly, let him not know, conceal herself as she knew she must. "No, not at all." Grani shied beneath her as though the lie had reverberated straight through the horse and into the ground.

Rycca shuddered. "Truly, I am fine."

Her head throbbed. So did lies ever cost her.

Dragon frowned. His bride was very pale and her eyes held a haunted look he could not mistake, for he had seen it himself in the eyes of men in the aftermath of battle. No doubt there were those who had seen it in him as well.

His gaze swept out over the sun-dappled harbor, the neat and prosperous town, the mighty fortress rising over all. Strange setting for a terrified woman unless, of course, he took into account his proud ships awaiting them.

She was afraid to leave, to go with him as Ruth had gone to face the foreign land that held her destiny. He had hoped the last few days would ease her dread but such did not seem to be the case. So be it. They were both prisoners of duty.

He urged Sleipnir on, taking care to note that she did the same with Grani. On the quay, they dismounted. Krysta and Hawk joined them.

"Fair sailing," Hawk said, observing the sky.

"It should be," Dragon agreed without enthusiasm. He gestured to several of his men who hurried up to take the horses and guide them onto one of the ships. Meanwhile, others were busy loading the last of the chests and bales, barrels and baskets. A goodly crowd had assembled to see them go. Even for so worldly a lot as the inhabitants of Hawkforte, the sight of a Norse jarl departing with his Saxon bride was worth turning out for. The bolder among them called their good wishes and cheered.

Dragon allowed scant time for farewells. Krysta hugged Rycca briefly, promising her rather fiercely that all would be well, then he was handing his bride onto the largest of the three vessels.

"I will tell Wolf what we discussed," Dragon said as he stepped onto the deck right behind her. "No doubt he'll be in touch soon."

Hawk nodded. "Good. Meanwhile I'll see what more I can learn here."

The two men clasped hands. A moment later, Dragon called the command and the mooring ropes were cast loose. Sooner than Rycca would have thought possible, the dragon ships moved swiftly out beyond the harbor.

• • •

S HE WAS IGNORED AND FOR THAT RYCCA WAS deeply grateful. For hours after they departed Hawkforte, Dragon said nothing to her. Instead, he took his turn with the men on the oars. She tried not to notice the powerful rhythm of his body as he rowed but her eyes were drawn back to him again and again. All around was an alien world and he the only certainty in it.

The sea went on forever. Land, once faded from view, might not have existed at all. Even the scent of it was gone. There was only wind and water, the creak of the rigging and slap of canvas mingling with the occasional grunts of the men straining at their efforts.

A small tent had been erected in the prow and there Rycca sat. The sides could be lowered when she wanted privacy but for the moment she was glad to leave them up. Such comforts as were possible had been provided—a sturdy box bed she could not help but notice was large enough for two, several chests with flat tops that doubled as benches and low tables, even an oil lamp carefully secured to a wooden post so that it could not tip over.

Rank had its privileges but rest did not seem to be among them for Dragon took no ease. He stayed on the oars while yet there was light. Before it faded entirely, Rycca was surprised to see the faint shadow of land on the far horizon. Surely this could not be the northlands? She had thought that far more distant. The moon had risen and by its glow they dropped anchor in a shallow bay. She saw no sign of habitation, nor did any sounds of people reach her on the still night air.

When at last Dragon came to her, he brought a bowl of stew and a mug of cider. "You should eat," he said, handing her both and turning to go. The men had taken in the sail and were bedding down for the night in the bow.

A few talked softly among themselves but their voices were hushed.

"Wait." Solitude had never troubled her but here, where land was no more than a smudge between sea and sky, she craved some human contact.

He turned back, looked, waited.

"Where are we?"

"Off the coast of Normandy. Tomorrow we swing north. If the weather holds, a week or so should see us at Landsende."

"Normandy . . ." So very close. So utterly unattainable . . . now.

He must have heard something in her voice, some hint of the longing she felt, for in an instant he was before her. He grasped her chin, compelling her eyes to meet his.

"Where were you going?"

Startled, she spoke stiffly. "When? What do you mean?"

He loosened his grip but only a little. "When I encountered you. You were making for Hawkforte, I think. Were you intending to take ship from there, for Normandy perhaps?"

Her sudden gasp was answer enough. He let go of her but did not leave. Instead, he stood, hands on lean hips, and glared at her. "That's where Thurlow's gone, isn't it?"

She reeled from shock to shock. "How do you know about him?"

"Hawk told me. Your brother has taken himself off, which is reassuring since it means at least one member of your family has some sense."

Her cheeks flamed but she could hardly dispute him. Hawk continued to eye her narrowly. Finally, he went to the flaps of the tent and pulled them down. "When you have eaten, get into bed."

"I am not tired."

He was opening the chest across from her and did not

so much as glance up. "Did I ask if you were?" Straightening, he drew out of the chest a thick leather belt.

About to take a spoonful of stew, Rycca set the bowl aside. She stared at the belt, unable to draw her eyes from it. The night was warm but she was suddenly very cold. Her father had beaten her with a belt, a stick, whatever was nearby. Was her husband the same?

"What is that for?" Even to her own ears her voice sounded high and reedy.

He was twisting the belt in his hands as though testing its suppleness. "I don't want any surprises tonight."

"Surprises?"

He came toward her. In the small tent, on the ship, at sea there was nowhere to go. "Not hungry? Then hold out your arm."

She had to stand up, had to put some distance between them, had to think. . . . "Why?"

"Don't argue about this. While we lie within reach of Normandy, do you seriously believe I will take the chance of your deciding to flee yet again?"

She stared at him dumbfounded. He intended . . . what? To beat her so that she could not escape?

"Th-there is no need for this."

He stopped suddenly, staring down at her. Her breath was rapid and shallow, her eyes opaque. "Rycca . . . ?"

Suddenly, she was back, as though rising up out of some depths he could not glimpse, and her gaze spat fire. "It's only an excuse, that's all, just a pretense for hurting. You despise my father, rightly so, but he always did the same. *Rycca, you are disrespectful. Rycca, you look rebellious. Rycca, you did not obey quickly enough. Rycca, there is something wrong with you.* Unless he was drunk, of course, then he did not bother with excuses. Do you get drunk, my lord? Should I know such times will be particularly bad?"

"God's blood . . ." A Christian curse, sprung from

his lips as naturally as her name. "Rycca, stop this! I have never struck you, nor will I. I think only to secure you to me while we sleep."

"Never—"

"I do not hit women."

"Everyone hits women."

"I don't, nor does Wolf nor Hawk. And no man in my service does so lest he wants to feel my fist. Women are the great gods' greatest gift."

"There is but one God."

"All right! Fine, his greatest gift."

A tiny smile trembled at the corners of her mouth. "But He made man first. So scripture says."

"I suppose he wanted to practice. Now hold out your arm and let's get this over with."

She did not obey but merely continued to look at him as though he stood before her for the very first time. Finally, she said softly, "I cannot swim."

"You cannot what?" She might as well have said she could not speak or walk or breathe.

"I cannot swim. If you will not accept my word that I will not attempt to flee you, word I freely give, then consider that I cannot swim. We may lie within sight of Normandy but all I can do is look at it."

"But . . . you can ride."

"Of course I can ride. Everyone rides."

"Everyone swims."

"I don't. Where I grew up there were only rivers and few folk swam in them. I never learned."

A great weight was coming off his chest. He had hated the idea of binding her, knowing she would hate it, but had not been able to think of any alternative. Never had it occurred to him that she actually could not . . .

"You must learn to swim," he declared emphatically as he returned the belt to the chest.

"Yes, my lord." She spoke more docilely than he had

ever heard her do before but with an underlying thread of humor that warmed his heart. Yet he was still shaken by fading echoes of his fear that she might flee. Losing her would be very . . . personal.

"All right," he said gruffly. "Finish eating and get some rest. You may not be tired but I am." As though to emphasize that fact, he pulled off his sandals and lay down on the bed on his side facing her. The bed that was far smaller than the one they had occupied at Hawkforte.

My, it was warm out here on the water. She would have imagined it to be cooler but she felt flushed all over. Nonetheless, she ate every scrap of the stew and drank every drop of cider, taking her time doing so. He was tired, surely he would fall asleep. But when she finished he was still watching her, a faint smile playing over his lips.

As she hesitated, he held out a hand to her, at once commanding and encouraging. "Come to bed now, Rycca."

She did but slowly and did not touch him. Instead, she lay down on her side with her back to him. A moment passed, another. She thought he meant to do nothing, and started when he sighed.

A steely arm wrapped around her waist. She was pulled gently toward him, nestled into the curve of his powerful body, his warmth and strength enveloping her. She turned her head into the pillow to stifle a gasp.

The boat, riding at anchor off the far shore, rocked gently in the night.

Chapter

NINE

S O DID THE BETTER PART OF A WEEK PASS. They sped on fair winds and swift oars, and each night anchored within sight of shore. Twice they made landfall for fresh water and game but did not linger. The coast along which they sailed was part of Jutland, ruled by the Danes. Dragon expected no trouble, for his ships plied these waters regularly in trade. Still, it paid to be vigilant.

All day the men bent to the oars, Dragon taking his turn among them. At night he joined Rycca in the tent, but except for holding her as they slept, he did not touch her. When he wasn't rowing, he taught her Norse.

"Many of my people speak Saxon," he said, "and other languages as well thanks to their experience as traders. But they would be pleased if you learned our language."

Rycca agreed readily and proved a quick study. Toward the end of the week, she was managing simple sentences.

On the sixth day, they left the shore behind and headed out into open water. "This is the Vik," Dragon told her. "The strait that lies between Jutland and the lands to the north, including our own. From this we take our name. When we see land next, we will be home."

The same thought seemed to be in the minds of his men for they bent to the oars with even greater will. The wind stayed with them and they flew over the water. Dragon steered their course by the sun and when that was gone by the northern star. Watching him, Rycca could not help but ask, "What happens if it becomes cloudy at night? You will not know which way we go."

In answer, he drew from beneath his tunic a small pouch and took from it a stone suspended at the end of a string. Holding it up for her to see, he said, "Watch how the stone turns by itself."

True enough for through no effort of Dragon's own, the stone twisted in the air for a few moments, then came to rest. The side with a small chiseled mark on it now pointed in the direction in which they were going.

"Why does it move?" Rycca asked in wonder.

"No one knows but it always points the way north."

He carefully replaced the stone in its pouch and returned it to his tunic. "If the story I was told is true, it has traveled far, all the way from the East beyond a great wall so long it would take a man more than a hundred days to walk its length. It was smuggled from the court of a mighty king and went through many hands before coming to me."

"It must be very valuable."

Dragon shrugged. "At least one man believed it was worth his life." When he saw the look on her face, he explained quickly. "The stone was given to me by a Byzantine trader in thanks for *saving* his life. He had no son, wished to retire from trading, and wanted the stone to go to a man he knew would keep it and use it well."

Ashamed of what she had thought, Rycca lowered her eyes. "I am sorry."

"For what? Assuming I took the stone by force? But that's what Vikings do, isn't it?"

He sounded exasperated and she could not blame him. But neither was she prepared when he suddenly asked, "Why did you not want us to marry? Because I am Viking?"

She had wondered if he would ask, then decided her reasons would likely mean nothing to him. But he was a man of surprises, this hero of her strange world, and very good at biding his time.

"It is true, I did not wish to wed a Viking."

"Because of what you have heard about us?"

"No, because of what I have seen."

It was his turn to be surprised. "Mercia is inland, well away from where most of the raiding occurred."

"Wolscroft is near the river Thames, which runs inland from the coast. The Danes raided along it when I was a child."

He remembered now. The Danes had managed to claim fully half of what had been the kingdom of Mercia with the remainder thrown upon the mercy of Alfred.

"That dream you had—"

"What dream? What do you know of that?"

Her sudden alarm quickened his interest but he was careful to conceal it. "Only that you had a nightmare. You couldn't seem to wake from it but that happens to all of us from time to time."

"Yes . . . I suppose it does."

"It could have been anything. I just wondered if it had to do with the Danes."

"It might have." Her mind scrambled, seeking equivocation, finding none. Just then she would have given anything to be able to lie.

"Do you dream of them often?"

"It's nothing, really. Just a memory . . . from when I was a child."

"And the Danes came?"

She nodded, her throat very tight. To speak of such things made them even more hideously real.

Dragon's hand was over her own. "What happened?"

"They came up the river. They did what they usually did. They left. That's all. That stone is wonderful. May I see it again?"

"In a bit. How old were you?"

"About six . . . I was six." *Please let him stop.*

He was closer to her, his arm around her shoulders. His voice was deep and gentle, unrelenting. "You saw people die."

It was not a question. He knew what she must have seen, what anyone would have seen who survived a raid. Silently he gave fierce thanks that she had been spared, but not without injury, as he now realized. "Someone you cared for?"

She nodded against his shoulder, not knowing how her head had gotten there. "My friend Aelflynne."

"She was your age?"

Another nod. It was hard to breathe. She was shaking. "They cut her throat open. She bled to death in my arms."

His own arms were very tight around her and his voice was very hard. "How did you escape?"

"I don't know. I've never known. They were all around me after I ran to her, killing, burning . . . raping . . . but somehow they overlooked me. I don't know why I lived and she not. She was better than I, sweeter and kinder. It should have been me."

"No!" He held her fiercely, stroking away the tears that trickled down her ashen cheeks. "Do not say that! Does not your own faith teach that we are always in the hands of God?"

"A careless god or an unfathomable one. Why create a world of pain?"

"It is not. You know yourself, there is great beauty here and joy."

She knew, at least now she did, since she had known him.

"I am a Viking." He said it sorrowfully, as though he would change it if he could.

"I do not think you are like the others." *Truth.* She did not, had never, not since the knowing of him.

"Yet you did not wish this marriage."

"That was before, when you were faceless to me. When all I heard was my father ranting on about the bloodthirsty Vikings and you the bloodiest of them all."

"That is ridiculous. I have never fought but in self-defense."

"It matters not to Wolscroft. He is obsessed, ever since that night." She looked up, met his eyes, grasped her courage. "He ran away . . . my father did. When his people needed him most, he called for a horse and fled. He even killed the stable boy who knew what he had done."

"You are beyond him, utterly different."

Her soul warmed, slowly to be sure, but the little flickers of comfort were growing. "I think he hates Vikings so much because they showed him for what he is."

"Forget Wolscroft, he is gone from your life forever. Look there, toward the north; by tomorrow you will see the first signs of life. The gulls and terns will come out to greet us, the sea will change its color for it plunges much deeper there, and the air will begin to smell of pine. We will be home."

Home. She had never known any such. But he did, and so powerful was his vision that she could almost see it for herself. Almost.

"You do not touch me." The words were out before she could reclaim them. She bit her lip hard, drawing blood.

"Don't," he said, nearly pleading as he caught the

tiny crimson drop. His lips touched hers, brushing lightly, giving her the taste of him. "I will," he said, and she was gone, lost in the glow of yearning.

T HEY MADE LANDFALL THE FOLLOWING AFTER-
noon. It came upon them in a rush, so it seemed to Rycca. One moment the world was all blue, sky and sea together, and the next it was green lit through with slashes of white and gray. The contrast was dazzling. As Dragon had promised, birds swirled overhead in welcome. The men threw bits of fish to them and laughed as they swooped down almost into the water before soaring back into the sky. The tang of salt yielded to the sweet perfume of fecund earth and towering pine.

And the land rose, sudden and sharp, climbing like the birds. Rycca gasped to see it. The world seemed out of kilter, no longer mainly flat as she had always known it but dominated by height. The rugged peaks, some she could see still harboring snow in rocky clefts despite the summer season, seemed to hold up the sky. Here and there along their slopes and in the valleys between, she could make out the gold of fields ripening in the sun, the green of pasturage and deep, sweeping swathes of pine. Fingers of the sea, glittering in the sunlight, reached between folds of the mountains as though to challenge their supremacy. A beautiful land to be sure but a land in which nothing would come easily.

Standing beside her in the bow of the drakar, Dragon said, "My brother's holding is to the east beyond the plain of Jæren. Between us, we control the coast facing Jutland. It has been many years since the Danes raided here. They are ambitious men, to be sure, but sensible all the same. They have discovered that trade is more profitable than war. The alliance between Saxon and Norse further assures they will never forget that."

"Would the Danes in England could learn the same."

"They are learning it. Alfred is a very good teacher."

She smiled at that, as he had hoped she would for he was inwardly cursing himself for making any mention of the Danes. Clearly, she had been badly scarred by what she had witnessed. But scars, even old ones, could be healed given time and proper care.

His heart lifted as the signal horns from the watchtowers near Landsende called out their welcome. They were close enough to shore now to see men and women in the fields and along the water's edge, waving to them. Up the finger of the fjord they flew, still racing until they were almost upon the docks, when Dragon called a command. At the same instant, the sails dropped and the oars rose, sending bright streams of water sluicing down them. All three drakars slowed and came to rest gently against the stone quays.

The crowd rapidly gathering there cheered the display of seamanship and cheered all the harder the return of their jarl. They raised their voices as one in lusty welcome, guards banging the hilts of their swords against their shields, men and women alike stomping their feet and calling out welcome while the children ran about wildly, dogs barked, roosters cawed, and a generally exciting time was had by all.

Until they noticed the woman standing at Lord Dragon's side.

Surely, Rycca thought as the cheers died away, they knew why he had gone to England? They must have realized he would be bringing home a bride? Or had they thought something would happen to prevent the marriage? Something very nearly had, but pray God they would never know that.

Silence descended along the quays. The combined weight of several hundred pairs of eyes fixed upon her made Rycca feel she could scarcely stand. Yet she straightened her shoulders and held her head high. Saxon pride, she reminded herself, and filled her lungs with alien air.

Dragon frowned. He knew his people to be a kindly lot but cautious. Knew, too, that there were mixed feelings about a Saxon bride despite the high esteem in which the Lady Cymbra was held. She was presumed to be unique, therefore no indication of what they could expect.

He had to tell them that and quickly. His gaze fell on Sleipnir and Grani, being offloaded from the adjacent drakar. Half-a-dozen grooms oversaw the operation while everyone else kept as far back as possible. After more than a week at sea and only two opportunities to run off their vast reserves of energy, the horses were even more exuberant than usual. They pawed the ground, tossed their mighty heads, and generally looked as though they were about to bolt.

"Feeling up to a ride?" Dragon asked. Before Rycca could reply, he lifted her into his arms and strode onto the quay. Silent, watchful, the crowd fell back. "I hope so," he went on, talking to her as though there were only the two of them. "Do you have a preference, Sleipnir or Grani? I suppose you adore them both?"

"Yes," Rycca said, glad of distraction from the blanket stillness. "They're both wonderful."

He looked down at her with a smile. "And you ride as well as I think you do? Enough to stay on one of these monsters after he's been cooped up for days?"

She met his gaze unhesitant. "I ride superbly and they aren't monsters."

His smile deepened. The horses quieted a little at his approach although they did try to paw at him for treats. "Enough," he said in a tone that brooked no refusal. When they had steadied, he handed Rycca up carefully onto Grani's back. "Hold tight," he muttered, "and don't let him forget you're there."

Rycca's face broke into a delighted smile. Her apprehension about the silent scrutiny of so many faded. Absorbed in patting Grani and telling him how wonderful he was—sentiments with which the big baby totally agreed—she did not notice the change in the crowd. Quiet watchfulness gave way to shock and the dawning of amazement. A child pointed until his mother snatched down his arm. Grown men caught themselves staring slack-jawed. Warriors who had thought themselves inured to anything craned their necks for a better look.

Dragon took note of all but Rycca remained completely unaware. Without concern, she rode beside him along the quay and up the road leading to the stronghold perched above. Only then did she realize that the crowd was coming right along with them and that more people were lining their way. So, too, was the silence dissolving into excited exclamations.

Uncertain how to react to any of this, she patted Grani again and laughed when he tried to break into a gallop. "Not yet," she admonished, skillfully reining him in, "but soon . . ." She glanced over at Dragon. "If you will permit, my lord?"

"Tomorrow we will ride to your heart's content." He looked well pleased and even amused.

"I do not understand," she said. "Your people were so quiet and now . . ."

Now they were cheering again, the women nodding in approval and the men going so far as to toss their caps into the air. Children were running alongside the horses, although not too closely.

Dragon grinned. "Did I mention no one ever rides these two save me?"

She could not have heard him right. "No one?"

"Only me," he confirmed. "Several of my warriors have tried but they were all thrown." He leaned a little closer and whispered to her, "Maybe if they'd been afraid of heights, they would have held on tighter."

Laughter bubbled up in her. Silly, giddy, astonished laughter. She could not believe he had done this yet she should have known, for he had ever treated her with kindness. Now he had bent a warrior's pride, for surely it must have been a great thing to be the only one to ride such horses, and given his people reason to admire her. She looked out over their smiling faces and knew the effort had succeeded.

Men, women, and children she had never seen before and whom she had been schooled to think of as enemies were cheering her as though she were one of their own. She could make out only a little of what they said but she knew they were encouraging and welcoming her. Tightness welled up in her throat. She looked from the crowd to her husband, who was gazing back at her with genuine pride in his eyes. Without thought, she reached out a hand across the space that separated them. He took it and raised it to his lips.

The cheers rose to heaven.

For the first time in her life, Rycca felt what it was to come home.

L ANDSENDE DELIGHTED HER. EVERYWHERE SHE looked, everything she saw was so very different from what she had known at Wolscroft. There were strong stone walls, to be sure, and high towers, but so too were there smiling people. Children ran about laughing. Women waved and called out boldly. Men saw that and did not mind but joined in the merriment.

Instead of the general air of a badly maintained barracks, to which she was so well accustomed, the town looked as though every inch had been swept clean. Nothing seemed out of place or neglected in the smallest way. There were even—wonder of wonders—flowers growing in small plots before the houses.

On a hill above the town stood a walled compound. The gates were open, guarded by men-at-arms who joined in the cheers as they entered. Dogs barked and ran alongside the horses, and chickens squawked as they dashed across their path. At the center of the compound stood a large wooden building roofed in tile and decorated with ornate carvings around the doors and windows. Nearby were several smaller structures, one of which Rycca recognized as the kitchen. Some distance away were several lodges, also intricately carved and painted.

Dragon drew rein in the center of the compound and dismounted. He came to Rycca and held up his arms. With a smile, she went into them. Still holding her, he climbed the wooden stairs to the walkway along the wall. From that height, the town and port were spread out below them, as were the golden fields and, beyond, the misty realm where land faded into sea.

"Landsende," he said with pride. "My mother's people came from here. They had a farm and did some trading when war didn't intervene. When Wolf and I were done seeing the world, I came here. There were only a few falling-down buildings left and a handful of people trying to wrest a living from the place. Fortunately, that's changed."

Looking out over the prosperous settlement with its bustling air of purpose, Rycca had to ask, "What made the difference?"

"Peace," he said bluntly. "People who feel safe will plant fields, improve their houses, invest in trading ventures, and the like. They won't huddle around their hearths waiting for the next disaster to befall them. And other people, seeing that a place is good, will come themselves. But peace has to come first. With it, everything is possible."

"And without it, nothing is?"

"Nothing worth having." He smiled apologetically.

"Forgive me, this is no time to dwell on the past. Come, there are many people who will be wanting to meet you."

He understated the matter. Over the next several hours, Rycca was convinced she met everyone in Landsende. Oh, it was possible she missed a baby or two who were napping but apart from that she was quite certain no one passed up the chance to greet the jarl's bride. Young and old, men and women, farmers, tradesmen, warriors, weavers, one and all they came to get a look at her. She smiled, nodded, and tried out what Norse she had so far acquired. That was so well received that she vowed then and there to work diligently until she had mastered the language.

Overwhelmingly, the people were friendliness itself, which made the handful who weren't stand out all the more. Several young and very pretty women frowned at her and sighed at Dragon. Rycca balled her fists and took great pride in the fact that she refrained from doing the huzzies bodily harm. Then, too, there was the warrior introduced as Magnus.

"My chief lieutenant," Dragon said as he presented a man slightly younger than himself, almost as tall, and well built. "Magnus and I knew each other as children. He settled in Landsende several years ago."

Rycca frowned slightly. He looked familiar to her and she thought she ought to know him already.

"Magnus was in Essex," Dragon explained. "He kept the horses company on the way home."

Of course, Essex, where he would have accompanied his lord to his wedding but not been introduced to the bride because of the . . . unusualness of the event.

Rycca smiled, prepared to like the man her husband obviously trusted. But even as she did so, a small shimmer of apprehension moved through her. She could see no reason for it. Magnus was by no means as handsome as Dragon; indeed his features were most remarkable for being utterly unremarkable. Yet did he appear cordial enough. Appear. Her cursed gift made appearance irrelevant; nothing mattered save truth.

And the truth was . . . what?

Magnus bowed his head courteously and regarded her with what gave every appearance of being warm but entirely proper admiration and appreciation. "My lady, you are most welcome here. Indeed, it is fair to say your arrival is the cause of much rejoicing."

So smooth. Yet what was wrong with that? He was a politic man. That did not mean he was disloyal.

"I am most glad to be here. Never did I imagine such a welcome."

"You did not? But surely you must be aware of how vigorously we all wish for peace."

Not him.

Oh, stop! She had no reason to think this way, no basis at all for her sudden suspicion. He was an entirely pleasant man. Surely Dragon was adept at winnowing the wheat from the chaff. If he trusted Magnus, and clearly he did, she had no reason to do otherwise.

Blood . . . fire . . . pain . . .

She closed her eyes for a moment, willing her wayward mind to stop. Cease its relentless assessing and simply allow her to enjoy the moment.

"What's wrong?" Dragon said with real concern. His gentleness tore at her, making her hate all the more her inability to enjoy so rare and precious a thing as this homecoming.

"Nothing," she assured him with a quick smile. "I am merely a little tired."

"I should have thought of that." He did something, she wasn't sure what, some gesture perhaps. The crowd parted. She was in his arms, despite her weak protests, being carried away in the direction of one of the lodges she had seen. It was larger than the others and farther apart.

She had a quick glimpse of the shields bracketing the door before Dragon shouldered his way in. The air smelled of pine. Windows stood open, their oilcloth shades rolled up and their shutters open. A mat of fresh rushes covered the floor. Fresh flowers adorned a table set near one of the windows. Fresh linens covered the bed . . . the very big bed with its massive, intricately carved headboard. So too were the half-dozen chests she saw adorned with complex shapes and scenes. The iron braziers were curled into serpentine designs, as was the delicate filigree work surrounding several glass vessels on shelves near the table. Everything was functional yet beautiful, redolent of wealth coupled to discernment.

For Rycca, who had known only the crudeness of Wolscroft, it was almost too much to take in at once. She had thought never to see any place so lovely as the lodge near Hawkforte where she had found such brief happiness but now she had to reconsider. Yet this was clearly a man's domain as she saw from the weapons and banners that adorned the walls. Saw, too, what made her eyes widen in disbelief.

There was a book on the table. She recognized it immediately even though she had scarcely ever seen one. It was in a large wooden case, vividly carved and painted, and her fingers itched to touch it.

Following the direction of her gaze, Dragon said, "Oh, good, it arrived." He set her down gently, went to the table, and opened the box. A smile wreathed his sunburnished features.

"My good friend Kareem ben Abdul found this for me. It purports to be the marvelous tales told by the bride of a rapacious lord who was so entertained by them that he spared her life."

Fascinated though she was by the book, indeed by the whole circumstance, Rycca could not help but remark, "How terrible. Why should a lord wish to slay his bride?"

Dragon shrugged. "He had some grudge against all of womanhood. Who knows the workings of such a disordered mind. Do you read?"

She hesitated, honesty warring with self-preservation. As always, honesty won. "Yes."

Women were not supposed to read, not where she came from, not according to the dictates of her father, who thought such things for eunuch monks who could be kept properly controlled but never for women, who might garner inappropriate ideas. She had learned in secret, thanks to one such monk who though not a eunuch was an honorable and courageous man.

"Yes." She said it again, just in case he hadn't heard, daring fate.

"Oh, good. You might as well know, I have ambitions to do as Alfred has done, to bring books and schools to this land."

He could have said he wished to sprout wings and fly to the moon for all the sense that made to her. He wore a sword, she could see it across his back. He used it with rare skill as she had seen on the Hawkforte road. He was a warrior. And a Viking.

He dreamed of schools and books.

"What an . . . admirable design."

"Some would not think so. Learning is considered a sign of weakness by some, although I have no idea why. To confront the world in all its complexity calls for real courage."

She nodded because she could think of nothing to say. He surprised her so easily.

He caught her look and put the book aside. "Enough of this . . . for now. I will send the women to you with food and water for bathing. All right?"

"Yes . . . of course, more than all right."

"There will be a feast." He gestured as though it was of no import. "The people expect it, you understand?"

"Yes . . . certainly."

Yes and yes and yes. She could say nothing else to him. Books, dreams, food, water, feasts . . . and that bed, so very close.

She allowed herself to look at him just then, really look as she had avoided doing at Hawkforte and during the voyage. He stole her breath, this *husband* of hers. Too vividly, she remembered what it was to lie with him.

"I realize you are tired," he said. "We will not tarry long at the feast."

Her smile held nothing of fatigue, everything of promise.

A GOOD SAUNA, THAT WAS WHAT HE NEEDED. That and a chance to catch his breath. She liked Landsende, he could tell. Cursed be Wolscroft, yet he was shamefully grateful to him for setting her expectations so low. And her fear had ebbed, for which he gave thanks to whatever god deserved them.

He would take her to bed this night, make her his wife in truth. The long nights of the voyage when he had practiced such unaccustomed chastity would be forgotten.

She would be his.

He felt a surge of fierce possessiveness and marveled at it for he had never felt any such with a woman. Yet she was his *wife*, altogether different from any who had gone before.

A meek little woman to rub his feet.

He laughed out loud. Praise every deity that had ever existed for sparing him that. He would pour libations to Odin, king of the gods, he and his battling wife, Frigg, and to Loki, too, for it was always wise to propitiate that

one. But perhaps he would also bring a priest to Landsende. The best of those were literate men with a store of
wisdom. It would do no harm to have one of them about.

Mayhap even more than one if he seriously intended
to set up a scriptorium. He had seen such at Hawkforte
and heard of the much larger enterprise in the king's
house at Winchester. Monks had the necessary skills.

She liked books. He warmed inside. His hurt at her
flight from their marriage was assuaged by the knowledge
of what had driven her. He had seen her dread turn to
smiles and seen, too, the desire in her eyes. They stood on
the brink of a new beginning. He was determined not to
squander it.

But first the feast. His people meant well, he credited
them for that. They liked her and wanted her to know it.
He gazed out over the heavily laden tables and thought
the women must have labored frantically to produce such
bounty. But then he saw Rycca suddenly from their perspective, beautifully garbed, at ease on a horse only their
jarl could ride, and realized they must want desperately to
impress her. So, too, he realized did he.

Cleansed by the sauna, freshly shaved and garbed
more formally than was his wont, he awaited his bride in
the great hall. And waited. The people had gathered, all
was ready, and they had just enough time to begin to stir
uneasily when she appeared.

God's blood but she was beautiful. Her hair fell like
copper fire down her back. She carried her head high and
she moved as grace personified, he thought, and felt pride
swell within him.

She was garbed in sky. Not really but the fabric,
whatever it might be, looked like that. He was put in mind
suddenly of a glorious sunrise into softest blue interwoven
with stray tendrils of cloud. The beginnings of a perfect
day.

Thank heaven he could take her to bed soon. Or as

soon as the feasting and merriment were sufficiently pro-
gressed that no one would think him lacking in control.
Especially not her. He thought back to the lodge when she
had come to him, taken him, and swore this night he
would show her wonders she could not imagine.

Wine flowed and ale and mead. Platters of whole fish
and pig were carried by, along with smoked meats, breads,
cheeses, the bounty of summer fruits and vegetables, even
rare confections crafted of spices from the farthest corners
of the earth. A king could not have offered better.

Nor was the entertainment lacking. Jugglers and
minstrels vied for the greatest applause and no fewer than
three renowned skalds, who were always well assured of a
welcome at the court of the Dragon, declaimed the great
stories of the ages. Dragon himself remained largely silent
except to converse with Rycca, who sat beside him and
replied to his comments with the same stilted courtesy
with which he offered them.

He could not remember ever feeling so discomfited
by a woman.

And not merely for the reason that the mere scent of
her, the slightest glimpse from the corner of his eye, the
most accidental brush of her hand against his were each
and every one enough to arouse him.

There he was, possessor of what amounted to several
lifetimes' worth of most pleasant memories of the fair sex,
made to feel a green boy by his own bride.

Night could not come quickly enough.

Chapter

TEN

THE DOOR CLOSED WITH A FIRM THUD. Rycca heard it but only distantly. She was absorbed in the discovery that sometime between leaving the hall with Dragon and arriving here in the lodge, the passage of mere moments, her heart had speeded up alarmingly and her breathing had become rapid little pants. She felt, and she thought also sounded, as though she had run miles.

As she had that day on the Essex shore when she fled from him.

But then she had raced into freedom, so she dreamed, whereas now . . .

That was too foolish. She had already lain with this man, at her own initiative, with none of a virgin's proper modesty or concern. On the contrary, she had gloried in her possession of him, the taking of him into her body, the milking of his seed, the explosion of incandescent pleasure that was her reward for boldness so shocking that the memory alone still stunned.

So why the sense that she was not merely excited but also afraid?

He was moving around the room, closing the shutters although he left the oilcloth shades up so that the soft evening breeze wafted through the wooden slats. The fiery glow of embers in a brazier illuminated his movements. She could not look away but stood, in the center of the room, following him with her eyes. He was so graceful, amazingly so for his size, as though the largeness of his spirit was at home in a body so big, so perfectly formed, so utterly male as to bedazzle her.

Her throat was very dry. She had drunk almost nothing and eaten even less but now she had the sudden wish that she had quaffed a skin of wine. Coward! Yet did instinct shimmer at the edges of her awareness, warning that this time would be different.

From the corner of his eye, Dragon saw her unease and smiled faintly. Ordinarily, he would not wish any woman to feel discomforted in his presence but Rycca was the exception. His smile deepened, becoming wry. She was that in every possible way.

It was time, he had decided, for a righting of the balance between them. A woman of strength and courage was all well and good, he would not have wished her otherwise. Yet she was married now and therefore must change. His *wife* did not go hieing off on her own, attempt to unman him, flee unrepentantly, deny his authority, and then, sweetly haunting memory, proceed to seduce him with skill all the more devastating for being artless. The catalog of her daring made him shake his head in yet heightened determination. His *wife* stayed at home where she belonged, welcomed her lord with a smile and soft word, graced his hall, and warmed his bed with appropriate, *wifely* enthusiasm.

That was the proper order of the world, never mind that he had managed to avoid it all these years. He was married now and he was damn well going to do it right.

Dragon walked into the center of the room where his

wife stood. Deliberately, he came up behind her and set a hand on her shoulder. The startled little jump she gave was gratifying but merely a beginning. His long fingers brushed aside the silken fall of her hair, baring the slender line of her neck. He leaned closer, exhaling lightly, and smiled at the shiver that ran through her. Slowly, deliberately, he touched his mouth to the base of her throat, first on one side, then on the other. Her head fell back as she trembled.

"My lord . . . ?" Her voice was breathless and a little high. A good start.

"Hmmm?" She tasted of honeysuckle, whirls of piney smoke, and her own elusive, purely female scent.

"It was so kind of you to let me ride Grani. Have you had him and Sleipnir long? Are there other horses here, not like them for surely none could be, but I wondered if perhaps you bred them? There is much to be said for that for good horses are always needed. I thought perhaps if you did already, I could help or if not, perhaps you would consider beginning. With such fine stock it would only be a matter of time before people from all over were clamoring for your horses. As you are much interested in trading—"

Grinning, he turned her to face him. She was flushed and her amber eyes looked wide enough to swallow a man. "We can discuss such matters at another time, *wife*. At the moment, all I am interested in is taking you to bed."

He wouldn't have thought it possible but her flush deepened. "Oh, well, as to that, surely there is no rush? I mean, after all, it is not as though we haven't already . . ."

"Once and as though in a dream. Frankly, my lady, you had me at a disadvantage. I fell asleep embracing a wine skin and awoke to find myself embraced by you."

"You seemed to enjoy it well enough," she said just a little tartly.

"True for all that it was a mere taste, the slightest hint of what is possible."

Excitement warred with alarm. Surely he exaggerated? It wasn't really possible to feel more than she had that night, was it? And if it was, did she want to when she had already come so close to experiencing the seeming oblivion of herself lost in a sea of pleasure? Of her own making, that had been, but this would be of his for she had no doubt now that he meant to take control. Wasn't he doing it already, touching her so lightly, so tantalizingly, tracing the curve of her cheek and her mouth, his breath warm on her, his body so close until it was all she could do not to cry out for him?

By heaven, she would not! Pleasure was well and good, and marriage holy, but pride demanded he not know how easily he could sway her. Did he learn that, she surely would be lost.

"I merely thought you might be tired," she said and raised a winged brow. "After so long a day and the journey itself."

His body, already powerfully aroused, tightened even further. Did she understand that she challenged his manhood? Probably not, for she was in many ways still an innocent. He smiled, but guardedly. "Such wifely concern but unnecessary, I assure you. The feast was to your liking?"

The feast? Vaguely did she remember it for all that it still went on. She could still hear the sounds of reverie, but softly and in the distance. They were quite alone. She looked up, met his gaze, and felt the tingle of surprise she always did at his height and size. His shoulders blocked out the moonlight creeping through the slatted shutters, leaving only the glow of banked fire to illuminate his features. Cast between shadows, he looked carved from stone.

"Your people are kind."

"They can be. Why are you afraid?"

"I am not!" Spoken too quickly, the words rang false.

"I thought you merely uneasy but now I see there is more than that. Why? It is not as though I am a stranger to you."

"But you are, stranger than any man I have ever met before."

Dragon grimaced and caught her hair in his hand, drawing her head back slightly, the better to look at her. "Ever do you prick my vanity. There will be nothing left of it soon."

She stared back at him in bewilderment. "What have I said?"

"It is what you have not, but never mind, I am resolved, what sighs and moans of pleasure, what cries of delight I wish to hear, I will have from you, *wife*, before this night is done."

Rycca gasped and would have pulled away but he had anticipated that and held her fast, by the hair not cruelly but entangled in his hand and by the waist, gripped firmly in a steely arm. She was all womanly curves but they did not melt against him, rather met him strength for strength as she strained to break his hold. He laughed at the fire in her gaze but prudently moved to one side. "That trick will not work twice on me," he cautioned, remembering how she had broken free of him in the Essex wood.

Her bewildered stare followed swiftly by the hot flush of understanding made him regret the words. He had no reason to believe she would behave in such a way again. Still, there were times when a man could be forgiven for choosing prudence.

Yet he could also make amends. He loosed her hair but held her still, drawing her ever closer, and with his free hand stroked her arm lightly. The sleeves of her gown were snugly fitted. He knew she felt his caress as keenly as if he had touched bare skin. "Why should we spar?" he murmured against her mouth. "I only want to give you pleasure."

She trembled, unable to stop herself. He let his hand slip to her breast, his long fingers stroking and teasing the nipple that strained against the thin fabric. Dropping his head, holding her firmly, he touched her there, just letting her feel the rasp of his teeth through the silk that moistened quickly at the touch of his tongue, darkening and clinging to her tightly. Her hands curled into his shoulders as her knees threatened to give way. Yet there was no weakness to her words.

"You want to control me." She spoke dispassionately as though observing the plight of another woman far distant from herself.

Dragon looked up, surprised. "You are my wife."

"Say rather your possession for so do you think, do you not?"

He shrugged, wondering why she stated the obvious. "All wives belong to their husbands."

"I wanted to be free."

His eyes darkened. There was greater challenge here than even he had thought. "You wanted to be safe from Wolscroft and the rest of them, even from me when you thought misguidedly. That is why you fled."

She shook her head. "Oh, no, safety was a convent from which not even my father could have forced me. But it was not to one such that I fled, was it? I wanted freedom, and having tasted it, however briefly, I want it still."

His hands tightened on her, driven by the sudden, piercing pain her words brought. Did she think to leave him again? To flee as she had done and leave him once more bereft. No, by heaven, she would not! "No one is free," he said fiercely. "We are all enmeshed in duty and responsibility."

"Your duty is of your own choosing, for did you not

return here after many years away and willingly take up your inheritance? Your destiny is of your own making and you the master of it as much as any man can claim to be. I want the same for myself, no more, no less."

"But you are a woman. . . ." His bewilderment was genuine. Such yearnings as she described belonged to the realm of men. Women were for hearth and home, the nurturing of children, such ordered security of days as could be wrested from uncertain fate. A man in the thick of battle, in the fury of adventure, in the depths of night had to be able to count on that, for without it, of what purpose was anything?

"You are a woman," he repeated firmly. "And my wife. You have been too long apart from womanly ways with no proper influence to guide you. I applaud your strength and your courage; both will breed true in my sons, but—"

"Your sons? *Your sons!* They will be *my* sons, Lord Vanity, and my daughters as well. Mayhap only daughters, for by heaven it would suit me to thwart you so!"

Lies, all lies. Yet strangely truth as well, for she seemed torn in two, at war within herself. The girl she had been was in danger of being lost forever, and the woman she was becoming was as much a stranger to her as the man who sparked the transformation.

His gentleness was forgotten, banished along with the memory of the sweet urgency she had felt lying in the night in his arms as they sped over the sea and the kindnesses he had done her that pierced the shield of loneliness forged in a child's anguish. Yet all this lingered deep within, weighing her down as though with chains of her own heart's making.

"I think it is not me you fear," he said suddenly, "but yourself." Skald-souled, he saw as though a curtain had been pushed aside and the landscape of her inner self bared to him as surely as he meant to bare her body. "You are afraid of being a woman because you think it makes you weak and vulnerable. Nothing could be less so, but were it not, you still have no choice for your own God has made you so."

He laughed suddenly, relieved to have discovered what he believed to be the source of her rebellion. "But, lady, at least give Him credit. He did a splendid job."

His cheerful evoking of the divine robbed her of breath momentarily. That was just enough for Dragon, who had learned long ago the advantage of surprise. She was in his arms, across the room, and deposited on the bed before she could do more than gasp.

He loomed over her, very big and very determined. His arms were braced on both sides of her, not touching but effectively constraining.

"So you are not afraid. You wish merely to be free."

She glared at him as pride demanded. "I have said as much, have I not?"

"And you want daughters, that is also so?"

"Why do you echo me? To what purpose?"

His teeth flashed white in the fiery light that also danced over her hair, making it appear as tendrils of flame licking the pillow's damask smoothness. "Ah, my lady, what purpose indeed? Perhaps I merely wish to fulfill your wishes. You want freedom? I can give it to you. Daughters, too, although that I cannot absolutely promise."

"How would you make me free?" Send her away perhaps? Banish the shrewish wife he must surely regret taking? Pain stabbed at her. She tried to steel herself against it and could not.

Because his mouth was on her throat again, trailing shivers of delight, teasing and tormenting so enticingly. And his hands, his too-skillful hands, were easing her gown up her long, tapering legs, baring her skin to the cool night air.

"Did you not notice," he murmured, concentrating on his task, "before when we lay together, how you soared at the end? That is a kind of freedom."

Truly, she had never felt freer but not for the world would she tell him that.

"Momentary," she said, "no more."

His eyes gleamed, swooped by dark lashes, crinkling at the corners, windows of his soul. "Momentary? My apologies. Be assured, I will do much better this time."

Why, she wondered, as he lifted her and eased the gown over her head, did that sound like promise and threat all at once?

B ECAUSE IT WAS, BOTH TOGETHER, AS SHE REAL-ized later when she surfaced just a little from the sea of pleasure into which he had cast her and, gasping, grabbed for air. A man as good as his word, he was that and more. So much more . . .

"Again, sweetheart," he murmured, his voice deep, compelling, and raised his dark head from the cleft between her thighs. Panting softly, Rycca gazed down the length of herself and wondered whose body she inhabited. Who was this woman who trembled beneath him, whose breasts were swollen, her nipples almost painfully hard, her legs spread shamelessly, her hips rising to the most daring caress? Who was she whose whole being focused on the rapidly coiling tension deep within her, the deceptive languor that enveloped her, drawing tighter and tighter until he bent his head once more, flicking her so lightly, and she . . .

"Ahhh, nooo!"

Her fingers tangled in his hair, pulling hard as she struggled against the paroxysms of pleasure that would not be denied. She had no chance against him and could scarcely remember why she would want one. He dazzled her senses with each touch, each look, each word.

And he was smiling for he had won again, wresting from her the surrender she did not wish to give. Smiling as he moved up, pausing to drop kisses along her smooth belly, in the hollows beside her hip bones, the vale of her navel, lingering over her body, savoring her until finally, having made her wait, he took her mouth with the deep, possessive thrust of his tongue.

Still, she tried to pull his hair out by the roots. He laughed then and grasped both her wrists, pressing them flat to either side of her head.

"My sweet little wife . . . so obedient . . . so compliant—"

"Damn you! You are unfair. Why will you not let me touch you?" As she ached to do, her need growing with each passing moment and unassuaged even by the pleasure he gave her again and again with such remorseless generosity.

He laughed once more and let go of her, rising to stand before the bed. Looking down at the delightfully wanton picture she presented, Dragon shook his head wryly. "Because I know my own limitations and do not care to reach them too quickly, unlike the last time." Holding her gaze, he unabashedly pulled off his tunic and tossed it to one side. Satisfied that he had her attention, he made quick work of his sandals but did not immediately rejoin her. Instead, he went to the nearby table and poured ruby wine from a silver ewer. Filling two goblets of precious glass chased at the rims with gold, he carried them to the bed.

With the tip of her tongue Rycca moistened her lips as she stared at him. Truly, whatever deity was responsible for this man had overdone. From the massive sweep of his shoulders and chest down past narrow hips to thighs bulging with corded strength, he was magnificent. A splendor of nature that compelled her scrutiny as surely as he had her surrender. He moved with grace, utterly at ease with his nakedness and her gaze that trailed over him in helpless fascination. An arrow of hair running down his flat abdomen thickened at his groin. Rycca's eyes widened. She had held this man within her body, lain beneath him in ecstasy, but save for that glimpse when he left the sauna, she had never seen him as fully as she did now. Then he had been relaxed and unaroused, now he was neither.

"Should I be flattered?" he asked with a smile as he handed her one of the goblets. Rejoining her on the bed, he lay back against the pillows as though he had no thought other than to converse with her. "You weren't afraid before and you were a virgin then."

"It seems innocence and ignorance have much in common," Rycca murmured, then swallowed fully half her wine without noticing. She felt flushed and uncertain, wanting to draw the covers up over herself but unable to reach them where they were bunched at the foot of the bed without making her self-consciousness glaringly obvious. His casual disregard of their mutual nudity and his blatant arousal made her all the more acutely aware of both. She struggled to match his composure even as she desperately sought some—any—distraction.

It came but from an unlikely source. Her gaze settled suddenly on a long white scar that bisected his left thigh, cutting clear across it in the arc of a descending blade that must have come very close to severing the limb entirely. Her breath caught. It was hard to say which surprised her more, the evidence of so terrible a wound or the fact that it was healed.

Hardly aware that she did so, she traced her finger along the scar, touching very lightly as though afraid she might somehow do him further damage. "What happened?"

He shrugged. "A fight. I slipped on wet ground."

"This is a killing wound yet you survived it and it seems to give you no trouble. How can that be?"

Dragon laughed, trying to ignore the effect her touch had on him. He was intensely aroused and unsure how much longer he could maintain his pose of calm control. Being stroked by her definitely didn't help. Neither did the tender concern he saw flash in eyes that not so very long ago had been spitting fire at him.

She was a contrary woman, capable of fierce pride and will yet also vulnerable and strong all at the same time. She could frustrate, bewilder, and mystify him, and he thanked Loki for it. Or perhaps Frigg, for he suspected the queen of the gods would approve of one such as Rycca.

"You see here," he said as casually as he could manage, "the benefits of travel and my own brother's fortuitous choice of a wife."

Rycca's brow furled. "I don't understand."

"In Constantinople I met a physician who showed me how wounds could be stitched. It seemed a sensible measure, much preferable to searing skin with a fiery blade. Years later, when I found myself bleeding to death on a road near Hedeby in Jutland, I remembered that I had thread and needle in my kit, the kind we use for repairing sails. It worked well enough."

"You stitched up your own leg with canvas twine and a needle?" The mere thought of what that must have felt like filled her with horror. To manage such a feat, a man would have to have nearly superhuman control.

"It was preferable to the alternative," Dragon said. "However, I didn't make a very good job of it. The leg healed badly and troubled me until Cymbra took charge of it."

"The Lady Cymbra, wife to the Wolf?"

"The very same. She is a healer of extraordinary

ability. Although I admit there were times when I contemplated wringing her lovely neck, she coaxed, pummeled, and generally coerced me back to full health."

That would be the Cymbra who was renowned for her beauty and who had provided Krysta with all those wonderful recipes, the same Krysta who was herself so lovely, so kind and gentle, so completely what a wife should be.

Unlike Rycca, who had no domestic skills at all and who was as far from such feminine perfection as it was possible to be. She who dreamed of freedom, announced her determination to bear only daughters, and snarled at her husband when he gave her pleasure.

Heaven help her.

Something of her thoughts must have shown in her face for Dragon's mood changed suddenly. He took her wine goblet from her and set it with his own on the table beside the bed. She stiffened when he drew her into his arms but he ignored that and settled her head firmly against his shoulder.

"Watching you," he said, "is like watching swiftly changing weather move over the sea. One moment you seem tranquility itself, and the next you are roiled by storms."

Her voice was muffled against his skin, so close that he felt the movement of her lips. "Ever have I kept my feelings hidden, until now. Indeed, there were long stretches of time when I thought I had none."

"Except the desire to be free?"

Her hair brushed against him like warm silk. "Except for that, and had I let any inkling of it emerge, a beating from my father would have been the least result."

"I wonder," Dragon mused as he stroked her hair, "how long it will take you to realize that you are safe here."

She had no answer for him, nor did she particularly

seek one. The shadows of her past cast into the present were no pleasant topic to contemplate, especially when far more enticing pursuit presented itself. It seemed he had forgotten his reluctance to be touched by her. Yet he would not yield as he had that incandescent night she cherished still. Perhaps he should drink more wine. But when she teasingly reached across his chest for the goblet to hand to him, he pulled her back. So quickly that she had no chance to realize his intent, he turned them both, pressing her into the soft mattress as he loomed above her.

His teeth flashed white as he smiled. "Let us strike a bargain, wife."

"What sort of bargain?" She made no attempt to hide her suspicion.

"I will do as I please with no resistance from you, and when I am satisfied, you may do as you wish."

For just a moment, his evenhandedness surprised her. Just a moment . . .

"Do you remember what I said about ignorance and innocence, my lord?"

"Very clearly, my lady."

"I have shucked off both. You toy with me. When you are satisfied, you will go to sleep and leave me to fume at having entered into so poor a pact."

"You wound me, all the worse for wounding yourself. Do you not know you are a temptress no man could resist?" He frowned at the sudden thought. "Although they had damn well better lest they be fodder for my sword." His big hand caught in her hair, drawing her head back, baring her throat to his caress. "Be advised, wife, I am a possessive man."

She took a breath, wrapped her arms around his shoulders, and parted her legs, drawing him into the cradle of her hips. "Be advised, husband," she murmured close beside his ear just before she bit it lightly, "I am a possessive woman."

His big body tensed in her embrace, becoming suddenly urgent. She had a scant moment to spare for thought of her daring at having said such a thing, for women were not supposed to place such demands upon their lords. Thought fled as he cupped her breasts, teasing his fingers over her nipples before suckling first one, then the other. The pleasure was, as always, almost too much. So too was his filling of her though he went gently, his face strained with the harshness of his control, entering her slowly but inexorably. She felt herself stretching to contain him as she had before but this time there was no pain, only a sense of stunning completion that filled and filled her until all the empty places inside her seemed taken up by him.

Dragon raised himself on his powerful arms, gazing down at her and farther at them united. Though the night air was cool, sweat gleamed on his forehead, yet he moved within her hardly at all, holding himself almost entirely still save for the very tip of him that probed lightly, seeking, then flexed against some hidden part of her being she had not known existed.

The world exploded and she with it. Without warning, she was sent hurtling over a shattering peak. Scarcely had crest after crest of pleasure begun to ebb than he was moving within her, hard and deep, holding back nothing now but taking his due as man, lover, husband. Taking her with him as well as the wildness grew, rippling through her like waves vibrating ever outward from a center. Her head tossed back and forth helplessly on the pillow, her back arching as she strained to be even closer to him, take him even more deeply into herself, make them even more completely one.

"Dragon . . . !"

No denial this but entreaty and demand together. She clung to him, her nails digging into his shoulders, as the world shattered yet again and took with it his formidable control. He claimed her mouth with the same rhythm as he drove within her, deeper, harder, faster. . . . His orgasm seized him and went on and on, seemingly endless.

R YCCA LAY ON HER BACK. SHE WAS SURPRISED TO find herself still conscious, or returning to it. Truly, after what she had just experienced she would not have thought it amiss to discover herself no longer a part of the mundane world. Yet there she was, the sheet feeling crumpled and hot beneath her, her lips and nipples tender, and the faint resonance of throbbing between her legs to remind her of what had just happened.

She turned her head slightly, relieved that she could do so, and found Dragon not asleep or at least drowsily replete as he should have been—oh no, not he—but wide awake, propped up on an elbow, and looking at her with what appeared suspiciously to be amusement.

"I don't think you are human," she said sulkily.

He grinned. "I felt like a god a few moments ago but that's to your credit, not mine."

That sounded rather nice but still his apparent nonchalance in the face of an experience that had left her utterly drained was irksome. She sat up suddenly and left the bed just as quickly, ignoring her weak-willed wish to stay right where she was, curl up against him, and feel the warmth and strength of his arms around her.

It was his turn to be irked. "And where do you think you are going?"

She tossed her hair aside so that it fell down her naked back to brush against her bottom. Over her shoulder, she said, "To find a night robe."

She thought he might object but he surprised her, which really should not have been surprising at all since he seemed ever to be doing that.

"Wear the green one."

About to take it from the chest, she looked at him instead. He was stretched out on his side on the rumpled bed, his head propped up in his palm, unbashed by the intimacy that made her acutely self-conscious yet oddly content all at the same time. With haste, she seized the green night robe and dropped it over her head.

Dragon hid a smile. He doubted she had any notion of how she looked draped in what seemed no more substantial than sea foam and lit by starlight filtering through the shutters. But he wasn't about to tell her for she was already skittish enough. Instead, he sat up, moved to the side of the bed, and held out a hand.

She hesitated, but when he said nothing, demanded nothing, did nothing more save wait, Rycca weakened. If only she could find something to dislike about him, she could steel herself against the insidious, treacherous, delightful yearnings he set off within her. But that perfect visage and magnificent body were mere trappings for a spirit of true nobility. How could she do other than fall completely under his spell, forget her own dreams, and become just one more in what was no doubt a *very* long line of simpering females grateful for his merest attention?

She shivered in pure revulsion.

"Rycca . . . ?"

"A sudden chill."

He rose, drew her into his arms, and led her back to the bed, producing a luxurious fur throw to place over her, even tucking it in around her before fetching them both more wine.

"Warmer?" he asked when he joined her beneath the fur.

Curled in the shelter of his body, feeling more cared for and protected than she ever had in her life, Rycca could only nod. The wine, the warmth, and all that had proceeded between them made her suddenly drowsy. She was only dimly aware of Dragon taking the goblet from her.

"I don't want to sleep," she murmured.

"What do you want to do?" His voice was soft in the darkness, so very near.

"Lie here . . . like this . . ."

She thought that being a man, he would object, would want more. But he merely kissed the smooth curve of her shoulder and fitted her against his body, her back to his chest and his arm resting on her waist, his fingers lightly brushing her belly.

Rycca exhaled slowly. Her limbs felt like water. Through the thin silk of the night robe she felt his hardness, yet he did nothing, said nothing, only held her.

"Do you ever lose control?" she asked.

He was silent, considering. Finally, he said, "Not in a long time."

"Do you want to?" The question surprised her. She did not know where it came from or why. Likely he did not either but he answered all the same.

"Control is important. That is most obvious in battle where it makes the difference between who lives and who dies, but it always matters."

"As it did when you stitched up your own wound?"

"Yes, without control I would not have survived."

"What about when you were a child?"

"I was lucky then and I had Wolf to shield me."

She turned in his arms, amid the soft rustle of silk, and faced him. Her slender fingers lightly stroked the square line of his jaw. "You have not answered my question."

"I do not understand it. Why would I want to lose control?"

"You might discover that you do not always need it. You trusted your brother. You knew you could always rely on him. Have you ever trusted anyone else like that?"

He answered quickly, emphatically. "No."

Her legs entwined with his, her toes tracing the muscled line of his calves. "Do you want to?"

"Do you really have to ask what I wish, and twice?" His chuckle was deep and affectionate. "Forgive me for being blunt, sweetheart, but isn't it rather obvious?"

It was and becoming more so by the moment, but Rycca refused to be distracted. While she felt so emboldened, she meant to make the most of it.

"Indulge me," she murmured against his chest. "Tell me what the man inside craves."

"Are you asking if I would like to trust you? Yes, of course I would. But you have to admit, we did not get off to the sort of start that inspires trust."

"Could we not try?"

He cupped her breast, drew his thumb over the rigid nipple. "We could do that," he agreed when he felt her shiver. "You could begin by not fighting me."

"I do not," she protested. "It is absurd to say so given what has passed between us."

"You do," he insisted, "inside. You hold back, trying to steel yourself against me or against the pleasure I would give you or both. I am not certain what it is that you see as weakness, threat, danger of some sort. But it is there all the same. I can feel it and I would that I did not."

"Yet you win anyway." She looked at his hand, cupping her, then into his eyes. "What difference except that you must put forth more effort for your victory? Is that what you object to?"

"Nay, sweetheart. Believe me, savoring you is no hardship. I would simply know you are willing . . . without reserve."

"You would have me keep nothing of myself."

"Keep all," he corrected, "but share with me."

The temptation was supreme. There in the darkness he wove thoughts of what could be, as though in a dream, so utterly different from anything she had known in the harsh daylit world that she had to wonder if mayhap she had fallen asleep after all, save in the nest of his arms.

But no, her body was unmistakably awake and rousing to his touch, heedless of her reservations. Reckless, careless body with no thought for past or present, living only in the incandescent moment. Lucky body.

He sensed her wavering and pressed home his advantage then, his skilled hands and mouth moving over her. Quickly enough she was lost to pleasure, the restless stirrings of her mind muted by the thrumming of swiftly rising passion. His victory this time was easier and even more complete. As it was when he drew her to him again and again through the night.

Yet before the first gray light of dawn appeared, it was Rycca who rose above him in the shadows around their bed. She smiled at his sleepy-eyed surprise.

"You have forgotten our pact, lord?"

More sated than he had ever been, Dragon looked at her in frank amusement. "My sweet, I hate to disappoint you but—"

"You will not," she promised, and bent to her chosen task. Before very long, the Lord of Landsende knew beyond any hint of doubt that his wife was a woman of her word.

Chapter

ELEVEN

RYCCA WOKE TO SUNLIGHT PRYING BENEATH her closed eyelids. She stirred slowly, uncertain at first where she was. Her first awareness was that the steady rocking of the boat was missing. Perhaps they had docked?

They had . . . yesterday . . . Landsende . . . riding Grani . . . the feast . . . Dragon . . .

Dragon.

She sat up, threw back her hair, and looked around hastily. A sigh of relief escaped her when she saw she was alone, but hard on that came realization of the late hour. Her first full day in her husband's manor and she had slept most of it away. Already she risked losing the approval of his people, who would surely think his Saxon bride a sluggard for failing to rise long beyond the time when decent men and women had already done a full day's work.

Not that she would have been able to contribute much had she awakened earlier, but that was another problem and one she did not feel ready to deal with before she washed the sleep from her eyes and readied herself to face the day, however belatedly.

The water in the pitcher on the table beneath the windows was cool. How not when it must have been there for hours if not since the day before? She bathed with only brief notice of the discomfort, for hot water was a luxury with which she had little acquaintance.

Her stomach rumbled as she pulled clothes from a chest and dressed as swiftly as she dared. All the garments brought from Hawkforte were vastly more elaborate and delicate than the roughly woven shift she was used to. She managed well enough but felt very clumsy in the process. Would she ever become accustomed to wearing clothes that seemed fit for a princess in a bard's tale? Perhaps in a future too distant and precarious for her to waste any time thinking about.

For in truth she had no time to waste, having already squandered more than enough. Yet for all that, her courage wavered as she stepped out into the fair, sea-scented day. A brisk breeze blew off the water carrying with it the tang of salt and, closer in, the smell of fresh-turned earth. Sunlight danced off the western hills where she could just make out the shapes of fat sheep grazing. Closer in, the ripening heads of golden grain waved gently in well tended fields.

Far out over the water, fishing ships were making their way toward the harbor where several plumb merchant vessels rode at anchor. Surrounded by peace and security, Rycca felt the coil of tension within her lessen just enough to make her aware of its presence. She was so used to being wary, to guarding her every step and always looking over her shoulder that she seldom even noticed her own unease. But here, in this place, everything was new and different. The old ways she knew all too well no longer fit and she felt cast adrift, unsure of where the next turn of the current would take her.

To the kitchens, first, she decided. They were in a separate building set a short distance away from the main hall. Several fires with iron tripods set up over them burned outside. Nearby was a large brick oven for baking. Several women were working there as she approached. One among them, a middle-aged woman with graying hair tucked beneath her head scarf, saw her, said a hasty word to the other women, and came to greet Rycca.

"My lady, I am Magda Kirstendotter. If you have come to see the kitchens, may I show them to you? I have had the keeping of them for several years and if I can continue to help you in any way, I will be happy to do so." As she spoke, she removed from her sturdy leather belt a chain weighted down with keys, which she handed to Rycca. "I believe you will find everything in order, my lady. Landsende is a rich holding and we are very well supplied."

Rycca stared at the keys uncertainly. She understood their significance well enough. As wife of the lord, it was her prerogative to control all domestic goods, food, drink, cloth, all of it. Thus, she would hold the keys and dole out what was needed as she saw fit. It was a responsibility for which she felt singularly unprepared, yet she had no choice but to accept the keys from the smiling woman who proffered them. When they were safely attached to Rycca's own belt, Magda looked well pleased.

"Long have we waited for Lord Dragon to take a wife, my lady. Your coming brings us great joy."

"I hope so." Magda's open and cheerful face prompted honesty. "I got the impression yesterday on the dock that people were not so sure of how they felt."

The older woman looked a little surprised at such frankness but she recovered quickly and laughed. "Oh, they got over that right quick when they saw you on

Grani. Imagine, a woman able to ride that wild one! You may know the men talked of little else last night. They finally convinced themselves that Lord Dragon must have told the horse to behave himself, that being the only explanation that could sit well with them."

Rycca laughed and Magda joined her. Soon the other women did the same. Magda introduced them all. Quickly enough, Rycca found herself at the center of a circle of chatting women being led toward the kitchens. The women's confidence and good humor struck her just as the evidence of their touches in the town had done. Never before, save for her brief stay at Hawkforte, had she been among women who were not fearful. Even as she tried to appear as though this were all most ordinary to her, she marveled at them.

And at the kitchens, which were unlike anything she had ever seen. In Wolscroft, they were dank pits from which emerged meat that was either raw or charred, sometimes both, which she thought a rather odd accomplishment, and other things too rank to be remembered. Rarely had she ventured within them. Never would it have occurred to her father to give her responsibility for them, much less the actual authority to effect anything good.

But here all was different. The kitchens gleamed, every surface scrubbed clean with sand, the floor swept clear of any hint of debris, and only good, fresh smells to be had.

"Here we have water," Magda said as she showed off a well cleverly dug right in the center of the kitchen, convenient to the several large wooden basins used for washing. She spoke in Saxon but repeated the words in Norse and nodded approvingly when Rycca tried them out for herself.

"And here, you see, many pots and spits of good iron.

The smithy here makes them for us but there are platters and bowls brought from far away by the traders."

Too distracted the night before to notice much of anything, Rycca was startled to see the stacks of beautifully ornamented serving dishes of glazed pottery, precious metals, and glass. So, too, was she drawn to the large chest that stood upright against one wall behind an iron screen of intricate design. The chest was almost as tall as Rycca herself and held within it a multitude of drawers of different sizes.

"Most of our spices are kept here," Magda explained, "except, of course, for the salt. Only a small quantity of that is on hand, the rest being in barrels in the storerooms." She gestured to the collection of keys she had given to Rycca. "That long, slender key opens this lock. I usually take out each morning whatever spices are likely to be needed during the day, but of course whatever you arrange will be fine."

"I see no reason to change how you have done things," Rycca murmured. She was trying to absorb the extraordinary notion that the entire large chest was filled with spices and that there was even more elsewhere. Yet that paled before the astounding realization that she was now in charge of all this, expected to know what to do with it and how to care for it properly.

She swayed slightly.

"Oh, my lady," Magda exclaimed. "I am so sorry! What am I thinking? Lilla, quickly, a stool for her ladyship and she must have something to eat. Some of the soup, perhaps? And the rolls just baked."

A stool appeared beneath her and Rycca was urged down onto it. Food materialized before her. The women clucked about, looking at her with concern and interest.

"You are all right?" Magda asked as Rycca first nibbled, then devoured the best roll she had ever tasted.

"Fine, thank you, I just hadn't eaten in a while

and—" Virtually nothing the evening before and it was already late afternoon so she had been almost a full day without food. No wonder then the sudden dizziness that had— She broke off her thoughts, struck by Magda's sudden look of disappointment.

"Is something wrong?" Rycca asked.

"Oh, no, not at all, my lady."

False.

Rycca waited, convinced the friendly woman was not truly given to lies. Patience quickly proved her right.

Magda glanced at the other women, several of whom nodded encouragingly. She hesitated a scant moment longer. "It is only that . . . we thought, perhaps . . . well, you know. Lord Dragon dotes on his little nephew. It is so sweet to see them together. We all look forward to the day when our jarl will be a father himself."

Therefore had they thought she might be . . . Rycca flushed and felt foolish for it. She was a married woman now and could reasonably expect to have children. Reasonably? Say rather certainly given what passed between her and Dragon. Indeed, she could be pregnant already and not even know it. The thought cast her into confusion, filling her as it did with both longing and trepidation. A child she could love, cherish, and protect, who would grow up so very differently than she had herself. Yet it was an awesome responsibility and she had no reason to believe she would be a good mother, having never known such.

"Here now," Magda said softly, "you try this good soup. Tell me what you think of the seasoning, if you will, my lady."

Rycca tried a spoonful, surprised by the medley of flavors that played over her tongue. She recognized chicken, wild carrots, juniper berries, and something else. . . .

"Thyme," Magda said. "I thought it would be just the thing after I heard the Lady Cymbra uses it."

The renowned Cymbra, again. Rycca knew a moment's craven gratitude that the lovely Krysta, at least, was on the other side of the sea. That left only one of them to deal with, which was quite enough. No sooner had the thought surfaced than it shamed her. She drank a little more of the soup and would have gladly enjoyed even more, save for the thought that she had already indulged herself well enough. First sleeping half the day away, then scarcely pausing for a look around before needing to be fed. A fine impression she was making.

She stood, smoothing the exquisite gown that felt even more like borrowed plumage. "I would like to see the storerooms now."

Magda guided her to them. The woman was kindness itself, taking care to point out everything she thought might be of interest, to introduce everyone whose path they crossed, and to offer ever more words in Norse when she realized how adept Rycca was at remembering them.

As they approached the storerooms, Rycca saw a familiar face step from the stable, look in her direction, and as quickly turn back from whence he had come. For just a moment, it seemed to her that the young man, Magnus, was avoiding her. But that was foolish for what purpose could he have in doing so?

"Was that Magnus?" she asked but Magda had not seen him and merely shrugged.

"It may have been, my lady."

"He used to be at Sciringesheal, did he not?"

Magda hesitated but at length she said, "Until about a year ago, then he came here."

"For any particular reason? I mean, is it usual for a man to serve one lord, then another?"

The older woman stopped and looked at her more closely. "Lord Dragon spoke to you of this?"

"He told me Magnus used to serve his brother."

Slowly, Magda nodded. She resumed walking again, Rycca keeping pace at her side. "There was an . . . incident at Sciringesheal. It was not Magnus' fault but afterward, he felt uncomfortable there."

"What happened?"

"He had been set to guard the Lady Cymbra. She was attacked and he wounded in the process. No one thought he was to blame but when it became clear he was no longer happy there, Lord Dragon offered him a post here."

"I take it they know each other well?"

"Magnus was the jarls' shadow back when they were all children. When their lands were attacked and everything destroyed, the brothers had the courage to make their way in the larger world. That was the right decision for them but Magnus wanted so much to go along. Of course, it was impossible. He was not even six years old. The Lord Wolf himself was only twelve then and the Lord Dragon was scarcely eight. They had scant hope of surviving themselves without trying to also protect so young a child."

"So Magnus stayed with his parents?"

"They were dead, killed in the raids. But an uncle took him in." She sighed deeply. "Unfortunately, he was a cold, harsh man. But you must understand, because of all the raiding, people lived in grinding poverty and constant fear. There was never enough food or warmth . . . or anything, including hope. Living in such a way brought out the worst in some. Fortunately, all that has changed now."

"Because of Lord Dragon and Lord Wolf?"

Magda nodded. "The orphaned boys who left to take their chances in the world came back as men, and not just any men but warriors of great power and cunning. And wealth, wealth enough to rebuild Sciringesheal and Landsende both, to transform them into what you see today, and change the lives of everyone here beyond imagining."

She could not have timed her words better for just then they arrived at the stout wooden doors that guarded the storerooms. Unlocked, they opened to reveal a treasure trove that made Rycca gasp. Never had she expected to see such bounty at this season when most of the harvest still waited in the fields.

She knew it as a time of anxious watching and waiting, hoping the rain came but not too much, the sun shone but not too brightly, no blight appeared to devastate what had been brought forth through so much labor, until all was finally home and safe before the first frost seared whatever carelessness or ill-luck left behind. Too often she had seen her father and his men chew meat by the winter fire while the peasants scrabbled for what little they could find to feed themselves, the old and young died needlessly, and all others turned gaunt and pale from the struggle to survive. She had thought a fat harvest well kept was the only surety against such fate but now she realized her error. A fat purse wisely opened also meant a full larder.

"From where comes this grain?" she asked Magda.

"Far to the south where they already have their harvest. The jarl trades for it."

"What sort of goods?"

"Smoked fish and furs but horses as well and fine ships. Lord Dragon and his brother build drakars of such speed and strength that they have been bought to ply waters very far from here."

"I see . . . and, too, they control the trade along this coast, do they not? Any who wish to trade here must surely pay tribute to them."

Magda shrugged. "As is only right for it is the skill of their arms that keeps the peace and allows for such trading to happen at all."

So her husband was indeed a wealthy man as well as a powerful one but he used his wealth to better the lives of his people. No wonder so many came to Landsende. Nor had she seen the all of it yet. Beyond the storerooms were cellars dug into the hills that held vats of mead, ale, and wine. There were also large barns, empty now as the animals foraged along the hillsides but soon to be filled with winter fodder for the large flocks, smokehouses that would shortly be working day and night, and vast rows of racks for the drying of fish and meat.

All hers now to manage and somehow keep functioning properly. Her hands shook slightly as she checked the keys hanging from her belt and tried to remember which opened what.

She was still with Magda, looking over the weaving shed, when Dragon joined them. He had come directly from the training field and was sweat-stained, bare-chested, and, to Rycca's dazzled eyes, glorious. Stammering a greeting in response to his own, she was all too aware of Magda grinning broadly at them before slipping away.

They stood in the quiet shed, motes of dust dancing in the sunlight streaming through the windows and the scent of wool sweet on the air. Silence stretched between them until Dragon asked, "Magda has been showing you around?"

Rycca nodded, wishing she could take her eyes from him but unable to do so. "She is very kind."

"Yes, she is a good woman, but everyone understands you are mistress here now. You must make whatever changes you wish."

"Indeed?" Her lips trembled in a smile. "You mean if I were to order the rushes left on the floors until they become old and moldy, no food served unless it is both cold and covered in grease, clothes not washed even if they are so full of dirt as to stand up by themselves—that will please you?"

He laughed and came toward her only to stop when he remembered his state. "Speaking of full of dirt, I am hardly fit company but in the spirit of wifely tolerance I wonder if you will accompany me to a pool a little ways from here."

He meant to bathe. The memory of him emerging from the sauna at the lodge flashed through her mind. Her mouth was suddenly dry. "I thought Vikings liked to boil themselves first."

"Ordinarily I would agree with you, but if I get into a sauna now, I will fall asleep."

"You are tired from your exertions on the training field?"

The look he trailed over her was purely male and so evocative as to warm her clear through. "I am tired from my exertions in our bed, lady, as I suspect you well know."

"That is a relief!"

He looked at her in surprise, prompting a red face and a quick explanation. "I meant that I could not help but think of you toiling as usual while I slept half the day away and felt myself shamed for such sloth."

"Oh, well, if it's any consolation to you, I fell asleep under a tree, to the great hilarity of my men, who are not likely to let me forget it anytime soon."

She laughed, tension uncoiling, and without hesitation she held out her hand to him.

T HE POOL WAS ON THE OTHER SIDE OF A HILL, close enough to walk to comfortably yet secluded especially at the hour when preparations for supper were under way. Distant sounds from the town reached them on the soft-stirring breeze but they were entirely alone.

"We did not ride today," Dragon said as they reached

the pool after a quick stop at their lodge. "Mayhap tomor-row."

For once in her life, the thought of being on the back of a magnificent horse did not command Rycca's atten-tion. She was far too busy looking at her magnificent hus-band as he removed his sword belt and blithely shucked off his trousers. Naked, he walked straight into the pool, submerged completely, and came up a few moments later, tossing streams of water from the thick mane of his hair.

"Hand me the soap, would you?"

Such a simple task, yet to fulfill it he would have to come closer. Or she would.

"That's a lovely gown," he said, smiling.

"All my gowns are lovely thanks to the Lady Krysta and your own generosity."

"It would be a shame to get it wet."

She looked at him in alarm, wondering if he would ac-tually do such a thing. His answer was a look of pure inno-cence, which immediately confirmed her suspicions.

"Do you have any idea how many women must have labored so long to make this gown?"

"No, do you?"

"Well, no, not actually because I never had a gown like this before, but even so, surely you wouldn't do any-thing to damage it?"

"Just to be safe, why don't you take it off?"

Oh, yes, that would certainly be safe. Indeed, never was she any safer than when was she naked and in his arms. Except, of course, from the danger of her own emotions.

"I bathed when I awoke."

"The day is warm."

"The pool looks deep. Recall, I cannot swim."

"Recall I mean to teach you."

Her alarm redoubled. "Not now?"

"Why not? What better time?"

"But I had not thought . . . I am not ready . . ."

"You will be," he said patiently, "if you would only take off that gown."

She took a step back and another. "There must be more to it than that. I must think about it, prepare . . ."

"Rycca?"

"Yes . . ."

"I will take two breaths. Then I am coming out of here, taking that gown off you, and you are going to learn to swim. Clear?"

Clear. She took another step back and glanced over her shoulder, looking for a likely route for flight. It was a mistake.

Wet hands gripped her. He was there so suddenly she had no time to anticipate it. Just as quickly he removed her gown, prompting the gnawing thought that he was very adept at dispensing with women's garments.

The water was . . . not unpleasant.

"Relax," Dragon said. He held her snug against him as he waded in deeper.

Her stare was chiding. He saw it and laughed. "All right, perhaps that is too much to ask. But try not to drown us both."

"I could do that?"

"No, of course not, it was a joke. Just breathe normally. You're doing fine."

She was clinging to him as the water rose ever higher around them. Why did people do this? Why couldn't they stay on land where they belonged?

"I don't think—"

"Good, thinking is a mistake in situations like this."

"I meant this is not a good idea."

He stopped and looked down at her, his eyes suddenly tender. "Rycca, fish swim."

"Of course they do."

"Fish are very stupid. How else do you think we catch them? Yet they swim and you, a woman of intelligence and spirit, will do the same."

He thought her intelligent, he who could read and dreamed of creating books? And spirited? Such a warrior as the Dragon himself found that quality within her? Maybe she could swim after all. Surely she could not bear the thought of failing to fulfill his expectations.

"What do I have to do?"

"Lie back, relax, take a few deep breaths . . . that's it . . . now just stretch out your legs. I've still got you."

She felt his hands beneath her back as she reclined in the water. The sky was very blue. Gulls circled lazily.

"Put your head back," he said quietly.

Her hair was wet. She felt it floating all around her. The water was rather nice, especially after the warmth of the day. She really didn't have to do anything except lie back and let him support her.

He was standing several feet away, much too far to still be holding her.

"Dragon!" Her head shot up, her feet went under, and suddenly she was flailing. He was at her side in an instant, steadying her.

"Easy . . . You were floating perfectly well until you thought to worry about it. The water will hold you up if you just let it."

"Don't go off and leave me like that again."

His mouth twitched at the corners. "All right, I won't. Ready?"

No, she wasn't, but there didn't seem to be much choice. She was on her back again, blinking at the sky, and she felt the moment when his hands withdrew. But this time she continued to float and after a while she even enjoyed it.

"Good," Dragon said with satisfaction. "Now we'll try it the other way."

"Other? But this is perfectly fine."

"You can't get anywhere lying on your back." His smile turned devilish. "Well, actually you can but perhaps this isn't the time to dwell on that. Take a deep breath."

"Why?"

Because her face was about to go straight into the water, that was why. When she came up sputtering, he was unrepentant. "Try again," he said.

"I don't want to." She too could be stubborn.

His sighed was rebuke enough. She filled her lungs, stuck her face in the damn water, and kept it there even when he took hold of her legs and stretched them out behind her. Amazingly, she did not sink.

While the sun kissed the western treetops, Rycca swam for the first time. She took only a few strokes to be sure but the delight she felt was great all the same.

"I did it! I actually swam!"

He stood, hands on his hips, the water lapping at his navel, and grinned. "You and the fish."

"You are a wonderful teacher."

The compliment surprised him. She could be such a bristly little thing, when she wasn't melting in his arms, and he knew he had forced her to do something against her will. He would have expected more stubborn opposition yet she behaved gracefully. It seemed she was relaxing just a little.

The sun was slanting below the western hills and a cooling breeze riffled the water. Inclined though Dragon was to linger there, when he saw his wife shiver he changed his mind.

They swam just a little longer, she too excited by the newness of it to notice the cold until it threatened to settle in her bones. Then, laughing, she went into his arms and stood obediently as he enveloped her in a length of linen and dried her briskly. When she was dressed again and somewhat warmer, she observed him as he pulled on clean trousers but did not bother with a tunic.

"Do you not feel the cold?" she asked, gathering up the linen, soap, and his discarded clothes.

"It is summer, sweetheart. There is no cold."

"Then I can scarcely imagine what winter must be like."

He touched a finger to the tip of her nose. "Don't be concerned. You will be wrapped in furs and snug by the fire." Drawing a little closer, he lowered his head near to hers. "The winter nights are very long. We will have to find some way to occupy ourselves."

He imagined her then, not wrapped in furs but lying upon them, her glorious skin rosy-hued in the light of glowing braziers and himself with naught to do through winter's night other than savor her. Truly, a man could ask for little more in this world and maybe in the next.

Yet even as they were climbing back up the hill, Dragon was reminded of his duties. Magnus met them near the crest, on the same side as the pond. He smiled apologetically to Rycca as he addressed his jarl.

"My lord, I am sorry to disturb you. The ship from Gaul you have been expecting has just put in."

"Any word on their cargo?"

"I did not speak to the captain directly but all appears in order."

"Good, then I will go at once." He turned to Rycca. "My dear, forgive me, I have been waiting months for this. Magnus, see my lady back. Oh, and, Rycca, tell Magda the captain and his men will be joining us at table. It is Paulo. Tell her that, she will know what he likes."

And he was gone, with the heady eagerness of a boy, hurrying off to whatever it was the ship had brought. She was left on the side of the hill with Magnus.

With her husband's most trusted lieutenant, Rycca reminded herself. Even so, she did not take the hand he offered, pretending not to notice it, but went up and over the hill alone, aware of him following along a few paces behind her yet disinclined to acknowledge his presence.

On the same side as the pond. That was where she had seen him first. Not coming over the crest of the hill as he would have had to were he just arriving from the town. But already there as though, perhaps, he had arrived a little sooner and lingered.

To watch them? The thought chilled her far more than had the cool water. Yet she realized how easily she might be doing the man a disservice by her suspicions. Distracted by Dragon—and when was she not?—she might easily have missed Magnus's appearance. He could be entirely innocent.

"Is something wrong, my lady?" he asked as, lengthening his stride, he came beside her.

She answered pleasantly yet held fast to her caution. "No, not at all. I am merely preoccupied."

"Of course, so much is new to you."

"Yes, it is, but everyone has been very kind."

"That is good to hear. If you have any problems, I would be happy to help in any way I can."

Lies.

The awareness rippled through Rycca as it always did, a darkling shadow that left her feeling vaguely ill. She darted a quick glance at Magnus and picked up her pace.

He looked utterly sincere, a man unblemished by the merest hint of deception or, indeed, of any complexity of character. His skin was smooth, his eyes untroubled. Perhaps that was why he looked so young, as though the world had not touched him as it had all others.

There was some fundamental wrongness in that but Rycca could not grasp it. She knew only that she was glad to see the town appear and gladder still when she was once more within the fortress walls.

She found Magda in the kitchens and told her the news. That set off a flurry of activity that quickly made Rycca forget all else.

Chapter

TWELVE

RYCCA WOKE EARLIER THE NEXT DAY BUT only because she had set her mind to do so. Left to its own devices, her traitorous body would have remained sunk in languid sleep. Ignoring its protests, she bathed, dressed, and left the lodge. It was midmorning and everywhere she looked, people were busy with their tasks. She thought to seek out Magda but before she could do so, her attention was caught by a circle of men standing in front of the great hall.

She approached them cautiously, drawn by the excited rise of their voices but wary all the same. Far too much of her life had been spent avoiding men and their cruelties for her to go among them easily. Yet she had little choice for they were all much too big for her to see over them.

Slowly, she drew nearer, craning her neck. Whatever they were watching had them well pleased for they were cheering and shouting encouragement. The circle moved, expanding and contracting with the rhythm inside it. A space opened up between two warriors and suddenly she was able to see through to—

Dragon. Her husband . . . stripped bare to the waist,

his burnished skin stretched taut over powerful muscles, wielding a mighty sword as he—her stomach clenched— took on all comers. Man after man stepped up, exchanged blows that looked to her shocked eyes as though meant to kill, and yielded, good-naturedly, grudgingly, reluctantly but yielded all the same. Comments flew, advice to the combatants, speculation about the weapon, and still they came, man after man, testing the strength and skill of their jarl. And still he fought, on and on, never hesitating or seeming to weaken. Indeed, he gave every appearance of enjoying himself thoroughly.

She would never understand men, and that one in particular. They made a game of violence, as though ter- ror and pain were not a single misstep away and lives did not hang in the balance. A deadly game played out with astounding skill, for even as she watched, the circle emp- tied of all save Dragon. No further man stepped up to challenge him.

He stood, the sword held straight in front of him, rock steady despite all his exertions, and turned fully around the ring of men. When still none stepped out, Dragon laughed and lowered his weapon.

"Damn those Moors, they make a fine sword."

"They do indeed," said Magnus. He separated him- self from the circle and nodded to Dragon admiringly. "No wonder you were willing to wait so long for it."

"I would wait longer still to learn the secret of how they do it but they guard that well." Dragon lifted the weapon again and studied the edge of the blade. "Some- thing to do with the folding of the metal, so I've heard."

"Secrets can be gotten at," Magnus said. He too eyed the weapon, covetously, Rycca thought. "You paid a king's ransom. For that, you might have bribed the right smithy."

Dragon laughed and clapped his lieutenant on the back. "Always the direct approach, isn't that right,

Magnus? Never mind that the Moors would come down on us in a fury, bar our drakars from their ports, and chop off the heads of any Viking so unfortunate as to appear before them."

"Then we would make war against them, lord. Are we not mighty enough?"

"Are we? They are many, we are few, yet we do well together when we respect their laws and ways. For me, that is enough."

Magnus said nothing more, but Rycca, watching him, saw the quick flash of derision that moved behind his eyes and knew her husband had missed it.

For he had, just then, seen her instead.

The smile he gave her held nothing of the deadly warrior and all the glee of a boy. "Rycca, come and see this! It is a sword from the Moors in Spain. They have a rare hand for the working of steel."

The circle parted. Men looked at her with guarded curiosity but were careful to move far enough away that none so much as brushed against her accidentally. She clamped down hard on her unease, pinned a smile to her lips, and stepped forward to greet her husband.

"So it seems, and you wield it well."

"It's impossible not to, for it is lighter than most such weapons and perfectly balanced." Without warning, he held it out to her. "Here, try it yourself."

She felt, not merely heard, the men gasp and knew how their thoughts must run. This was not done. A weapon of such worth was for men and only then for the very strongest among them. Yet he put it in the slender hands of an alien woman, one they had never glimpsed before the preceding day, who spoke only a smattering of their language, and who, rumor whispered, had not even wanted to wed their jarl.

Before such challenge, she could not back down. Rycca took the sword and gripped it firmly, praying not to

disgrace herself. It was heavy but definitely not so much
as other swords that she had tried in secret. This one was
different. She could actually heft it. And did so, gracefully, letting it swing in small, controlled arcs. Thurlow
had taught her all he dared, for he had feared, not
wrongly, that she might be provoked someday into taking
a blade to one of their brothers or even, if her desperation
grew enough, to their father. That would have meant her
death yet there had been times when she had contemplated such as a reasonable choice.

Not now, though, this was only play. She kicked her
skirt to the side, laughed, and pointed the tip of the blade
at Dragon, almost but not quite touching his broad chest.
"Too bad you do not have another."

"Oh, but I do. I bought two of them, that one for me
and another for Wolf." He allowed just a moment for her
to contemplate that he might seriously consider calling for
the other sword, then proved he did not need it to deliver
a blow that stunned her.

"By the way, he and Cymbra ought to be here soon."

"W-what . . . ?" Caught off guard, she let the tip of
the blade drop.

"My brother and his wife, they will be here today. I
thought you'd want to know." He was grinning broadly,
damn him.

"Of course I want to know! But now, only a few hours
before they come? Why did you not tell me sooner?"

He stepped forward and kindly took from her the
sword she had forgotten. "What matters that? Magda and
the women will see to the cooking. The lodge Wolf and
Cymbra always use is kept ready for them. And you—"
He looked her over so blatantly as to wring chuckles from
his relieved men. "You look well enough."

She wanted the sword back. She was going to stab
him with it.

He seemed to read her mind and deftly sheathed the

blade. Speaking so softly that only she could hear, he said, "Everything will be all right, Rycca."

Well did she wish to believe him but doubt filled her. The Lady Cymbra would never point a sword at her husband, much less in front of a crowd of his own men. But then she probably wouldn't knee him in the groin either. Her beauty was renowned, as was her skill as a healer, and as though that were not enough, there was said not to be a better cook in all of Christendom.

And she was coming here. Rycca groaned inwardly. Truly, her cup runneth over.

T HE DRAKAR FLYING THE WOLF-EMBLAZONED sail dropped anchor in the port of Landsende scant hours later. Dragon was on the dock to greet it and his wife was beside him, though it had taken some persuading to get her there. Even now he kept firm hold of her hand lest she try to absent herself. Not that she would. Flight at such a time would be cowardly. Besides, there was nowhere to run.

So did she stand with all the dignity she could muster, silently giving thanks to the Lady Krysta, yet another perfect wife, who had seen to it that Rycca was properly garbed. Although something was sure to be out of place. She had taken great care to avoid any damage to her gown but her hair was probably mussed or her cheeks too flushed or her manner insufficiently feminine. Somehow or other, she was certain to be found wanting.

Especially by the tall, dark-haired man clad in stark black who stepped from the drakar, offering his hand to the woman who appeared beside him.

He was as tall as Dragon and, by all evidence, as formidable a warrior. But then she had expected nothing less. His features were handsome enough, she supposed, though she scarcely glanced at his face. It was on the

COME BACK TO ME

woman she focused, and what she saw made her heart drop.

The Lady Cymbra was beauty personified. Chestnut hair shot through with gold tumbled in thick waves almost to her knees. Her eyes, blue as the sea beneath summer sun and thickly fringed, were set in an oval face of damask perfection. Her nose was slender and tapering above full, rose-hued lips that were moist and slightly parted. Her body, suffice to say, was everything a man was likely to dream of but never quite find.

She was perfect—exquisitely, extraordinarily perfect. She looked like a statue come to life, scarcely a real woman. Until, that was, she smiled. Then she suddenly looked human and . . . nice. Quite simply nice.

"Dragon!" she said and moved ahead of her husband to greet her brother-in-law with a warm hug. "You look well. The leg still is not bothering you?"

"It would not dare, after the terror you put it through." He spoke with obvious fondness laced with humor. Over the top of her head, he said, "Well met, brother. You wasted no time getting here."

The feared Lord of Sciringesheal, whose warrior's prowess was known from the ice-rimmed lands of the north to the balmy seas of the distant south, grinned. "Did you not think I would? Your ships were seen off the coast full two days ago. Plenty of time for me to hear of your return." His gray eyes shifted to Rycca, and with that his smile faded. "Lady Rycca of Wolscroft, I presume?"

Dragon set Cymbra aside gently and took his wife's hand again. Holding it, he said, "Nay, brother, Lady Rycca Hakonson now."

The Wolf said nothing, merely looked at her. Rycca felt time slow to a full stop as she met those ice-cold eyes. Her stomach plummeted.

"Wolf, stop that." Lady Cymbra laid a hand on her

formidable husband's arm and smiled at him sweetly. "You'll frighten the poor girl, and heaven knows she's had enough to cope with."

Turning to Rycca, she said matter-of-factly, "Pay him no mind. He and Dragon are devoted to each other, which is just as it should be, but that doesn't mean we aren't delighted to welcome you into the family. Now come, you must tell me all the news from Hawkforte." She took Rycca's arm, disengaging her from Dragon, and began walking with her up the dock toward the road, ignoring the men and chattering all the while. "Krysta writes regularly as does Hawk but I can never have too much news. You saw them, didn't you? Are they well, and Falcon also?"

Stunned at the daring of a woman who would deal so confidently with the formidable Wolf, not to mention the Dragon himself, Rycca could do little but stammer. "Yes . . . well . . . all of them."

"Oh, good, and yourself? I hope the journey here did not tire you overmuch."

"No, it was fine."

Over her shoulder, Cymbra called, "Wolf, bring Lion, will you? Rycca and I are going on ahead."

The Wolf muttered something and Dragon laughed in response. Rycca found herself whisked away back up toward the fortress. She scarcely knew what to think except that she was in the presence of a woman who was as close to legendary as any being could get. What stories were told of her! That she had been sequestered in her own manor to prevent men from fighting over her, that she possessed strange powers, that the Wolf had kidnapped her for vengeance but married her for love, that her own brother, mistaking what had happened, had returned her to England by stealth and that Norse and Saxon had come perilously close to war over her.

Yet for one who had lived such a tumultuous life, she

seemed remarkably down-to-earth. "Have you found all as it should be at Landsende? I know Magda is very competent but if there is anything you need . . ."

"Thank you, no. There seems to be more than enough of everything."

"Everything except what Dragon has needed most," Cymbra said frankly, "a wife to give comfort and meaning to his life. He and Wolf had a hard time of it when they were growing up. Has he told you much about that?"

"A little . . . he told me about going to sea when he was very young."

"They made their own way for years against obstacles that would have destroyed lesser men. It is said that along with my brother, Hawk, they are the most formidable warriors in the world today and I think that may be true. But now they want peace and are willing to go to great lengths to get it."

"Even to Dragon marrying an unknown woman he did not choose for himself," Rycca blurted. She could scarcely believe she had spoken so, yet Cymbra's own openness prompted the same in return.

"You are the third bride wed for peace," Cymbra said with a smile. "And to be frank, it has not been an easy road for the two of us who went before. Yet knowing what we do now, neither Krysta nor I would ever have chosen a different path."

"How much choice did you have?"

To Rycca's surprise, Cymbra laughed. "In my case, none." She sighed in mocking languor. "I still remember Wolf's deeply romantic proposal. He told me that if I did not wed him, he would kill my brother."

"*He what?*"

"Oh, don't worry, he's gotten much better." She laughed again, fondly. "Much, much better. Besides, Dragon is the one who was always good with women."

Rycca could not dispute that but neither could she

ignore what she had just been told. Shocked, she asked, "What did you do?"

"Do? Why, I punched him, of course. What else could I do? He went to our wedding worried that the blow still showed."

"You . . . punched him?" The ethereal beauty beside her had struck the fierce Wolf?

"Rycca, dear sister, something you must learn at once. Wolf and Dragon are both wonderful men but they are also overwhelming. It is part of their charm. Nonetheless, with them it is always best to be firm. For that matter, the same can be said of my brother, as Krysta learned readily enough."

"She and Lord Hawk seem devoted to each other."

"As are Wolf and I. That doesn't mean one should be a meek little woman rubbing feet."

"What a horrible notion! However did you think of it?"

"Oh, didn't you know? That's the kind of wife Dragon always said he wanted."

Too many more shocks of this sort and she was going to turn to stone right where she stood. "He said that? Whatever could he have been thinking? Any such woman would drive him mad."

"Which is more or less what Wolf told him, only he said she would kill him with boredom. No, Dragon needs someone who can match his spirit, which I am now reassured you can do. Come, let us seek out Magda, who will serve us cool milk and cakes and give us a snug place to talk while the men amuse themselves."

"Dragon has a sword for his brother."

"The Moorish sword? Perfect, they will be occupied for hours. We won't see them again until they are satisfied neither is stronger or more agile than the other."

"Have they always been so competitive?" The questions tumbled out. She was so eager to know all and could scarcely believe that the legendary Lady Cymbra was so approachable. Perhaps her being here was not such a bad thing after all.

"Yes, I think so, since they were both grown. But make no mistake, their loyalty to each other is absolute. And now, I am happy to say, they have extended that to include my own brother, who knew very little of loyalty in his life until he met those two and Krysta also."

"Forgive me, but that seems an odd thing to say about a lord so mighty. I would think he could command the loyalty of everyone around him."

They had reached the kitchens. Magda and the other women were rushing out to greet them. Cymbra turned and looked at Rycca directly. Her clear blue gaze seemed suddenly to look past all masks. What she saw must have pleased her for she smiled warmly, yet did a shadow of concern move behind her eyes. "Does the name Daria mean nothing to you?"

Slowly, Rycca shook her head. "No, nothing."

Cymbra sighed. "I feared as much. Dragon would not want to alarm you. Yet you must know."

She broke off then, holding out her arms to Magda, who swept her on into the kitchens. Rycca followed.

D ARIA," CYMBRA SAID A SHORT TIME LATER AS they sat on stools in the kitchen, sipping milk drawn from the deep cooling well where it was kept to chill, "is my half-sister and Hawk's. Our mother was our father's second wife. His first bore Daria. She was already grown when I was born and I knew her little, but this much I did know: She was married in her youth to a lord of Mercia who fancied himself a rival for the power of Alfred of Wessex. As Alfred worked to unite the country against the ravages of the Danes, her husband worked to betray him."

"Treachery seems commonplace among the lords of Mercia," Rycca murmured.

"That fellow Udell whom Hawk killed last year was Mercian, wasn't he?"

"He was, and as great a traitor who ever lived."

Cymbra nodded. "Such was also true of Daria's husband. In time, Alfred realized it. He met that lord in combat and defeated him, killing him in the process and seizing his lands as the law requires. Daria lost what she valued most, not the husband but the power and privilege she thought her due. She never recovered. Though Hawk provided her with a good home and even for a time gave her the running of Hawkforte, yet did she nurture great hatred of Alfred."

She broke off to settle her son more comfortably on her lap. Wolf had stopped by to leave the child with her, surprising Rycca with the easy competency he showed toward the boy. Remembering what Cymbra counseled about not allowing herself to be overwhelmed, she managed to look past the Wolf's formidable manner to see within the man who clearly loved his wife and child with all his heart. That he was also hurrying off to engage in mock combat with her husband was mildly worrying, to be sure, especially since they were both so obviously eager to wreak havoc on each other. Rycca consoled herself with the thought that they must have done the same before, probably many times, and survived it.

Besides, she was too preoccupied with the story Cymbra told to worry overmuch.

"About two years ago," Cymbra went on, "Wolf conceived the idea of an alliance between Norse and Saxon to stand against the Danes. He thought such an alliance would be best confirmed by a marriage between himself and me. This did he propose in a letter to my brother. With the help of a traitorous house priest, Father Elbert, Daria intercepted that letter and stole Hawk's seal as well. She sent back to Wolf a refusal in Hawk's name and mine that not merely rejected the alliance but also insulted him deeply. His response was all too predictable, although it is certain Daria herself never thought of it."

"What did he do?" Rycca asked, trying very hard not to sound breathless.

Cymbra smiled in fond memory. "Wolf came to Essex and took me by stealth. We were married as I told you and only then did he send word to Hawk as to where I could be found. Naturally, my brother was very angry and concerned. He came to Sciringesheal, where I did my utmost to convince him that I was happily wed, which certainly was true but unfortunately he did not believe. So are men ever stubborn. One thing led to another and Hawk spirited me back to Essex. Winter set in and it was months before Wolf could follow. During that time, Hawk realized his mistake. Once Wolf arrived, all was settled amicably, which was a good thing because this little one"—she smiled at her drowsy son—"had just been born and I was in no mood to put up with any more foolishness on the part of bull-headed men. It was while we were at Hawkforte, waiting as I regained strength to return home, that Wolf suggested Hawk and Dragon should also make marriages for the alliance."

"Such suggestion I am sure they both heartily welcomed," Rycca said sardonically.

Cymbra laughed. "About as much as they would being boiled in oil. Hawk was especially bad. He had been married years ago when he was very young and had no good memories of the experience. But I must say, Krysta brought him round in far shorter time than I would have thought possible."

"Do you have any idea how she did it?" Rycca ventured, hoping not to sound too desperately curious.

"Oh, I know exactly how." Cymbra looked at her new sister-in-law and smiled. "She loved him."

"Loved him? That was all it took?"

"Well, to be fair, I think she also maddened, irked,

frustrated, and bewildered him. All that certainly helped. But I will leave Krysta to tell her own story, as I am sure she will when opportunity arises. Let us return instead to Daria."

Cymbra looked off into the middle distance and sighed deeply. "Wolf and I came back to Sciringesheal still not knowing who had sent the false letter. Yet were we all determined to find out. In the meanwhile, Hawk and Krysta's marriage was arranged. Krysta came to Hawkforte and in time they were wed, but Daria remained determined to destroy the alliance. At the root of that determination was her hatred of Alfred. She reasoned, if any such as she can ever be said to reason, that the alliance strengthened the king in his stand against the Danes, which actually is true enough. Therefore, she set out to kill Krysta in such a way that Hawk would be blamed."

"To kill her? She actually meant to take her life?"

"Oh, yes, in fact she was quite set on it. As Krysta is Norse, Daria believed her murder seemingly at the hands of her Saxon husband would destroy all chances for the alliance and she was probably right. Fortunately, Krysta survived. Daria's guilt was discovered, as was Father Elbert's. He was turned over to Church authorities and Daria was banished to a convent, where she remains to this day."

Rycca let her breath out slowly, only then realizing she had been holding it as she learned of the woman who had blazed such a swath of hatred and havoc. "How terrifying all this must have been for you and for the Lady Krysta. To be wed under such circumstances and to face such danger . . . it makes me ashamed of my own reluctance and the troubles I myself have caused."

"Troubles? I have not heard of this."

Rycca glanced around at the other women who were still in the kitchen, though busy at their tasks. Her voice dropped. "Mayhap Lord Dragon does not wish it known."

"Then it shall not be." Quietly, Cymbra added, "But should you ever feel the need to speak, be assured I will not betray a confidence."

Truth. Shining, unequivocal truth.

Even as Rycca recognized that, Cymbra's expression changed. She looked puzzled suddenly and spoke as though to herself. "What was that?"

"What?" Rycca asked.

Cymbra withdrew slightly, sitting back on her stool. She held her sleeping son more closely but her gaze never left Rycca. "Just now when I spoke, I felt something. It seemed to come from you."

She could not have. That was impossible. And yet . . . *truth.* Again, the Lady Cymbra had spoken exactly what she knew to be fact.

"Again," she said, and this time her gaze locked on Rycca's. "It is you."

"No." In her haste to get to her feet, Rycca almost knocked her stool over. "Pray excuse me. I must see to your quarters."

And she was gone, hurrying out of the kitchen, wishing desperately even as she fled that there was somewhere, anywhere, she might be free of her own strange self.

S HE COULD NOT HIDE FOREVER, NOR WAS SHE foolish enough to try. In short order, Rycca collected herself and decided what she would do. First, she would apologize to the Lady Cymbra, explain that her coming was just a little unnerving but that she was not usually so foolish. Then would she do her utmost to stay away from her sister-in-law however long the lady remained at Landsende. That the friendship that had seemed to spring up so readily between them would die aborning was merely one more lack in a life well accustomed to them.

It seemed a good enough plan for what it was. Intent

upon it, Rycca spared only a little wonder for Cymbra's seeming ability to know what another felt. Maybe it simply came with being ethereally beautiful, supremely courageous, and perfect in every way.

Wolf, Dragon, and all their men were still on the training field where the practice combat with the Moorish swords continued and remained the center of all attention. For that, Rycca breathed a small sigh of relief. Magda and the other women would be busy preparing the feast to welcome the Lord Wolf and his wife. To that, she could contribute nothing. Best she take herself off and find some quiet place to remain until her presence was required.

She chose the pond where she and Dragon had frolicked what seemed now like too long ago. It was very quiet there. Save for a few sea birds, she was alone. But not for very long. Scant minutes passed before Cymbra marched up over the hill, carrying her son, and came straight to Rycca. She sat down right beside her on the damp ground, heedless of her exquisite garb, and settled her child.

"I know you want to be alone right now and I apologize for ignoring your wishes. But I think there is something I need to tell you."

Uncertain what to do, Rycca hugged her knees and stared at the water. "How did you know where I was?"

"This is a favorite spot for Wolf and me whenever we are here. I thought you and Dragon might like it too."

"He taught me to swim here, just yesterday." She spoke wistfully, as though the memory was already fading.

"Does he know?"

"Know what?"

"That you can feel what is truth."

Rycca turned her head and looked directly at Cymbra. "How can you possibly know that?"

"Think about it. How *could* I possibly know? What would I have to be able to do in order to know what you are feeling?"

"You would have to . . . feel the feelings of others."

Cymbra smiled gently. "And what better gift could a healer possibly possess?"

"You are saying . . . ?"

"That from earliest childhood I have been able to feel what others feel. It has been both blessing and curse. At first, I could not control it. That is the real reason why Hawk secluded me away in my own manor, not that nonsense you may have heard about not wanting men to fight over me. He would cheerfully have killed anyone who tried that. But until I learned how to build a wall to shut out the feelings of others, I was helpless. Eventually I did learn but I paid a high price. I lived behind that wall far too much. It was only after Wolf took me away that I learned I didn't really need walls, that I could live in the world and still have the strength to be as I am without being harmed by it."

Rycca nodded slowly even as she struggled to come to terms with what she had just learned. Such was the Lady Cymbra's reputation as a healer that some special gift did seem to be at work. But what a gift and what a formidable challenge to face, to be ever connected to everyone, able to feel what they felt, prey to their every emotion, fear, pain, all of it.

"It is not so terrible," Cymbra said. "I do know how to hold myself apart without sealing myself off. Can you do that?"

"No," Rycca admitted quietly. There seemed no point to concealing anything now, and the chance to unburden herself was far too tempting to deny. "Truth is truth, nothing stops it. Just as nothing stops knowing a lie for what it is."

"It felt to me like a shimmering, as though light had moved through me. Is that how it is for you?"

Rycca nodded. "By contrast, lies feel like a dark, suffocating cloud. There is never any question of which is which."

"But no one knows you have this ability?"

"I have kept it to myself although I think my brother, Thurlow, suspected. Had my other brothers or my father guessed, they would not have hesitated to kill me for being a witch."

Cymbra reached out and put her hand over Rycca's. Softly, she said, "I am sorry. But you are free of them now. Do you not think you could share this with Dragon?"

"Dragon, who was reluctant enough for this marriage and who now finds himself with a wife he can never hide anything from. Who will always know whether he is telling the truth or not. You think he would welcome such a wife?"

Cymbra thought for a moment. "Well . . . I don't know . . . Perhaps if you rubbed his feet?"

Rycca stared at her in shock, saw the look of pure deviltry in Cymbra's eyes, and burst out laughing at the same moment as her new sister-in-law—and friend—did the same. They laughed and laughed, not quieting until Lion stirred, gazed at them reproachfully, and opened his mouth to unleash a bellow that reverberated off the nearby hills and sent the sea birds scattering to safety.

"Oh, my heavens," Rycca said when it was finally quiet enough to say anything at all.

Cymbra sighed. She rose, picked up her son, and tried to settle his head back against her shoulder. "It has been ever such. He almost brought the rafters down in the chapel at Hawkforte where he was christened."

"It is most impressive," Rycca said as she, too, stood. "I suppose that accounts for his name."

"It's actually Hakon, to honor Wolf and Dragon's

father, but he is called Lion and I suspect he always will be."

Just as he would be satisfied only to be set down. On his own two feet, he toddled off determinedly toward the top of the hill, leaving the bemused women to follow.

Chapter

THIRTEEN

WOLF, CYMBRA—AND LION—REMAINED at Landsende for a week. For Rycca, the time went by far too quickly. She and Cymbra became fast friends, exploring the area for the herbs Cymbra always needed, talking about everything under the sun, and dissolving into such frequent gales of laughter that their husbands took to rolling their eyes every time they saw them. She even learned to relax in the presence of the Wolf, who, observing his brother's obvious happiness, dropped his stern demeanor. The evenings passed in conversation interrupted only by the stories Dragon was persuaded to tell. He had a seemingly endless supply and recounted them so well that Rycca found herself hanging on every word.

Taking note of this, Cymbra waited until Dragon had finished a tale before she said, "Don't you think Rycca would like to hear about Hadding, the warrior Odin rescued from his enemies? Indeed, so would I for as I recall, the last time I asked about him, you told the story in great haste without the scantiest details." There was a gleam in her eyes that Rycca had come to understand meant she was up to something, but she had no idea what might lurk behind so seemingly innocent a suggestion.

Dragon grinned and looked at his brother, who leaned back in his chair and laughed. When Rycca appeared puzzled, Cymbra said, "I confess, when I noticed how attentive you are to Dragon's stories I was reminded of myself. At Wolf's and my wedding feast, I persuaded Dragon to tell a great many tales. He was the soul of patience."

"*He* was?" Wolf interjected. "I was the one with the patience. My dear brother knew perfectly well I was sitting there contemplating various possibilities for doing away with him and he enjoyed every moment of it."

"Now how could I have known that, brother?" Dragon challenged. "Just because the wine goblet you were holding was twisted into a very odd shape?"

"It was that or your neck, *brother*," Wolf replied pleasantly. He looked at Rycca reassuringly. "Don't worry, if I hadn't already forgiven him, that sword he gave me would force me to."

"It is a magnificent blade," Dragon agreed. "They both are. Every smithy in Christendom is trying to work out what the Moors are doing but . . ."

"It's got something to do with the temperature of the steel," Wolf said.

"And with the folding. They fold more than we do, possibly hundreds of times."

"Hundreds, really? Then the temperature has to be very high or they couldn't pound that thin. I wonder how much carbon they're adding—"

Cymbra sighed. To Rycca, she said, "We might as well retire. They can talk about this for hours."

Wolf heard her and laughed. He draped an arm over her chair, pulling her closer. Into her ear, he said something that made the redoubtable Cymbra blush.

She cleared her throat. "Oh, well, in that case, you

might as well retire, too." Standing up quickly, she took her husband's rugged hand in her much smaller and fairer one. "Good night, Rycca, good night, Dragon. Sleep well." This last was said over her shoulder as she tugged Wolf from the hall.

Her obvious intent startled Rycca, who even now could not think of herself as being so bold, but it made both the Hakonson brothers laugh.

"As you may gather," Dragon said in the aftermath of the couple's departure, "my brother and his wife are happily wed."

"As are the Lord Hawk and Lady Krysta," Rycca said softly.

They were alone at the high table, those of Dragon's lieutenants who had shared it with them having taken themselves off earlier. Magnus had not been among them. He was away somewhere, visiting relatives or so Rycca had heard. She was glad of his absence for she could no longer deny the unease he prompted in her. A few servants still moved around the hall but the hour was late and soon they, too, would seek their beds.

The torches guttered low, casting long shadows across the center hearth left unlit on so pleasant a night. Shutters were thrown back to bare the windows, admitting a soft breeze. One of the many long, sleek dogs who frequented the stronghold was curled at Dragon's feet. Rycca found herself hard-pressed not to stare at her husband. To be fair, he was an excessively handsome man. His rugged features were perfectly formed, and as for the rest of him . . . She swallowed hastily. Probably the less she thought about his magnificent body right now, the better.

Quietly, Rycca said, "They are fortunate to have such happy marriages and doubly so, given the threat they faced."

Dragon reached for his wine goblet, twirling it idly between his fingers, but did not drink. Over the top of it, he regarded his lovely wife. She looked especially thoughtful this night. Her cheeks were flushed and fire seemed to dance in her eyes. He found himself staring at her mouth and looked away quickly. "Cymbra told you about Daria?"

"Yes, she did."

"I thought she would and that it would be better coming from her. You understand, of course, that the danger is passed. Daria will never be in a position to try to hurt anyone again."

"Cymbra told me she is in a convent."

"I would you had no misimpression. The convent in question treats the sick, including those disordered in their minds. The nuns are compassionate but no one's fools. They know what Daria did and tried to do. She is kept in closest confinement."

"And the priest?"

"The same at the chapter house of his order. He claimed little involvement save that he was in thrall to Daria but none believed that. Obviously, a man had to be at the center of their plotting."

"Why obviously?"

Dragon smiled. She was such a prickly little thing. How he adored soothing her, as he looked forward to doing shortly. *Very* shortly.

"Take no offense, my lady. I say that merely for practical reasons. The man who carried Wolf's message to Hawk, the letter proposing the alliance that set all this in motion, never returned. We presume him to be dead. While it is true Daria attempted to kill Krysta, we do not believe she could have killed a hale and hearty Norseman who was twice her size. By the same token, the response bearing Hawk's seal was brought by a Cornish trader who puts in frequently at Hawkforte and Sciringesheal. He is an honest man, known to both Wolf and myself. He said he was paid to bring it by a man wearing the Hawk's colors. We believe him but Daria had no authority over any of the Hawk's men and there is no reason to think any of them would have taken instruction from her."

"Has any man of the Hawk's ever come forward and admitted giving the message to the Cornisher?"

"No, which leads us to believe that man had reason to think the message could be false and has long since absented himself from Hawkforte."

"Or that he was never a Hawk's man to begin with, merely wearing the garb of one."

"Exactly. At any rate, whether he was one of the garrison or not, we doubt he took his orders from Daria. She was heartily disliked and treated with derision behind her back. No, there had to be a man involved, and that was Father Elbert." Dragon lifted her hand from where it lay in her lap and touched his lips gently to her smooth skin. "But you have nothing to fear from him either. The entire matter is over and done with."

He spoke with such assurance, and was so clearly convinced of the truth of what he said, that Rycca found it hard not to believe him. Yet did doubt linger. Even as they strolled together to their lodge and found there the private joy of their bed, some tiny portion of her mind continued to wonder at the man who seemed at the center of a plot to destroy the peace between two peoples. Try though she did to see him in the garb of a priest, he remained a shadowed figure, faceless and indistinct.

T HE WOLF-EMBLAZONED DRAKAR SAILED ON THE next morning's tide. Even as it pulled away from the stone quay, Cymbra and Rycca were still talking to each other, the one on deck, the other walking alongside on the dock. They continued until they could no longer hear, finishing with a pledge to meet again soon.

"She is only a day away," Dragon said comfortingly. "As soon as the harvest is in, we can visit Sciringesheal. Will that please you?"

In the circle of his arms, Rycca nodded. A little shyly, she said, "It is just that I have never had a woman friend before, or many friends at all, for that matter. Thurlow was one such but—"

"I would be another," Dragon murmured as he lightly traced the curve of her lips with his finger. "Which, I admit, is not how I envisioned being a husband, yet have my expectations been enlarged."

Deeply touched, Rycca smiled. Because she was so pleased, yet also to hide the intensity of her feelings, she said, "I am glad to hear that, my lord, for I feared you disappointed."

"How so, lady, could I have given you such a notion?"

"Only that I have yet to rub your feet."

Dragon's laughter drew the startled gaze of the others on the quay. "You have heard that, have you? I plead in my defense that I was young and foolish."

"And now you are much older and wiser."

"Not much but a little, enough to know what is good in my sight and my life."

She blinked very quickly then because the sun was in her eyes and it made them tear. So she told herself but did not try for a moment to believe.

They walked back up toward the stronghold arm in arm but before they got very far, a shadow fell across their path.

Magnus smiled apologetically as he inclined his head to Dragon. "Your pardon, lord, but I have only just returned and I regret there is a matter that requires your attention."

"Now?" Dragon asked, his gaze still on Rycca.

"Regrettably so. There is cargo missing from a merchant vessel that docked a few hours ago. As you will understand, the captain is upset."

That did get Dragon's notice. "He is claiming it was stolen here?"

Magnus shrugged. "He is strongly suggesting that."

"No port is better guarded than Landsende."

"I know that, lord, as do you. But . . ." He spread his hands.

Dragon sighed. He turned back to Rycca. "Forgive me, but if there is a thief among us, it is best I discover that quickly."

"Of course, I understand."

"Magnus, see my lady—"

"No!" Rycca spoke so swiftly and so firmly that both men looked at her in surprise. She moderated her tone and even managed to smile though she was determined to avoid the trusted lieutenant's company at all cost. "It is only that I would prefer to spend a little time in the town. I have seen very little of it and it seems quite appealing."

"I am glad you feel that way," Dragon said, "but it would be better for you to have an escort."

Rycca laughed, though she was far from amused. "My lord, never in my life have I seen a better ordered or more secure place. Every man, woman, and child here honors you. If I cannot go among them in perfect safety, then nothing in this world is assured, not even the regular rising and setting of the sun."

Dragon looked at her in amusement. "You flatter me but it is true nonetheless, Landsende is a safe place. You may do as you wish, but do not tarry too long for I will be delayed only briefly."

She did not doubt him, for in his topaz eyes she saw not the lover she had come to know but the leader who would tolerate no disregard of his law or of his will. A tiny shiver ran through her as she spared a moment's pity for the hapless and ill-advised thief.

The men went off, Magnus walking beside his lord, and Rycca was left to her own devices. After, that is, Dragon was no longer in her gaze. Until then, she stood, simply looking after him. With a sigh for her own susceptibility, she set off into the town. Before she had gone very far, her progress was slowed by the greetings of every man, woman, and child she passed. Everyone knew her and it seemed all were pleased to see her.

The men were cordial but cautious, inclining their heads, sometimes murmuring a word of welcome, but doing nothing that could possibly, by the wildest stretch of imagination, offend their lord. The women were friendlier, exchanging comments with her about the pleasant weather and offering little gifts, a brightly polished apple, a cup of cool well water mixed with the juice of freshly crushed berries, a small cloth bundle of sweetly scented herbs to tuck into her gown. She accepted all with shy thanks as a warm sense of pleasure grew within her.

The children added to it for they were the most open of all, following her with frank curiosity and good cheer. When they realized she welcomed their company, the bolder among them made suggestions as to what she should see and do. She was introduced to a litter of pups born scant days before, to a lame hawk recovering from a broken wing in the cottage of the smithy, to an aged woman who kept a pot of honey drops and handed them out generously to all the children. Children who were unlike any Rycca had ever known at Wolscroft, happy children who danced around her, squirming in their young bodies, laughing and smiling, their faces flushed with health and confidence.

Tucked in the curve between water and hills, prosperous and at peace, Landsende would be beautiful to any eye. But to Rycca the children made it a place that seemed almost magical to her, as though she stood in the heart of the strange world she had soared into so unexpectedly when she went hurtling off the cliffside.

Gladly would she have spent the entire day with the children and well she might have were it not for the dark cloud that seemed to sail across the bright day. It happened so suddenly and so surprisingly that for several moments Rycca hung suspended, uncertain what to do. Coming around a corner with the children, she glimpsed a man who appeared familiar to her. He was in his midtwenties, of medium height and slim build, dressed in simple garments a farmer or perhaps a sailor would wear, his brown hair loose at his shoulders and an intent, quick look on his slender face. A face she knew although for a moment she could not have said how. Then he slipped into place in her mind and she saw him there against the backdrop of the hall at Wolscroft, talking with her father.

A Wolscroft man here? In Landsende? How could that be? Mercia had no trade with the Norse, doing business with the Welsh and the tribes of Gaels across the Irish Sea. True, half of Mercia was under the rule of the Danes, but her father and the other Mercian lords in the half that remained English had nothing to do with them, fearing and loathing them as they did in equal measure.

Why then a Wolscroft man in Landsende? She must have been mistaken. After all, she had seen him for only a moment before he vanished around a corner toward the docks. Yet she found herself going in the same direction, to see if she might glimpse him again. She did not, and after a little while she began to feel foolish in her effort.

The children tried to draw her away, offering to show her the best places to fish in the streams just beyond the town. But before they could do so, Rycca caught sight of a large crowd gathered on one of the quays where a merchant vessel was docked. She moved closer, the children trailing after her, and tried to hear what was being said.

Dragon was at the center of the crowd. His simple garb worn for comfort and, Rycca suspected, ease of movement in combat, said little of his rank, yet there was no mistaking that he was lord here. In a crowd of supremely fit men bred for battle, his sheer size and strength singled him out. Yet was it his manner that revealed his power. His features were unreadable as he listened to a red-faced merchant sweating in his fine velvets.

"Studded with gems, lord! A goblet fit for the noblest of kings! The crowning piece of all my cargo! How am I to replace such a treasure? And what am I to tell my investors, those who trusted me to bring them home a fair profit?"

The jarl of Landsende did not reply at once but merely looked at the man from his considerably greater height and with such calm that the merchant who had begun his protestations with a righteous air soon sputtered into silence.

Only then did the Dragon speak, quietly and with the air of a man who is summoning patience. "Come." He turned and walked away, up toward the stronghold, with no notice given to who might or might not be following him.

Everyone did, of course, including Rycca, who was consumed with curiosity to see how her husband would handle the matter. For all the merchant's bombast, such a theft was serious. So too was the fear that might grow among other merchants that the port of Landsende was not, after all, a safe place to drop anchor. She had no doubt that Dragon would move quickly and firmly to snuff out any such thought. But how, exactly, he would do so remained a question.

With the rest of the crowd, she followed along up to the great hall. As she did so, she noticed a boy who was roughly dressed and had also been roughly handled. A livid bruise covered his left cheek and his hands were tied behind his back. The supposed thief looked utterly terrified, as he might well under the circumstances, but she also noted the defiant tilt of the head he fought to keep erect despite the cuffs he received from his escort, urging him to move more quickly.

Entering the hall, Rycca slipped past many of the others and found a place for herself behind a tall wooden pillar that helped to hold up the roof. She did not wish to attract attention, most especially since she was not certain her husband would want her there. But she was determined to see and hear all.

Dragon took a seat in the high-backed chair he used at meals. For this occasion, it had been brought out from behind the table and placed alone in clear view of everyone. The merchant, blustering with importance, jostled and shoved until he had a clear spot nearby. He glared at the youth who was brought forward to stand before the man who would judge him.

Rycca's heart tightened as she saw how truly afraid the boy was, yet she understood that such fear might merely indicate his guilt. Dragon looked at him silently for several minutes. Beneath such scrutiny, any man might be pardoned for shrinking but the boy still kept his head high. Even more remarkably, he looked straight at the powerful warlord who would decide whether he lived or died.

"What is your name?" Dragon asked at length.

"Olav, lord." His voice had a slight wobble but he spoke clearly.

"Of what line?"

"The line of Ragnarson of Hedeby."

Dragon nodded slowly. The boy was from the largest trading center in Jutland, therefore a Dane and of a respected house. Care was due in the judging of any man but this called for especially cautious handling.

"How came you to be on this voyage with Master Trygyv?"

The merchant tried to answer for him but Dragon waved him into silence. "You will have your turn, Master Trygyv. Right now it is for the boy to speak."

Yet did the lad hesitate. A flush crept over his face. Reluctantly, he said, "It was good for me to leave Hedeby for a while. Master Trygyv agreed to give me passage in exchange for my labor."

"I see. . . . And why did you think it wise to leave your home?"

The boy chewed his lip. The merchant looked as though the answer was about to burst from him. Only a stern look from Dragon kept him silent.

Finally, Olav said, "I displeased my father and he told me to get from his sight."

"A stern rebuke," Dragon noted. "What did you do to merit it?"

"I did not wish to marry the woman he had selected to be my wife."

Having so recently dealt with a similar problem himself, Dragon looked a little surprised but he hid it quickly. "An honorable son obeys his father."

"I am honorable!" Olav shot back. "But there are limits. . . . There must be." He glanced around him as though to see if any in the assembled crowd might agree with him. His gaze fell only on closed but watchful faces.

Desperately, the boy said, "The lady was twenty years older than I, thrice widowed and with only her wealth to recommend her. Am I to be blamed for wanting a wife to bring more than mere coin to my hearth?"

"And your bed!" someone shouted out suddenly and the crowd laughed. Olav looked startled and uncertain but managed a wan smile.

"Enough," Dragon said. "We are not here to judge your matrimonial difficulties but whether or not you took the missing goblet as Master Trygyv believes."

"As I know, lord!" the merchant shouted, unable to contain himself any longer. He pointed a plump finger at the hapless Olav. "I took him on against my better judgment merely out of pity for his situation. I gave him a chance to redeem himself, even mayhap to set his own feet on the road to wealth. And how does he repay me? He steals a kingly sum, enough for a drakar itself!"

"In that case," Dragon said dryly, "it must have been a very large goblet or at least a heavy one. Where do you think he could have hidden it?"

"I know not, lord. We docked only a few hours ago and I was occupied for most of the time since then. There was ample opportunity for him to remove it from my vessel and conceal it somewhere here in Landsende."

"That is a serious charge, Master Trygyv. It would mean someone here, in my town, was conspiring with a thief."

As though belatedly aware that it was not wise to offend so mighty a lord, the merchant backtracked hastily. "Many pass this way, great jarl. I only suspect another traveler of aiding the boy, not one of your own people."

"When did you last see the goblet?"

"When it was packed away in a wooden case built to protect it from harm during the voyage."

"Where was the case kept?"

"In the small accommodation I have for myself on board my vessel, but in the confusion of docking any man could have entered there."

Dragon's eyebrows rose. "There was no lock?"

"Yes, there was, on the case, but it was found broken." Trygyv glared at the boy. "I suspect he used a hammer of some sort."

"So he broke open the case, took the goblet, concealed

it somewhere upon himself, left your vessel, and gave the goblet to an accomplice?"

"Exactly!" the merchant exclaimed. "Lord, even as we speak the goblet may be taken from Landsende, never to be found again! Put this thief to the questioning, let him taste fire and steel! He will reveal its whereabouts."

Olav paled but not even the threat of torture caused him to lower his head. Rycca took note of that, for it affirmed what she already knew. She edged forward, ready to intervene quickly if that should prove necessary.

But Dragon did not appear disposed to take up the merchant's suggestion. Instead, he asked, "How would he have known the goblet existed? Did you speak of it openly?"

"Well . . . no—of course not. But obviously he learned of it somehow. He must have heard about it in Hedeby before we left. That is probably the reason why he approached me."

"Are any of your men missing?"

Trygyv shook his head gravely. "They are all accounted for, lord, and may I add, they are all good men long known to me. None of them had anything to do with this."

Dragon nodded slowly. He turned to the boy.

"Olav Ragnarson, you have heard the charges against you. Do you still maintain your innocence?"

"I do, lord! I knew nothing of any goblet and I never left the vessel after we docked except to help with the unloading. I went no farther than the quay."

"Then you handed it to someone there," Trygyv insisted.

Dragon held up a hand. "Enough." He looked around at the assembled crowd. "Does any other man have testimony to give in this matter?"

When no one spoke, Dragon said, "It appears no one saw this boy near your quarters, Master Trygyv, much less saw him take the goblet or give it to another. Lacking any such witness, how did you come to believe he was guilty?"

"Because of his manner, lord! He is an arrogant pup who thinks himself too good for honest working men and—"

"That is not true!" Olav interjected, the first time he had interrupted the proceedings. "No man can say I did not carry my full share of the work or that I put myself above any man. I did all that was required of me and shirked nothing." He seemed truly offended by the idea that he could be capable of such behavior.

This time, several heads nodded. Seeing that, Trygyv burst out again, "He is foresworn, lord! By his own father. I was the fool to trust such a man, but can I be blamed for wanting to help a boy? Little did I know I took a viper to my breast."

The merchant turned to the assembled crowd, addressing all there. "Who can put faith in a man who fails to uphold the will of his own father? Who dishonors his family? Who is sent from the sight of all respectable people, cast as a wolf upon the mercy of wind?"

This appeared to have some effect, for again several men nodded. But not Dragon, who merely stared at the plump merchant with a curious smile. "Master Trygyv, I myself was so cast, as was my brother, who, you may recall, bears the name of Wolf. That was not the name he was given at his birth any more than I was called Dragon. Yet did we both become such men when we found ourselves loosed into the world without family or friend."

"Through no fault of your own, lord! This is a different situation altogether. This boy was already foresworn and now he is a thief."

"That, Master Trygyv, remains to be seen. I have heard no evidence against him, save your own suspicions."

In the shadow of the pillar, Rycca breathed more easily, yet still she waited to see how her husband would resolve the matter.

"Then put him to the torture, lord! Force him to speak the truth!"

There was a rustling in the crowd, a murmur as though men spoke to themselves about the wisdom of such a course. It was, after all, tradition. From one end of the vast world to the other, men were tortured to make them yield up truth. The very idea of not doing so seemed odd in the extreme.

But not to the Dragon, who said quietly, "A man may say anything if he is made to bear enough pain."

"Not I!" Olav exclaimed. He was pale and rigid, but he held his slender body with the pride of a warrior. "I will never yield! I had no hand in this matter and I will never say otherwise regardless of what you do to me!"

"See how boastful he is, lord?" Trygyv said. "See what an exalted sense of himself he has, he who rightly should be ground down by the enormity of the offense he gave to his own family. Truly, lord, Ragnar of Hedeby would thank you for ridding him of so false a son."

"I know Ragnar of Hedeby," Dragon said. He did not raise his voice in the slightest yet his words carried to everyone gathered in the great hall of Landsende. "We have done business together. He is a hard man, true enough, and not one who would tolerate being crossed by anyone, including his own son. But neither is he a monster. If this boy dies, Ragnar will mourn him."

Olav looked stricken by this, torn between hope and yearning. For the first time, he lowered his head, but not before Rycca saw the quick sheen of tears in his young eyes.

Compelled by them, she stepped forward. Her sudden appearance caused a start of surprise in the crowd. She ignored it, as she ignored the rapid beating of her heart, and moved quickly to her husband's side. Before he could say anything, she bent close to his ear and whispered, "I know I am intruding and I am sorry but I must speak with you."

Hiding his surprise at her sudden appearance, Dragon said quietly, "Lady, I am occupied here. A man's life hangs in the balance."

"It is of that I would speak. Please, hear what I have to say but privately for it is only between us."

So filled with entreaty was her voice that Dragon could not deny her. Even as he puzzled over why she should behave in such a way, he rose. "I will return in a moment," he said to all assembled and, taking his wife's hand, left the hall.

Outside, behind the kitchens, which were empty as everyone attended the trial, he said, "You must be quick. Have you knowledge of this matter?"

"Yes, I do. Trygyv is lying."

"Did *you* see something? Is that why you came forward?"

"No, I didn't see but I still know." Praying he would understand, she said, "Dragon, we spoke of trust. Now I must trust you with the deepest secret that I have. There is only one other person in the world I have ever spoken with about this and that is Cymbra." At his startled look, Rycca explained, "And then only because she already knew, having felt what I felt."

She waited to see if he would express ignorance of Cymbra's gift but he only nodded. "What did she feel?"

Quickly, before she could think again about the wisdom of what she was about to do, Rycca replied, "Truth. She felt it through me because it is what I feel. Always since I was a small child it has been thus. When anyone speaks, I know if their words are true or not."

He looked at her for what seemed like a very long time. Finally, he said, "I have never heard of such a thing."

And he knowing the stories of the wide world. Her heart dropped, yet she persevered. "Perhaps there has been no other like me, I do not know. I only know what I am. If it displeases you, I am sorry, but I cannot change. I can no more stop knowing what is truth than I can stop breathing."

"Let us say just for the moment that you are right about this and you really can tell who is speaking truth and who is not. You say Trygyv is lying? About what, exactly?"

"Not about the goblet. That really does exist and he did bring it here with him. But he is lying about everything else. He does not suspect Olav, not really, and he did not hire Olav because he felt sorry for him. He had some other reason, I know it not, but it was not that."

"What reason would a merchant traveling with a goblet worth a king's ransom have for taking on a foresworn man?"

Rycca shook her head slowly. She truly did not know.

But Dragon did, or at least he strongly suspected. "Unless he knew the goblet would come amiss . . ."

Her eyes widened. "And needed someone to blame it on, a likely suspect."

"We do not know this. It is only a possibility."

"Yet you can ask him and I can listen to his answer."

He studied her very closely. "You are asking me to decide a man's life on this strange gift you claim."

"No, I am not. There must be some evidence. I am only asking you to look for it."

They had been away from the hall too long and could not linger further. With the usual decisiveness of his nature born in battle, Dragon accepted this. "So be it. But you will keep silent and speak only when we are in private."

"I was about to ask that of you. I would greatly prefer no one else know."

"That I cannot promise you, but for the moment at least, it will be so."

They returned to the hall together, Dragon to resume his seat and Rycca to take up a place a little to the side of him but clearly within his sight. Within the sight, as well, of all those gathered there with ample time to wonder why the jarl had absented himself in the midst of such serious business to speak with his Saxon wife.

Not that anyone said as much or even looked amiss. They simply waited for the jarl to get on with it.

FOURTEEN

MASTER TRYGYV," DRAGON ASKED, "DO you really fear that your goblet may be taken away from Landsende and you never see it again?"

The merchant drew himself up, set his features in an expression of the utmost solemnity, and said, "I do so fear, my lord. Indeed, I dread that it may have already happened."

Very slightly, just enough for Dragon to see, Rycca shook her head.

"In that case," the jarl said, "we must seek the goblet immediately. All else can wait."

"But the boy will tell us if he is put to the question!" Trygyv insisted.

"Are you so anxious for torture, merchant? If the son of Ragnar has committed this crime, I do not believe he will be forced to speak of it short of his own death, which will profit you nothing, as he will take with him the whereabouts of the goblet. If he is innocent, torturing him will avail us nothing for he will know nothing of any use. Therefore, there is no reason to tarry at it. Rather, the town must be searched immediately and your vessel as well, from bow to stern, every nook and cranny. I will put my men to it at once."

Before Trygyv could comment further, Dragon raised a hand, summoning Magnus. To him alone, he said, "Organize the men. Concentrate on the vessel and any place Trygyv is known to frequent in the town. He has been here before. There may be somewhere he prefers for drinking or a woman he fancies."

Magnus nodded quickly. He cast a curious glance in Rycca's direction but hurried to do his lord's bidding.

Most of the townspeople, along with the crew of the merchant vessel, made their way back down to the quays to watch the men-at-arms. Only a few dutiful housewives went home instead, just to be certain no brash man stuck a grimy hand into their clean laundry.

Several hours passed. Just as Dragon had ordered, the search was thorough. Every inch of the vessel was examined, from the cargo hold to the below-deck area where the crew slept to the spaces beneath the benches where the oarsmen sat. So, too, every barrel and bundle on the quays was checked, as was every building nearby where an accomplice or Trygyv himself might have gone.

While all this went on, Olav was untied with the warning that he stay close to Dragon. This he did most willingly. The two of them fell to talking of business and where a young man might be likely to make his fortune. Seeing them in amicable conversation, Trygyv became even more red-faced and agitated. When he could contain himself no longer, he approached Dragon.

"We are wasting time, lord! The goblet is not here." He pointed at Olav. "This one has already spirited it away. Your refusal to force him to speak has assured the success of his crime."

Rycca took it as a sign of the man's extreme nervousness that he would be so foolish as to suggest the jarl of

Landsende was responsible for the loss of the goblet. She waited to see how Dragon would react but he merely shrugged. Yet did she have the keen impression he had taken close note of what Trygyv had said. Dragon's gaze went to the merchant vessel, where his men were still searching, going over the same places again and again.

Quietly, he said, "It has to be somewhere. The only place we have not searched is the water itself and I hardly think whoever took it threw it overboard."

Just as he spoke, Rycca caught the quick flash of panic in Trygyv's eyes. So did Dragon. An entirely humorless smile lifted the corners of his mouth, baring his teeth. Gesturing to his wife to follow him, the jarl stepped onto the vessel.

"My ship has already been searched thoroughly," Trygyv protested. "You are wasting yet more time."

Dragon did not reply but continued along to the small shelter on the deck that was Trygyv's quarters. He ducked his head to enter, then emerged a moment later. This time his smile was genuine.

"Olav, come here."

Without hesitation, the young man obeyed. Dragon pointed to a rope extending from beneath the shelter and over the side of the vessel to disappear beneath the water line. "Pull that up, will you?"

If Olav thought it odd the jarl would ask him to perform so simple a service rather than just doing it himself, he said nothing of that. Instead, he hauled on the rope, which came up swiftly, dripping strands of seaweed and—

Olav gasped. "Frigg and all her handmaidens, what is that?"

The glow of the sun rose out of the dark sea, gleaming as the light hit it, exploding with color. . . .

Rycca stared in amazement. She had seen many beautiful things of late but nothing quite so stunning as the goblet. Formed of beaten gold and studded with precious stones, it was so large that she doubted she could lift it easily. Fit for a king indeed, and a strong one at that.

Dragon took the goblet from Olav, who continued to stare at it in amazement. Shaking the last of the water off the dazzling cup, Dragon said, "A good plan, Master Try-gyv, so far as it went. But not good enough."

The merchant was already backing away, trying to reach the dock, although where he thought he would go from there, Rycca could not imagine. It mattered not, for several of his own men seized him.

"Let me go! I have done nothing!"

Dragon silenced him with a single look. "I think," the jarl said, his voice carrying to all those assembled on the vessel and the surrounding quays, "you plotted to make off with the goblet from the beginning. You schemed to claim it was stolen, then sell it for yourself and keep the profit from those who invested in your voyage. To that end, you leaped at the chance to hire Olav, a man disgraced, and one you believed you could blame for your crime."

"No! I did not . . . I swear . . ."

Dragon went on remorselessly. "I saw Olav's expression when he caught sight of the goblet and I am certain he never saw it before. No one saw him enter your quarters or leave the area of the quay. There is no evidence to suggest he is guilty of the theft. On the other hand, the goblet was found concealed within easy reach of you, Master Trygyv. It would have been a simple matter for you to wait until your vessel sailed again, then under cover of darkness pull the rope up and recover the goblet. No one would have seen you do it or been any the wiser."

"You cannot prove it," Trygyv insisted, but his voice shook and his whole manner was that of a man caught in a vise of his own making.

"No, I cannot," Dragon agreed almost pleasantly. "But I don't have to. Olav—"

Again the young man stepped forward. He looked at Dragon with unconcealed respect and admiration. "I would never have thought to look where you did."

"When every other possibility has been eliminated, the one that is left has to be the right one. Here—" He handed the goblet to the stunned young man. "Take this and Master Trygyv with it to your father in Hedeby. Tell him all that has happened and let him be the judge of it." He gestured at the crew, every man among it looking well satisfied with what had transpired. "These men will vouch for what has occurred here and for this as well: Tell Ragnar of Hedeby I congratulate him on having a son of courage and pride who brings honor to his name. If he cannot find a warm and comely bride for you, I will be happy to do so."

This brought cheers and laughter from the assembled crowd, among them several young women bold enough to call out their own offers. Olav blushed fiercely but he looked as well pleased as any man could be.

Yet the Dragon was not finished. "Oh, and, Olav, you drew the goblet from the sea. By law, that makes it yours. I trust you to do right by Master Trygyv's investors but the rest of the profit belongs to you."

Rycca almost laughed then for the boy so lately in disgrace and threatened with death appeared scarcely able to comprehend that he had been suddenly transformed into an honored—and wealthy—man. So too did she come very close to bursting with pride. Her husband might as easily have pulled the goblet up himself and thereby become its rightful owner. Yet he gave it to a boy who needed it far more, and who with it received an entirely different life. Such generosity was the very hallmark of honor.

Thus did the Dragon's people think as well, for they cheered their jarl mightily as he left the vessel. He smiled and acknowledged their acclaim but his gaze sought

Rycca. She came to his side, slid her hand into his, and together they walked back up to the stronghold.

There they lingered only a little time at supper, absenting themselves so early as to prompt smiles and a few encouraging remarks from Dragon's lieutenants. All except Magnus, who sat silently, seemingly deep in thought, yet he looked swiftly at Rycca when she stood. For just a moment, their eyes met. An odd shiver moved through her but she forgot it promptly, wrapped in the warmth of her husband's smile.

Wrapped in his arms, as well, long before they reached their lodge. Scarcely had they stepped from the hall than Dragon, hardly breaking stride, lifted her high against him and continued swiftly on his way. Rycca laughed and held on to his broad shoulders. "I can walk, you know," she teased.

"Not as fast as I can." He looked absolutely serious, as though the scant extra moments it would have taken her to reach the lodge unaided were more than he could bear.

Before she had time to contemplate this, he was kicking the door closed behind him. No braziers or candles had been lit but moonlight poured through the unshuttered windows. Dragon went straight to the bed but did not put her on it. Instead, he set her on her feet right next to it.

"I should be better than this," he muttered as he stripped off his clothes. "I've never had any trouble with control. But the more I make love to you, the less control I have. I don't understand what is happening to me."

Truth. He was genuinely bewildered and even perhaps a little alarmed. Rycca hid a smile or tried to. It danced in her eyes.

"Oh, you think that's funny?" Dragon said. "But then you're the woman who ran straight off a cliff. Good sense isn't your strong point."

"Perhaps not."

One dark brow rose. "So agreeable?"

"You were wonderful today. What you did for that boy was amazing."

He looked at her in genuine surprise. "I did nothing but what was right."

"You refused to have him tortured or to presume he was guilty. And when you realized he was innocent, you gave him back his life, with his father, his family, the future he would never have had otherwise."

Dragon shrugged dismissively. "Rycca, sweetling, I hate to puncture your pretty fantasy but the fact is I don't especially want Ragnar of Hedeby as an enemy. I gave him the perfect excuse to take his son back and I sent the boy home to him rich. He will be indebted to me forever."

"Be as cynical about it as you like, but you still did what was right and we both know it."

"Enough of Olav. Take off your clothes. Better yet, I'll do it."

"Oh, no!" She stepped back quickly in alarm, which prompted a swift frown from him. It vanished when Rycca said, "I saw how you manhandled that tunic. You aren't about to do the same to this gown. Just wait a moment. . . ."

Even as she spoke, she deftly undid the laces down the side of the garment and lifted it carefully but quickly over her head. Her husband was in a mood, ridden by tension she could not understand. She wanted to placate him, yet she also wished to surrender to the urges he so effortlessly unleashed within her.

Naked save for the gauzy chemise that hid nothing from his eyes, she stood before him, her head lifted proudly to conceal the quivering she felt within. She gloried in his gaze, hot and potent, raking over her. But when he reached for her, she stepped back again.

"I ask a boon, lord."

She had never asked him for anything—save freedom and that he could not give. Caught, knowing he could hardly refuse, Dragon rasped, "What?" He had not meant to be so curt but speech was almost beyond him. He wanted her with a desperation he had never felt before save every time he lay with her, and even then he usually managed to maintain some semblance of control. Not now. He burned, his body drawn bow-taut. If he did not sheathe himself soon within his wife's silken depths . . .

She looked at him directly, her eyes wide and candid. "All day I have wanted to . . . touch you."

His dark brows rose. All day? Well, that was certainly pleasing but it didn't make his condition any easier to bear. Harshly, he said, "You don't have to ask permission to touch me."

She shrugged her lovely, almost bare shoulders. "I know, but under the circumstances . . ." Her gaze drifted down his body, rather pointedly, he thought.

Which definitely did not help matters at all.

"You can touch me later," he said and reached for her again.

She pressed her palms against his chest, tossed back her gleaming hair, and laughed. Really, he was going to die from this.

"Just a little now . . . please?"

Dragon squeezed his eyes shut and reached deep down inside himself for the control that was so intrinsic a part of his warrior's nature. It had to be in there somewhere. Any moment now he'd stumble across it.

Her nails grazed his flat nipples. He groaned deep in his throat. "Your body amazes me," Rycca said softly. "Before I met you, it never occurred to me that a man could be beautiful. But you are . . . everything about you is so perfectly formed, so powerful . . . so very different from myself."

This he knew. It was the marvel of nature, the greatest of the great gods' accomplishments. Or of God, he knew not nor did he care. Naught mattered save the effect of his wife's touch.

She moved closer, the fragrance of her tantalizing him as her hands stroked lightly over his chest. "You have such strength," she said softly, "but you have never hurt me. I find that remarkable."

"I am very careful not to hurt you," he said, his voice thick.

Rycca nodded. "I appreciate that."

She touched his lean hips and beyond, lightly caressing the hard muscles of his buttocks. He gritted his teeth and swore to himself that he could bear this. She was very close to him now, the thin cloth of her chemise brushing against him. He found that barrier intolerable. Plucking at the fabric, he muttered, "Take it off."

She looked a little surprised, then smiled. "The truth is, I feel safer with it on, a little bolder."

"Little?" He wanted to say more, something about her being any bolder and he would burst, but he couldn't get the words out. Probably because he wasn't breathing very well.

Rycca hesitated but only a moment. With the gracefulness so natural to her, she lifted the chemise over her head and discarded it. In the silvery moonlight, her skin glowed like polished alabaster, pale but for the rosy fullness of her nipples and the fiery curls between her thighs. He reached for her urgently, but once again she eluded his grasp.

"Please . . ." she said again and took his thick wrists in her hands. Drawing them away from her body, she raised her head and met his eyes. "You can't realize how much I want to . . ."

"Thor's thunder, lady, do whatever you will before I perish!"

Her eyes widened yet more and a startled laugh broke from her. Then her expression was suddenly wistful. "Do not think badly of me."

Badly? How in all creation could he manage that? She was a dream brought to life, the most exquisitely seductive enchantress he had ever imagined. And she was his by the law of man and God. In all the wide world, how could a man ask for more?

A moment longer she lingered, meeting his eyes, and then, before his startled gaze, his warrior wife, proud and valiant, mysterious and beguiling, sank to her knees. Dragon gasped. His head fell back and the muscles of his throat tightened. He had known the services of concubines so skilled that they boasted they could bring a man to madness. While he had enjoyed their company, never had he thought himself lost with any of them.

This was different. At the first warm touch of her breath, the first stunning flick of her tongue, reality dissolved. There was nothing save the heat churning with him, the convulsive tension of his body, and the fleeting thought that the world could end and he would not bestir himself to care.

His hands clenched into fists as he fought the urge to take swift hold of her. She wanted this. So did he, even if it was likely to kill him. He could bear it . . . he could. . . . He was a warrior, a man of strength and endurance. He would not be undone by a woman, no matter what pleasure she gave. He would hold on . . . fight the savage pressure building within him. She would surrender to him, not the other way around.

But she was not as other women. There was something in her, some gift of the gods that set her apart. She took him fully within her mouth and he cried out, trembling on the very brink.

His response enthralled Rycca. His scent, his taste,

everything about him was as a potent stroking deep within, arousing her almost unbearably. She gloried in her power to give him pleasure even as her blood ran molten and consciousness of all save him faded away.

A tiny, salty drop settled on her tongue, tantalizing her just as a savage groan broke from Dragon. The control of a lifetime, hard-won, rooted at the very core of his being, broke. He reached down, lifting her and in the same movement twining her legs around his hips. Beyond thought, mercy, any consideration other than the savage need of his own body, he took two steps and pressed her against the wall. Holding her there, he reached down, opened her to him, and with a single thrust of his hips, penetrated her to the hilt.

Unable to move, Rycca could only wind her arms around his powerful shoulders and cling to him. Touching him, savoring him, had left her yearning for the completion he now pushed her toward. Even as her body stretched to accommodate his fullness, he gave no quarter but drove into her again and again. She buried her head against his chest and sobbed his name. Their lovemaking was raw, swift, and tumultuous. In the space of mere heartbeats, the world shattered.

Long moments passed before Dragon could think of moving. His chest felt constricted, his breathing ragged. He was dazed and disbelieving. Surely he had imagined what had just happened. But the deep, profound satisfaction of his body said otherwise. So did the fact that he was still holding the woman he had just used so savagely up against the wall. *His wife.*

He shook his head fiercely, trying to deny what could not be denied. How could he, who had always treated women with the utmost consideration and gentleness, have done such a thing? And how must she feel? Distantly, her sob echoed in his ears. Horror roared through him, as intense in its own way as the pleasure that had preceded it.

Quickly, he carried her over to the bed and laid her down. "Sweetheart, it's all right . . . I'm so sorry . . . I've never . . ."

Her eyes flicked open, heavy-lidded and slumberous. Something very ancient danced in their honeyed depths. Slowly, languorously, she stretched. Dragon watched her exquisite body arch against the fur throws on the bed and blinked in astonishment. Surely he misunderstood . . . it was too much to hope that . . .

"Hmmm, what did you say?" Her voice was velvet soft and just a little raspy. Gently, she touched his face.

"That I am . . . sorry?"

Her eyes cleared. "What on earth for? That was wonderful, magnificent." She stretched again and a small, amazed laugh escaped her. "I think my bones melted."

Relief roared through him. He, too, laughed and flung himself down on the bed beside her. He should have known better, should have realized that his warrior woman was a match for him in every way. Gathering her to him, he stroked the slender line of her back as she sighed contentedly. But scant moments later, her mood changed. She raised herself on her elbows and looked at him. "You seemed . . . tense before."

Dragon was drifting very close to sleep when he heard her. He didn't open his eyes but a smile lifted the corners of his mouth. "Tense? Sweetling, I was rock hard. 'Tense' really doesn't come close to describing what I—"

She swatted at him. He opened his eyes cautiously. "That's not what I meant," Rycca said. "When we left the hall, you were in such a hurry."

"To make love with you."

"Hmmm, that's nice. But usually you linger. This time you were in a rush before I did anything. You seemed strained, as though something bothered you."

Dragon sighed. He should have known better than to think he could hide his feelings from her. His wife seemed to need no special gift to understand his emotions. But she did possess a gift that set her apart, or so she believed, and it was that which troubled him.

He turned over onto his side, drawing her into the curve of his body, and lightly touched her cheek. "Did you mean what you said today?"

"What I said?" She turned her head and looked at him over her shoulder. "About what?"

"Truth."

"Did I mean that I know when people are telling the truth and when they are lying? Yes, of course I did. You saw with Olav . . ."

"I saw you defend a Dane. That was startling enough."

She had not thought of that, had not even considered, in her eagerness to save the innocent boy, that he was one of those she feared so terribly. "I did not—"

"Yes, you did."

"I mean I did not think of it."

He squeezed her gently. Perhaps his hope that she could put the past behind her was becoming real. Yet could that really happen if she was right about her strange ability? What did it mean to live in a world where truth always stood apart from lies? He could not imagine such a thing, nor did he wish to deceive his wife in any matter. Yet he disliked the idea of being always and utterly exposed in every word he said. There were times when a man needed to be . . . subtle.

Yes, that was the word. Not dishonest but careful in the choosing of his words and the shading of their meaning. A man should be able to do that and still be sure of his wife's trust in him, not concerned she might be judging him a liar. It was that uncertainty rankling him that had driven him when he took her from the hall. He had wanted to affirm his possession of her but never had he imagined he would do so as he had. Indeed, he was still amazed—and not a little concerned—at how easily she had shattered his control.

"How long," he asked quietly, "have you believed you were a truthsayer?"

"I cannot remember a time when I was not as I am now."

"Were you never tempted at Wolscroft to reveal this strange gift of yours?"

Drowsily content, Rycca shook her head. "My father cared naught for truth or lies. He condemned men as he chose, regardless of whether they had actually done anything. Just as likely, he freed men who were every manner of criminal because they paid him to do so or provided some other service for him. Had I spoken, it would have availed nothing save cause me to be burned for a witch."

His arms tightened around her as he silently cursed Wolscroft for the brutal dolt he was. How any man could have so lovely a daughter and not cherish her was beyond knowing. For that matter, how could any man fail to cherish such a wife? He certainly did even as he remained uneasy. Far in the back of his mind, he could never forget that she had not wanted their marriage. She wanted to be free.

"Rycca?"

"Hmmm?" She sounded almost asleep.

"Never mind." He would let her rest and hope to do the same himself. There would be time later to solve the mystery of her, to discover whether a tormented child had spun a fantasy of power for herself or if, incredibly, there was really something to it. For the moment, it was enough that she was where she belonged, in his arms.

And in his heart. Ah, yes, that was the problem, wasn't it? He *loved* her. He, who had loved so very many women, *loved* the fire-haired warrior woman who ran like the wind and sailed over cliffs. Who met his passion with her own, beguiled and bewildered him, and made him long for what he had never thought possible.

Somewhere, Loki was laughing.

FIFTEEN

M Y LADY," MAGDA SAID, "THERE IS SOME-
thing you should see."

She spoke very quietly yet Rycca heard
the alarm in her voice. She gave up brushing
Grani's mane and, ignoring the horse's protest, followed
the older woman from the stable. "What is the matter?"
Rycca asked when they were outside.

Magda glanced around to make sure they were not
overheard. Still very quietly, she said, "There is a problem
in the weaving shed."

It was late afternoon. The yard at the center of the
stronghold was almost deserted. Most people had finished
their tasks and gone off to the nearby pools and streams to
bathe and relax before beginning preparations for supper.
The weaving shed was likewise empty. Earlier in the day,
the women who had charge of the weaving had moved
their tall looms outside into the fresh air to do their work.
But now the looms were back inside the shed, heavy with
the effort of many days' labor to craft the fabric needed to
make garments.

Except that no garments would be made from this

cloth. Rycca gasped and stared in disbelief. All the looms were slashed, cut straight through the warp and woof, so that the fabric on them hung in shreds.

"Sweet heaven . . ." she murmured.

"I found them like this just a few minutes ago," Magda said grimly. "I couldn't remember if the women had enough thread for tomorrow and I wanted to check."

"Who could have done such a thing?"

"I have no idea. Nothing like this has ever happened before. The women are at the stream, bathing. They put the looms away no more than an hour ago."

"Then someone came in here between then and now, and did this." As she spoke, Rycca touched the tattered remains of the cloth. Her hand shook. The fabric was cut through with what must have been a very sharp blade. Speed would have been essential since anyone could have walked in at any moment. But there was also an aura of deliberate violence in the way each and every loom was slashed, as though someone had worked in a swift fury.

"Master Trygyv's vessel sailed this morning, didn't it?"

Magda nodded, her expression making it clear that the same thought had occurred to her. "I checked and it did." Her gentle face creased with worry. "I cannot imagine who could have done this. Landsende is a peaceful place. There are no troublemakers here."

Rycca did not doubt that for she knew full well her husband would never have tolerated any such. But someone had done it and that raised the question of who would be so foolish as to provoke the ire of the Dragon.

"We must tell the jarl," Magda said softly.

"Yes, of course. He is on the training field right now but I will tell him when he returns. When the women come back from the stream, I will also tell them. They have worked enough today and should rest. Tomorrow will be soon enough to remove what is left and begin anew."

Rycca thought for a moment, then added, "I will ask my lord to have a sturdy lock put on the door here. I don't really think whoever did this would be so foolish as to try it again, but it is still better to take precautions."

Magda nodded. She looked relieved to have someone else take charge of the matter. It had not occurred to Rycca to do otherwise, yet she was a little surprised to realize how readily she was slipping into her role as the mistress of Landsende. All the same, the destruction in the weaving shed troubled her greatly. Beyond the waste of the women's work, it bespoke an angry and unstable temperament unseen and unsuspected existing among them.

Rycca was still thinking about who that might be several hours later when Dragon returned to their lodge. He had bathed and was freshly garbed but it made no matter. Grubby and sweat-stained, he looked just as glorious to her. She restrained the impulse to hurl herself at him and instead poured him a cup of wine.

He took it with a nod of thanks and an appreciative look that warmed her to her toes. With an effort, she dragged her attention back to the matter at hand.

"My lord, there has been an . . . incident in the weaving shed. I am sorry to trouble you with it but I think you must know and I also need your approval to put a lock on the door to the shed."

Dragon set down the wine he had just tasted, reined in his thoughts of how soon he could properly take his wife to bed again, and frowned. "What sort of incident?"

Briefly, Rycca told him. Before she finished, his frown had deepened. He stood before her very much the Lord of Landsende, calm, controlled, but completely focused on the trouble that had come into his domain. "You saw no sign of whoever could have done this?"

"No, none, but I must also tell you that yesterday

morning when I was in the town, I thought for a moment that I saw a man I remembered from Wolscroft. I have no idea if he could have had anything to do with this."

"We have no trade with Mercia. There is no reason for anyone from there to be here, save for you, of course. How sure are you that you recognized the man?"

"I could be mistaken," Rycca admitted. "I only caught a glimpse of him. But if he is not the man I remember, he looks extraordinarily like him."

"Then we must try to find him. Tell me of his appearance."

When Rycca had done so, Dragon sighed. "That describes perhaps a third of the men in Landsende. Is there nothing that would set him apart?"

"Not really, but I would know him if I saw him again."

"I do not want you going about the town until we have gotten to the bottom of this."

She thought to argue with him but one look at her husband's face stopped her. His authority would not be challenged by her or anyone else. Yet still she might have tried but for knowing that he was right. If someone from Wolscroft was at Landsende, it was unlikely he had come for any good purpose.

"Perhaps this is only an isolated incident," she said.

"Let us hope so," Dragon agreed. "My men will ask after anyone unknown. If he is here, we will find him."

Unless, Rycca thought, he had already left. But she did not say that. For just then, Dragon shucked off his concern as a man might drop a wet cloak. He smiled in that way that never failed to make her toes curl and reached for his wife.

Later still, as she drowsed, she felt him rise from their bed. He moved quietly and she remembered how easily he had come upon her without her hearing. Shortly, he was dressed and left the lodge. When she emerged a little while later, she saw some of the men-at-arms moving down toward the town. If the man from Wolscroft was there, he would be found.

B UT HE WAS NOT, NOT THAT DAY OR THE NEXT. Indeed, the looms were repaired, the weaving was resumed, and the destroyed cloth was replaced before there was a hint that the man might still be present.

"My lady," Magda said. Her gentle face was lined with worry and her hands, clasped in front her, twisted anxiously. "I am sorry but . . . there is a problem in the kitchen. If you would come see—"

Rycca lay off currying Sleipnir and went quickly. "I cannot explain this," Magda said as they hurried across the yard. "Perhaps it happened by accident but I don't see how."

They stepped inside the low building. A large barrel of salt stood by the door. It had been brought, at Rycca's direction, from the storeroom only that morning. The salt was to be used to make brine that would preserve many of the vegetables that were shortly to be harvested.

"I opened it myself," Magda said as she again removed the top of the barrel. "At first, I assumed it was fine. Why would it not be? Everything is checked carefully before it is put away in the storeroom. But then I thought . . . something does not smell right." She lifted a handful of what the barrel held and offered it to Rycca. "Look here, there is salt but there is something else as well."

Rycca looked closely at what had come from the barrel. She moistened a finger, pressed it to the grains, and tasted them. Salt . . . and—

"Sand. Someone has mixed sand with the salt."

"It's the same way all through the barrel."

"Quickly," Rycca said and hurried from the kitchen.

Magda followed at her heels. In the storeroom, both women opened barrels of salt and tasted them.

Rycca sighed with relief. "Thank heaven!"

Magda managed a wan smile. Neither woman wanted to think about the havoc that would have resulted from having no salt this close to the harvest. But even so, to have one barrel destroyed was very worrisome.

"There must have been people in and out of the kitchen all day," Rycca said as she and Magda walked back in that direction.

"I think so," the older woman agreed, "but if anyone had seen this done, they would have come to you or me immediately. Besides, it must have taken some time to empty the barrel of half its salt and replace it with sand mixed all the way through."

"Whoever did it meant to conceal what had happened so that we would go ahead and make the brine."

"Which has to set for a fortnight. We would have been left with nothing for pickling."

"All right . . . someone would have needed at least a few minutes and then only if they worked very quickly. Also, the barrel is heavy. To upend it and spill out half the salt swiftly would require considerable strength."

"There are always times when the kitchen is empty."

"True, but someone would have to have known that."

Magda spread her work-worn hands. "We do many of the same tasks every day. Someone watching could take note of when the kitchen would be unoccupied."

"I suppose . . . but it would still have required swift work and strength."

The women looked at each other. "You will tell the jarl?" Magda asked softly.

"I have no choice," Rycca replied. With a heavy heart, she went to find her husband.

Dragon heard her out calmly. He went with her to the

kitchen to see the damaged salt. He even inspected the lock on the storeroom door and agreed it was sturdy. Yet when Rycca proposed putting a lock on the kitchen, he shook his head.

"More locks are not the answer. I must be able to trust my people. For that matter, they must be able to trust each other."

"Then we must find who is doing this, assuming it is the same person who destroyed the cloth."

"That seems a fair assumption since we have never had any trouble like this before. I think it unlikely two miscreants would have suddenly appeared here."

So did Rycca but she was at loss where to look for the guilty party. Of the man from Wolscroft she thought she had glimpsed, there was still no sign. Although Dragon had told her it was possible he was seen boarding a ship from Landsende only the day after she thought she saw him. The description was too general to be sure, but even so, he could hardly be responsible for damaging the salt.

There was a question Rycca wanted to ask her husband. It trembled on the very tip of her tongue yet remained unuttered. Instead, she went in search of Magda.

The older woman was in the laundry shed. She looked up when Rycca entered. "My lady?"

They were alone. Even so, Rycca spoke softly. "Magda, I have been wondering, is it possible there is someone here who was . . . fond of the jarl before he married? Someone who might be resentful that he has taken a wife?"

Magda raised her eyebrows until they almost vanished into her gray hair. "My lady, there are a good many here who were fond of the jarl before he married. Some, not really all that many, might have had more reason to be that way than others. But it was always well understood that if the jarl ever married, it would be because—" She broke off, flushing.

"Because duty compelled him?"

"Yes, my lady, that is so, but it doesn't change the fact that everyone is happy for you and the jarl. Genuinely happy as, if I may be so bold, it is obvious both of you are."

Truth.

Magda meant exactly what she had said. She and everyone else, including the comely young women Rycca had seen occasionally casting wistful looks in Dragon's direction, were glad of the marriage.

Who, then, wanted to discredit Rycca? That the two incidents were aimed at doing exactly that she did not doubt. Both struck at the domestic heart of Landsende, where, as the heavy keys hanging from her belt signified, she was responsible.

She had no answer, only worry, but as a week passed and nothing else happened, her concern eased.

It returned with a rush.

The morning was warm, scented with the ripe perfume of the fields. Insects hummed in the bushes, gulls circled overhead. Everywhere, the men and women of Landsende were preparing for the harvest with keen anticipation. Their crops were bountiful and they looked forward to reaping the rewards of their hard work these many months.

But not quite yet. Another day, perhaps two, and the timing would be perfect. Until then everyone sought some means to keep occupied, even Dragon.

"Let us ride," he said before he had scarcely opened his eyes to morning's light. He rolled out of bed and, standing beside it, stretched. The sculpted muscles of his back and shoulders flexed powerfully. Rycca watched him with warm appreciation. She would have been content to remain just where she was, especially if he returned, but the thought of galloping over the hills in the fresh youth of day was more than she could resist. Besides, they could always find a secluded spot.

With a grin that matched his own, she darted from the bed and dressed rapidly. They stopped by the kitchen just long enough to snatch a few warm rolls from Magda, who laughed and shooed them on their way. In the stable, Dragon led Grani and Sleipnir from their stalls as Rycca lifted the saddle blankets off the pegs where they were kept. She draped a blanket over each horse while Dragon got the saddles. He lifted them into place and Rycca tightened the cinches and girths.

Outside in the sun, Dragon spoke firmly to Sleipnir. "Now behave yourself." The proud stallion tossed his head but stood rock steady to please his master. He lifted Rycca into the saddle and stood by to be sure she was safely seated, prompting her to roll her eyes and laugh at his caution.

Dragon cast her a chiding look, reached up for Grani's reins, and swung himself into the saddle. Scarcely had he done so than the horse let out a high-pitched scream that split the air. Grani's ears went up as his head went down. He bucked hard and frantically, clawing the air with his rear legs, then landed hard on all four hooves and took off at a furious gallop across the yard, through a gate, and out onto the training field. Through all this, Dragon managed to stay on him even as he struggled to calm the mighty horse. Horrified, Rycca spurred Sleipnir to follow even as others began running toward the field to see what was happening.

Grani tore around the field, never slowing despite Dragon's strong hands on the reins. He bucked several more times yet his master remained rock steady. The horse raced toward the line of trees at the far end of the field, gathering speed with every moment until he was almost upon them. Suddenly, without warning, he dug his hooves into the dirt and came to a violent, bone-wrenching stop. The change in momentum was too much. Despite all his strength and skill, Dragon was thrown straight over the horse's head and flung to the ground.

Rycca screamed. She drew rein close to him and threw herself from Sleipnir's back onto her knees beside Dragon, frantically reaching for him. Her horror redoubled when she saw how perilously close his head had come to striking a rock nearby.

"Dragon! My lord . . . oh, please, wake up—speak to me! Don't you dare just lie there!" Tears all but blinded her and slid unheeded down her ashen cheeks. Clasping his shoulders, she tried to lift him. "Please . . . wake up . . . don't—"

He was too heavy, she couldn't budge him. And he just lay there, his eyes closed, all the life seemingly gone from him. A sob broke from her. She grabbed hold of his tunic and pulled so hard that the sturdy cloth came close to rending. "Don't you dare! You can't be hurt! Think of all the battles you've been through, all the adventures! Are you going to let a horse you don't even *like* do this to you?"

One eye opened and looked at her balefully. "Would it be better somehow if I did like him?"

Rycca gave a shriek of delight and threw her arms around Dragon's neck, damn near choking him. By the time he managed to disentangle himself, his vision had cleared enough to see that his wife was crying and laughing at the same time. That rather pleased him.

"It's all right," he said gruffly. "I'm fine. Only let me get up."

"Careful," Rycca admonished and stood by to help him. "Here, put your weight on me."

Dragon started to laugh and thought better of it when he realized his head was pounding. "Lady, if I do that, I will crush you." Wincing, he got to his feet. Only then did he and Rycca see the large crowd of people gathered around them in the field. Observing their lord to have survived his misadventure, they sent up a cheer.

The jarl of Landsende, heartily embarrassed to find himself in such a position, managed a wave and a wan smile for his people before turning his attention to Grani. The horse stood nearby, his reins held by Magnus, who had retrieved him.

"Is he hurt?" Dragon asked.

Magnus shook his head. "I don't think so, lord. He seems perfectly calm now." Indeed, even as they watched, Grani began nibbling at the grass.

"Mayhap he was stung by a bee," Rycca suggested. "I had that happen one time. The horse I was on took off just like Grani did."

"I'll wager you stayed on his back," Dragon muttered.

"No, actually I didn't. Nor did I get up as quickly as you have."

That soothed her lord's pride but only a little. He hurt all over, not that he was about to admit it. Moreover, he too had seen the rock and realized how very near he had come to serious injury. But mostly he was gripped by the quicksilver memory, ever repeating, of how it had felt to fall from that height.

It had not been pleasant.

"Let's get him back to the stable," Dragon said. "I want to take a close look at him."

There, in the light streaming through the open windows into the stall, he found the burrs. They were under the saddle blanket, six in all, clustered close together. The kind of needle-sharp burrs that grew on wild vines. Dragon touched his finger to one and watched the drop of crimson blood that quickly formed.

"I don't understand," Rycca said. She had climbed onto the railing around the stall so that she could look over Dragon's shoulder. "The blankets are always well shaken and brushed."

"You saw nothing of these when you put this on Grani?" Dragon asked.

"Of course not. If I had, I would have used a different blanket."

He nodded, looking again at the blanket. The burrs were toward the center, just where they would need to be to take the full force of his weight and cut into the horse with what must have been terrible pain. There was an outside chance that a single burr might have been blown onto the blanket while it was being aired. But a half-dozen placed so deliberately had to have been done on purpose.

The stable was rarely unoccupied. Even when the horses were being ridden or were grazing in the fields, there were always stalls and tack to be cleaned. Yet in the midst of such activity, only an unfamiliar face was likely to be noticed. Anyone well known, often seen in the stable, would pass by easily.

Rycca spent a great deal of time in the stable.

The moment the thought occurred to Dragon he put it from his mind firmly. It was ridiculous. First, he had absolutely no reason to think she would want to do him harm. Second, if she had put the burrs on the blanket, why would she have then put the blankets on the horses? Surely she would have tried to avoid suspicion by having someone else do that task.

Unless she feared that someone else might notice the burrs.

Mayhap he had hit his head after all. He shook it angrily, heedless of the pain that heightened. Grani needed care. His hide was cut where the burrs had dug in.

Rycca loved horses, Dragon reminded himself. He could not believe she would ever cause one to be hurt deliberately.

But she would know the hurt would not be lasting, that it would pass quickly.

"Here," Rycca said and held out a small stone jar.

"What is that?" Caught still in his unwelcome thoughts, he spoke more harshly than he'd intended.

She seemed not to notice. "Salve for Grani."

Dragon nodded. He took the jar from her and saw to the horse's care, glad of something to do that at least for a short time silenced the wayward voice in his mind.

When he was done, he lingered, checking the horse over very carefully. Grani showed no sign of further damage. But he did seem to understand that something had happened for he butted and nuzzled at Dragon even more than usual.

"It's all right, boy," Dragon said as he stroked his mane. "You weren't to blame and there's no lasting damage to either of us."

"Thank God for that," Rycca said with every evidence of sincerity. She had lingered in the stall, watching her husband care for the horse. Her eyes looked very tender. Now she said, "Come away, Dragon. Grani is fine and you need to be seen to yourself."

The notion surprised him. "There is nothing wrong with me."

"You took a hard fall."

"I'm unhurt."

She sighed, took the curry comb from his hand, and put it back on the wooden shelf that ran around the top of the stall. "Cymbra told me how stubborn you were about your leg."

"That was different."

"I certainly hope so. That was an injury that could have killed you or at the very least kept you in pain for the rest of your life. Now, I doubt you have more than a few bruises. But would it really be so terrible to see to them?"

As she spoke, she came up very close to him, her

body brushing lightly against his. He smelled the fragrance of her perfumed soap mingling with the aroma of fresh hay and sunlight. "I have yet to see the sauna," Rycca said.

She was a damn distracting woman. He could scarcely remember what he'd been thinking about a few moments before, except that it had been ridiculous. "You can't actually see much in there," he said absently, studying how the rays of sun played in her hair. "It's dark."

"Really? I guess we'll just have to go by touch then."

Anticipation rippled through him and with it his merry fellow surged happily. Dragon sighed. A day begun hurtling over a horse's head might as well include a little relaxation.

"Is it very hot?" Rycca asked as she ducked her head to enter the low stone building cut into the side of the hill.

Vividly aware that the deep bruising he had felt only a short time before was eclipsed by far more urgent sensations, Dragon smiled. "Extremely."

She looked at him over her shoulder. "I won't get burned, will I?"

"Quite probably," he said and came up close behind her, urging her into the chamber. When he shut the heavy wooden door behind him, the only light came from a small window cut high up in that door and the glowing embers of the fire in a stone box set in the center of the room.

Rycca looked around as her eyes slowly adjusted. The sauna was surprisingly spacious and outfitted with long benches along three sides. "I had no idea it was so big."

"It's not unusual for a group of friends or relatives, sometimes a whole family, to enjoy a sauna together."

"Men and women at the same time?" Rycca was not prudish. It was impossible for her to be so, having grown up at Wolscroft, where no thought was given to modesty or decency. But she was startled by the notion of men and women being at ease in each other's company while naked. She was nothing of the sort at that very moment and they were both still dressed.

Dragon smiled faintly or so it seemed in the dim light. "That is the old way and still the custom where people are used to living in very close quarters."

A sudden thought occurred to Rycca. She turned to him with alarm. "No one is likely to come in while we are here, are they?"

"Certainly not."

"How can you be so sure? If it's the custom for people to use the sauna together—"

He came toward her, his smile deepening. "No one will come."

When still she hesitated, Dragon said, "If I were here by myself, my men would not hesitate to enter unless they had some reason to believe I wished to be alone. However, as I am not by myself—"

"People wouldn't necessarily know that."

He laughed heartily. "Of course they know it. You think people don't take note of what we do?"

"I hadn't really thought about it."

"If it makes you uncomfortable, don't. But the reality is that it is only natural for my people to be curious about us."

"I suppose—" She was only half listening to him and had been ever since he stepped closer to her. It was hot in the sauna; no doubt that accounted for her rather dazed state. That and the shock of seeing him thrown. Those horrible moments kept playing in her mind. As much as she truly believed the sauna would ease his discomfort, so too did she need the reassurance of being able to touch him, feel his strength, and know for herself that he was all right.

And still she saw the moment again and again. . . .

"Dragon?"

"Hmmm?" He was distracted, stroking the soft curve of her cheek.

"You don't think . . . I mean, there couldn't be any . . . no, there couldn't be." She answered her own question firmly, certain the stray thought that had flitted through her mind was absurd.

"Couldn't be what?"

"It doesn't matter. Here, let me help you with that." Gently, she urged him down onto one of the benches and, kneeling in front of him, removed his sandals and set them aside. Then she urged him up and carefully eased his tunic over his head. Tall though she was, to accomplish this she had to climb up on the bench. He laughed when she was done and caught her around the waist, sliding her down the length of his aroused body.

"Such a dutiful wife. So meek and obedient."

Rycca made a little gurgling noise and sank her teeth into the lobe of his ear. He grunted but did not let her go. A moment later, when her tongue stroked that portion of him she had just offended, he groaned and cupped her buttocks, pulling her hard against him. "Don't tell me," he said harshly, "that you're wearing one of those damned delicate gowns again."

"Not for riding," she said, a smile in her voice.

"Good." His very large, very capable hands went for the ties down her back.

This time she let him undress her. Despite the heat of the sauna, his touch made her shiver. Naked against him, she could not stop trembling. Over and over, she saw him flying through the air . . . the rock so close to his head.

He made a rough sound deep in his throat and pressed her head to his chest. "What are you thinking of? You were wondering about something. What is it?"

"Nothing . . . it doesn't matter." Her lips moved against his skin, tasting the tang of salt. She closed her

eyes, senses whirling. The earth had shaken when he
landed, she swore it had. Or at least her earth, the center
of her being. If he had been hurt— Her hands clutched at
him, over the rounded curves of his shoulders, down the
bulging muscles of his arms. It didn't help. Hard in her
mind was the knowledge that any man, no matter how
powerful, could be harmed . . . and even worse.

"Rycca . . . ?" There was worry in his voice. He
tipped her head back and in the glow of the firebox,
looked at her. Slashes of silver shone along her cheeks. She
was crying. Dragon cursed under his breath. He lifted her
quickly and, still holding her, sat down on the bench.
Wrapping her legs around his waist so that she faced him,
he spoke gently. "Everything will be all right, sweetheart,
I promise. Only trust me, let me take care of you."

Far in the back of his mind, the ridiculous thought he
had so briefly entertained rang mockingly. Truly, the fall
had been harder than he'd realized to make him doubt his
wife for even a moment.

"I'm sorry," she murmured. "I don't know what's
come over me. I never cry."

In point of fact, she did, or at least she had since
meeting him. But he wasn't about to point that out to her.
Instead, he tenderly brushed away her tears and kissed her
lingeringly. He meant to offer only comfort—or at least
the nobler side of his nature did—but inevitably other
needs made themselves known.

He felt her body soften against him at the same time
his own hardened yet further. Swiftly, he laid her down on
the bench, slid his hands beneath her smooth buttocks,
and lifted her to him, spreading her sleek thighs. Rycca
gasped as his mouth found her. She tangled her fingers in
the thick mane of his hair and held on as pleasure bright as
the sun swiftly seized her.

She was flung high and free, soaring unhindered, riding a seemingly endless crest that carried her farther and

farther before reaching a peak that left her sobbing her husband's name even as he held her shuddering body in the safety of his arms. Slowly, the pulsations of ecstasy eased, only to begin anew as he entered her, not all at once but little by little, giving her time to feel all of him.

Her head fell back as she cried out. She reached for him, drawing him down to her, loving the weight of him, the heaviness of him inside her, driving away memory, making the taunting vision of his fall shatter into a thousand pieces even as she herself did, again and again. Firelight gleamed, revealing and concealing the ancient poetry of possession. Flame-burnished limbs entwined, voices cried out together, and fierce driving strength and power yielded up their tribute, there in the dark heart of the earth's womb.

Chapter

SIXTEEN

THE HARVEST BEGAN THE NEXT DAY. AL-most from the beginning, there were prob-lems. Bottoms fell out of baskets. Water drained out of skins. A wheel came off a wagon, almost crushing the man walking beside it. Most seriously, the blade of a scythe broke loose while being used and badly cut the leg of a young farmer.

Dragon insisted that such incidents were normal but Rycca was not so certain. She found herself looking over her shoulder far too often, checking and rechecking the most ordinary things and even, toward the third day, be-ginning to jump at sudden sounds. Her nervousness did not go unnoticed. Magda began to glance at her worriedly and the other women whispered among themselves.

She wanted to tell them that she was fine but the incident with Grani still haunted her dreams. She would wake in the middle of the night needing to reassure her-self that Dragon was there beside her, whole and un-harmed. He would sense her unease and draw her to him, offering all the comfort she could want. Yet still her fears lingered.

On the fourth day, they exploded.

Almost everyone in Landsende, the town as well as the stronghold, was hard at work. Rycca went alone to the kitchens, needing some spices to add to the stew that was being cooked over open fires in the fields, close to the people who would be eating it. People who had worked almost without rest, far into the nights graced by a clear sky and an almost full moon. They got only a few hours' sleep, ate where they could, and scarcely paused even to speak or take note of what was happening around them. She wanted them to have a good meal.

Magda had been in the fields all morning, supervising some of the women. Except for the guards manning the watchtowers as always, the stronghold was deserted. So was much of the town as everyone joined in to help with the harvest. A dog sleeping in the sun raised his head briefly and eyed Rycca but quickly settled back down into his nap.

She was not used to being so alone. A vague sense of unease accompanied her into the kitchens. They were, as always, meticulously clean and orderly. The long tables where food was prepared had been rubbed down with sand and water so that they were without even the smallest stain. Bowls, pots, and ladles were neatly stacked out of the way. Fragrant herbs hanging from the rafters sweetened the air. But the floor . . .

Something was scattered over the floor toward the far end of the kitchens. Something small, indistinct . . . round and dark . . . almost like . . .

Peppercorns. Precious peppercorns torn from the safety of the locked spice cabinet, which now stood open, its double doors hanging ajar, all its drawers pulled out and their contents either spread over the floor or missing entirely.

Rycca gasped in shock. Still disbelieving of her own eyes, she moved forward carefully, smelling the crushed pepper beneath her feet, and reached out a hand to touch the cabinet doors. Their wood was smooth and unmarred. They showed no evidence of having been forced but instead appeared to have been opened by a key.

The key that hung at her side.

As far as she knew, it was the only key to the spice cabinet. Yet obviously that was not so, for she had not opened it.

A deep, shuddering breath escaped her. First the fabric, then the salt, then Grani, and now this. Someone was attacking her ever more directly, implicating her in doing harm to Landsende.

The day that had seemed so warm suddenly felt chill.

With a heavy heart, Rycca took herself out to the fields to find Dragon and tell him what had happened. He was with the young man who had been injured by the scythe just that morning. Now bandaged and no longer bleeding, the man was still very pale but he looked up at Dragon with utter confidence.

"You will have to work hard to regain full use of the leg," the jarl was saying. "But it can be done. That I can testify to personally since I went through it myself. I can show you what to do, and you have all of the coming winter to recuperate. By the time these fields are ready to be sown again, you will be fully recovered."

The young woman who stood beside the man, clutching his hand, nodded in agreement. "The jarl knows of what he speaks, Harald. This is bad luck for us but not so bad as it might have been." She took his hand held in hers and touched it lightly to her belly. "Our child will know his father. Nothing else matters."

Dragon rose quietly, leaving the couple to themselves. He had gone only a little distance when he saw Rycca. "How is he?" she asked, looking at the injured man.

"The wound is deep but not to the bone. It will take time and effort but he will recover."

When this news failed to relieve her, Dragon asked, "Is something wrong?"

She nodded reluctantly, dreading what she had to say. "I'm afraid so. The spice cabinet in the kitchens has been broken into. Some of the spices are scattered on the floor but most of them are just gone."

He looked at her for what seemed a very long moment. Finally, he asked, "When did you discover this?"

"Just now. I went to the kitchens to get some spices for the stew Magda and the other women are preparing for the midday meal. There was no sign of anyone else about except the guards, in the towers of course, but I presume they don't watch the kitchens."

"No," Dragon said slowly, "they don't. You say the cabinet was broken into?"

"It was opened. There was no damage to the cabinet itself but the lock is hanging apart."

"Where is the key?"

"Right here." She held it up.

"Have you had it with you all day?"

"Yes, along with all the rest of them. You know Magda gave me the keys right after I arrived here. At night, they are near my clothes in our lodge. During the day, they are right where they are now." A sudden thought occurred to her. "Do you think someone could have come into our lodge while we slept?"

Again, Dragon looked at her. Slowly, he shook his head. "No." He said nothing more but he really didn't have to. She had known the moment she spoke that it was impossible. With his warrior's instincts, he would have come awake at once if anyone entered the lodge. He slept with the Moorish sword right beside the bed. An intruder might well have been hacked to pieces before he could get more than a step inside.

"Then there must be another key," Rycca said.

Dragon shrugged. He turned to Magnus, who was

standing nearby, and gave instructions for the injured man to be carried back to the town, then he set off toward the stronghold. Rycca had to run to catch up with him. Neither of them spoke again until they were in the kitchens, looking at the damage.

"Give me the key," Dragon said, holding out his hand.

Rycca obliged immediately although she found herself a little clumsy, having difficulty getting the large iron key off the ring that held it and a dozen others.

"Are you sure this is the right one?"

"Yes. See, it has this little nick right at the top."

He saw and nodded, then fitted the key into the lock. It turned easily. "It's the right key," Dragon said.

"I know that. I opened the cabinet just yesterday."

"Are you sure you relocked it?"

"Yes, of course I am." When he still appeared unconvinced, she added, "The lock is large and heavy. I could hardly leave it undone and not notice. But even if I had somehow, Magda or one of the other women would have seen it and told me."

"They have given you no trouble?"

"Absolutely none. Everyone has been very kind and welcoming." Everyone save Magnus, about whom she still harbored doubts. Yet could she not bring herself to speak of this to her husband.

Especially not when his features were whipped free of any expression and his eyes shuttered.

Alarmed, Rycca said, "Dragon . . . I swear to you, I did not—"

He held up a hand. "Enough. You are my wife. Yet are you also mistress of Landsende. It is your responsibility to properly safeguard that which is within your domain."

"I know that but—"

"You must have mislaid the key."

"No, there must be another key."

"Were there one, I would know of it."

"Then there has to be some other way to open the lock."

"It is true . . . I have heard that some locks can be opened with very narrow picks. But," Dragon added quickly, "it takes special training and skill to do that."

Rycca's shoulders began to sag but she caught herself and straightened immediately. "I am sorry to have brought trouble into your home. It is the last thing I wanted."

Her husband sighed and wearily ran a hand through his hair. She saw then that he was tired, was as everyone else, after four days of unrelenting labor. More gently, she said, "I truly am sorry, Dragon. But I don't know what is happening here and it's beginning to frighten me."

He nodded, his manner softening, and touched her face lightly. "We will find out who is doing this, Rycca. I promise you that. In the meantime, keep a close eye out and tell me if you see anything—or anyone—odd."

She assured him she would do so, then stayed in the kitchens to sweep up the remains of the spices while he went to speak with the men on the watchtowers. He returned as she was finishing.

"They saw nothing, as we expected, but they will be watching now."

For the moment, it was all that could be done. The harvest was no time to begin seriously looking for whoever was causing the disruptions at Landsende. But once it was done . . . Dragon's face turned grim. Once it was done, he would find whoever had dared to cast suspicions upon his wife. Find and punish.

For three more days the people labored to bring in the bounty of the golden fields. Rye and wheat were bundled into tall stacks to dry, aided by clear skies and a steady breeze. Soon the mills would be grinding and the barns filled with fodder for the sheep and cattle being brought down from the high pastures. Ale and mead would be brewed, mattresses stuffed with fresh straw, and poppets made for the children from the last stalks. When all was done, the feasting would begin. It was the thought of that, and of the comfortable, well-fed winter to follow, that kept people at their labors even as weariness began to dog every step.

When the last sheaves of grain were finally gathered in and the fields laid bare, a tired cheer was raised. People began packing up their blankets and pots, all the provisions they had brought out into the fields to save themselves walking back and forth. In threes and fours, families walking together, they trudged back to the stronghold and the town.

Rycca walked along with Magda and the other women. Despite their assurances, she had insisted on staying in the fields, helping with the cooking, and taking her turn carrying water skins to the thirsty workers. True, she had scorched the chickens she tried roasting on the spit over the fire, and she had probably spilled as much water as ended up drunk, but at least she had tried. When the next harvest came around in a year, she promised herself, she would be better able to manage.

By the time she reached the stronghold, Rycca felt unaccustomedly exhausted. More than just the fatigue of hard work was affecting her. Her step dragged as she entered the lodge. Dragon was still off somewhere with his men. She paused just long enough to wash her hands and face in a basin of cool water, then tumbled onto the bed and slept almost instantly.

It was evening when she awoke. She lay for a little time on her back staring up at the slanted roof of the lodge. It was home to her now, so she thought, as she had never known home to be. The ease with which she had become part of Landsende still amazed her. She had settled into it as a bird into the nest, glad of the refuge after a stormy flight.

Or was she deluded?

"You saw nothing of these . . . ?" Dragon had asked her about the burrs, as though she could conceivably have placed a blanket containing them on a horse he—or anyone else—was about to ride.

"You must have mislaid the key," he had said, as though he took it for granted she was a careless housewife. Better he think that, she supposed, than that she had opened the cabinet herself.

He had accused her of nothing, she realized. His only reprimand had been to say she must safeguard what was in her domain. This she knew, but how, exactly, was she to do that when someone seemed intent on upending her?

With a sigh, she rose from the bed where she felt more inclined to stay and sleep away the shadowed night. Instead, she splashed water on her face again but failed to find in it any hint of ease. Leaden-spirited, she left the lodge and went to the great hall, where she knew supper would shortly be laid.

It was a simple meal, prepared without spices, and word of that lack had clearly spread among the people. Several glanced at her when she came in, then swiftly looked away again.

She took her seat beside Dragon but he was deep in conversation with Magnus and said little to her during the meal. It was not over soon enough. When the last dishes had been served and the ale brought around again, she murmured her excuses. He rose as she stood.

"Are you all right?" he asked. She thought him

belatedly aware of her and put the notion aside as unworthy.

"Fine." She mustered a bright smile, felt its falseness,
and let it fade. "Merely tired."

She went from the hall feeling his eyes on her back.

For all that, scarcely had she crept into bed than
sleep overtook her again. She woke very slightly in the
night to feel her husband gathering her into his arms.
Sleep claimed her once more and she did not stir again
until day.

Not bright day but muted, softened day in which all
sight and sound were blurred. Fog had rolled in during
the night. There were misty days in Mercia but nothing
like this thick, all-enveloping whiteness that seemed to
erase the world. The gulls were silent, roosting somewhere, and the absence of their familiar calls made the
quiet more sharp.

Rycca went out into it dazed and made her way by
memory and touch until she reached the kitchens. Magda
was there with the women who assisted her. They greeted
their mistress with calm cheer.

"The porridge is on," Magda said and offered a bowl
heavily laden with honey and cream. Rycca ate it greedily.
She could have managed more but restrained herself from
saying so.

Instead, she asked, "How does anyone find their way
in this?"

Magda laughed. "Not well, my lady, that's for certain. Thanks be there is little enough to do this day."

The women nodded, glad of their own ease after the
grueling work of the past week. Rycca lingered a little
time with them but she still sensed they could not relax
fully in her presence, too aware of her status as the jarl's
wife and her difference as a foreigner. Before long, she left
them and set out to find the stable.

Were it not for the whinnying of the horses, she

might have stumbled in circles and gotten nowhere. As it was, she almost walked straight into a wall before she realized she had arrived. Feeling her way to the door, she went inside. Lamps had been lit against the fog-shrouded gloom. The horses were all still in their stalls. They were unaccustomed to such restraint except in bitterest winter and it left them uneasy.

Rycca fussed over Grani and Sleipnir. Caring for the horses took her away from her own uneasy thoughts. She groomed them both and braided their manes, gave them fresh water and grain, and treated them to apples. They tried hard to persuade her to let them go out, butting up against her, nuzzling her with their warm noses, and generally making sweet pests of themselves, but she stood firm.

"Be patient. When the fog lifts a little, I'll take you to the paddock. But not quite yet."

They nickered in protest but settled down quickly enough when the apples appeared. She left them and went to the other side of the stable, where the geldings were kept. The mares were in another building altogether. There she began forking hay into the stall of a sturdy chestnut who tossed his head and was pleased to accept an apple.

The busier she kept, the better she felt. She had a problem, the string of incidents that seemed to point to her, but she would work it out. She was a truthsayer, after all. She would find a way to discover who was responsible.

Not Magda, she was already sure of that. Besides the woman's guileless manner, like smooth milk in a pail, Magda had been in the fields all morning when the spice cabinet was robbed. Rycca had seen her there for herself. Nor did she believe for a moment that Magda could have emptied out the barrel of salt and replaced it half with sand in the time that would have been needed.

Magnus, then. That seemed a far likelier possibility.

She had felt his lies from the beginning and knew full well he did not want her at Landsende. But would he truly risk angering his jarl just because of that? To what end, and why?

Her head began to ache. She gave up cleaning the stalls and leaned up against the door of the stable, looking out into nothingness. Morning aged, the sun rose higher, yet the fog was as thick as ever. With a sigh, she turned to go back inside.

Just as she did, there was a movement behind her and to the left. She had an instant to sense a dark, looming presence swiftly closing on her. Before she could even begin to react, a hard hand slammed down over her face as a steely arm wrapped around her waist.

Shock roared through Rycca even as she struggled fiercely. She clawed at the hand over her nose and mouth and at the same time kicked out, trying to do as much damage to her captor as possible. Panic threatened to grip her as she realized that she could not breathe. Her lungs burned for air as her senses whirled. Just as her head sagged, an instant before the light vanished from her eyes, she found herself staring at two serpents intertwined, each devouring the other. She fought desperately for consciousness but a dark vortex loomed before her. Helpless, she fell into it.

D RAGON WAS DOWN IN THE TOWN WITH A GROUP of his men, helping to pull a merchant vessel up onto the rocky strand. The damned thing was taking on water and had to be beached lest it sink. Such a task was hard enough in any circumstances but the fog made it almost impossible. The men could scarcely see one another or the vessel. Yet they had managed to get strong ropes around it, several stalwart lads going under the hull to secure them. Enough brute strength and the job would be done.

"Heave!" Dragon yelled into the fog and added his own great strength to the pull on the ropes. The vessel nudged a few more inches out of the water.

"Heave!" Backs straining, muscles bulging, bodies streaked with sweat despite the cool morning, the men moved as one. A few more inches.

"Heave!" Water gushed out of the hole near the bow as it emerged into the air. Men rushed behind the vessel to push it as the rest continued pulling. In two hours from the time they had begun, it was done.

Dragon dropped the ropes that had worn grooves in his shoulders. No vessel had ever been lost at Landsende, not even in the sudden storms that could sweep down out of the north without warning. Merchants coming there knew they could count themselves, their cargo, and their ships safe. He wasn't about to let anything change that.

Yet neither was he about to hide his ire from the hapless Gaul who tried to sputter his thanks.

"Look there," Dragon said, pointing to the hole in the bow. "That wood is practically rotted through. When was the last time your hull was pitched?"

"Alas, lord, I am but a poor man and—"

"You will be when you find yourself without a vessel. You will lay up here for the next week and let my men see to what repairs are needed. Understood?"

"Yes, yes, of course, lord. I know your men are skilled and you will not rob me. Only pray you remember I am but a—"

"Poor man. I know, I know. For a poor man, you never seem to lack for a cargo, but never mind, the price will be fair. Now get on with your work. I have other matters to tend to, assuming I can find my way to them."

He had come on foot, unwilling to risk any horse in

such treacherous fog, and was returning to the stronghold the same way when the first whiff of smoke stopped him. He stood, just where the road began to rise toward his strong stone walls, and wondered at the sudden awareness. There was always smoke for fires burned day and night in every cottage. But the fresh sea breezes blew the scent away so that, really, it was not usual to smell fire.

Yet he did now. He most definitely did.

It was because the air was so still, held down by the fog.

There had been other foggy days, many of them, but he had never smelled anything like this.

No, that wasn't right. He had but never at Landsende. Once in Byzantium when an old quarter of the city had caught fire and burned. Again in Italia when lightning struck a stand of ancient trees. This was not the smoke of hearths. It was too big, too threatening to be anything so tame.

He began to run, heedless of the fog, following the ever-thickening scent around the stronghold walls and into a nearby field. There he saw the flames. They were rising out of a barn waiting to receive the harvest bounty. Already, they shot into the air, their heat scorching.

Dragon turned to call for help but his men were already coming to him. They too had smelled the fire, as had the men and women rushing up from the town, stumbling in their haste, many carrying buckets.

They formed a chain all the way from the high field down to the strand and the water there. Hundreds of people, children included, hefting hundreds of buckets in a desperate line to fight what quickly became an all-consuming fire.

The weather had been dry. The barn burned fiercely. The heat of the flames seared the faces of those closest to it, Dragon among them. He knew almost immediately that the barn could not be saved. All efforts were directed toward stopping the spread of the fire. There was enough dry stubble in the field to give it fuel, and even in the absence of wind, the danger lingered that it might veer toward the town or rain sparks down on the stronghold.

"Get shovels!" he ordered and set his men to digging a trench around the barn, a break for the raging flames. The tactic worked but it was several hours before the fire finally burned itself out.

Dragon did not wait. While yet the remains of the barn smoked, he walked all around them, looking for any hint of how the fire could have started. The barn had been empty, therefore no torches or lamps would have been lit within it, nor was there reason for anyone to be inside, particularly on so foggy a day when just finding the field would be difficult. There had been no storm, no lightning, nothing natural that could have started the conflagration.

Yet start it had and he meant to find out how. Quickly enough, he discovered the cause. A thick stream of pitch, the same kind used to seal the hulls of ships and readily available in Landsende, soaked the ground beginning a few yards from the barn and leading right up to it. Up to and in, he would wager. Pitch on a vessel submerged in water was perfectly safe but on land there was little that burned so well.

The fire had been started deliberately.

The fabric, the salt, Grani, the spices . . .

His head went up. He walked slowly, seeming still to examine the barn but in fact looking at the men and women who had come to fight the fire. Along with the folk of Landsende were the crews of every vessel in port. They, too, had rushed to help. Not a single person was missing save for the very young, the very old, and—

"Where is my wife?" he asked Magda, coming upon her as she helped gather up the buckets.

Soot-stained like all the rest, her eyes red from the fire, she looked around uncertainly. "I . . . don't know, my lord. I have not seen her." Even as she spoke, he saw the dawning realization in her eyes. The absence of the Lady of Landsende at such a time was strange indeed.

He raised a hand to summon Magnus, who appeared, as always, directly at his side. "I want her found." Grim-faced, Dragon turned back to survey the smoldering ruins.

C OLD DAMPNESS PRESSING AGAINST HER FACE woke Rycca. She hovered a moment on the edge of darkness before memory returned with a jolt. She was on the ground. It was the wet earth she had felt against her cheek. The fog billowed all around her. She had no idea where she was or how long she had been unconscious.

Or who had seized her.

Gingerly, she sat up and took stock of herself. Save for a few aches and pains, she appeared to be unharmed.

Serpents. The thought sprang unbidden in her mind and with it came the image of twin snakes devouring each other. She had seen that just before the darkness took her. But where and why?

There would be time enough to ponder that later, if she was fortunate. At the moment, nothing was more pressing than to be sure she was truly alone. Cautiously, she strained her eyes against the fog and listened intently. Not a flicker of movement or murmur of sound suggested anyone was near.

Relieved, she took a deep breath and willed herself to be calm. Though it was summer, the day was cool. Her clothes were wet and clung to her. She shivered, wrapping her arms around herself and trying to guess what time it might be but it was impossible to determine the angle of the sun. However many hours had passed since she was taken from the stable, day would be fading and with it would come even greater chill. She had to make her way back to Landsende and quickly.

But in the fog she had no idea in which direction to move and risked worsening her situation with every step she took. Yet to do nothing was unbearable. Still mindful of the danger if her kidnapper was nearby, she called out hesitantly, "Hello . . . is anyone here?"

Her words vanished into silence so thick it rivaled the fog. She might have been utterly alone in a world from which all sight and sound had vanished.

The thought chilled her even further. How many times during the years at Wolscroft had she longed to be alone? She had dreamed of living all by herself in an aerie somewhere, like a wild falcon or hawk never to be tamed by man. Except for Thurlow, there was not a person she would have missed and many a one to whom she would gleefully have said farewell forever. But that had changed now, utterly changed. She longed for Dragon, the sound of his voice, the touch of his hand, the warmth of his smile. For a moment she closed her eyes and saw him behind them. The vision gave her strength and she decided she had to move, slowly and carefully to be sure, but she could not simply stay where she was.

She had taken only a half-dozen steps when she noticed that her hands felt oddly stiff. Puzzled, she stopped and held them up. Through the swirling tendrils of cloud, black streaks stood out against her pale skin. She brought her hands closer and inhaled. The acrid smell of pitch filled her breath.

Pitch? That was odd. How could she possibly have gotten pitch on her hands? There was none in the stable, or at least she had no memory of any.

Again, she listened. Far off in the distance, muted by

the fog, she thought she heard the sound of waves breaking against the shore. It might be a trick of the wind, so
scarcely perceptible was it, but she had nothing else to
guide her. Step by cautious step, still wondering how she
had gotten pitch on her hands, Rycca began trying to find
her way home.

SEVENTEEN

TIME SEEMED TO MOVE VERY SLOWLY IN the mist and Rycca with it. She stopped every few feet and listened, trying to make sure that she had not imagined the sound of the sea and was still headed toward it. Her clothes felt ever more uncomfortable. She was damp through to the skin and beyond, chilled to the very bone. Shivering, she moved a little faster, only to stumble over a rock and fall hard.

Groaning, she got to her feet again and proceeded more carefully. However cold she was, it would be little help to injure herself. As she went, she thought again of the serpents and tried to imagine who could possibly have taken her from the stable. Who would be so mad as to risk the rage of the jarl of Landsende? But having risked it, why simply leave her unharmed in the fog?

Perhaps the miscreant had lost his nerve and fled rather than face his just punishment. The more she thought about it, the more she was convinced that must be what had happened. She even felt a sense of relief, for surely the same person must have been responsible for all the other things that had happened. With him gone, she could hope that life at Landsende would return to normal.

She stopped for a moment, listening again. The sound of the sea seemed louder but she couldn't be sure. However, she also thought she heard something else, a slow, rhythmic pounding of some sort. Weary, aching, worried, yet did she feel a little spurt of hope. Still, she forced herself to continue slowly.

The world had the quality of a dream, Rycca decided. With all the everyday landmarks stripped away, there was nothing between her and her thoughts. She wondered suddenly what life would be like if it were always so and decided she preferred not to know. Too much inward gazing was likely not good for the soul. She missed the world, all the vibrant color and movement. Even winter was not so barren as this fog that made her want to do nothing so much as lie down on the ground, curl up into herself, and forget about all else.

Not that she would, even for a moment. She kept going, listening for the sea, hearing again the pounding. It was familiar somehow. She had heard it before and knew what it meant, yet a little while longer passed before she realized what she strained to catch.

Hoofbeats! A horse moving not at a gallop but at a steady trot all the same. Who would let a horse do that in such blinding mist? Who would take such a chance?

"Rycca!"

Dragon's voice rang out clear and strong, seeking her.

"Here!" Never had she been so glad to hear anyone in her life. "Here! I am here!"

He came out of the cloud, first only a hint of darkness against the white, taking form quickly until she saw him, tall and strong astride Sleipnir, who pawed the ground in pleasure at having found her. Oddly, his master looked less pleased.

From his great height on the horse, he gazed down at her and demanded, "What the hell are you doing out here?"

That was hardly the warm and comforting greeting she had hoped for, yet she was willing enough to accept it. "Trying to get back to Landsende." She held up a hand and he took it, hoisting her into the saddle as though she were thistledown. Even now, knowing his body so intimately, his strength still startled her. She was silent for a moment, pretending to settle herself in front of him.

An acrid smell clung to him. It pierced her sudden unease and heightened it.

"What is that?"

"The smell? Smoke. The barn burned."

"The barn? The big one where all the fodder is supposed to go?"

"The big one."

She twisted in the saddle and looked at him. His face was stained with soot and very grim. "What will we do now?"

"Build a new one, quickly."

That was a sensible enough answer and typical of the man, yet she was still taken aback. "I don't understand. How could it have burned?"

"It was torched. Someone spread pitch around the barn and probably into it as well, then lit fire to it."

She was frozen in his arms, utterly rigid.

"What is that on your hands?" he asked in a way that told her he already knew.

"Pitch." She was very proud that her voice held steady.

"I don't suppose you would care to explain how you come to be stained with pitch and out here miles from Landsende."

Her throat tightened painfully. Just then she needed

nothing so much as for him to hold her and reassure her that everything was all right. What a foolish wish! How weak and ridiculous of her to expect any such thing!

"I was in the stable with Grani and Sleipnir. Someone came out of the fog and grabbed me. I couldn't breathe and I lost consciousness. I came to perhaps an hour ago and have been trying to make my way back ever since."

She spoke by rote, her voice devoid of expression. So too did she avoid looking at him again. There was no point save further pain.

But she could not deny the trembling deep within her. If he did not believe her, what hope had she? Cast among strangers who could so easily become enemies, what would be her fate?

He was silent for a long moment but she felt his arm tighten around her. Finally, he said, "Have you anything else to tell me?"

"I saw two serpents eating each other."

"What? In the fog?"

"No, I'm not sure where. Just before I lost consciousness, I saw them."

"You imagined them."

She started to shake her head, stopped. Pride forbade her to try to convince him of anything. Or perhaps she merely sensed the futility of it. Already she felt herself retreating inward as she had done as a child, fleeing in the only way left to her.

The fog made no difference to Sleipnir. He found his way back to Landsende unerringly. Smell, Rycca supposed. Every place had its own unique scent. Wolscroft had smelled of dank stone and fear. Landsende was the sea, ripe fields, the gentle smoke of hearth fires, horses and leather, sweat and steam, all the rich, complex aromas of home.

Home? She swallowed against the tightness in her throat and pushed the thought down firmly.

Yet still it lingered. The walls around the stronghold were looming out of the fog when she finally asked, "What do you intend to do?"

He did not answer at once. They were inside, near the stable, and he dismounted before their eyes met. He looked tired, she thought, not in the body so much as in the spirit, and felt a spurt of sympathy for him.

She went into his arms. He lowered her to the ground but did not let go of her. His warmth and strength offered no comfort. He said, "My people have been harmed by this."

That much was obvious. Folk wearied from the harvest would now have to labor quickly to construct a new barn lest their efforts go for nothing. If the fodder couldn't be stored properly, the animals couldn't be fed during the winter. Some would be culled as it was, but cull too many and the flocks would be sadly depleted come spring. The loss of one barn could reverberate for years.

Yet for all that, his choice of words stung.

"*We* have been harmed by this," Rycca said.

He did not answer but took her hand and led her into the great hall.

Damn her! How could she have no explanation for this, nothing he could use to spare her what must otherwise be? Did she have no understanding of his position? He was jarl, the leader of his people, their security in an uncertain world. Whatever his private feelings, he could never forget that.

Dragon took a deep breath, struggling for calm. Dread had been building in him ever since discovering that Rycca was missing. He had gone over and over in his mind the series of events—the destroyed fabric, the damaged salt, Grani, the spices, and over and over he had told himself she could not possibly be responsible. Especially not for Grani. She loved horses.

She didn't love him. *Thor's hammer*, why was he

thinking that now? Who cared if she loved him or not? Certainly not he, who had never thought to find love. It was fine for Wolf and Hawk, and he was happy for them, but few people were ever so fortunate and he had not expected to be among them. Never mind the lingering yearning that stirred within him, the wistful wishing for some true sense of connection that shattered loneliness and gave shape and purpose to his life. He absolutely was not going to think of that. It was enough that she was his wife and that she respect what that meant.

But she had not. She had fled from him even after they were all but married. She had lain with a man she had every reason to believe was not the one to whom she had been given. She had fled again and finally wed him only when the alternative was to be turned back over to her father and likely death.

Yet since then—Memory filled him. Rycca in the ship on the way to Landsende, patiently repeating each word in Norse he taught her, determined to learn to speak the language of his people. Rycca lying in his arms at night, sweet and pliant. On the quay, riding Grani, her surprise and pride when she realized the gift Dragon had given her. Her struggles to assume her duties as mistress of his manor. She was not skilled in household matters, this was hardly a secret, yet she had seemed to try so hard. Their nights together and those days he could steal away, filled with passion unlike any he had ever known.

Was this truly the woman who had betrayed him? Who all along, as she lay in his arms, sat beside him at table, won the approval of his people, still plotted to release some venom within herself in acts of ever-increasing destruction?

Plotted? The word rang harshly in his thoughts. There was no plot, merely a series of events, probably impulsive, that had led them both into this nightmare.

Plotted. He shook his head, trying to clear it. Wolscroft hated Alfred. Alfred's prestige was invested in the success of the Norse and Saxon marriages. Rycca was Wolscroft's daughter.

And as unlike him as day from night. She loathed her father, had even accepted an unwanted marriage to escape him.

Had she?

What if he had it horribly, hideously wrong? What if all of it, her flight from their marriage, her fear of her father, her gladness at escaping him, what if all of it was false and she no different than the seed from which she had sprung?

It was his bitterness taunting him with such unwelcome thoughts, nothing more. Even if his worst fears were true, they did not explain why she would have risked herself in acts of destruction.

Because she thought she knew him and believed he would not physically harm her? Because the worst she might reasonably expect from him was to be repudiated as his wife and sent back to her family? Such repudiation could be seized upon by Wolscroft, taken as a profound insult and used as an excuse to demand that Alfred sunder the Norse and Saxon alliance.

He had lingered too long in Byzantium. That capital of intrigue and deception had twisted his thoughts.

And yet, it could be true. Though it stabbed him to the core even to contemplate such a possibility, neither could he reject it.

She would have to give an accounting of herself so as to satisfy his own questions and those of his people. They, too, had a right to know.

With such heavy thoughts, the jarl of Landsende entered his hall.

The people of Landsende assembled swiftly as word spread that the wife of the jarl had been found and under what circumstances. Dragon's lieutenants, Magnus among them, came first but others followed on their heels. They filled the hall, with those arriving a little later relegated to the yard beyond.

Dragon sat in his high-backed chair. He had not offered a seat to Rycca and she did not expect one. She understood full well what was to happen here even as her mind reeled from the thought.

Her husband, the hero of a strange land, from whom she had fled only to welcome into her body and her heart, was putting her on trial.

Deep within herself, beyond the barriers of shock and dread, fear stirred but she could scarcely feel it. That was good. She embraced the numbness, letting it fill her as the fog still filled the waning day. Hidden by curling tendrils of mist inside her, she could keep some essential part of herself safe.

"Rycca—"

She surfaced just enough to realize the jarl was speaking to her. Whatever he had said, she had not heard.

"I asked you what happened."

"I have already told you." Her voice was very low. She could scarcely hear it herself, but then she was very far away in the fog.

"You said you were taken from the stable by someone you could not see and left unconscious some distance from here."

She nodded, feeling her head go up and down as though on the end of a string.

"You have pitch on your hands."

She held them up, staring at them. They seemed to belong to someone else. All around her, she heard the people gasp, felt the quick ripple of murmurs spreading among them.

"How did the pitch get there?"

"I don't know."

Nor did she know him. Vainly, she tried to remember

the playful intimacy of their time together, lying beside him, holding him in her arms and her body, feeling set free by joy. It was all lost in the fog.

"You have no explanation?" He was frowning, and for just an instant she felt a spurt of sympathy for him, then it faded before the sheer impact of the moment.

She was trapped. How could she prove that she had not done something when the evidence said she had? The fog had shrouded all. No one could have seen her taken from the stable or seen who really set the fire at the barn. Indeed, it might all have been done on the spur of the moment, the guilty one seizing the chance of invisibility.

Rycca lifted her head. She was still very cold but the inner chill of her spirit was worse by far. She had to fight her way past it in order to speak.

"I did not do this. I did not do any of it. Naught that has happened is my fault."

"So you say and so I would believe. But the evidence speaks against you."

"Not all the evidence." Driven by desperation to reveal that which she had wished to keep secret, she said, "I am a truthsayer. I cannot speak lies."

Again a murmur rose behind and around her. This was the first the people had heard of such a thing and it prompted much comment.

"Silence," Dragon ordered. He left his chair and walked to the center of the hall, close to Rycca. As though he spoke only to her, he said, "You have told me this about yourself but I have no way of knowing if it is true or not."

"But I showed you with the boy, Olav—"

"I came to my conclusions in that matter separate from anything you said. It was clear to me Trygyv was likely lying, hence did I suspect him of stealing the goblet himself and simply searched for it where it would be kept in easy reach of him. That had nothing to do with any truthsaying."

His words destroyed her last faint hope and replaced it with despair. If he did not believe something so essential to her nature, how could she hope for him to believe anything at all about her?

Driven by that despair, she exclaimed, "What about the serpents I saw? Surely they mean something?"

"Serpents devouring each other. Who are they, lady? I know your loathing of Vikings, you made no attempt to hide it. Is Alfred the other serpent, the king whose death you spoke of so readily?"

"You are twisting everything! How can you do this?"

"Say rather how can you?"

His thoughts in turmoil, Dragon waited for Rycca to reply. When it became evident she would not, he searched vainly for some alternative to finding her guilty at once. That would raise the specter of punishment and of that he could not bring himself to think at all. Not yet, at least. It might be he would have no choice.

He should have been a skald, free to wander the world spinning his tales.

But he was not. He was jarl and his people were waiting for him to do what had to be done.

He began to speak, to say she would be confined in their lodge until such time as he could come to a judgment of the matter. But before the first words were uttered, he reconsidered. Just then he saw her look at Magnus and look quickly away as though flinching from him. Magnus? The man he had known since boyhood. The man who had served him ever faithfully. The man Rycca had clearly wished to avoid. Why?

What if she really was a truthsayer and, being such, had some reason to think Magnus less than trustworthy?

He was snatching at straws yet they were all he had. If Rycca was innocent, someone else had to be guilty. Someone who had deliberately sought to turn both him and his people against her, to sunder their marriage, and to place at risk the alliance that was meant to bring them peace.

If such a person existed, whoever he might be, Dragon had to discover him. Far too much was at stake to do otherwise.

He longed just then for a private moment with his wife, a chance to tell her his thinking and explain what he was about to do. But there was none. His people were watching . . . and waiting. Against the sudden tightness of his chest, he spoke.

"You will be taken from here to the punishment post where you will remain until such time as you choose to speak honestly and completely about your actions."

Rycca gasped. She could not believe she had heard him aright. Neither, it seemed, could his people, for they too were suddenly agitated. A few murmured their approval but most seemed shocked even as she was.

Dragon turned away as though in disgust. He gestured to Magnus. "See to this, will you? She is my wife, I do not wish her hurt, yet must it be done. You understand?"

"Of course, lord," Magnus said quickly. He looked properly somber but also determined as he approached Rycca. "Come, lady."

So stunned was she that Rycca could not gather herself to protest. She spared a last look at Dragon but he was watching Magnus and did not meet her eyes. Her husband's loyal lieutenant took her arm and led her from the hall. Outside in the fog, he found his way to the post unerringly. The sight of it filled Rycca with horror, bringing as it did memories of such a post at Wolscroft and the terrible agonies endured at it. In her time at Landsende, she must have walked past the post a hundred times and never even taken note of it, so different did all seem here.

Had seemed. Everything was changed now. She could

hear the people who had followed them from the hall but the fog was still so thick they appeared as no more than dark ghosts against the blankness of the world. A rope hung from the post. Magnus took hold of it. Briskly, he said, "Give me your hands."

She obeyed because she had no choice. Though her spirit cried out in protest, she had too much pride to engage in futile resistance. He looped the rope around her wrists and tied them snugly. She glanced up and found him gazing at her with fierce glee. In an instant, his expression was masked but Rycca was sure of what she had seen. She stepped away from him quickly. Her back pressed against the post. The fog was her friend now. Never mind that it was cold and dank, it hid her from the eyes she was sure were staring at her. The people of Landsende had come to see the Saxon bride humbled. But she would not be. She would keep her head high and endure no matter what. It was not as though she had any choice. Pride was all that was left to her.

Yet after some little time, she decided to sit down. There was no shame in that and it was vastly preferable to falling over. She had not eaten since the porridge at breakfast but the mere thought of food made her nauseated. Settling herself on the ground, she tucked the damp skirt of her gown around her and shivered.

The jarl—she refused to think of him in any other terms—had said she would remain at the post until she spoke honestly about her actions, but she had already done so and it had availed her nothing. How long could a person be made to stay like this? Without shelter, lacking privacy for the most basic needs, exposed to public humiliation, existence would quickly become hellish. A tremor of dread ran through her. She wished for the reassurance of his arms around her, strong and sure, arms in which she had found such fleeting happiness. Tears stung her eyes. She wiped them away angrily.

Moments later, Magda stepped out of the fog before her. The older woman carried several blankets, a bowl of steaming stew, and a ewer of water. Briskly, she wrapped Rycca in warm wool and put a spoon in her hand. "Eat, my lady. I will come back shortly and you will be released to see to your needs."

Startled, Rycca said the first thing that came into her mind. "I thank you, but you must not do this, Magda. I would not see trouble brought down upon you."

The older woman straightened slowly, a look of worry on her gentle face. She hesitated but finally said, "Do not be concerned about that, my lady." Then she was gone, back into the fog.

Rycca sighed deeply. She had one friend at least, so it seemed, and for that she was grateful. But gratitude did not undo the huge knot in her stomach and make it possible for her to eat. Not even the delectable aroma of Magda's stew could tempt her. She set the bowl aside and burrowed deeper into the blankets. They, at least, offered warmth.

She wasn't eating. Dammit, she needed to do that to stay warm. There was no telling how long this could go on. On the verge of sending Magda back to try again, Dragon reconsidered. The serving woman had followed his instructions precisely. If this was to have any chance of working, he could not appear overly concerned. As it was, he was taking a chance staying so near. From his position near a corner of the stable, he could see the post through the fog but, he hoped, could not be seen himself. The sight of Rycca tied there tore at him. Not even a stern reminder that she might truly be guilty helped. He simply could not bring himself to believe it.

With a deep sigh, he settled back against the wall of the stable. Inside, Grani and Sleipnir whinnied as though they sensed their master's unhappiness. Toward evening, the fog began to lift. Dragon made sure he was well concealed and continued to watch. Magda came as he had arranged with her and led Rycca away for a short time. When they returned, the serving woman retied the rope although it obviously upset her to do so. He saw Rycca speaking to her consolingly. Magda frowned over the untouched bowl of stew, left a basket of fresh food, and made sure Rycca was well wrapped in blankets before she departed again.

No one else was about. Either the people of Landsende were sensible that their jarl would not appreciate their gawking or they had simply found it too disturbing to see a woman they had come to like in such distress. Whatever the case, they kept well away. No one dined in the hall that night and even the guards in the watchtowers kept their backs to the yard.

The long twilight finally gave way to night. Dragon stretched to ease the stiffness in his back and legs. His people would presume he was in his lodge, brooding over the treachery of his wife. It was his hope that whoever among them had thought to harm her, if indeed there was such a person, would make himself known shortly. She was tied, helpless. Surely, the opportunity would appear too good to pass up.

His stomach twisted. Never in his wildest imaginings would he have conceived of using Rycca in such a way, to lure out a traitor. But he truly could not think of anything else he might do. Over and over, he told himself she was not in any real danger. He would see anyone entering the yard immediately, long before an assailant could get near the post. And when he did see him—

There was some grim comfort in considering the price he would exact but it did not distract him from his vigil. Utterly still, all but invisible against the wall of the stable, the Dragon kept watch over his Saxon bride.

The moon was high in the sky when Rycca jerked awake suddenly. She was startled to discover she had slept, disbelieving really, for never would she have thought that possible. Yet exhaustion had finally overtaken her. Stirring in her cocoon of blankets, Rycca realized several more had been added to the pile. Magda must have come back without her being aware of it.

She had been dreaming of Dragon, imagining him there with her. What a cruel, stupid trick for her mind to play. Better she not sleep at all than surrender to such pitiful fantasies. It was very quiet in the yard. The moon was full and shining over all. Sharply etched shadows stretched across the ground. She heard a sudden *whish* and looked up in time to see an owl embarking on his night's flight.

So beautiful . . . so treacherous. To be given a glimpse of such a place only to have it snatched from her was worse than never having known it at all. How much kinder life would have been had it ended in her flight off the cliff.

Oh, no, that was too much! Never would she yield to such self-pity. Life was a gift from God no matter what hardships it brought.

Absently, for no better purpose than to distract herself, she twisted the rope that held her wrists. The knot was very loose. With only a slight effort, she could free herself.

And do what? Flee again? She swallowed a bitter laugh. There was nowhere to run to. She was in a prison of her own making, bound by ties she could not break to a man who believed her capable of the lowest treachery. Yet, oddly, she was not afraid. When the wanderings of her weary thoughts reached this point, Rycca stiffened in surprise.

She was not afraid.

How could that possibly be? She who had suffered through years of nightmares because of the violence she had witnessed at the hands of Vikings was now tied to a punishment post in a Viking town and yet she was not afraid. What shock and dread she had experienced were gone. In their place was only a strange serenity.

It would be all right.

She was innocent and somehow Dragon would find that out, as he had with Olav and, she was willing to guess, with others. When it became clear to him that she had nothing more to say, he would reassess what he knew and realize there had to be another explanation. Unlike her father, he was not a cruel or vengeful man. He would not hurt her. She had only to wait until the truth became evident to him.

Indeed, she had been foolish to think he might be angered by Magda's kindness to her. He would not blame the older woman who had been loyally in his service for so many years. Loyally . . . Rycca's eyes widened in the moonlight. Magda was utterly, unswervingly loyal to Dragon. Never would it occur to her to do anything that might displease him. Which meant—

She stared into the silvered night, straining to see. Nothing moved in the yard. There was not a hint of anyone about. And yet the conviction grew swiftly in her that she was not alone.

Hesitantly, feeling just a little foolish yet emboldened by yearning she could not deny, she whispered, "Dragon? Are you there? Can you hear me?"

Scarcely believing that she had guessed his presence, bewildered as to what that must mean, Dragon told himself he should not answer. The very person he hunted might already be about, only waiting for what seemed a safe moment. He could wreck it all by speaking. And yet he could not withstand the soft pleading in her voice.

Tensely, he answered. "Rycca, be quiet. No one must know I am here."

Joy flooded her. She had to suppress the urge to shout with relief. Her faith was not misplaced. He had not left her alone in the cold and dark.

"Dragon, why—?"

"Hush! We will speak of this later."

Ever obedient—the thought almost made her laugh out loud—she pressed her lips together and kept silent. Yet there was no such restriction on her thoughts. He was there, keeping watch over her, which meant he expected something to happen. What? That she would be so foolish as to try to escape? Not for a moment did she believe he would seek to trap her like that. No, he was waiting for someone else, the real villain who had sought to harm them both.

Waiting and hoping to lure him out by the simple expediency of using her as . . . bait.

That husband of hers—that dear, darling husband of hers—was going to have some serious apologizing to do when this was over.

Fearing that the sheer expanse of her smile would give the plan away, Rycca pulled a corner of a blanket up over her face. A short time later, she drifted off to sleep again, secure in the knowledge that she lay under the watchful eye of the Dragon.

EIGHTEEN

U NLIKE HIS WIFE, THE JARL OF LANDS-
ende did not sleep. Bred to the hardship of
battle, Dragon kept close vigil all through
the night. Nothing moved in the yard, nothing stirred. There was scarcely a sound until the cock
crowed morning.

Magda appeared immediately thereafter and took
Rycca away for some little time. When they returned, the
older woman attempted again to persuade her to eat.
Rycca promised she would try, and with her mood much
lightened she really meant to do so. Yet the very smell of
food made her stomach oddly unsettled and she set down
the bowl of porridge without taking a spoonful.

That infuriated Dragon, still watching from the stable. As though the circumstances were not bad enough, a
night without sleep had left him even more on edge. It
was all he could do not to stomp out into the yard and demand she swallow every bite.

After which he would take her in his arms, kiss her
lingeringly, beseech her to tell him he could not possibly
be wrong to trust her, and generally make a slobbering

fool of himself to rival those great dolts Grani and Sleipnir.

No, that he would not do. He would instead have a word with the men on the watchtowers, telling them to keep an eye on his wife and leaving them to make of that what they would while he went off to the river, there to immerse himself in blessedly cold water and cast off the shadows of sleeplessness.

When he returned, freshly garbed but not having taken time to shave, he found the day unfolding much as usual. People were coming and going about their daily tasks, now that the barn was rebuilt, apparently determined to ignore the fact that the lady of their manor was tied to a punishment post. Not Magda, though. That stalwart passed him with as close to a glare as she would ever come and bustled out to ask Rycca advice about something or other. The sheer ludicrousness of that struck Dragon and he was chuckling when Magda passed by again, which earned him another stern frown.

That was the height of levity for the day. Hours passed and nothing happened. Magda came and went, clucking over Rycca's failure to eat and glaring more at Dragon every time she saw him. Several of the other women began to do the same. He took that as an indication that those who had gotten to know Rycca best held her blameless. His venture into Byzantine intrigue of the previous day rankled all the more. He tried not to think about it.

The day dragged on. With the stronghold as busy as ever, Dragon told himself no one would be so foolish as to approach Rycca with intent to do her harm. Yet he found excuse after excuse to be in the yard himself. Magnus met up with him there at midday and asked if Dragon wanted him to take his place training the men. Dragon agreed and Magnus went off.

The sun hung motionless in the sky, or so it seemed.

"Get some sleep," Magda advised as she bustled by on her way to bring Rycca yet another meal she likely would not eat.

"Find out why she isn't eating," he shot back. For good measure, he added, "And tell her she damn well better."

Magda rolled her eyes but knew better than to say anything more.

Dragging the whetstone out in front of the stable, Dragon settled down to sharpen his sword. It was a proper enough activity, one he engaged in frequently. No one ought to think anything of it. The Moorish blade truly was remarkable, enough so to give him a few minutes' surcease from his constant worry over Rycca.

The day warmed. He noted that Rycca had on a fresh gown and was trying once again to eat. Magda was doing her job. From the nearby paddock, Grani and Sleipnir nickered. They refused to quiet until he got up, went over, and fed the fools apples.

"She'll be all right," he told them under his breath. "I probably won't be but I don't expect you to concern yourselves with that."

They bobbed their heads in what, he suspected, was agreement.

The sun was slanting westward, and Dragon was wondering how he was going to get through a second night without sleep, when a sudden shout from the watchtowers alerted him. He took the ladder two rungs at a time and reached the nearest tower while yet the guards were pointing out toward the road that led past the town toward the fields.

"Look, lord, there!"

Dragon looked. He saw two men pushing a hand-cart of the sort farmers used for trundling tools back and forth between the fields and the barns. Each man had one hand on the cart and was waving frantically with the other. Something was slumped in the cart but Dragon couldn't make it out. Yet it was clear that the men were in distress.

Quickly, he summoned half-a-dozen of his men, threw a saddle on Sleipnir, and rode out to find out what was wrong.

"We found him in the ravine near the river," one of the farmers said. He gestured to the bundle in the hand-cart.

Dragon approached and moved aside the coarse blanket flung over what proved to be the body of a man. He was of medium height and slim build, in his mid-twenties, with brown hair worn loose to his shoulders. Exactly the man Rycca had said she had seen in Landsende and who reminded her of someone from Wolscroft.

The fellow's eyes were closed and his skin held the pallor of death. There was a livid bruise along the right side of his head, partly caving in his skull. No doubt it was this that had dispatched him to eternity.

"Look at his wrist, lord," the other farmer said. He spoke diffidently but with an undercurrent of excitement that Dragon could not miss.

The dead man wore a plain shirt and trousers. The shirt was long-sleeved. Dragon lifted the fabric covering the man's left wrist and saw tattooed there . . .

Twin serpents entwined, devouring each other.

"Begging your pardon, lord, but the Lady Rycca said someone took her from the stable by force and she saw twin serpents. Mayhap it was these."

The surge of relief that roared through Dragon almost made him dizzy. In the dark night of his soul, he had battled doubt and chosen to believe in her, and now he was fiercely glad of it. Yet this confirmation of his trust was deeply welcome all the same.

He had scant time to enjoy it for hard on the evidence of her innocence came anger so intense that he felt as though the top of his head was about to come off. For the first time in his life, he understood what propelled the legendary berserkers, men who became something other than human on the battlefield as they were utterly overtaken by the drive to kill.

The struggle he waged to maintain control of his rage required every ounce of his formidable self-discipline, and victory remained precarious. Had the man from Wolscroft still been alive, Dragon truly did not know if he could hold off killing him long enough for him to talk. Talk he would have, of that there was no doubt. But whatever secrets he possessed had gone with him into the world beyond. Not much effort was needed to conclude what his presence at Landsende and his actions meant.

"Bring him," Dragon ordered and turned Sleipnir, spurring him to a gallop back to the stronghold.

The stallion came to a jarring stop near the punishment post, clumps of dirt spraying out from beneath his hooves. Dragon was out of the saddle in an instant and beside Rycca. He said not a word, unable to bring himself to speak until she was free of that loathsome place. His hands actually trembled as they undid the rope binding her.

"What is it?" she asked as he pulled her to her feet but resisted the urge to yank her into his arms, uncertain how she would respond. That she had realized his intent the night before did not absolve him of responsibility for being willing to use her in such a way, far less for entertaining even briefly the notion that she might be guilty.

"There's a dead man," he said and immediately regretted the words. Frigg and all her maidens, he was supposed to be skald-skilled! Surely he could have found a gentler way to inform a woman who had just been through so much.

However, far from looking concerned, Rycca appeared instantly interested. "Really? Who?"

"Your man from Wolscroft, I think. At least he fits your description."

She thought about that for a moment while she shook her skirts free of dirt. "I had begun to wonder if I'd imagined him."

"Apparently not, nor did you imagine the serpents. They were tattooed on his wrist."

"So that's what happened. He had a hand over my nose and mouth. I couldn't breathe but I remember looking down at his other hand grabbing me around the waist. I must have seen the tattoo just as I was losing consciousness."

She spoke matter-of-factly. Dragon did not. Indeed, he had trouble speaking at all. "I'd give almost anything to have him alive."

"Yes, it would have been better if he could have talked."

"I was thinking more about the pleasure of killing him."

Rycca gave him a swift look. "Done is done. What happened to him?"

"I'm not sure. He appears to have died from a blow to the head."

"Perhaps he fell after he left me. The fog was so thick it would have been easy enough to do."

It was a likely enough explanation but Dragon wanted more time to consider that before coming to any conclusions. He had done quite enough jumping as it was. The farmers, aided by his men, were bringing the body into the yard. Already, people were clustering around.

He took Rycca's hand, held it high in his, and said,

"The Lady Rycca is blameless. The true culprit has been found."

His people nodded, happy with this news. Yet the women still appeared stern. The men looked at him sympathetically, as well they might. He sighed inwardly. She already thought she had too many gowns and seemed to have no interest at all in jewels. The two best horses in the world were hers to ride. How exactly might he make amends?

"You did what you had to."

He started, sure he had heard her wrong.

"Oh, don't mistake me, I have no more liking for being staked out like a goat than would the next person. Still, it was a good plan, all things considered."

Shocked by her perception, he made no effort to hide his intent. "But it didn't work. I thought the culprit would come after you."

"Fortunately, he was already dead, or so it seems."

She had seen enough of the body as it was trundled by to be sure of that. This was not a fresh death. Several hours old at least, she thought, and perhaps even an entire day.

"You have experience to judge such things?" Dragon asked.

"Death was common at Wolscroft."

"Which brings me to the matter of your father—"

She turned, her eyes very wide against the paleness of her skin. He realized suddenly that though she had slept some the night before, she was as exhausted as he was.

Very low, she asked, "Do you have any idea how humiliated I am to be related to such a man, much less to have to call him father?"

"Take comfort. Perhaps your mother strayed."

"Oh, dearly would I like to believe that! It was my fondest dream for years. But she was meek by all accounts. I am his get, like it or not."

"As far from him as day from night. We have spoken of this before. You know my feelings."

She was silent, looking at him. Her eyes said all.

He took both her hands in his and raised them to his lips. Their gazes locked, he said, "I made a mistake."

"Confusing your wife with a goat?"

What was that he had thought about the difficulty of having a wife who was a truthsayer?

He took a breath, let it out slowly, and sent with it a prayer. "There was a time—a brief time—when I considered you might be guilty."

Truth.

Rycca smiled. She freed her hands, cupped them to his face, and rose on her toes to touch her mouth to his.

"What is that for?" he asked, caught between relief and bewilderment. Likely she would always keep him so off balance and likely he would always be glad of it for truly fortune smiled upon him. A great knot seemed to be untangling in his chest.

"For believing me."

"I only briefly didn't," he repeated.

"No, I mean for believing I am a truthsayer."

"And you know that because—"

She laughed and took his hand again. "Because you are a wise and canny man, Lord Dragon. You could as easily have insisted you never even flirted with the thought that I might be guilty and thereby saved yourself what must surely have been an uneasy moment for a husband."

He was slightly stung but not too much, for her ready forgiveness was as a balm over all else. "Generally speaking, I do tell the truth for its own sake."

"I never thought otherwise. And I would be as truthful with you. Last night, I realized suddenly that I was not afraid. All things considered, that was rather ridiculous but it was how I felt nonetheless."

The knot was definitely gone. Indeed, a great warmth

seemed to suffuse him. If a woman who had every reason
to fear Vikings could be tied to a punishment post by her
own Viking husband and not be afraid, that could mean
only one thing:

"You trust me."

"And you trust me."

At that moment, looking down at her, his face held
nothing of the mighty warrior and jarl. He looked instead
like a boy handed the world. She wanted only to give it to
him again and again.

"I would say," Rycca murmured, "that for a rocky beginning, we are managing well enough."

It was an incongruously happy note upon which to
discuss a dead man.

Silently giving thanks that his wife—*his wife*—had
not a squeamish bone in her lovely body, Dragon studied
the corpse. "Is he the man you saw in town?"

Rycca nodded at once. "Definitely, and I was right to
think I knew him from Wolscroft. His name is Fuller, for
his family who have been fullers of cloth for as long as
anyone can remember. But he aspired to bigger things
and put himself in service to my father."

"Who sent him here. With hindsight, I should have
thought of it." He remembered Wolscroft at the wedding,
drunk and belligerent, disarmed by his own daughter.
How had he failed to realize the man would seek revenge?

"I must tell Hawk and Wolf of this," he said.

She nodded but he saw the misery in her eyes and was
loath to leave her even briefly. "Come, I will write in our
lodge, where you will oblige me by resting."

"I would rather have a bath," Rycca said and mustered a smile though he thought it rather thin and cursed
her father again inwardly.

The women brought a tub usually used for washing
clothes but a delight to Rycca, who wanted more than a

pailful of water. When the tub was filled almost to the rim, the women departed. Dragon settled at the table with parchment, ink, and quills before him. Wolf had insisted they both learn to write, even enlisting a terrified priest to teach them. Dragon had resented the effort. It was only years later that he saw the good sense of not having to depend on anyone else for such communication. The letters were urgent, he intended them to go on the morning tide, yet words eluded him. Not that he didn't know exactly what he wanted to say, he was merely distracted.

His wife shed her clothes and began tying up her hair on top of her head. He found himself staring at the slim line of her back, the tapering of her spine and waist, the graceful arc of her hips. He glanced away with effort.

The parchment looked yellowed compared to the alabaster purity of her skin.

To my brother, the Lord Wolf of Sciringesheal. I send you greetings.

Her legs were slender and firm. He watched her step into the tub and remembered the silken strength of her thighs as they parted for him.

A man of Wolscroft has appeared here, bent on mischief. He is dead now.

She sighed deeply as the water touched her, a rapturous sigh of the sort that would have awakened his merry fellow were he not already at attention.

Grace to God, my wife is unharmed.

With a little wiggle, she settled her head against the rim, the rosy tips of her nipples just visible to him above the water.

Grace to God . . .

He'd written that already. With a frown, he crossed it out and tried yet again to give his attention to the letter.

Mercia ever breeds traitors. I write to Hawk as well.

She picked up the soap from the edge of the tub and

began lathering her arms. Dragon splotched ink over the paper, cursed under his breath, and blotted it up with sand.

Alfred must be told but I think it better he hear of it from Hawk.

The soap slipped down over her breasts and farther beneath the water.

I will write more later. For now, come to Landsende if you can that we may discuss this matter.

Done, signed, sealed with a blob of wax hastily drawn from a candle and imprinted with his ring. He took the letter, stepped outside the lodge, found the first man-at-arms he came upon, and gave it to him.

"By fast boat to Sciringesheal. Understand?"

The man assured him he did and Dragon returned to the lodge. Rycca was just rising from the tub. He had yet to write the letter to Hawk but he could do that in the morning and it would still catch the tide.

He went to her with a length of cloth set aside for drying, enveloping her in it and drawing her back against his chest. His hands moved over her lightly but continuously. He could not touch her enough.

"You are a very understanding woman." He might have added *and a very forgiving one* but she turned just then and the cloth fell open. Her breasts pressed against his chest through the thin tunic he wore.

"Did you sleep at all last night?" she asked.

"No, of course not."

The corners of her mouth lifted. "Oh, well, then you must be too tired."

He remembered baiting her over the Amazons and grinned. "Fishing, my sweet?"

She smiled beguilingly, slipped a hand down his trousers, and found precisely what she sought. Stroking him, she murmured, "Come to bed, husband."

Let it never be said he refused a perfectly reasonable request from a lady. Or, indeed, failed to fulfill it with alacrity. He laughed and backed up until he felt the edge of the bed against his knees, then simply let himself fall. Rycca came right with him. They stroked, tasted, explored each other for as long as Dragon could stand it, which was scant minutes.

"Enough," he growled, then rose from the bed and undressed, leaving his garments where they fell. When he returned to her, she drew him to her urgently. Pleasure engulfed him but just around the edges of it lay a sense of unease. He felt a desperation in her that surprised him. He had known her to be desperate only for freedom.

"What is it, sweetling?" he asked, his big hands tangling in her hair, his thumbs circling the edges of her forehead, pressing lightly as though to drive out whatever concern lingered there.

"I'm sorry," she murmured and turned her head away. The thick fringe of her lashes drooped over her eyes but not before he saw the flash of frantic misery in them.

"God's blood," he said before he could think better of it, "do not bring your loathsome father to our bed."

The shock lifted her out of her morass. She propped herself on her elbows and glared at him. "I do no such thing." Even as she spoke, she angled her hips, trying to push him off.

Dragon refused to give way. He stuck an iron-hard thigh between hers before she could realize his intent, took hold of her shoulders, and pressed her back down beneath him on the bed. "Yes, you are. You're trying to distract me from his treachery and perhaps yourself as well. But dammit, woman, I care not! How many times, in how many ways, do I have to tell you that?"

"He struck from hundreds of miles away! I thought him safely behind me, that part of my life closed and gone, and I was wrong! How can I ever draw an easy breath? Ever truly believe I have escaped him?"

The full realization of her anguish leaped out at him. Their eyes met for a long, tortured moment. Words boiled up in him, of comfort, promise, reassurance, but they vanished unformed. He, skald-souled, could scarcely grunt. To do so would be to speak of the death that surely awaited Wolscroft, the only possible response to his attack. He did not wish to talk of death in bed. Instead, he took her mouth hard, kissing her deeply and not stopping until she put her arms around him and held on tightly.

Their lovemaking was frantic at first. He brought her to orgasm with his hands and mouth, driving her further and further until she screamed his name. Only then did he enter her, holding himself strictly in check despite the driving thrust of his need. Hardly moving, only stroking deep within her, he brought her up again, determined to wipe away every vestige of fear, unhappiness, concern. Determined as well to banish from her thoughts any lingering memory of the preceding day and night. She clawed at his shoulders, drawing blood, and he thought it well spent. His control shattered suddenly and he gripped her hips, pulling her up to him, driving again and again, finding release in oblivion.

Into which he sank between one heartbeat and the next. The long day and night without rest took their toll. He fell against the pillows, a steely arm draped over her, and knew nothing more.

RYCCA LAY AWAKE JUST A LITTLE TIME, ON HER back, eyes wide, stunned by the depth of the pleasure he had given her. Would it never be ordinary with this man? Never the comfort of sweet routine? Her smile was still aborning when she, too, slept.

Late in the night, when even the owls nested, Dragon

dreamed. He was deep in a cave, comfortable and secure, with no desire to leave. But something called to him, some sound or sense, drawing him upward. He resisted it, wanting to stay where he was, but the need got stronger. His mind stirred, flaring at the edges of consciousness.

Urgency suddenly drove him. He opened his eyes but otherwise did not move. A shadow loomed by the bed, straightening into the form of a man with sword in hand.

One thought rang like hammer on anvil in Dragon's mind: Rycca lay beside him. Above all else, he had to protect her.

He jackknifed from the bed, landing on his feet and in the same motion reaching for the Moorish sword that should have been close at hand.

But was not. Was, in fact, in the hand of the intruder.

"You slept too deeply, jarl," Magnus said. He smiled grimly. "But then, I counted on that."

Maybe he was still asleep and dreaming, for this truly made no sense. Staring at the man he had known since boyhood—the man he had fought beside, gotten drunk with, and, truth be told, shared the occasional woman with—he struggled to understand. "What are you doing here?"

Magnus's mouth thinned. "Did you think I would never tire of being second to you?"

"You are mad."

"Yet I hold your sword and you are unarmed. Which of us do you think will die this night?"

And with that, Magnus lunged. He was a skilled and able fighter long schooled in battle. Dragon was naked and unarmed. The first slash of the Moorish sword would have gutted most men. Dragon sidestepped it easily. Even so he did not underestimate his peril . . . or Rycca's.

He could not think of her just then. All his attention had to remain on the man who meant to kill him and, no doubt, her as well. Yet from the corner of his eye Dragon saw that his wife had awakened and quickly taken in the situation. She was sitting up in bed, holding the covers to her breasts and keeping very still. He spared a moment to give silent thanks for her good sense, then picked up the small wooden table beside the bed and slammed it against Magnus.

The force of the blow staggered him but only for a moment. He closed in, swinging hard. Dragon blocked the sword with what was left of the table, which crumbled away in his hands. He looked around for something else, just barely managing to avoid several more blows any one of which should have killed him, and picked up a trunk near the windows. Magnus came at him fiercely but in that instant Dragon called upon his vast strength and lifted the heavy trunk over his head. His muscles straining with the effort, he hurled it directly at his attacker.

It struck Magnus full in the chest. He lost his balance and fell back toward the bed. A canny fighter with swift reflexes, he reached for Rycca, no doubt intending to use her as a shield. But she was ready for him and did not hesitate, kneeling upright in the bed, modesty forgotten as she raised a ewer of water and brought it crashing down on his head. It broke into pieces as Magnus staggered yet again and went down.

Dragon was on him instantly. Magnus fought fiercely to hold on to the sword but Dragon wrestled it from him and kicked it out of reach. He pinned the traitor to the floor with an arm at his chest and another at his throat. Calmly, as though he had not just been in a battle for his life, he asked, "Why?"

Magnus was breathing hard, his chest rising and falling convulsively. A bitter smile etched his mouth. Already, his eyes gazed upon eternity. "Wolscroft has a bounty on you," he rasped. "He sent his man to find someone to take it."

"Not good enough. He must have had some reason to approach you."

"We shared a tun of wine one evening in Essex. He knew my feelings."

"You killed him."

"I didn't want the Wolf hunting me when I was done."

"He won't be," Dragon said, and snapped his erstwhile lieutenant's neck.

S LOWLY, DRAGON GOT TO HIS FEET. DIMLY, AS though from a great distance, he heard Rycca's voice.

"Are you hurt?" She stood close beside him, garbed only in the glorious fall of her hair. Her hand was on his arm and her eyes were wide with concern.

He looked down at her and shook his head. "No."

Hurt? Why should he be? Because he had been betrayed by a man he thought he knew and could trust? Such was the way of the world. There was very, very little a man could ever truly count on.

"You fought," he said and reached out, needing to touch her. His big hands stroking her hair, he drew her closer to him until he enveloped her in his arms and held her as tightly as he dared. It was just so damn good to feel the warmth of her body, to know she was safe and there with him. She anchored him to the world.

Rycca laughed a little shakily. "Oh, well, you know me, ever ready to plunge in." She touched her lips to his chest, kissing him lightly and repeatedly, needing the taste, the scent, the touch of him.

He had come so very close to death. Over and over, she had watched Magnus strike, believing that at any moment Dragon would fall. His strength and skill were as no man she had ever seen, yet for all that he was still human. Her hand drifted down to the scar on his thigh and she shivered. So very close . . .

"Don't think about it." As he spoke, he lifted her and

carried her to the bed. She was shivering uncontrollably now, her whole body quaking.

"What's happening to me?" Her teeth were chattering, making it almost impossible to speak.

"Just a reaction. It will pass." He got into bed with her and held her close, stroking her back, murmuring to her soothingly. After a while, she began to calm, indeed too much. She felt as though she could barely lift her head.

"This never happened to you," she murmured.

He smiled in the dim gray light of the new morning. "Oh yes it did, and more than once. After my first battle, I was shaking so hard you would have thought it was winter instead of high summer. But that was better than the way I was before it."

"Scared?" she asked very softly.

"Spewing-up-my-guts scared. Make no mistake, I've seen the most valiant men react to battle in all sorts of ways. The best suffer even in victory. It's the ones who don't you have to worry about." He glanced over the side of the bed at what had been Magnus. "If you're better now, I have to leave for a few minutes but I will return immediately."

She nodded, understanding what had to be done, and burrowed under the covers as he pulled on a tunic. When he was dressed, he lifted the body and hoisted it over his shoulders. She watched as he went out into the fading night.

He returned very quickly, as promised. She heard voices outside the lodge and saw the flare of torches just before the door closed behind him. He came to stand beside the bed. "All right?"

Scarcely had she nodded than there was a brisk knock at the door. Frowning, Dragon went to answer it. He came back bearing a heavily laden tray and instructions from Magda.

"You are to eat the soup first," he said bemusedly. "It is one of Cymbra's recipes and Magda says it will settle your stomach. You are to drink all the milk, eat the poached chicken, and not neglect the stewed apples."

"Did she bring anything for you?" Rycca asked as she sat up in the bed. To her astonishment, she was suddenly hungry. Watching two men battle to the death apparently stirred her appetite. Mayhap it had to do with who had won.

Dragon sighed. "It doesn't appear so." Nobly, he added, "But that's fine, I'm not hungry, and I have to write to Hawk without further delay."

"You could have some of the chicken," she said generously.

He saw her eyeing it and laughed. "No, sweetling, you go ahead."

She shrugged, which had the effect of causing the covers to fall away from her, and reached for the soup. Dragon went to the table by the window, moved the chair so that he had his back to his wife, and sat down to write his letter.

It was full dawn by the time they both were done. "I cannot sleep more," Rycca admitted though her eyes were shadowed with fatigue.

"I don't believe I can either." Dragon returned the trunk to its appointed place, tossed the remnants of the table outside the lodge, and sat down beside her on the bed. He touched the side of her face gently. "But you should try."

She shook her head. "Then I will dream and I don't want to, not yet."

Blessedly, he understood, but then he always seemed to do so. He stood up again and reached for her hand. "Let's ride."

They did, wild and free, over the long, stubble-scented fields nestled between the rising hills and the rolling sea.

They spoke of nothing that had happened but only of the gift of the moment, a bird in flight, light on sea foam, the scent of the wind. At midmorning, they stopped and ate the repast Magda had insisted on sending along with them. Sleepy in the aftermath, Rycca dozed. She woke from dreamless rest to find her lap filled with wildflowers—blue and gold violets, white starworts with bright yellow centers, wild geraniums, purple heather, pale lavender bellflowers, creamy butterworts . . . a treasure trove of nature's jewels.

"Where did these come from?" she asked her warrior husband.

He leaned back on his elbows and studied the sea. "Some trolls came by and left them."

"Trolls picking flowers?"

"More believable, surely, than me doing it?"

She laughed and surprised him by competently weaving the summer's late blossoms into a garland for her hair.

"How is it you know how to do that," he asked, "when you are so thoroughly undomestic?"

She threw a purple aster at him and laughed again. "I thought I was managing to conceal that."

"Oh, certainly. You learn fast, that's for sure, and Magda thinks the world of you, which she would not if she didn't think you had real ability. But tell me of the flower weaving."

She sighed with great exaggeration and obliged him. "One day at a fair I saw a girl wearing a flower garland. Never in my life had I wanted anything so much. There were others for sale but I knew better than to ask for one. It was quite astonishing enough that I'd been brought along. At any rate, I resolved then and there to learn how to weave them myself. I absolutely will not tell you how long it took me but eventually I mastered the art."

To prove her point, she set the completed garland on her head, where, he quickly assured her, it looked lovely. But he made a mental note that Rycca's barren childhood was one more crime for which Wolscroft would pay.

They rode back in the golden glow of afternoon. Scarcely had they topped the rise above the town than Dragon drew rein. Beneath him, bobbing on the ink-blue water, was a drakar, its wolf-emblazoned sail only just being furled.

"He couldn't possibly have received your letter," Rycca said as they rode swiftly to the stronghold. "And I know Cymbra has a rare gift but surely she cannot sense your thoughts."

"Something else must have happened," Dragon said and urged Sleipnir on.

Cymbra was already in the kitchens with Magda and the other women. Rycca hurried to join her while Dragon went down to the beach to welcome his brother. Wolf stood there on the strand, impassive as always, and watched the fire that had almost burned itself out.

"Magnus?" he asked, pointing to the pile of smoldering ash that had been a funeral pyre.

Dragon nodded, unsurprised that his brother had already heard. Such news must have greeted him the moment he stepped on shore. "I thought of burying him but decided he should have none of my land, not even that much."

"Rycca is all right?"

"She seems fine. I took her away from here while this was going on." He gestured to the pyre.

"I've had a letter from Hawk," Wolf said.

"And missed one from me. Come, let's crack a barrel of mead and talk."

Hawk had written to say that Alfred had heard rumblings of opposition to the alliance of Norse and Saxon coming from within his own kingdom. He suspected

Wolscroft but was unsure. As Dragon was now yoked by marriage to that unworthy, he thought it best if Wolf broke the news to him.

"No news," Dragon said as they sat in the great hall, flagons of mead before them. "Magnus confessed before he died."

He told his brother what the traitor had said. Wolf heard him out grimly. "We underestimated Wolscroft," he said. "I thought him a bully and drunkard, nothing more."

"As did I. Bringing him down will not be easy."

Wolf nodded. "He holds much of Saxon Mercia since Hawk killed Udell last year. If he were to go over to the Danes—" There was no need to say more. Alfred of Wessex had united much of England to stand against the invaders but the peace he had wrought was precarious. It might easily be undone.

"He won't," Dragon said. "Wolscroft hates the Danes."

His brother looked surprised. "How do you know this?"

Briefly, Dragon related the story Rycca had told him of the Danes' raid when she was a child, of Wolscroft's cowardice and his determination to keep it secret. "Can you see him making alliance with the very men who caused him to so shame himself?"

"Unlikely," Wolf agreed. The brothers looked at each other as certainty dawned.

"Then," Dragon said, "his target must be Alfred . . . and Alfred's alliance with us."

"That false priest Elbert said the bitch Daria was allied with the Danes."

"He may have lied."

There was time after that to eat the very fine meal Cymbra and Magda prepared with Rycca's able assistance, to linger over the table as Dragon spun stories, and for lovers to dream the night away in each other's arms.

But on the morning tide, while yet a ghostly mist lingered over the water, shouts rang out on the quays, oars slipped into their locks, and sails billowed as a dozen war-armed dragon ships sailed for England.

NINETEEN

THE HAWK OF ESSEX LOOKED OUT TOWARD the sea and thought for a moment that he had stepped back in time. As it had more than two years before, a Viking war fleet was bearing down on his shore.

He called to his wife, who was, after all, Norse and whom he knew had a good grasp of things. "Would you agree that Wolf and Dragon are reasonable men?"

Krysta lifted their son from the basin in which she had been bathing him, grinned at the baby's eager kicks, and wrapped him snugly in a blanket before joining Hawk at the window. "Eminently reasonable."

He looked again over the sea. "Something has stirred them." Buckling on his sword, he went to find out what it was.

Krysta hurried down to find Rycca and Cymbra in the great hall. The women hugged one another, cooed over Lion and Falcon, and exchanged the usual comments about the voyage, which thankfully had been uneventful. Krysta was not fooled. She saw the strain in the eyes of the two women she was happy to regard as sisters, and she was determined to ease it as much as possible.

Summoning servants, she sent the children off to be spoiled and adored, and declared, "Let's take the sauna before the men do."

Cymbra and Rycca helped gather towels and scented soaps and oils. While yet their husbands were conversing on the quay, they hurried off to the chamber set in the side of the hill. When the women had disrobed, Krysta added wood to the firebox and threw water on the heated stones. A sizzling cloud of steam scented with pine rose to fill the dimly lit interior.

Rycca sighed with relief and stretched out on one of the low wooden benches. The others did the same. They spoke idly for a few minutes until Krysta said, "Tell me what has happened, all of it. I know Hawk wrote to Wolf about Alfred's concerns, but why have you come in such force?"

"Because Alfred may need help," Rycca replied. She told Krysta of the events at Wolscroft, adding, "It shames me deeply to admit this but I think my father sought to kill me, slay Dragon, and make it appear as though I had died at his hand while defending myself. Had he succeeded, the alliance could have been destroyed and even Alfred's hold on the throne weakened."

"No shame attaches to you," Cymbra said gently. "Clearly, you are not your father's daughter in any way that matters."

"Absolutely not," Krysta agreed promptly. "You bear no responsibility for his actions. Look you, I have a half-wit brother who tried to brand me a witch and deny Hawk my dowry. I share no blame for his idiocy."

Cymbra wound the gleaming mass of her hair high on her head, secured it with a ribbon, and nodded. "Nor do I count myself responsible for the actions of Daria, who is, after all, my half-sister. The bonds of family can be wonderful but there is a time to know when to stand apart." She held out a hand to Rycca on the nearby bench. "Besides, we are your family now, all of us, and we know your worth."

Deeply touched, Rycca had to blink several times before she could respond. She knew both women spoke pure truth and loved them for it. After a lifetime of emotional solitude unbroken but for Thurlow, it was still difficult for her to comprehend that she was no longer alone. Yet was she beginning to understand it.

Softly, she said, "I worry over Dragon. He refuses to talk of my father or of what will happen now that we are here, but I fear he is planning to take matters into his own hands."

Cymbra and Krysta exchanged a glance. Quietly, Cymbra said, "Your instinct is not wrong. Dragon simmers with rage at the harm attempted to you. In Landsende I caught a mere glimpse of it, and it was like peering into one of those mountains that belch fire."

Despite the heat of the sauna, Rycca shivered. "He came close to losing his life once because of me. I cannot bear for it to happen again."

There was silence for a moment, broken only by the crackling of the fire and the hiss of steam. Finally, Cymbra said, "We are each of us married to an extraordinary man. There is something about them . . . even now I don't really know how to explain it." She looked at Krysta. "Have you told Rycca about Thorgold and Raven?"

Krysta shook her head. "There was no time before." She turned on her side on the bench, facing the other two. "Thorgold and Raven are my . . . friends. They are somewhat unusual."

Cymbra laughed at that, prompting a chiding look from Krysta, who went on to say, "I'm not sure how but I think somehow I called them to me when I was a child and needed them very much."

"Krysta has the gift of calling," Cymbra said, "as I do

of feeling and you do of truthsaying. Doesn't it strike you as odd that three very unusual women, all bearing special gifts, came to be married to three extraordinary men who are united by a common purpose, to bring peace to their peoples?"

"I had not really thought about it," said Rycca, who also had not known of Krysta's gift and was looking at her with some surprise. All three of them? That was odd.

"I believe," said Cymbra, who clearly had been thinking about it, "that there is a reason for it beyond mere coincidence. I think we are meant to be at their sides, to help them as best we can, the better to transform peace from dream to reality."

"It is a good thought," Krysta said.

Rycca nodded. Very quietly, she said, "Blessed are the peacemakers."

Cymbra grinned. "And poor things, *we* appear to be their blessings. So worry not for Dragon, Rycca. He will prevail. We will all see to it."

They laughed then, the trio of them, ancient and feminine laughter hidden in a chamber held in the palm of the earth. The steam rose around them, half obscuring, half revealing them. In time, when the heat had become too intense, they rose, wrapped themselves in billowing cloths, and ran through the gathering darkness to the river, where they frolicked in cool water and laughed again beneath the stars.

The torches had been lit by the time they returned to the stronghold high on the hill. They dressed and hastened to the hall, where they greeted their husbands, who stood as one when they entered, silent and watchful men before beauty and strength, and took their seats at table. Wine was poured, food brought, music played. They lingered over the evening, taking it into night.

The moon was high when they found the sweet, languid sanctuary of their beds. Day came too swiftly.

By noon, the tide had turned. The drakars emblazoned with wolf and dragon joined the fleet of the Hawk as they set sail for the city of the king.

Rycca but dimly remembered Winchester, having been there only once as a child. Much more she recalled the scriptorium that adjoined the royal palace and her furtive, fascinated wanderings through it while the monks were at prayer. It was there she had conceived the extraordinary notion of learning to read, for so long her proudest accomplishment.

But no longer. Now it had to give way before her pride in being the wife of the Dragon. They entered Winchester on horseback and rode along the broad, straight avenue that led to the palace. People pressed in all around them, staring at the stern-faced warriors rank on rank behind the mighty lords whose names ran like quicksilver through the crowds. The Hawk was known in Winchester and his banner drew cheers, but Viking warlords in the king's city were something new. Heavy silence descended in the wake of the jarls of Sciringesheal and Landsende.

Riders had hurried ahead to alert Alfred. He came down the steps of his palace to greet them. Rycca was surprised by the ordinariness of his appearance. He was of moderate height, simply dressed in a plain brown tunic, a cape thrown over shoulders still broad despite his years. His neatly trimmed beard was liberally salted with silver but his eyes, when she came close enough to see them, were as keen as those of a much younger man.

"Long have I hoped to meet you both," he said to Wolf and Dragon when Hawk had presented them to him. "And honored am I to welcome you to my court."

True, as far as it went, Rycca thought. But the king was also curious, if not apprehensive, about what had brought the Viking lords to his doorstep. Well he might be.

COME BACK TO ME

Alfred drew to his side a plump and pleasant woman he introduced as his queen, Ealhswith. Krysta greeted her with unfeigned warmth that was returned in full. Graciously, the queen welcomed both Cymbra and Rycca and invited them to accompany her to their quarters so that they might rest and refresh themselves.

When they came back down to the great hall, the king was deep in conversation with his guests but he broke off to greet the ladies as they came forward, gloriously gowned, perfumed, and bejeweled, but for all that beautiful because of the radiance that shone from within each.

"Three brides," Alfred said, "and surely there have been none lovelier. Yet have your marriages, each and every one of them, been fraught with danger."

"Only at the beginning, sire," Krysta said. "I daresay, none of us has any complaints now."

This was just what was needed, Rycca thought, a light and gentle touch. Already the faces around the high table looked more at ease. She took her place beside Dragon, who squeezed her hand.

"Your husband has been telling me of events at Landsende," Alfred said to her. "I deeply regret what you experienced."

"It was hardly your fault, majesty," Rycca murmured. Indeed, she thought everyone knew very well whose fault it was.

"As to your father," the king said delicately, "his activities must be investigated."

"He sent his man to Landsende," Dragon said firmly, "and he conspired with my lieutenant to kill us both. Of that much we can be certain."

"Yet would I be certain of it all," Alfred said. He looked at Wolf. "You believe he may have conspired against all three marriages?"

"It is possible," Wolf said. "Father Elbert claimed the

Danes were behind Daria's plotting but he never named an actual Dane."

"He swore he did not know," Hawk said. "He insisted he was Daria's dupe."

The men, king included, exchanged glances. Clearly, none believed this. But the women shared their own silent communication and theirs was a good deal less certain.

"I face a problem," Alfred said. He leaned forward, resting his arms on the table, and looked at each of them in turn.

"What am I dealing with here? An outraged father regretting his daughter's marriage and who perhaps even believed she had been given to a man who would harm her, which you can be sure will be his defense, and who therefore sought to free her of a union she did not wish? Or a traitor seeking to destroy peace between our peoples, plunge us into war, and unseat me from my throne?"

He sighed deeply, and for just a moment the weight of his years hung heavily on him. "The one I can kill under the law and men will uphold me for it, just as they did when the traitor Udell perished last year. But the other . . ." Again the king sighed. "That is a different matter."

"Fine," Dragon said promptly. "I shall solve your problem for you." He made to rise.

Rycca did not mask her response. She grabbed hold of his wrist with both her hands and yanked hard. "Sit down," she said emphatically, and then just to soften it, "I pray you, my lord."

After a moment's shock, Alfred laughed. He shook his head ruefully. "You three must know how men envy you? The beauty of your wives is spoken of with awe, yet I am pleased to see they are not lacking in spirit either."

"Mayhap too much spirit," Dragon growled, but he did not look truly angry, merely frustrated.

"Your killing Wolscroft will only cause more trouble," Alfred said. "No, this must be handled within the law."

Slowly, Dragon resumed his seat but he looked in no way pleased about it. Rycca returned her hands to her lap and tried hard to look abashed. He wasn't fooled but he did reach over, take hold of her chair, and haul it up close to his so that he could rest an arm around her shoulders. A rather heavy arm, she thought, reminded of his strength and will. Not that she minded. Above all, she wanted him near her, not off risking his life against her father.

"There would have to be a trial," Alfred said, "and that means the taking of evidence. Before we contemplate any such thing, I would know what Father Elbert and the Lady Daria have to say for themselves."

"You think they would tell the truth?" Hawk asked.

The king looked frankly skeptical. "They are both kept under harsh rule. A promise of some lightening of their circumstances might loosen their tongues. But," he added, "it would be difficult to know whether they spoke the truth or not."

"Rycca . . ." Dragon spoke, only her name to be sure, but buried within it was a question. He would not speak of her gift and neither would any of the others. Of that she was absolutely certain. It was up to her to reveal to the king what she had always kept hidden, if she so chose.

"Majesty . . ." She hesitated, uncertain of what to say. Alfred was looking at her, his eyes patient but tired. She thought suddenly of all he had done, the lifetime of battle and struggle, his entire being dedicated to the golden vision of a united England living at peace. Were it not for him, there would have been no release from the time of chaos and killing that had so scarred her childhood, of that she was certain. He was the hope of her peoples, both of them now, Norse and Saxon alike. She could not fail them or him.

"Majesty, I am a truthsayer."

The king looked from her to Dragon. The jarl of Landsende inclined his head. "It is as she says. Rycca can tell the difference between a truth and a lie. I cannot explain how this is but I have seen it work for myself and I know that it does."

Alfred's gaze shifted back to Rycca. The tiredness was gone. He stared at her intently with the look of a man who has seen far too much of the world to doubt that it held marvels. "Does your father know of this?"

She shook her head. "No, my lord. I concealed it from all, for it would have meant my death."

"At Wolscroft's hands?"

Though it pained her greatly, she said, "I was never of any value to him, my lord."

"His loss," Alfred said quietly. He thought a moment longer, then nodded. "Very well, I will send for Father Elbert and the Lady Daria. We will hear what they have to say."

"Why not send for Wolscroft?" Dragon asked, fingering the hilt of his sword as he spoke.

"To what purpose?" Alfred replied. "I can accept that the Lady Rycca is a truthsayer for I have no reason to doubt her word or yours. However, I do not wish to put her in the position of judging her own father. Beyond that, even if she did catch him in a lie, her word alone will not justify his execution in the eyes of my nobles. There must be more."

Rycca nodded, inwardly relieved. It was her fondest hope that she would never have to see her father again, but she was beginning to realize that might be impossible.

"The priest, then," she said, "and the Lady Daria. At least we will finally know the truth of them."

She had three days to ponder what that truth might be. Three days during which Dragon scarcely let her out of his sight. He went so far as to try to accompany her to the queen's solar, only to be shooed away by Ealhswith even as she smiled and took pains to reassure him.

"I promise you, my lord, the Lady Rycca will be as safe here as a babe in arms. Believe me, the quarters of the queen are not entered into by miscreants."

"That is all well and fine, majesty, but—"

"Should you not be aware, my lord, we had an incident here last year when the Lady Krysta was taken from Winchester by stealth. Since then, my lord husband has spared no effort to assure nothing of the sort can ever happen again." She gestured toward the grim-faced guards on watch in the corridor. "You will find the same beneath my windows, Lord of Landsende, and even above us on the roof. Not even an errant bird can enter here."

Even as she spoke, through the open door where she stood Dragon saw a raven alight on the sill of one of the solar's windows. Rather oddly, he thought, Krysta walked over and began talking to it.

"There are four new books in the scriptorium, my lord," the queen said, unaware of what was going on behind her, "and a young priest—a friend of Father Desmond, who is now at Hawkforte—who is responsible for one of them. By the way, he has a yen to travel."

That said, she shut the door not quite in his face but as close to it as that gentle lady could ever come. Dragon hesitated. He eyed the guards, who eyed him back, reminded himself that he was in the house of the king, and finally decided to go look at the new books. While he was at it, he just might have a word with the priest.

Three days later, a stunned but delighted Father Thomas prepared for his journey to the fabled northlands, there to establish a new scriptorium. The Lord Dragon having readily agreed to his request for parchments, pens, inks, and the like, the good priest was racing about Winchester trying to spend the absurdly large quantity of gold he had been given to secure supplies. As it happened, he was the first to see the prisoners arrive, but so taken was he with his task that he failed to notice them.

Not so Rycca. She was standing at a window of the solar, gazing out over the town, when she saw the convoy of armed men surrounding two riders as they approached the palace. She said nothing but inwardly she gathered herself for what she knew must come.

Scarcely a quarter-hour later by the queen's water clock, she was summoned to the great hall.

"They are here," Dragon said without preamble. He took her arm and drew her close to him. She nodded but remained silent, absorbed with studying the man and woman who remained under the tight scrutiny of the guards. The man was garbed and tonsured as a priest but the light of faith did not shine in him. His face was pale and strained, his shoulders slumped, and he continually glanced around anxiously. After one quick look in the direction of the woman, he jerked his head away. If the Lady Daria noticed him, she gave no sign. Tall and thin, austerely dressed, she nonetheless held her head high and smiled widely. A cold, fierce pleasure seemed to seep from her.

Cymbra came into the hall just then with Wolf beside her. He stopped her at the entrance and said something Rycca could not catch. Cymbra shook her head, took a breath, and continued into the hall. Wolf followed, frowning.

Krysta and Hawk arrived almost immediately thereafter. Hawk very deliberately put himself between his wife and his half-sister, which reminded Rycca that Daria had tried to kill Krysta.

"We will begin," Alfred said. He looked first to Father Elbert.

"Priest, you will answer my questions fully and

truthfully. Do you so, I am willing to consider an amelio-
ration of your circumstances. Do you not and you will
suffer for it. Do you understand?"

The priest bobbed his head up and down. Rycca
looked at his hands clasped before him, twisting compul-
sively. She started to move a little closer to him only to be
stopped by Dragon, who glared at her. With a sigh, she
contented herself with mere listening.

"What is the name of the Dane with whom you conspired to prevent the alliance between Saxon and Norse?"

A pulse beat spasmodically in the priest's right eye-
lid. "I do not know, majesty. Before Almighty God, I
swear my crime was only to follow the will of that
woman"—he pointed a shaking hand at Lady Daria—
"who is a servant of evil!"

A short, barking laugh of contempt greeted this pro-
nouncement. All eyes shifted to Daria. She drew herself
up even more erectly, her gaze alight with glee. To Alfred
she declared, "Fool that you are, king of fools, even you
should know this perversion of a priest lies!"

Alfred's mouth thinned dangerously but he held his
temper with what Rycca thought was admirable fortitude.

"Indeed, lady?" the king asked. "And what do you
know of this?"

Daria looked around at them all. To Rycca, she
seemed to be savoring their attention. She opened her
mouth as though to speak, shut it suddenly, and was silent
for several moments before she said, "I, lord? A mere
woman? How could I know anything at all?"

From the corner of her eye, Rycca saw Cymbra shiver
suddenly. Wolf reacted at once. He drew her into his arms
and turned his back on the group, effectively shielding her
from them. Again, he spoke to her low and urgently.
Again, she shook her head.

Krysta too had seen and was frowning. A little man
came into the hall just then. He was very short, barrel-

chested, and sported a great, dark beard. He went to Krysta, patted her hand, and nodded to Hawk, who seemed to know him.

"I think you underestimate yourself, Lady Daria," Alfred was saying. "I remember you very well from when both of us were young. You were not a timid woman or a stupid one."

Again Daria seemed to wage a battle within herself but this time she could not stop herself from preening. "True, lord, I was never that. If only things had gone differently. My fool of a husband . . ." She frowned deeply.

"Was not worthy of you," Alfred said. "It was my sad duty to usher him from this world when he rose in rebellion against me. You deserved better, lady."

"Oh, I did! I truly did! How amazing that you realize that. It has been such a struggle. . . ."

"I imagine so." The king leaned forward as though hanging on her every word. "I would like to hear of your trials. Perhaps your current circumstances are not justified."

"Indeed they are not! No one will even explain to me why I am kept in that horrid place with those dreadful nuns who will not let me do anything but eat, sleep, and pray."

Hawk looked up at the ceiling. Quietly, he said, "Perhaps trying to kill my wife and our then unborn child has something to do with where you are now."

Daria whirled on him. The man who was her half-brother and who had given her a home for years after the treason of her husband became the target of a full blast of her vitriol.

"Bastard! Oh, yes, do not think otherwise, for our father was only ever married to but one woman, my mother. Mine, not yours or that stupid cow Cymbra's!

She held all his heart and soul, and he was never free to vow himself to any other!"

"God help him were that true," Hawk muttered. "Thankfully, it is not."

No, Rycca thought, it was not, but rather more importantly, Daria believed it was. She was truly convinced of what she said.

"Besides," Daria continued, "I never tried to harm your wife."

Lie. She knew full well what she had done.

"You do not remember?" Alfred asked.

"What is there to remember?" She pointed to the priest, who shrank before her scrutiny. "This one clouded my mind. He played upon my loneliness and my devotion to God. He gulled me with false promises and stole from me all reason."

"So it was all Father Elbert's doing?"

"I did not!" the priest cried out. He turned to Alfred frantically. "I swear, lord, upon peril of my immortal soul!"

The king held up a hand, silencing him. "Answer me, Lady Daria. Was it Father Elbert's doing or your own?"

"My own? Have you heard nothing I have said? Oh, but of course not! The mighty Alfred! Why would you listen to me?" She turned away in disgust.

The king rose from his seat. His face like thunder, he stared down at her. "Answer me, woman! Do not gainsay your king!"

But Daria had retreated into the fortress of her vanity. From there, she peered out, cold, calculating, and well pleased with the frustration she had wrought.

She and the priest were taken away. The rest were left to mull over what had happened.

Cymbra was pale but stalwart. She looked at Krysta with deep sympathy. "There is a terrible sickness in her. It is a wonder she did not succeed in killing you."

"She came very close," Krysta replied softly. Hawk put an arm around her and drew her to him. Together, they and all the others turned to Rycca.

She took a deep breath, willing herself to calm. Never before had she felt the brush of such malevolence. She prayed she would never do so again.

"Daria is mad," she said. "I have never before tried to tell truth from falsehood in a mad person. But when she spoke of her father never being able to vow himself to anyone but her mother, that was truth. False though it is, she genuinely believes it, and that gave me something to gauge the rest against. She lied about not remembering what she did to Krysta. She knows it full well. The problem is that she never answered your majesty's question about who was really responsible for what happened, she or Father Elbert."

"No," Alfred said wearily, "she did not. I can recall her, question her again, even, if need be, put her to the torture. But will it avail us anything at all?"

"Not likely," Cymbra said. She shuddered. "That one is so engulfed in hatred and rage I doubt she can feel anything else at all, even pain."

"Besides," Rycca added, "I do know that Father Elbert is telling the truth. He really does believe himself to have been her dupe, and when he called her a servant of evil, he said what he genuinely thinks. He is terrified of her."

Alfred looked skeptical, as did the other men. "Mayhap he is only a very good liar."

"No," Rycca said quietly, "he is not."

The king let that go for the moment and said, "Would your father have used such a woman?"

"I don't know," Rycca said honestly. "He has contempt for all women. Ordinarily, I would think it would not even occur to him to involve a woman in anything he did, but I could be wrong. Daria was perfectly positioned to carry out his will. That might have been enough to make him overlook her sex."

"There is no way to know," Alfred said regretfully. He looked at Dragon. "And without that knowledge, I cannot bring Wolscroft to trial."

Wolf moved closer to his brother, putting a hand on his shoulder. "Easy . . ."

"Easy? How am I to be easy when the man who sought to kill my wife is to go unpunished?" Turning back to Alfred, the outraged Lord of Landsende said, "Think not, majesty, that the alliance between us means Norse will suffer harm at the hands of Saxons and not seek just recompense. By Odin, that will never be!"

"By Christ, that is not what I seek!" Alfred shot back. "But what good will it do the alliance if I am tumbled from my throne by lords who think one of their own has died at the whim of a Viking?"

The two men glared at each other as Rycca's breath caught in her throat. She felt them all teetering on the very edge of disaster.

"Daria has pushed us to this," she exclaimed, "and perhaps also my father. For pity's sake, let us not fall prey to them!"

Desperately, she turned to her husband, pleading with him. "Lord, I love you truly with all my heart. Every moment with you is precious to me but I would give up even that if it meant peace between our peoples. Nothing else can be allowed to matter so much as that."

Dragon did not reply. He was staring at her very oddly. Of the others, she had no awareness at all. Only he existed for her just then. She felt as though there was no ground beneath her but this time instead of falling as she had off the cliff, she soared frantically, desperately, not knowing if at any moment gravity might reclaim her but soaring all the same.

"What did you say?" he demanded.

"Nothing else can be allowed to matter so much as the peace between our peoples! I understand full well how angry you are. The insult done you was profound, but I beg you, think of what you do. Do you go against my father, he wins!"

Slowly, Dragon shook his head as though trying to clear it. His gaze locked on Rycca's like a man holding fast to the rudder in a mighty storm. A dull flush crept over his high-boned cheeks. "Insult? You think I want to kill your father because he insulted me? For pity's sake, woman, I damn near lost you! Don't you have any idea what that means to me?"

Her eyes widened, never leaving him as he stalked across the stone floor of the Saxon's king's great hall and took firm hold of her by her shoulders. He dragged her up against him even as he near yelled, "Dammit to hell, woman, I love you! What care I for insults? Nothing matters to me save keeping you safe and—"

"Love?" Rycca repeated in a daze.

"Loki take you, lady, you are not the easiest woman in the world to get along with, you know! You are strong, spirited, stubborn, not a meek bone in your body! Your body . . . Never mind that, the point is you have stolen into my heart and I lack any will to get you out, so do not dare you think of dying! I absolutely forbid it! Did you say you love me?"

Oh, my, Rycca thought, she truly did have wings after all. Strong, sturdy wings that would carry her as high as she wanted to climb. And that was very high indeed.

A smile crept over her clear to her toes. She cupped her husband's face between her hands and took his mouth with hers. Well and thoroughly did she kiss him right there in front of everyone. That took some time, and when she was done she was rather breathless. Yet she managed to say, "I love you, lord. More than life, more even than freedom. You are dearest to me above all."

And for just a moment, there in the hall of the king, Rycca of Landsende saw the sheen of tears in her Viking's eyes.

TWENTY

H E REALLY WAS AN IMPOSSIBLE MAN. FOR
all that she loved him to the height and
breadth of her being, there was simply no
denying that. Rycca sipped the herbal tea
Cymbra had brought her, good for an uncertain stomach,
and tried for the hundredth time since returning to Hawkforte to think how best to approach her husband on the
matter that absorbed them all.

Wolscroft remained free. Like it or not—and Dragon
still simmered—Alfred could do nothing. He lacked the
evidence to bring the Mercian lord to justice, and without
it any attempt to punish him would only deepen the crisis.

So what to do?

Rycca knew perfectly well. The problem lay in con-
vincing Dragon.

Every time she tried to bring up the subject, he cut
her off, which made her suspect he already knew what was
in her mind. That he did this by drawing her into his arms
and dazzling her with his lovemaking was beside the
point. Or at least it was after she recovered enough to
think again.

"Some place with no bed," she murmured to herself, "no pile of straw, no mossy riverbank, no chair, bench, or table, no field or tree, no . . ."

She sighed and tried hard not to smile, without success. Loving Dragon and being loved by him put all the world, even Wolscroft, in a different perspective.

But it did not solve the problem.

That morning when she rose there was a certain crispness to the air, an early hint of the season's turning. She needed no one to tell her that within weeks the sea lanes to the northlands would begin to bear ice. They had to return home soon whether this was resolved or not.

And if it was not?

If it lingered on to the next year?

Then Dragon would have one more reason to seek to kill Wolscroft before the traitor could strike again.

Her smile deepening, Rycca touched her still-flat belly. Not a word of it had she breathed, not to anyone, but Krysta and Cymbra knew nonetheless. Yet did her dear sisters of spirit keep her secret as she bided her time, seeking the proper moment to tell her fierce husband.

The moment Wolscroft died, she thought, and wondered that she could contemplate so dispassionately the demise of her father. Yet never had he truly been a father to her. As a field sown with salt bears no crops, so did she bear no love for the man from whom she had never known aught but hatred.

Die he must and the sooner the better. But in the proper way, as the traitor Udell had died, causing men to rally rejoicing around their king.

It was very pleasant in Krysta's solar, the room scented with the fragrance of drying herbs and filled with sunlight. But the scene just a little beyond was not so gentle by far. With a sigh, Rycca contemplated the guards on the high walls around Hawkforte. Besides the Hawk's own men, the men of the Wolf and the Dragon kept watch as well. Night and day, hour to hour, never eased for a moment, three warlord husbands kept guard over their beloved wives. Out beyond the harbor, boats patrolled. In the hills beyond Hawkforte, sentries stood their posts. No one entered the town without being identified. No one came near the stronghold without being approved.

At this rate, they would never catch Wolscroft.

Cymbra understood that full well, as did Krysta. Rycca saw it in their eyes but understood they would not speak to her of it. The matter was for her to decide.

How to persuade him . . . ?

The raven landed on the windowsill nearby. It was the same bird who came every day. If Krysta was about, she lingered. Otherwise, she usually flew away quickly. Not now, though. Now she cocked her gleaming black head to one side and gazed at Rycca, who looked back for a moment before reaching for the dry husk of bread Cymbra had brought her. Crumbling it, she stretched her arm forward slowly so as not to alarm the bird and sprinkled the crumbs on the sill.

"Come and eat," she said softly.

The bird hesitated but then sidestepped forward and pecked at the bread. Rycca returned to her musings. When all the crumbs were gone, the raven began to preen her feathers. Rycca watched her idly, still thinking of how to make Dragon see reason.

"There you are," Krysta said as she came into the solar.

Rycca and the bird alike looked up.

"Oh, Rycca, how are you feeling?"

"Much better. Cymbra's cure worked wonders, as usual."

"Good . . . You know, I think she is downstairs now and would like to talk with you."

Glad of something to do, Rycca rose at once. She thought Krysta would come with her but the golden-haired woman merely smiled and leaned against the window.

Out in the corridor, Rycca thought she heard Krysta speak to someone. That was rather odd, for there was no one left in the solar. Perhaps it was just the wind whistling around the corners of the high tower.

Cymbra was in the hall. She looked happy to see Rycca but a little surprised, too. Lion was playing at her feet. Rycca sat down beside them, watching the child with pleasure. Never before had she given much heed to children but now they seemed to be everywhere and ever fascinating.

On impulse, she asked suddenly, "What is it like to have a baby?"

Cymbra smiled. "Glorious, messy, thrilling, almost beyond belief."

"No, I mean afterward, when they're . . . here in the world, depending on you."

"Terrifying and wonderful."

Rycca nodded. The little boy was playing with an assortment of carved wooden animals. There was his namesake, the lion, as well as horses, bears, and several fish and birds. . . .

Birds.

Really, there was such a thing as being so preoccupied as not to see what was before her.

"You know," Rycca said softly, "Krysta never did really explain what makes the friends of her calling so unusual."

Cymbra laughed. Her son heard her, looked up, and bestowed upon her a smile of such radiance as to make both women forget all else for a precious moment.

Krysta came down a short while later. She looked glad to see them together. Taking a seat, she said, "Thorgold has told Raven that everything is in place."

Cymbra nodded briskly. She put her hand over

Rycca's and said, "Should Wolscroft come now, he will be caught."

Her father . . .

She spared one last moment of yearning for what could never be, then nodded.

N O! BY ALL THE GODS, YOU MUST BE MAD!" Rycca looked up at the infuriated Viking glaring down at her from his great height and schooled herself to calm. Tempting though it was to give back as good as she was getting, it would avail her nothing. Besides, he was merely concerned about her and that was rather sweet.

"It is the only solution," she said reasonably.

"Solution? It is a formula for disaster! You have been through too much. It has addled your wits if you think for one moment that I will ever agree—"

"My father may be able to pose as a rational man, but in fact he is not. He is ever driven by emotion, one in particular: rage. He will be determined to finish this and will seize any chance to do so." She turned to Hawk, who stood nearby, Krysta beside him. "You have a lodge near here. I have already stayed there."

"No!" Dragon said before anyone else could reply. They were all of them, Wolf and Cymbra included, in the great hall of Hawkforte. Rycca had chosen that as the best place and this as the best time to confront her husband. Yet her heart thundered as she contemplated what she was trying to get him to do.

"There is no other way," she insisted.

"Nothing else but to use you as bait? Madness!"

"Don't make me say it."

"Say what?" Wolf asked. He was leaning against a pillar, Cymbra close by, observing his brother with the air of a man torn between sympathy and amusement.

Gritting his teeth, Dragon said, "That I used her as such to lure out Magnus. It almost got her killed."

"*Me?* What about *you?*" Rycca demanded, momentarily forgetting her purpose. That night of terror still lived too vividly in her memory. "It almost got *you* killed. You're the one who had to fight him, naked, unarmed, and him having your Moorish sword."

Hawk and Wolf exchanged a look. "*That's* how Magnus died?" Wolf asked. He grinned. "Pretty damn good, brother."

The women looked to the ceiling and sighed in exasperation.

It was left to Hawk to break the deadlock. "I hate to say this, but Rycca has a point. Unless Wolscroft is lured out, this can't be resolved."

"So you would use *my wife*—" Dragon challenged.

"Fully protected," Hawk hastened to add, "surrounded by all our might. There is only one road and the forest on both sides is very thick. We could hide a hundred men within a few feet of that road and no one could detect them."

Dragon was silent for a moment. He gave every appearance of waging a battle within himself. Finally, he said, "A hundred men isn't enough."

Rycca's heart leaped, for she recognized that as just the tiniest concession to the plan they were discussing.

"Don't forget Krysta's friends," she said quickly. "They will help too."

Her husband scowled. "What friends?"

"It's a little complicated," Hawk replied. "Let's just say my wife has friends in high places . . . and low ones. Wolscroft won't be able to belch without our knowing it."

"I still don't like it. . . ."

Rycca took her husband's hand in hers. She looked up into his eyes. Gently, with all the confidence and courage she could muster, she said, "We will never be free until this is over."

UNDER COVER OF DARKNESS, NOT A HUNDRED men but three times that number slipped away from Hawkforte. Saxon and Norse alike, led by the Wolf and the Hawk, they took up position along the road that passed the lodge. By dawn they had so blended into the surrounding forest that as day came, the birds, deer, rabbits, foxes, and all the other denizens of the wood behaved just as they always did, with no awareness of the deadly presence come among them.

Not long after, Dragon and Rycca rode out of Hawk-forte. They made no secret of their departure or where they were bound. A spy would have had to be deaf and blind to miss what they were about.

Before midday, they were at the lodge. Together, they unsaddled Sleipnir and Grani and got them settled. That done, Dragon stood for a few minutes looking out toward the road. He saw nothing, which satisfied him. Taking Rycca's arm, he led her into the lodge.

It was as she remembered, a haven of comfort and serenity. With a glad sigh, she kicked off her shoes and sat down on the side of the bed. Smiling, she patted the mattress beside her.

Her husband scowled. It seemed to have become his habit. "We aren't here to relax."

"Wolscroft may not even be in the area. It could take days for this to be settled."

"He's here," Dragon said with certainty. "He will know what happened at Winchester, and he will be looking for a way to stop us before we can threaten him further."

Privately, Rycca believed the same but she saw no

reason to stress it. Nothing would happen until dark. Of that she was confident. Which meant . . .

"We have hours to fill. Any ideas?"

When he realized her meaning, he looked startled. With a laugh, she scrambled off the bed and went to him.

"Oh, Dragon, for heaven's sake, do you really want to mope around here all day? I certainly don't. I still haven't gotten over being afraid Magnus was going to kill you, and I simply don't want to think about death anymore. I want to celebrate life."

"There are three hundred men out there—"

"Which is why we're in here." She raised herself on tiptoe, bit the lobe of his ear, and whispered, "I promise not to yell too loudly."

A shudder ran through him. Even as his big hands stroked her back, he said, "Warriors don't mope."

"No, of course they don't. It was a poor choice of words. But you'll be pacing back and forth, looking out the windows, or you'll go get that whetstone I noticed in the stable and sharpen your sword endlessly, or you'll be staring off into space with that dangerous look you get when you're contemplating mayhem. You'll be totally oblivious to me and—"

He laughed despite himself and drew her closer. "Enough! Heaven forbid I behave so churlishly."

"Speaking of heaven . . ."

With the covers kicked back, the bed was smooth and cool. They undressed each other slowly, relishing the wonder of discovery that still came to them fresh and pure as their very first time.

"Remember?" Rycca murmured as she trailed her lips along his broad, powerfully muscled shoulder and down the solid wall of his chest. "I was so nervous. . . ."

"Really? Fooled me . . . Ahh . . ."

"I'd never seen anything so beautiful as you."

"Not . . . beautiful . . . you are . . ."

"I can't believe how strong you are. Why am I never afraid with you?"

"Know I'd die 'fore hurting you? Sweetheart . . ."

"Ohhh! Dragon . . . please . . ."

His hands and lips moved over her, sweetly torment-ing. She clutched his shoulders, her hips rising, and wel-comed him deep within her. Still he tantalized her, making her writhe and laughing when she squeezed him hard with her powerful inner muscles. But the laughter turned quickly to a moan of delight.

She looked up into his perfectly formed face, more handsome than any man had a right to be, and into his tawny eyes that were the windows of a soul more beautiful than any physical form. A piercing sense of blessedness filled her that she should be so fortunate as to love and be loved by such a man.

Her cresting cry was caught by him, his mouth hard against hers, the spur to his own completion that went on and on, seemingly without end.

Y ET THE WORLD DID RETURN, FOR ALL THAT, even if it seemed to shimmer around the edges. Dragon lay back on the bed, Rycca tucked close beside him, and waited for the thundering of his heart to ease. So determined had he been on vigilance that he could scarcely believe how utterly removed from all thought of danger he had allowed himself to become.

But perhaps "allowed" was the wrong notion alto-gether. His feelings for Rycca were constant, permitting no variation for circumstance.

She was asleep, which was good. The longer she slept, the faster all this would be over for her. And over it would be, if he had to hunt down Wolscroft, wring the truth from him by whatever means necessary, and drag him in front of Alfred himself. But he hoped it wouldn't come to that.

The day wore on. While yet Rycca slept, Dragon did all the things she had said he would do—paced back and forth, contemplated mayhem, and even honed his blade on the whetstone from the stable. All except being oblivious to her, for that he could never manage.

But when she awoke, sitting up heavy-lidded, her mouth so full and soft it was all he could do not to crawl back into bed with her, he put aside such pursuits and controlled himself admirably well, so he thought.

Yet in the midst of preparing a meal for them from the provisions in the pantry of the lodge, he was stopped by Rycca's hand settling upon his.

"Dragon," she said softly, "if you add any more salt to that stew, we will need a barrel of water and more to drink with it."

He looked down, saw that she was right, and cursed under his breath. Dumping out the spoiled stew, he started over. They ate late but they did eat. He was quite determined she would do so, and for once she seemed to have a decent appetite.

"I'm glad to see your stomach is better," he said as she was finishing.

She looked up, startled. "What makes you say that?"

"You haven't seemed able to eat regularly of late."

"Oh, well, you know . . . so many changes . . . travel . . . all that."

He nodded, reached for his goblet, and damn near knocked it over as a sudden thought roared through him.

"Rycca?"

She rose quickly, gathering up the dishes. His hand lashed out, closing on her wrist. Gently but inexorably, he returned her to her seat. Without taking his eyes from her, he asked, "Is there something you should tell me?"

"Something . . . ?"

"I ask myself what sort of changes may cause a woman to be afflicted with an uneasy stomach and it occurs to me I've been a damned idiot."

"Not so! You could never be that."

"Oh, really? How otherwise would I fail to notice that your courses have not come of late? Or is that also due to *travel*, wife?"

"Some women are not all that regular."

"Some women do not concern me. You do, Rycca. I swear, if you are with child and have not told me, I will—"

She squared her shoulders, lifted her head, and met his eyes hard on. "Will what?"

"What? Will what? Does that mean—?"

"I'm sorry, Dragon." Truly repentant, Rycca sighed deeply. "I was going to tell you. I was just waiting for a calmer time. I didn't want you to worry more."

Still grappling with what she had just revealed, he stared at her in astonishment. "You mean worry that my wife *and* our child are bait for a murderous traitor?"

"I know you're angry and you have a right to be. But if I had told you, we wouldn't be here now."

"Damn right we wouldn't be!" He got up from the table so abruptly that his chair toppled over and crashed to the floor. Ignoring it, Dragon paced back and forth, glaring at her.

Rycca waited, trusting the storm to pass. As she did, she counted silently, curious to see just how long it would take her husband to grasp fully what he had discovered.

Nine . . . ten . . .

"We're going to have a baby."

Not long at all.

She nodded happily. "Yes, we are, and you're going to be a wonderful father."

He walked back to the table, picked her up out of her chair, held her high against his chest, and stared at her.

"My God—"

Rycca laughed. "You can't possibly be surprised. It's not as though we haven't been doing our best to make this happen."

"True, but still it's absolutely incredible."

Very gently, she touched his face. "Perhaps we think of miracles wrongly. They're supposed to be extraordinarily rare but in fact they're as commonplace as a bouquet of wildflowers plucked by a warrior . . . or a woman having a baby."

Dragon sat down with her still in his arms and held her very close. He swallowed several times and said nothing.

Both could have remained contentedly like that for a long while, but only a few minutes passed before they were interrupted. The raven lit on the sill of the open window just long enough to catch their attention, then she was gone into the bloodred glare of the dying day.

T HE RIDERS CAME AN HOUR AFTER FULL DARK. There were a dozen in all. They drew rein in front of the lodge, except for Ogden, who rode his mount right up to the door and pounded on it with the hilt of his sword.

"Come out, you Norse scum! Your precious Valhalla awaits!" This must have struck him as the height of wit for he followed it with high-pitched laughter.

"Shut up," Wolscroft ordered. "Hakonson! Come out now and you will die with a sword in your hand. Otherwise, I swear you will perish without honor."

Inside the lodge, Dragon shot a stern look at Rycca, warning her to be silent. He let a few more moments drag by, long enough to make those outside uneasy, then called, "If I'm going to die, Wolscroft, I want to know why."

"Come out! We'll talk."

"Don't go!" Rycca said urgently. "It's a trap."

Her husband looked down at her with amusement. "Of course it's a trap, sweetling. There are a dozen men out there. They assume they've got us neatly caught."

"You could be killed before anyone got near enough to stop them."

He shook his head. "I'm not going to be killed. But I am going to get Wolscroft to talk. It's the only way." He turned toward the door, turned back, and said, "Do not, under any circumstances, even think about so much as poking a finger outside. Do you understand?"

Ever obedient, Rycca nodded.

Again he turned to go, again he looked back. "Let me rephrase that. Do you promise me you won't come outside until I tell you to?"

Her response was a glare but she followed it with a nod.

If nothing else, this husband of hers was learning caution, which was all to the good since he surely had need of it.

Dragon drew his Moorish sword, opened the door, stepped just outside it, and shut it firmly behind him. Torches carried by the riders illuminated the scene. Seeing the fierce warrior and the weapon he carried, Ogden backed up hastily toward his father. Wolscroft was in the center, bearded and begrimed after what must have been several days in the saddle coming down from Mercia.

"So," he said with a sneer, "the mighty Viking wants to know why he is to die."

"It seems a lot of trouble for you to go to just because you don't approve of me as your son-in-law."

"God's blood, it's amazing you Norse filth can find your own asses if that's as far as you can see."

"If there is something larger at work here, what is it?"

"What is it?" Wolscroft repeated. He leaned forward in his saddle, staring at Dragon. Little flecks of spittle shone at the corners of his mouth. "It is vengeance, you fool! Years ago I suffered injury at the hands of Norsemen and I swore I would exact payment for it. But Alfred wants to make *peace*. God preserve us from the fancies of so weak-minded a dolt."

"How does killing me stop Alfred?"

"It stops his precious alliance. Men will realize all this talk of peace was idiocy. They will turn against him and his reign will end!"

Dragon nodded. "I have to admit that makes a certain amount of sense. Frankly, under the circumstances, it's too bad you couldn't have stopped the alliance earlier on."

"Not for want of trying! God's blood, that woman . . ." Wolscroft shuddered suddenly. Apparently even he who cheerfully contemplated the murder of his daughter and son-in-law had limits.

"The Lady Daria," Dragon said, grimacing. "Still, you can't say she didn't make an effort. After all, it was she who stole Wolf's letter to Hawk proposing the alliance in the first place, and Wolf's own marriage to the Lady Cymbra. Did she contact you then to warn you of what might happen?"

"Her husband and I knew each other well and shared many of the same sentiments. She understood that."

"So you directed her to forge the response from Hawk that came so close to provoking war. And later to kill Krysta and make it look as though Hawk were responsible. Whose idea was it to blame the Danes?"

"Daria's," Wolscroft admitted grudgingly. "Even a fool woman can have a good notion occasionally. But all the rest was mine." He drew himself up in the saddle, impatient now to be done. He raised one hand to order forth his men.

Not a fair fight, then, Dragon thought. Himself on foot against eleven men on horseback. No, ten, since apparently Ogden meant to absent himself. Perhaps he remembered too well what had happened on the Essex road not all that long ago.

If these weren't the worst odds he had ever faced, they came damn close. Still, he sensed the wings of panic moving through the riders and thought he might have a decent enough chance.

Thought but was destined never to know, for just then a great fluttering shattered the forest stillness, a sound somewhere between the howl of wind and the throb of drums. A terrible beating that grew louder and louder as the air thickened, becoming almost solid, and the men began to scream.

Ravens filled the sky. They swarmed from the surrounding trees, darting at the riders, going for their eyes. Even as they did, out into the clearing before the lodge ran a band of stout little men, weirdly dressed, sporting long beards, and looking as though they had just crawled from beneath a bridge. They seized the bridles of the horses and whispered to the animals, causing them to rear so violently that the riders were tumbled from their saddles and fell one after another to the ground. The birds swooped lower, still attacking, as the men huddled, arms wrapped around their heads, thrashing frantically. Before Dragon's startled gaze, the little men loosed the horses and turned to go. One, who looked somehow familiar, gave him a cocky grin and waved.

Friends in high places . . . and low.

It was over very quickly then. Wolf, Hawk, and their men emerged from their hiding places, surrounding Wolscroft and the others, disarming them before they knew what was happening. Even so, Wolscroft tried to brazen it out.

"Kill me and kill your precious alliance!" he shouted.

Sheathing the sword he had not needed—truly peace was a marvelous thing—Dragon strode forward. "Kill you? God's blood, man, we're not going to do that. You will be treated with tenderest care while you are conveyed to the king for trial."

Even Wolscroft had the sense to blanch at this, yet still he tried to bluster his way out. "You have no evidence! It is no more than your word against mine."

"And ours." Father Thomas spoke with quiet confidence as he stepped into the clearing. Beside him stood the man Dragon recognized as Hawk's house priest, Father Desmond.

"We two," Father Thomas said, "will swear to what we heard here this night. You are condemned from your own mouth, Wolscroft, and all England shall know it."

More was said then, most of it by Wolscroft, who blathered on, screaming threats even as he was tied and hustled into the wagon in which he would begin his ignominious trip to justice. But none of that mattered. It was, as Rycca had so fervently prayed, over.

Almost . . .

TWENTY-ONE

"MY LORD?"

Dragon turned to eye the man who had just addressed him. They were standing on the dock at Hawkforte. A fresh wind whipped the riggings of the drakars, where preparations were being completed for the voyage home.

"What is it?" Dragon asked.

"There is a man, lord, just off a ship from Normandy. He's in the tavern over there and he's asking for the Lady Rycca."

"Is he? What manner of man?"

"Tall, slender, actually he looks rather like her ladyship. He says she is his sister and he seeks word of her."

"Does Rycca have yet another brother?" Wolf asked. He was close to Dragon and had overheard the exchange. The news had him fingering the hilt of his sword.

"Yes, she does, but I gather he's an altogether different sort. Do you mind finishing up here?"

"Not at all. Go ahead."

Scant minutes later, Dragon set a horn of ale in front of the visitor from Normandy. The young man looked up, startled. He was pale skinned, with eyes like honey and hair that held the promise of fire. Had Rycca been a man, she would have looked just like him.

Happy, happy day that she was not.

"What brings you to Hawkforte, friend?" Dragon asked as he took the seat opposite his new acquaintance.

"I seek word of my sister, the Lady Rycca of Wolscroft. I have had troubling word of her in Normandy and wish to be assured of her safety."

Trouble involving Rycca? How astonishing. Dragon hid a grin and said, "You would be called—?"

"Thurlow. And you are—?"

This time, Dragon's smile would not be denied. "Ah, well, as to that, therein hangs a tale."

A N HOUR OR SO LATER, RYCCA LOOKED UP FROM the last of the chests she was packing in the great hall of Hawkforte and beheld a sight that seemed out of a dream. Her beloved husband was walking toward her accompanied by her beloved brother. Slowly, she got to her feet.

"Th-thurlow . . . ?"

His face, so very like her own, lit with pleasure. "Rycca, dear sister! I rejoice to find you well!"

They hugged fiercely while Dragon looked on with as much contentment as he could have mustered had he personally arranged the reunion of the twins.

"I don't understand," Rycca said when she could speak again. Her throat was very tight and tears gleamed in her eyes but she could not stop smiling. "Why are you here?"

"I heard a wild rumor in Normandy, about you fleeing from the marriage arranged for you by the king himself," he said, with a chiding shake of his head. "Really, Rycca, what were you thinking? Dragon here is an exemplary fellow. How could you have not wanted to marry him?"

Over her brother's shoulder, Rycca sent the fine fellow in question a look that would have turned a lesser man to ash. Dragon merely raised his eyebrows, the very image of wounded innocence.

"It was a little more complicated than he may have explained to you."

"Nonsense," Thurlow said with all the certainty of a very young man whose heart is nonetheless in the right place. "I love you dearly, sister, but we both know you can be a tad impulsive. Fortunately, I am assured Dragon will take excellent care of you."

Rycca laughed then and reached out a hand to her husband, who took it with a grin. As she drew him to her, she said softly, "As I will care for him, brother."

After a moment of sweet contemplation of the man she loved beyond life itself, she returned her attention to Thurlow. Gently, she asked, "Has Dragon told you—?"

"Of Father? Yes, he has." Her twin sighed deeply. "I will pray for his soul. No doubt his death en route to Winchester was an accident."

Rycca nodded although she knew they would never be certain of that. Mayhap Wolscroft truly had panicked when he attempted to escape. But his fatal fall off the very cliff from which she had soared free hinted at the darker side of his soul. Wherever he was now, she prayed he would find mercy and ultimately redemption.

"And our brothers sent into exile," Thurlow continued on a note of wonder. He was grappling with the extraordinary fact that those who had made his life and Rycca's so anguished were simply vanished.

"Which means," his sister said softly, "that you are Wolscroft now. Lucky are that land and people for I know they will blossom under your care."

Her brother nodded. He looked humbled by the sudden, stunning change in his circumstances but also determined to do his best.

As would they all. Rycca left her twin and went into Dragon's arms. From their safety, she watched as Wolf and Cymbra came into the hall. Wolf was carrying Lion and the three were laughing over something. Close behind came Hawk and Krysta, Falcon nestled in his father's arms. Smiling, they joined the others.

The sun came out just then from behind a cloud and shining through the high windows filled the hall with a golden radiance. For just a moment, it seemed to Rycca that everything slowed down and very nearly stopped. A single mote of dust hung suspended before her eyes, whirling, dancing, revealing in its simplicity the miracle of a timeless moment made radiant by love and the peace it had wrought.

Then Dragon lifted her hand and gently kissed it, and she felt his touch clear through to the very essence of her immortal self. Time moved on again, carrying them with it, yet she knew that for them there always would be the moment everlasting. Truly, blessed are the peacemakers.

D ARKNESS NOW DESCENDS BUT BRIGHT TORCHES light the night just as love and the dream of peace will shine through all the years to come. Far into the future, the descendants of these three couples will themselves meet their own challenges, live their own adventures, and find their own enduring blessing in everlasting love.

About the Author

JOSIE LITTON lives in New England where she is happily at work on a new trilogy of historical romances. She is also at home at *www.josielitton.com*.

Read on for a preview of

OF ME

the first passionate book
in Josie Litton's dual volume
DREAM OF ME and
BELIEVE IN ME

CYMBRA LEANED BACK, RESTING HER HEAD against the rim of the leather tub, and sighed deeply. Warm water lapped at her limbs. The scent of herbs sprinkled in the bath teased gently at her nostrils. The soft crackle of the fire and Miriam's quiet movements were the only sounds in the chamber. For the first time in far too many hours she could relax and, just perhaps, gather her thoughts.

What thoughts they were! She knew very little of Vikings except that they seemed to be of two types—merchants and raiders. Despite her claim to Sir Derward, she didn't really suppose that the difference was questionable.

The prisoners didn't look like the sort who would want to sell her a few lengths of cloth. Yet neither had they behaved as the brutal killers and despoilers that Derward had branded them.

Authority was very weak in parts of England, with the result that the Danes had seized control over broad swaths of land. They were poised to seize even more, and might if men like her brother didn't succeed in stopping them.

Which made these Vikings . . . what? Even as she told herself it wasn't her problem to solve, her mind could not resist turning over the puzzle. Nor could it keep from drifting irresistibly to the leader, the tall, heavily muscled man with the midnight-black hair and the icy gray eyes.

No, that wasn't quite true. His eyes weren't always icy. There had been times when they brushed her like white-hot fire.

She didn't want to think about that, mustn't think of it. Her body felt oddly heavy, especially between her legs, where a hot, moist sensation was building. She glanced down, surprised to see that her nipples were peaked, and flushed. Quickly she rose from the bath and seized the drying cloth Miriam had thoughtfully laid nearby. With that wrapped around her, she felt a little calmer.

Seated by the fire, she murmured her thanks as Miriam began to brush out her hair. As always, the motion soothed her but she stopped it before very long. Miriam's hands were sore now more often than not, and the unguents Cymbra made for her didn't always take the pain away completely. Gently, she laid her hand over the old nurse's.

"I'm sorry I worried you today."

Miriam sighed. She sat down beside the young woman who had been her charge since the tender age of three days, when Cymbra's own lady mother had passed beyond the veil of this world. She loved Cymbra dearly but she didn't pretend to understand her in the slightest.

"You terrified me." She shook her head in bewilderment, sparse strands of gray hair escaping from beneath her wimple. "How could you do such a thing? Much as I hate to say it, Sir Derward is right, Vikings are animals. They could have killed you without a second thought."

"What should we do then?" Cymbra asked softly. "Kill everything we fear? If we do that, others will fear us and seek to kill us in turn. It will never end. One cruelty begets the next endlessly."

The old nurse shrugged. "'Tis the way of this world. No man can change that, and certainly no woman can."

Cymbra sighed and rose, standing before the copper brazier that dispelled the evening's chill. Her shoulders and arms were bare, the cloth barely covering the swell of her breasts. She shivered slightly. "Perhaps not, but still I must try. There is too much pain."

Miriam cast her a quick look. "You never speak of that anymore."

Both women shared a memory of the very young Cymbra, screaming and screaming, unable to explain what was wrong. It happened many times . . . when a stable boy cut his foot on a scythe, when a kitchen maid was scalded with water, when a warrior died of a wound that would not heal.

That had been the worst, going on for days until finally the Hawk had drugged her with the juice of poppy brought from far lands and sat, holding her in his arms, through an endless day and night, his face grim as he decided what had to be done.

Holyhood became her sanctuary. Safe within it, she learned how to control what was at once gift and curse. Miriam didn't know how, could only dimly imagine the struggle Cymbra had waged. She'd won in the end, though at great cost. Now she could care for the injured and ill, even for the dying, without making their pain her own. She felt it still, Miriam was sure of that, but she managed to keep it apart from herself. Usually.

"There is nothing to speak of," Cymbra assured her with a smile. She drew the cloth more closely around herself and stared into the flames, but instead of seeing them she seemed to see only midnight-black hair, burnished skin, and eyes the color of slate. She shook her head, impatient with herself, and dropped the cloth, reaching for her bed robe.

"Go to your rest, Miriam," she said as she wriggled the garment over her head: Emerging from the mass of gossamer linen, she tugged her hair free—no small task in itself—grinned, and gave the old nurse a kiss. "Heaven knows, you earn it putting up with me."

Clucking a denial Miriam did as she was bid. When the door had closed behind her, Cymbra stretched her arms far above her head, standing on tiptoe, and made a small sound of contentment as more of the tension eased. She needed to sleep yet felt oddly energized, as though the day had lasted minutes instead of hours.

Tomorrow word would come from Hawk about the fate of the prisoners. She drew her brows together as she wondered what her brother would decide. Likely he would have them brought to him at Hawkforte to judge them for himself. She would never see the gray-eyed man again. Not that it mattered, couldn't, shouldn't matter. Why then did she ache?

Thought of sleep fled. She glanced around the chamber that had been hers most of her life. There near the brazier was her needlework, awaiting her hand. There, too, was the chest holding her medicines and precious manuscripts. Her lute was on a table next to the wooden coffer that held her paper, pens, and inks. All manner of distractions beckoned but she could not settle on any of them. Instead, she opened the door that led out onto the tower walkway just beyond her room. The night was cool but she felt unaccountably warm. The perimeter wall of the tower came almost to her shoulders. Her modesty was well protected as she stepped out, clad only in her night robe.

Protected surely from anyone on the ground. But not protected from the man who stood in the shadows of the walkway, watching her every movement. Wolf gazed at the play of light and shadow over her exquisite form and fought for the self-control that always before had been as natural as his next breath. No more.

Having scaled the tower, a simple feat, only to find the old woman in the room, he had waited, unable to tear his eyes away as Cymbra bathed, rose from the tub, draped herself in that ridiculously thin cloth. Then, as if to finish him off, discarded it in favor of a bed robe that couldn't have protected her from a balmy breeze, much less from his eyes.

In the northlands, people dressed sensibly—or not at all. She would have to adjust to that.

And rather more than that.

The men he had sent into Holyhood the preceding day disguised as merchants had done their job with expected precision. The guards outside the cell lay unconscious, bound and gagged. So, too, the guards on the palisade wall. His men kept vigil by the great hall just in case Derward or any of the others arose, but there was slim likelihood of that. They were all snoring deeply.

That left the Lady Cymbra—completely unprotected.

She was close enough for him to touch, a vision of pale beauty caressed by starlight. He smelled the fragrance of her skin, felt the brush of a strand of her hair lifted by the night wind. He heard her sigh, saw the rise and fall of her breasts as she breathed deeply.

It was more than any man could be expected to bear and he had no intention of doing so. Still, he was oddly loath to disturb her peace. She would know little enough of that in the days—and nights—to come.

Cymbra looked out over Holyhood, her sanctuary and prison both. An uncharacteristic impatience filled her, a longing for something she could neither define nor deny. Such foolishness. She was the Lady Cymbra, sister of the Hawk, and a healer. She had a place where she belonged and work that was her life. In all that, she was blessed.

Why then did she yearn for more? She was like a child wishing for the moon, rather than a grown woman who should know better.

She had to be sensible. It was late, she would go inside, lie down, and in time she would sleep. Morning would come, the prisoners would leave, life would go on. Yet she lingered a moment longer, gazing out at the walls of her home. Holyhood's walls, where Sir Derward's guards pretended to watch, nodding over their spears, their dark, drowsing shapes so well familiar to her that she scarcely noticed them—save when they were gone.

Gone. Cymbra stiffened suddenly. She leaned forward, staring. There was no mistake. She scanned every part of the palisade that she could see, and not a guard was in sight. Holyhood's security was more gesture than reality, but never before had there been no guards at all. Something was wrong.

Very wrong.

Vikings.

Hawk would have been taking the cell apart with his bare hands.

The gray-eyed man was so calm.

So unconcerned.

From the wrath of the Norsemen preserve us, oh, Lord.

She turned, already running, meaning to call the alarm.

Running . . . straight into steely arms and a merciless hand that slammed down over her mouth. Hot, piercing terror tore through her. She struggled with desperate strength but uselessly. In an instant, she was lifted high against a rock-hard chest and felt herself being carried through her room, down the winding steps of the tower, out into the night.

"Be silent," Wolf said implacably. "If you scream,

anyone who comes will die." He looked down into her eyes to see if she understood. She did. He released her mouth so she could breathe more easily but he did not lessen his hold on her or slow his stride. She was dimly aware of other men moving alongside them, more in number than the prisoners had been, swords gleaming. She caught a glimpse of the gates of Holyhood standing open. Then the fortress was behind her and there was only night and wind. And fear so great it threatened to swallow her.

Read on for a preview of

IN ME

the second passionate book
in Josie Litton's dual volume
DREAM OF ME and
BELIEVE IN ME

KRYSTA DID NOT APPEAR IN THE HALL THAT evening. She stayed out of sight, wrestling with what to do. All night she tossed and turned, trying to decide on some course that might yet bring a fair wind. She could confess all and throw herself on his mercy, but the mere thought filled her with dread. She could sneak off on her own before he sent her away, then return somehow as though just newly arrived. If Thorgold and Raven went with her, perhaps they could claim to have encountered their mistress on the way. But what chance was there that would work? Hawk had seen her too often and too clearly. She should have thought of that before embarking on what had seemed so sensible a plan, the selfsame plan now lying in tatters about her.

She rose at first light, dazed by sleeplessness, still trying to decide what to do. To her relief, she saw no sign of preparations for her departure. But that meant nothing. No doubt the Hawk's men were ready to ride in an instant. Her stomach churned with hunger but she could not bear the thought of eating. She heard Daria's shrill voice coming from the kitchens and turned instinctively in the opposite direction. Scarcely had she done so, and before she could take more than a step, she ran right into the steward, who must have come up directly behind her.

"Your pardon," Krysta said quickly and tried to move away, but the young man moved as well, blocking her.

"His lordship wants you."

"W-what do you . . . ?" she stammered.

"He wants you," Edvard repeated with a hint of impatience. "Upstairs in the tower room." When still she hesitated, he gave her a little push in the right direction. Worse yet, he stood right there, watching to make sure she went.

Krysta climbed the tower steps slowly. She was thinking desperately of what to say. If only she had a little more time, she might be able to come up with a plan of some sort or another. But time had run out and now there was nothing left to do save hope for the best. And pray, that might also help.

The door to the tower room was partly open. She took a deep breath, gathered her courage, and pushed through it.

The chamber took up the entire uppermost floor of the tower. It was dominated by the largest bed Krysta had ever seen, hung with richly embroidered curtains and covered with luxurious furs. She might have noticed nothing but that bed had it not been for a sight more arresting to the eyes. In a corner of the room, Hawk stepped into a tub of steaming water. She caught just a glimpse of his bare flanks before he lowered himself, preserving modesty but leaving plain for her befuddled sight the vast expanse of his heavily muscled chest and arms. That and his predator's smile.

"Don't just stand there," Hawk said. "Make yourself useful. I need my back scrubbed." Before she could get her mouth around a response, he ducked under the water, came up flinging drops in all directions, and began lathering his hair. She watched with unwilling fascination. His skin was bronzed and beneath it muscle and tendon moved with easy grace. His nipples were small and flat. Under his arms were tufts of hair that looked even silkier than that on his head. He ducked again to rinse and came up with water streaming down his face. Opening one eye, he glanced at her. "Mayhap you did not hear me."

She had heard him all right, well enough to know what the edge in his voice meant. He was bound and determined on this, for some reason. Mayhap he regretted letting her go the previous day and meant to remedy that, a thought which set her heart to racing. Or mayhap he merely wanted to humiliate her before sending her on her way. Whatever his intent, angering him seemed a poor choice.

Not that there were any good ones to be seen. With utmost reluctance, palpable in every step she took, Krysta approached the tub. She did not take her eyes from him but, once convinced she meant to obey, he ignored her completely. She blushed red and looked away quickly as he matter-of-factly went about his ablutions, grateful though she was that the water afforded some protection to her innocence. Or what remained of it after the awakening of desires she had not known she possessed.

Just then she was discovering yet another of them, the desire not to let him have his way completely. He wanted his back scrubbed, did he? With docility that should have alerted him, she knelt beside the tub, picked up a cloth, and dunked it into the water. Applying it and all her strength, she set about to scrub the skin right off his back.

Hawk laughed. Damn him, he thought her amusing. She redoubled her efforts. "Sheathe your claws," he said, still chuckling. "I've slept on rock and never noticed. I doubt you can have any ill effect."

"It won't be for want of trying," she muttered. There was no give in him at all. She might as well have been scrubbing stone. Warm, smooth stone so firm beneath her touch . . . She jerked back as though burned and tried to rise, only to be stopped by his hand clamped on her wrist. "You haven't finished," he said. His brows rose mockingly. "I thought the Norse prized cleanliness. Can't you even manage a simple bath?"

"If you took it properly, in a sauna like a person should rather than soak yourself like salted beef in a pail of water . . ."

"There is a sauna here and I enjoy it. But a man still wants a real bath from time to time."

His fingers were rubbing soothingly where he held her, as though to ease away any small hurt he might have inflicted. Had there been any? She couldn't remember. A shiver of pleasure danced beneath his touch. His eyes were as blue as the sky at high summer, thickly fringed by sun-kissed lashes. A night's growth of beard softened the harshly beautiful lines of his face. She had a sudden, almost irresistible urge to touch him slowly and lingeringly, so that she might learn every inch of him.

"You have a sauna?" Anything to distract herself from thoughts becoming more wayward by the moment.

He nodded without taking his gaze from her. "The only good idea the Danes ever had."

"Better than invading England?" The question was out before she could stop it. Foolish, foolish! She should have kept silent, concentrated only on getting away. What was she thinking to converse with a naked man holding her captive?

His gaze drifted to her mouth, watching her lips move as she formed the words. "I suppose it depends on your perspective," Hawk said absently. "To the Danes, that's an excellent idea. To us . . ." He shrugged, in that gesture accepting the great struggle that had dominated his life. The struggle he was bound and determined to win even to the extent of forging an alliance between English and Norse against their common enemy, and taking a Norse wife to cement that alliance.

A Norse wife . . .

"Enough talk of war," he said. "I have other matters on my mind." All night he had chewed over his suspicions, now convinced he had to be completely wrong, now not certain of anything at all. In the end, impulse had won out, which was unusual, for he always thought before he acted even in the heat of battle when the razor-sharp quickness of his mind had saved his life more times than he could recall. But such thought was lacking where she was concerned. She fogged his mind, sowing confusion with every smile. How fortunate she was not smiling at the moment. Indeed, she looked as though she might never do so again.

"You said you would not lie with me."

Her eyes widened. He watched, fascinated, as color crept over her cheeks. "I spoke in haste. . . . I meant—"

"Oh, then you will lie with me?"

"No! I mean, we should not speak of such things. My mistress . . ."

"Your absent, tardy mistress." His eyes narrowed. To be safe, he tightened his hold on her wrist but carefully, for he truly could not imagine hurting her. Provoking her was another matter altogether. "Forget her, she is of no account."

"*What?* She most certainly is of account! Did you yourself not say we both owed her a duty?" His precautions were well taken. She tugged hard, trying to free herself. He continued to hold her easily.

"Duty is a cold bedmate. I prefer mine warm and willing. Better yet, as hot and yielding as you were yesterday. Come here." He did not wait for her response but began drawing her closer until she was half bent over the tub, her eyes so wide with shock he thought he might fall into them.

"I will not! How can you even think such a thing? Let me go! Stop it."

He tugged a little harder. Just enough. She lost her balance and toppled over into the water. Indeed, she would have landed right on Hawk had he not removed himself agilely from the tub just as she entered it. There was only so much temptation a man could take and he thought it prudent to limit his. He stood, heedless of his nudity, watching her thrash about. Watching, too, what happened to the water. When the first traces of black color began running off into it, his expression changed. Uncertainty had held his anger at bay. Certainty unleashed it.

He yanked a towel from the nearby stool and wound it around his loins as he awaited the emergence of the soaking, sputtering, dye-stained Lady Krysta. His bride.